THE RAPE OF
GANYMEDE

A Greg Quaintance Mystery

Books by
John Peyton Cooke

STINK LAKE

OUT FOR BLOOD

TORSOS

THE CHIMNEY SWEEPER

HAVEN

THE RAPE OF GANYMEDE

THE FALL OF LUCIFER

AFTER YOU'VE GONE AND OTHER OUTRÉ TALES

THE RAPE OF GANYMEDE

A Greg Quaintance Mystery

John Peyton Cooke

**Éditions
Cuir Noir**
London

cuirnoir.com

ISBN 978-0-9810047-1-6

Éditions Cuir Noir
J. P. Cooke, Publisher
1 Roland Gardens
London SW7 3PE
United Kingdom

cuirnoir.com

johnpeytoncooke.com

This book is for

Keng

Here the curtains draw; there is discovered JUPITER *dandling* GANYMEDE *upon his knee, and* MERCURY *lying asleep.*

JUPITER: Come, gentle Ganymede, and play with me.

                I love thee well, say Juno what she will. . . .

                Hold here, my little love; these linked gems

                Gives jewels

                My Juno ware upon her marriage-day,

                Put thou about thy neck, my own sweet heart,

                And trick thy arms and shoulders with my theft.

GANYMEDE: I would have a jewel for mine ear,

                And a fine brooch to put in my hat,

                And then I'll hug with you an hundred times.

—CHRISTOPHER MARLOWE

Dido, Queen of Carthage

act I, sc. i

One

Juan had lathered up my scalp and was finishing it off with a straight razor when my beeper went off. I began to reach for it under the black latex hair-catching bib, but Juan laid a hand on my shoulder and said, "Don't you move a muscle, Gregory." He stood behind me in the mirror, staring me down with his mascara-dark eyes, holding the razor up like a threat.

I relaxed my arm. I'd gone for the beeper out of habit and didn't really want to know who wanted me. It was a hot Friday night in June, about seven o'clock. I'd been sitting in my office most of the week with nothing better to do than watch soap operas. At five tonight, I'd closed up shop, gone back to my apartment, and dressed down, into an olive drab Army tank top, cutoff blue jeans, and tan workmen's boots. I was wearing my old dog tags around my neck on a short, silver-beaded chain. I'd promised myself I was going to take advantage of my life's extended lull and go out clubbing. I had three rent payments due—my office, my apartment, and my space at Ahmed Kotby's parking garage—and I was going to put them out of my mind by drinking, dancing, and ogling go-go boys. I was in one of those hell-I-deserve-it kind of moods. Aside from a mile of credit, I was dead broke.

Juan gave my shoulder a firm squeeze and said, "Nice, by the way. But you feel a little tight. Maybe you want me to take you back and turn you over to Achilles for some bodywork?"

"No, thanks, Juan."

"How come all you ever want is a cut?" he said, sounding hurt, as he drew the final stroke down the back of my neck. Juan had been my hairstylist (if you can call it that) since I moved to Manhattan after being drummed out. He was a bleached blond Mestizo with earth-red skin and a classic Aztec nose, with a brass nose-ring like a bull's. His pumped-up chest was shrink-wrapped in red-and-white-striped rubber that bore the JPG logo of Jean-Paul Gaulthier, who may also have been responsible for Juan's black patent leather pants. While he worked, Juan stood on in-line skates to make up for the fact that he was a fireplug.

You might think that no guy in his right mind would trust his head to a descendant of Montezuma wearing skates and wielding a straight razor, but this was Chelsea 10011, known to direct marketers as the gayest zip code in the United States, and the boys were lined up around the block for Juan. He was as hot as Popocatepetl.

I was about to check my beeper when Juan skated around to the sink and tossed a steaming towel over my head as if it were raw pizza dough. It stung a little.

"You never want a manicure," he accused.

"No point. I bite my nails."

"You shouldn't do that. Look, Gregory, you have your little office upstairs, you're our neighbor, man, we see you around all the time, but all you ever want is a cut. You ever think of trying a body wax or electrolysis? A smooth chest and smooth legs are very, very sexy." He unfastened the latex bib from around my neck and brushed away stray hairs.

"I like my chest hair, Juan."

Juan thrust his hand down the neck of my shirt and grabbed hold of a fistful of curly hairs. "Mmm—me, too. You're right, you should keep it.

Skip the waxing. If I was your boyfriend, man, I'd be pissed if you shaved it off. I'm just supposed to do suggestive selling, you know? I don't care. At least I get to see you strapped in my chair every two weeks."

He removed his hand from my chest and the towel from my head and started singing along to the song on the radio. It was the new ballad from Jimmy Gilbert, "Love You Too Much." Juan tried to match Gilbert's pure falsetto, but he failed.

"You like that song?" I asked.

"Like the song, hate the video. Why's he got to put Madeleine Downey in it? It's just an excuse to show them kissing a thousand times to prove he's not queer."

"She *is* his wife."

"On paper. It may fool little housewives in Iowa, but it doesn't fool me. Listen to the song, man, it doesn't fit the video. It's all about forbidden love, love he feels too strongly, love that's got to hide itself. Then Jimmy goes and gets married to a supermodel and they put out this video full of all this hetero kissing shit and him acting like some kind of macho asshole. I never seen anything so disgusting."

"Are we done?" I was referring to the rant.

"Yeah, man." Juan used the corner of a dry towel to polish a spot on the top of my head. Then he noticed my right biceps and pressed his thumb against it, as if to rub off what he saw there. "Hey, man, that's a joke, right? A temporary tattoo?"

"Only in the sense that I must have been temporarily insane when I got it," I said. Juan was looking at a permanent tattoo with U.S. ARMY in big fat letters and, below that, the mother of all bald eagles screaming its heart out and holding in its claws a convoluted ribbon with the words OPERATION DESERT STORM.

"Where'd you get that?"

"A tattoo parlor in Fayetteville, North Carolina. I was out drinking with some buddies our first night back from Saudi. Each of us got one— at least I wasn't the only idiot."

"Buddies, huh?" Juan grinned lasciviously.

"Yeah," I said. I didn't want to get onto *that* depressing subject. But he wouldn't let go.

"You fought in the war?"

"Uh-huh."

"I watched it all on CNN, maybe I—"

"Boring, wasn't it?"

"Maybe I saw you climbing out of a foxhole or something." Juan gave me a nudge.

"Yeah, sure. I would have been the one in desert fatigues and Army boots."

"You see any action?"

"Yeah," I said, looking down and away. Juan seemed disappointed that I didn't develop my answer further.

"So what happened, man? You get a dishonorable discharge?" His inflection made it sound like a badge of honor. For a buff Chelsea boy, Juan had a definite East Village streak.

"No, not dishonorable, but not honorable, either. Undesirable. Otherwise known as S.O.L."

"What's that?"

"Shit out of luck."

I stood up and reached for my wallet. I tipped Juan with some cash I'd advanced off my Visa card. He thanked me, stuffing the wad of bills down his front pocket. His basket shifted a little—or was it just my horny imagination?

"Hey, Gregory, how come you and me never gone out?"

"I'm not your type, Juan." It came out sounding sadder than I would have liked. I don't usually go around asking for pity.

An eyebrow went up. "How do you know what my type is?"

"Look at me. Cutoffs, tank top—I'm no fashion plate."

Juan's gaze drilled into me, and I glanced away to my beeper's display, wondering who . . . It was a Manhattan phone number, but I didn't recognize it. I was too down in the dumps even to consider that Juan might really be interested.

"Fuck that, man." Juan punched my shoulder lightly, like a buddy. I looked back at him. "You heading out tonight?"

"Yeah, actually." My smile crept up at the corners.

"That your boyfriend?" He jerked his chin up, gazing down at my beeper. His nose ring swung back and forth, glinting.

"Yeah," I said, palming it. "My pocket boyfriend."

"No, *pendejo*."

"Sorry. No, haven't got a boyfriend. Don't know who's calling me. Potential client, probably."

"You really a private investigator, like it says on your door?"

I dug out my license, only eight months old and already worn around the edges. "I don't look like much of one out of my suit, but yeah. Private dick at your service."

"Private dick." He laughed. "Sounds like a call boy."

"It is, kind of."

"Hey, Greg, I get off at ten." Juan handed me back my license. "You want to meet me for coffee somewhere?"

"Coffee," I said, perking up. He really was serious.

We discussed where.

I was planning to take a nap at my apartment before going back out, but when I got home I was greeted by a red light on my answering machine. Absently, I switched to Playback, figuring it'd be nothing of importance. I pulled off my tank top, tossed it on the futon couch, undid the top button of my cut-offs, and turned on the air conditioner. I sat down and put my feet in their boots on the coffee table.

Beep. "Yes, I'm calling for Mr. Quaintance. This is David Loeb. I'm an attorney. You've probably heard of me—"

"Shit," I said aloud. I'd heard of David Loeb, all right, and I recognized his voice. I'd never met him, but I'd seen him on TV. I'd watched the coverage of the Hugo Wallis trial—but it was over and done with and had been off my mind for months. Wallis had been my favorite actor on my favorite soap until he'd gone and murdered his lovely wife Fiona in cold blood. The jury—mostly women—claimed to have reasonable doubts. The last I'd seen David Loeb would have been the press conference after Wallis's acquittal, when a reporter asked him if he would have defended Hitler. There he stood on the courthouse steps in his custom-tailored Italian suit, surrounded by gabbling reporters, uniformed policemen, TV cameras, halogen lights, and boom-dangling microphones. The usual catcalls could be heard from the trial groupies mounting the barricades. Blinking his eyes, Loeb took a moment to gather his thoughts before saying, in his usual careful and cogent manner, "The question you should be asking is whether Hitler would have hired me. Incidentally, any of you who read Toobin's *New Yorker* piece should know that I'm the son of Holocaust survivors. Hitler sent many of my elders to their death at Auschwitz." With that he drew a breath deeply through his nose and gazed out over the heads of the suddenly speechless press corps. "Now do any of you have a question relating to my client or to the case?"

I turned up the volume, jotting down David Loeb's phone number as the message gave it out.

"I'd like to hire you for a job," he continued. "A friend recommended you. Said I could trust you. Your office was closed, so I tried here. I'll be trying your pager. If I don't get a call back before eight, I'll have no choice but to find someone else. Hope to hear from you." *Beep.*

It was almost eight now. The number I'd recorded was the same as that on my beeper. I would be a fool not to call. After defending Wallis, Loeb had four million new dollars that he wouldn't know what to do with—according to the *Post*, anyway.

I was parched, though, so I downed a bottle of Gatorade from the fridge to lubricate my chops. Then I called Loeb's office.

A male secretarial voice answered: "Bulkeley, Stearn. David Loeb's office."

I told the guy who I was, and he put me right through. They must have been expecting me.

"David Loeb," came the voice, deeper and more mellow.

"Greg Quaintance. You still need somebody?"

"I'm glad you called, Mr. Quaintance."

"Just what kind of a job did you have in mind?"

"It's too delicate a subject for the phone. Can you come up here so we can discuss it?"

I hesitated. I wanted that nap. "I'd be happy to. When?"

"Tonight, the sooner the better. I'm free now."

"This wouldn't have anything to do with Hugo Wallis?"

Loeb chuckled. "Mr. Wallis is no longer a client of mine, if that puts your mind at ease. You didn't see me Wednesday on *Dateline*?"

"No, sorry."

"For his civil trial, Wallis has chosen to be represented by another member of the defense team. Someone not with Bulkeley, Stearn. What I want you for has nothing whatsoever to do with him. How soon can you get up here? You're where, Chelsea?"

I told him yeah and that I'd be there in half an hour. He said that was fine and hung up.

I had no idea what it was about, but I had a feeling it was going to knock the rendezvous with Juan off my schedule. I could wait to call Juan, though, until I knew for sure.

"Shit," I said.

I stripped off my cutoffs and briefs, opened up my meager closet, and tore the plastic sheath over the top of my dark gray Barney's suit—my very best business drag.

Two

It was a muggy night. As I stepped out of the cab, my trouser legs clung to me like leeches. The day's smog had drawn itself in from the rest of the city to settle here on Madison Avenue like a curse. The sidewalk and gutter were scattered with gnawed cigar butts—remnants of one of the last trends of the century, the lunchtime outdoor cigar smokers' orgy. Anyone seeking an explanation for this bizarre all-male behavior involving the sucking of long objects can be my guest to go dig up Freud.

It was already a New York cliché that the Sony Building looked like a giant Chippendale dresser. I wouldn't know a Chippendale dresser from a Chippendales dancer, but I liked the Sony Building just fine. I'd never known New York without it. David Loeb was here on the thirtieth floor, and I was going in.

The air-conditioning in the vaulted atrium turned the sweat on my forehead to ice water and made my suit relax. I talked to the security guy, a mocha-colored man with a Brillo-pad mustache, who phoned up to confirm that David Loeb was expecting me. He made me sign his book and pointed me to a waiting elevator car, which I had to myself. As the lights charted my upward mobility, I took out a tissue and daubed my face and palms and made sure my Takashimaya tie was straight. I was calling on a guy who could laugh off the fact that he'd just been dumped by a celebrity client who'd made him four million dollars.

The elevator doors opened on a hall of green marble outside the glass entrance to the high-ceilinged receiving area of the deserted offices of Bulkeley, Stearn. I pressed a buzzer that summoned from the back a young man in shirtsleeves, tie, and suspenders, who smiled raggedly at me and let me in.

"Mr. Quaintance? Alex Clements. I'm David Loeb's assistant." He was about twenty-two with dull eyes and an ashen complexion, as if his boss never allowed him out during the daytime. "He'll be glad you're here. This way, please."

I followed him down labyrinthine corridors, past office after office that were by now empty or dark. Clements held his fingers taut at his sides as if in perpetually perfect typing form. His steps along the marble floor were small and hurried. I kept his pace but with a lazier, longer stride, as I noticed how nicely his thin olive trousers hung from his young butt.

"Everyone else gone home?" I asked.

"Not at all. There's always some who like to go to the library and burn the midnight oil."

"Sounds very pagan."

Clements didn't find that funny, but he gave me a charitable smile. We came to a dark door; he knocked on it perfunctorily before opening it.

"What is it now, Alex?" came the voice from inside.

"Sorry, David. It's Mr. Quaintance."

"Good," said David Loeb, getting up from his desk.

Clements withdrew like a vassal, closing the door behind him with a soft click and leaving us alone.

Loeb looked at me covetously, like I was an hung juror. The thick head of dark hair that worked so well on TV seemed unnatural in person. He was in his fifties, clean-shaven, and deeply tanned, with a sheen to his flesh like a coat of shellac.

We shook hands like a couple of lumberjacks. Loeb had a good grip, and I imagined him as the sort who might engage a colleague or a rival in bouts of racquetball at the New York Athletic Club. He asked me to have a seat, which I did. He offered me a cigar, which I declined. He sat back behind his desk, glancing longingly at his cigar box, then back at me, before deciding against it. He looked like he could use one, but I wasn't going to encourage him. He could have had twenty today for all I knew.

The tall windows behind him faced onto the skyline of midtown from about half the height of the GE Building, which stood starkly illuminated to the westerly edge of the view. Loeb's law books lined the walls on either side, out of the way, leaving the rest of the office clean and uncluttered. His desk was shiny and black, papers neatly ordered, his desk lamp hovering brightly on a hinged graphite arm. An eight-by-ten color photo of his skinny blond wife stood in a black frame between his inbox and his cigar box, facing outward, directing a hollow smile my way. I had seen her on TV as well, hanging on Loeb's arm at a movie premiere at the Ziegfeld. She was a former model. They looked good together. I wondered whether she was a trophy wife or a beard. Loeb had such a virulently heterosexual persona in front of the TV cameras, it made me naturally leery.

I had a high degree of suspicion about people's sexuality—something I picked up in the Army, like a social disease. You never could tell for sure with straight guys until you got them into bed, maybe a little drunk. Maybe a lot drunk.

Loeb was staring at my head. "Is that natural, or—"

I hoped like hell I was not blushing. "Uh, no. I just got it done today, actually."

"You mean you *paid* someone to do that?" Self-consciously, he touched his hair, and I wondered if it was an expensive toupée or maybe a hair weave.

"If I did it myself, I'd end up bleeding to death."

"Do you mind if I ask how much a cut like that costs?"

"This was forty-five. Plus tip."

"Forty-five? I know a guy who'd do it for ten."

Ten might take care of the hair below a toupée, I thought.

"My guy works in the salon below my office," I said. "I like to patronize the local shops. You think I'm a chump."

Loeb shook his head. "Nice area these days, Chelsea. Full of beautiful young people." He smiled. "Where exactly are you?"

"My office is on Eighth between Sixteenth and Seventeenth. My apartment's closer to Ninth."

"Loft?"

"Not exactly." I left it at that. If I were to say I lived in a cramped studio with a kitchenette and slept on a futon, it would defeat the purpose of the Barney's suit. At the same time, I didn't want him to get the impresssion that I didn't need the money. The Army hadn't exactly offered me a pension or health benefits. All they gave undesirables was a kick in the pants.

The back of my neck itched from Juan's handiwork. At this point, meeting Juan was still up in the air. It all depended on what Loeb wanted. If he didn't broach it soon, I would have to get pushy and ask. I risked a glance at my watch: 8:50.

Loeb picked up on my anxiety. "You're wondering why I called you. As I said, a friend put me onto you."

"I didn't realize we had a friend in common."

"You did some work for Tay Farrell out in Southampton. He gave me the strongest possible recommendation. He said I could trust you implicitly."

"He told you I'm gay—and that I'm out."

"Yes. Also that you're good at keeping secrets that need to be kept—such as Tay's gayness."

"I wouldn't give out privileged information of any kind for any reason. The minute I did, I'd be looking for another career."

"Good. That's a good answer."

I couldn't help but wonder how much Tay Farrell had told. Sure, these guys could trust me, but how far could I trust them? Tay was a star of the same daytime soap Hugo Wallis had once been in, and he was just enough in the closet to keep his fans from knowing, while he juggled his glamour boys on the side at his parties in Southampton. It wasn't exactly my crowd. I'd done some security work for him, and after that we'd had a fling for about two days. The fact that Tay was a friend of Loeb's made it all the more conceivable that Loeb's wife was a front. But I wasn't going to ask; I assumed it wasn't germane to the case.

"I value Tay's counsel on certain matters, and I needed some reassurance on this case. I've already lost one investigator."

"Lost? That could mean a lot of things."

"Fired. First he fled, then I fired him."

"Fled. Who is he?"

"Angelo Ferrante."

"Never heard of him," I said, not that that meant anything.

"He took some information with him, which he sold to the *National Enquirer*. We got a call from them today asking us to comment on his story."

"Where's Ferrante now?"

"No idea. But that doesn't matter anymore. He's done all the damage he can. This isn't about Hugo Wallis, Mr. Quaintance. . . . I can just cut the crap and call you Greg, can't I?"

"Sure."

"And call me David, please. Now listen, Greg, what Ferrante sold has the potential of becoming bigger than Hugo Wallis. It has to do with Jimmy Gilbert."

He may as well have said Jesus Christ. I said it myself.

"The *Enquirer* is going to be at the checkout stand of every supermarket in America in five days. Before that, we could see a criminal complaint. We can't stop the presses on the *Enquirer*. I'm asking you to help me nip the criminal case in the bud."

"What kind of charges are we talking about?"

"You don't mind if I go ahead and have a cigar, do you? This has been a long day."

"Doesn't bother me," I said, as he reached for it.

He trimmed it and lit it and drew a few puffs and exhaled noxious green smoke. "First I want to know if you'll take the case. I'll pay double your usual rate—"

"Plus expenses."

"Plus expenses, with a bonus if the work is satisfactory."

"I'll need to know more particulars before I can accept." I was remembering Juan's mention of call boys. Even desperate street hustlers drew the line at certain things.

Loeb swallowed hard. Whatever trust he had in me didn't seem to make it any easier. Still, he wasn't going to tell me anything that Ferrante hadn't already sold. I could read about it next week like everybody else. He bit the bullet.

"The charges are initiating with the mother whose kid is involved."

"What kid?"

He didn't answer. I'd interrupted his train.

"The mother's threatening Jimmy with several counts of first-degree sexual assault of a minor."

"Boy or girl?"

"A boy." Loeb's gaze was a challenge. "Of fourteen."

"Any truth to the charges?"

Loeb shrugged. "As far as you and I are concerned, that's neither here nor there, okay? My job is to protect Jimmy from any and all possible harm. Your job is to help me."

"Assuming I take the case."

"Then I have to know now whether you'll take it."

It sounded like a morass in the making, but I'd have to be an idiot not to leap into it, so I said, "Yeah, okay."

"I'm not asking for much," Loeb insisted, leaning forward and tapping dead ash into a pewter ashtray. "I need you to go talk to the mother. She claims that she's prepared to go to the police and file formal charges against Jimmy unless we can come to terms. A settlement up front, she says."

"Well, it's a lot nicer than saying extortion. If you give her anything, she'll try to milk Jimmy Gilbert for all he's—"

"She's not getting a dime," he said abruptly, interrupting my cliché with one of his own. Smoke came pouring out of his nose. His flesh turned red like the innards of a blood orange.

"And you want me to represent your position."

He nodded. "I can't talk with her directly. It would make her think she had a chance. She wants to play this game with us, and we'll show her how we do it."

Loeb had kept his cool throughout most of the Wallis trial, but he was awfully keyed up now. Perhaps this was his normal self, the one beyond the range of the CNN cameras.

"You're not hiring me to convey threats or bust heads or anything like that."

"No, Greg, of course not. You'll be working on behalf of Bulkeley, Stearn. We're hardly the Mafia. You'll be our special envoy. Our ambassador."

"I admit I like the sound of that."

"The thing is, right now all we have is her word against Jimmy's. You will tell her that if she expects us to negotiate in good faith, she has to give us something in return. You'll tell her we don't know how much of it—in fact, whether any of it—is true and that we're not going to pay for something she can't prove. Either she has to show us some evidence, or she has to bring the kid up here for a Q and A."

"You're looking for a bargaining position?"

"That's what we want *her* to think. Once she gives us some evidence, we'll mold it into something we can use. We'll lay out all our cards for her. She'll see that she can't possibly win, that all she'll succeed at is embarrassing herself and her son and her entire family, and that she won't end up with any of Jimmy's money. In fact, she'll risk losing a defamation suit and paying *us* damages. By then, she will have given in. We'll have her in tears. Then all we'll have left is damage control."

"The tabloid story."

"That's right. They might sell a scoop to one of the TV shows, but that would never air more than a day in advance. That gives us four days. When the story hits, we make the mother and son recant and tell the press that it was all a lie."

I didn't exactly share his ebullience on the damage control point—but I was a free lance, whereas Loeb was deeply vested.

"I want you to go over there tonight and talk with the mother. It can't wait. This may be only the first round of many. It could be a long weekend."

Loeb took a key from his pocket and unlocked the top drawer of his desk, from which he removed a blue file folder.

"I'd guess that Jimmy Gilbert's not an easy client to work for," I said, but Loeb said nothing. He would not be drawn out on such a comment. The mind of a good lawyer was a filing system that sorted everything into what was relevant and what wasn't.

Loeb didn't want to share his file. He was paging through it himself and would tell me whatever he thought I needed to know. This was less than desirable. I wasn't a lawyer, and I preferred a certain amount of chaos when I was looking for answers. Sometimes the most irrelevant thing became the most important; if you overlooked it, it could come back at you like friendly fire. I'd rather have a look at the file myself, but Loeb was the boss.

"This won't be in the *Enquirer*, but the mother is Callie Blassingame." Loeb paused to gauge my reaction.

I had none. I'd never heard the name before, and my disordered mind was drifting back to Juan. I still had plenty of time to call and cancel and say I was sorry—but that didn't mean I'd be granted another chance. Life was rough. Too bad.

Loeb pressed a button on his phone and said, "Alex."

"Yes, David?"

"Get me Mrs. Blassingame, will you?" He lifted his finger and told me, "Callie's married to Dr. Troy Blassingame."

"That rings a bell. Plastic surgeon, isn't he?"

"One of the best. He did Natalie Reston. Perhaps that's why you've heard of him. He was in the press quite a bit while the Restons were in the White House—that whole flap over who paid for the work he did on her."

"Facegate," I said, making Loeb wince. The short-lived scandal had dogged Natalie Reston in the early years of her husband's presidency. Supposedly, the First Lady had managed to divert public monies intended for renovations of the White House to the more pressing project of propping up her face. When she was close to being caught, she hastily paid back the money, claiming it had been a loan in the first place and that she had no idea that anyone would consider it to be theft of public funds. She was never prosecuted; otherwise, she would now be a convicted felon. "That means Dr. Blassingame was the recipient of our largesse— my tax dollars and yours."

"Hey, she paid it back. I always thought the whole scandal was just a lot of smoke." The thought of smoke made Loeb suck on his cigar. "Incidentally, Troy Blassingame also happens to be the longtime plastic surgeon to Jimmy Gilbert."

It was no secret that Jimmy Gilbert had undergone cosmetic surgery. If you were to compare his album covers—from when he was a child star at eight years of age, until now, a man of thirty-five—you would easily perceive changes that could not be accounted for solely by the march of time. Gilbert was six years older than me, and the idea that he could have relied on the services of a "longtime" plastic surgeon was a little creepy.

"I can see how this all got started."

"You can?" Loeb seemed to think I meant more than I said.

Alex Clements's voice came over the speaker: "David, I've got Mrs. Blassingame on the line."

Loeb picked up. "Hello? Yes, Callie, it's David." His manner was polite but terse. "I'd like to send someone over to talk with you. Is now a good enough time?"

Loeb held the receiver slightly away from his ear and held up a finger for me, begging my patience. He rolled his eyes.

"Callie, that's why I'm sending over my representative. His name's Greg Quaintance, and he's a private investigator. You can talk to him as if you were talking to me. No, it won't be like Ferrante. That was a fluke. Trust me. Yes, Callie, I know. I'll take care of it. All right. I'll send him right over."

Loeb hung up noisily. He took up his fountain pen and scratched out an address for me on a Post-it. When I got up to retrieve it, Loeb stood and shook my hand again.

"Good luck, Greg." Loeb reached in his pocket and pulled out a big sheaf of crisp bills folded neatly in half. He pressed it into my palm. "Here's a small advance."

"Thanks." I riffled the corners: three grand, easy.

"I used to throw a lot of work Ferrante's way. If all goes well, this could be the beginning of a lucrative partnership."

"Uh, sure."

I wasn't counting on it. It sounded like a very big if.

Three

The cab took me to Fifth Avenue and East Seventy-ninth Street. I had the driver let me off across the street at Central Park near a couple of pay phones in the shadows near the low, sooty stone wall. I dialed the salon— the only number I had for Juan.

"Sorry," said a young man's voice, nineties disco blaring in the background. "Juan's gone. Can someone else help you?"

"No. He told me he got off at ten. It's only nine-twenty."

"He had some cancellations or something, I think."

"Do you have a number where I could reach him?"

"Let me find out."

I was put on hold and made to listen to a recorded message about their licensed massage therapists.

I looked out across the street to the elegant, beige brick-faced apartment building. The upper floors were lighted twin towers of terraced penthouses overflowing with shadowy foliage. The long awning at street level displayed the address in gold numerals, underneath which the uni- formed doorman was tipping his hat and smiling at a middle-aged man and a teenage boy as they walked out of the building, down the red indoor-outdoor carpet, to where a uniformed chauffeur stood holding open the rear door of a Lincoln limousine.

"I'm sorry, sir, they say I can't give out Juan's number, but I could leave him a message. He'll see it tomorrow."

"That's no good. Could you call him for me yourself?"

"I'll have to see—"

"Look, you don't have to ask anyone's permission, okay?"

"Uh, yeah, I guess so."

The chauffeur took a quick look up and another look down the sidewalk before closing the door after the man and the youth. He climbed in behind the wheel and pulled out into traffic, becoming one of many pairs of red taillights among a horde of yellow cabs.

"Good boy," I said. "Tell him Greg had to cancel, okay? Tell him I got called away on business, and I won't be able to meet him tonight. You got that?"

"Uh-oh—you're Greg? Juan is going to be disappointed!"

"I'm disappointed, too. Tell him I'm sorry, will you?"

"Okay."

"All right, thanks, bud." I hung up.

At a break in traffic, I jaywalked across the street.

"I'm here to see Callie Blassingame."

The doorman ushered me into the foyer. He was a wine-faced man of about sixty with white hair and a tobacco-stained mustache. He grabbed the receiver from the wall and punched a three-digit number. "Yes, Maria? There's a young gentleman—"

"Quaintance. Mrs. Blassingame should be expecting me."

The doorman gave me a thumbs-up. "Gentleman down here for Mrs. Blassingame. Says he's an acquaintance." He gave me a wink. "Okay, I'll send him right up." He hung up. "Go on, they're waiting for you. Penthouse A on thirty-eight."

"You wouldn't know if Dr. Blassingame is home?"

"You're in luck," the doorman said impishly. "You just missed him."
He laughed so hard he began to cough.

The Latina who opened the door held her shoulders square, reminding
me of my former drill sergeant, except that she was sucking in her cheeks
and pursing her lips. She was in her mid-forties, with high cheekbones,
short hair with frosted tips, and a mauve skirt and jacket with gold
buttons. Her posture told me she was really too proud to be anyone's
housekeeper.

"You are the detective?" She raised a dubious eyebrow, nicely
plucked, and held the door only partway open.

I wasn't sure what she didn't like about me. I was opening my mouth
when another voice came hurtling toward us, along with the skittering of
an animal's claws across a parquet floor:

"That's okay, Maria, I'll get it!" This was punctuated by a high-pitched
yap from a small dog that sounded like it wanted to take a bite out of
crime.

Maria opened the door wider and stepped back, eyeing me with
distaste. I found myself wishing I'd brought along a hat and coat to hand
her. And a bone for the dog.

"Mr. Quaintance? I'm Callie." She stepped in between me and Maria
as if to avert something. "Please come in."

"Thanks," I said and stepped over the pooch—a little Scottie that was
panting from all the excitement and had no interest in my ankle or in my
Kenneth Cole shoes.

Callie's eyes were red and puffy, the collar of her silk blouse was half
turned up, and the jade brooch that kept her cleavage from popping open
was slightly askew. Her hair was tangled. The shifts that hung over the
open French doors were billowing in, revealing the dark terrace beyond. It
looked like a good place to go for a crying jag if you were upset for some
reason that your husband and son had just left you alone with your

housekeeper and your crazy dog.

"What'll you have to drink?" Callie asked.

I told her a Pellegrino would be fine, and she frowned.

The Scottie was running circles around its mistress, barking and prancing and bucking like a bronco as Callie locked the front door and led me into the living room. She gave Maria my drink order and asked for a double Scotch on the rocks for herself.   Maria gave her a disapproving look and made small *clip-clops* across the floor as she disappeared down the hallway.

"Have a seat," Callie said, directing me to one end of the immense sofa while she sat on its opposite wing. The overhead track lighting was aimed down at her like carefully positioned spotlights. Her face was perfect like nothing is—bottled-blond hair, eyes in sweet symmetry, nose neither too big nor too wide, jaw well defined, cheekbones chiseled without looking gaunt—with no major fault lines to indicate she had ever had any worries. It was like looking at a refinished piece of furniture: you could stare at it all you wanted, but it wasn't going to give you any hint how long it had been around, where it might have been, or how it might have been treated.

"Poor Jenks," Callie said, scruffling the dog's head. He was trying to bounce up into her lap. "He's got attention deficit disorder."

"I didn't know it afflicted dogs."

"Oh, he's got the attention span of a chihuahua. Don't you, Jenks? Yes, you do!"

We were in the middle of the living room, which was easily five times the size of my entire apartment. The Blassingames had the requisite wall of shelves cluttered with unread novels (*August 1914, The Satanic Verses, Harlot's Ghost*) and oversized art and photography books. Several large twentieth-century portraits were hung importantly along another wall and individually lighted, but I had no clue who either the artists or the subjects were. I supposed one of the books could tell me. They kept a baby grand piano where the living room bled into the dining room. Beyond that lay the terrace. I caught a narrow glimpse of Maria's leg in the kitchen down the hall, and I figured on several bedrooms, a master suite, and maybe an office down that direction as well. They would have two or three bathrooms, and the terrace would extend from the dining room to the master bedroom. The building had probably gone co-op when I was about ten years old; by now, the Blassingames' square footage would be worth a few cool million.

"Listen, I don't want to waste your time," I said. "David Loeb called you about me. I'm a private investigator."

"Yes, I know." Callie seemed sad that we were getting down to business so soon.

I dug a card out of my wallet and handed it to her. While she was looking at it, Maria appeared with our drinks.

"Oh, Maria, would you be a dear and take Jenksie into the kitchen? I think he needs his Ritalin."

"Yes, Mrs. Blassingame." Maria, who looked like she was in no mood to be a dear, hefted the dog up by his trunk and carried him away down the hall, paws scrambling in the air.

"You're sure he's not just frisky?" I asked.

"Oh, no, he has A.D.D. The vet diagnosed it. When he has a spell, we're supposed to give him half a Ritalin."

"How many milligrams is that?"

"I have no idea."

"Looks like an awfully small dog to be given half a tablet of anything meant for us."

"It does the trick."

"Your vet's sure it's safe?"

"Oh, please, Ritalin is harmless! And Jenks is a much happier doggie today than he was."

Sure he was happy. He was getting a steady supply of human stimulants. By now, Jenks had probably conditioned the people he lived with so that whenever he acted out, they would reward him with a fix. Pavlov and

Skinner would be proud of him.

"Cigarette?" Callie said, opening a Russian lacquered box on the coffee table and turning the Dunhills toward me. I took one, and so did she. I pulled out my Zippo and leaned across the table for her, then lit my own. She tossed her hair back, exhaled a lungful of smoke, dropped the facade of pleasantness, narrowed her eyes, and said, "So."

"We both know why I'm here."

"Now you sound like Angelo Ferrante."

"Never met the guy."

"You're here because David is still too scared to come himself and look me in the eye."

"You've known David Loeb long?"

"We go back. He's been Jimmy's lawyer as long as my husband's been Jimmy's plastic surgeon."

"Have you or your husband ever been his client?"

"No. David handles only celebrities, not hangers-on like my husband. And there are better lawyers."

"Why don't you have one here now?"

"I'd rather handle this myself." She gave me a sly smirk and tasted her Scotch.

"That makes me think you don't trust your own lawyer."

"I'm in between lawyers at the moment. I'm divorcing Troy, and the first thing he gets to keep is our lawyer."

"How long have you been divorcing him?"

"We separated last week. I haven't officially filed for divorce yet. I had an attorney—good friend of mine—but he screwed up the separation agreement, so I fired him. I know plenty of others. I guess I should pick the best attorney, not the best friend."

"Is the one you fired still your friend?"

She took a leisurely drag on her cigarette. "You're more inquisitive than Mr. Ferrante."

"I'll take that as a compliment."

"Maybe you shouldn't. I liked Mr. Ferrante."

"How do you like him now that he sold what you told him?"

"How much did he sell?"

"We won't know until the paper hits the stands. But if he was that strapped for cash, you shouldn't assume that he held anything back just because he enjoyed your company."

"How do you know he was having financial troubles?"

"I don't. I figure he must have needed more money in the short term. Maybe he owed someone some money."

"Too bad. But I don't blame Ferrante. I blame David for hiring him. How do I know I can trust you?"

"The story's worthless now."

"I doubt that. The *Enquirer* has rivals. And there's the tabloid TV shows."

"Callie, listen to me. If I do good work for Loeb, the word of mouth will do me more good in the long run than selling out for a payoff. As near as I can make out, trust was the main criterion David Loeb used when he hired me. He knows Ferrante was a mistake."

"That asshole, he better know," Callie said. "Ferrante's going to ruin everything. David stands as much to lose as I do."

"Is money your only concern?"

Callie snuffed out her cigarette in the ashtray. "Of course not. But what good will it do to drag everybody through a long criminal proceeding when I could be taken care of up front?"

"You mean you and your son."

"You know what Jason would go through up there on the witness stand? The trial could even be televised. Jason's identity is supposed to be kept secret since he's a minor, but people will *know*. For him to get up on that stand and recount all the things Jimmy did to him—think of the humiliation!"

I got the impression she was thinking of her own.

"How do we know that this would ever proceed to a full criminal trial?" I asked. "That Jason would even testify?"

Callie lit another cigarette and ignored my questions.

I pressed her again: "If he didn't want to testify, could you even compel him to?"

"I don't want to get into any of that right now."

"We'll save it for later, then. Without a criminal trial, you're basing your monetary demands on the threat of negative publicity. Jimmy Gilbert's going to get the negative publicity anyway next week. If you file charges, the D.A. won't even think of prosecuting if you can't get your son to testify."

"Is Jimmy willing to take that risk? He could go to jail for years and be tagged as a sex offender the rest of his life."

"Your case is on shaky ground even before we've heard any evidence. What is your evidence, by the way?"

"I don't see why I need to get into that right now, either."

"As far as we know, there could be nothing. Accusations of this kind are made all the time against celebrities—"

"This isn't like that," Callie insisted matter-of-factly.

"How much do you want, anyway?"

"Twenty million."

"That's a lot of money."

"It's not even a tenth of what Jimmy's worth."

"That doesn't mean you're entitled to any. How much are you going to get in the divorce?"

She sat up stiffly. "That has nothing to do with anything."

"Loeb isn't going to part with any of Jimmy Gilbert's money as long as he thinks this is a scam. How do we know it's not?"

Callie laughed smugly. She looked up, staring deep into my eyes. "David knows. You can bet David knows. You know, Mr. Quaintance, you may be in over your head. You go back to David and tell him that he can't scare me off even if he sends over a hundred lackeys."

"I can't. David won't go any further until he can have a look at some evidence. In the absence of physical evidence, he wants you to bring Jason up to his office for a Q and A."

"Over my dead body. Who does he think he is?"

"Listen, I doubt if you have any physical evidence, because you haven't even gone to the police. You're not likely ever to have much in the way of evidence, because you've already tipped off Jimmy Gilbert. If he's done anything to Jason, he'll have already gotten rid of any incriminating evidence—photographs, videotapes, articles of clothing, whatever."

Callie closed her eyes against what I was saying.

I went on. "You haven't taken Jason to the hospital for a physical exam, have you?"

"I can't put Jason through that."

"Well, that's the first thing the police will do once you report it, even if the last incident occurred days or even months ago. It's standard procedure. But it's unlikely that any useful evidence would come from it. I mean, you're not talking about a forcible rape, are you?"

"I don't know what you're getting at." She did, though.

"This isn't a case where Jimmy Gilbert jumped out of the shadows and held a knife up to your son's throat, is it?"

"No, it isn't."

"I'd guess that Jimmy Gilbert has known Jason for some time, hasn't he? Given that he's known you and your husband since—when, since before Jason was born?"

"Jimmy was at his christening. We named him Jason's godfather. But they only started spending significant amounts of time together last year, when Jimmy took Jason to Asia with him."

"This was what, his concert tour last year?"

"That's right. Last summer, the second leg of Jimmy's tour. He offered to bring Jason along."

"And you let him go?"

"Of course. Why shouldn't we? I never suspected a thing. It never crossed my mind that Jimmy might do anything improper." Callie laughed once, harshly. "Maybe I should have. I guess the rest of the world thinks Jimmy's a freak. Well, I trusted him."

"When did you figure out what was going on?"

"Last week. Until then I had no idea."

"How did you find out? Did Jason tell you?"

"No. Everything began to add up. A combination of things."

"Like what?"

But she was mum on details. "You must think I'm an idiot to have let it go on for so long without catching on."

"No, I don't."

"Well, let me tell you, it's hardly the kind of thing I would have thought about my own son."

"After you figured it out, what did you do?"

"I confronted Jason."

"What did he say?"

"He just said, 'So what?'" Callie's eyes grew watery, and her voice choked up. "'So what, Mom, what's the big deal?' That's what he said! 'So what, Mom'!"

I handed her a facial tissue from my pocket pack.

"Jason sees it as consensual," I said. "If he doesn't see what the big deal is, how are you going to get him to testify?"

Callie wiped the tears from her cheeks and let out a single, sad laugh. "No wonder David hired you. You got just what you came for, didn't you? Now you think this will never go to trial. You're wrong. If I don't get paid, I want to see Jimmy in jail."

"I wasn't trying to trick you, Callie. I'm just trying to get one thing clear, though, for myself, at least."

"What's that?"

"I want to know why you don't take this to the police right now. Jason's still a minor, which means that legally, none of it was consensual. In that case, a crime has been committed. If I were you, I'd take it to the police."

"Thanks," she said, sniffling. "At least I know I can trust you. David might think of some sneaky maneuvers, but he would never suggest that I go to the police."

"Then why don't you?"

"I wish it was that easy."

"Why isn't it?"

"I can't tell you."

"Why not?"

"Look, I'm doing the only thing I can do. You go back and tell David that I'm not giving up. He'll know what I mean."

"I will. But you won't get anywhere with David unless you can produce some evidence."

"What can I do? I can't put Jason through a Q and A."

"How about if I talked to him?"

"No, I can't do that."

"No recordings, no transcripts, I won't even take notes. You can check me out first. Just allow me to find out the facts. You and I can go over them, if you like. Then I take them back to Loeb, and he can decide whether he wants to pay or play."

"Maybe," she said. "Only as long as Jason cooperates, though. I guess you'll need his father's permission, too."

"What's the chance of that?"

Callie weighed it. "I don't know. These days, it's hard to predict what Troy will say."

"Because of the separation? I'd like to know what set it off. Was it before or after you caught on to Jimmy and Jason?"

"Don't put it that way!" She twirled her hair with a finger and finished the last of her double Scotch. "'Jimmy and Jason'—as if they were a couple, for Christ's sake!"

"Tell me what it had to do with you and your husband."

"What do you think?"

"I have no idea."

"He knew," she said finally, quietly, swirling the melted ice around in her empty glass. "The bastard knew all along and didn't tell me. That was the straw that broke my back."

"Where are they now?"

"Who?" She looked at me but seemed unable to focus.

"Your husband and your son. I saw them leaving here in a limousine just before I came up to see you. Where did they go?"

"Oh. Back to the country house. You don't think this is all we've got, do you?"

"Where's the house?"

"New Jersey. Outside of Raritan. Somerset County."

"Raritan," I said, racking my brain. "Isn't the Doris Duke estate out that way?"

Callie nodded. "She was one of our neighbors. You want to know our other neighbors? There's our senile ex-President, Ralph Reston. And Natalie Reston, of course."

"One of your husband's best customers."

"That's right. Good ol' Facegate." Callie held up her glass to the former First Lady. She seemed quite drunk. "Also Jimmy Gilbert. His estate butts up against ours."

Poor choice of words, I thought.

"Has your son been staying with you?"

"For a few days."

"Why did your husband come tonight?"

"Because I'm not allowed to have Jason here. It's in our separation agreement. Troy has sole custody of Jason until we get the divorce worked out. That's why I fired my lawyer."

"So when can I talk to Jason?"

"I don't know. I'll have to discuss it with Troy."

"Listen, Callie, once you get a new lawyer, I'm sure he can get your separation agreement thrown out. If your husband knew all along what was going on, and if Jason's story is true—"

"Of course it's true. You don't believe me?"

"Yes, I do. That's another reason why I'd like to talk to Jason. I want to know if he's telling you the truth."

"Why would he make up such a thing?"

"To make you mad. To get your attention. To play you and your husband off each other. Or just for kicks. Who knows?"

She shook her head. "You don't know Jason."

"Is he your only son?"

"Our only child."

"Have you got a photo?"

Callie stood up, stumbled slightly on her pumps, and went over to the bookshelves. She pulled down a thick album and laid it out on the coffee table before us.

"These are his baby pictures." She opened the first leaf.

There were several shots of the naked baby Jason on his stomach, bare butt in the air, holding a rattle. I was about to tell Callie I wasn't interested in his life story when she turned the next page, to his christening.

"Oh!" she said, turning her face.

There was Jimmy Gilbert holding the swaddled Jason and smiling, his eyes hidden behind wraparound sunglasses, as he stood along with the priest, Dr. Troy Blassingame, and a much younger Callie. This would have been the year of Jimmy Gilbert's most successful album, *Provocateur*, which had four number-one singles: "Provocateur," "Spinning in Circles," "My Song," and "Once in a While." I remember because I was in high school out in Wyoming; MTV was new to our town, and no matter where you went, you couldn't escape Gilbert's videos.

I skippped to the back of the book. The shots here were professionally done—some in color, some in black and white—of a charming young teen-aged boy in various cocky poses, wearing different sets of casual clothes.

"He's done some modeling," Callie said proudly. "This one was in a

Macy's ad in the *Times* last month." She pointed to one of him wearing a pair of khaki summer shorts and a polo shirt.

His smile was brilliant, and he had sandy-blond hair that was long on top and short along the sides. The hairstylists had tried different looks— parted in the middle or over the side or slicked back. Sometimes they wanted him more boyish, sometimes looking older than his age, sometimes clean-cut, sometimes grungier, sometimes goofy, sometimes brainy (with glasses).

"How about a family snapshot?" I asked.

Callie turned back a few leaves and froze. She snatched a five-by-seven from the page before I had a chance to see it. She ripped it in half, then in quarters, then again until she couldn't rip anymore. The pieces fell from her fingers.

"Jesus, I forgot about that one."

"What was it?"

"Here, go ahead, have a look. I didn't mean to do that. It's just that I'm so . . . well, here." She handed me the small, colorful pieces of paper.

I spread them out on the coffee table, turning them all face up, and put the puzzle together. I vaguely recognized the photo.

"It was that ad campaign last year for those jeans," she said. "The one they had to pull because it was pornographic."

It wasn't pornographic, of course. A mother wasn't likely to put a piece of child pornography in her son's photo album. But it was sensuous and provocative, which was why the ad campaign had been yanked after it had already been plastered on every bus stop and billboard in Manhattan. If you looked at it coldly and dispassionately, you could wonder what all the fuss was about. It was basically a thirteen-year-old boy lying on a shag carpet with his shirt unbuttoned, showing most of his chest, and wearing a pair of cutoff jeans with the top button undone. He had a glazed, almost drugged look on his face.

"Who was the photographer?" I asked.

"Yuri Zetlin. Maybe you've heard of him."

"I've seen his work in *Vanity Fair*, I believe."

Perhaps Callie hadn't considered them obscene when she let Jason do the shoot or when she put it in the book; when the furor erupted, she changed her mind but forgot to remove it.

"You can have it if you want it," she said.

"No, thanks."

I remembered the ad campaign, and I remembered this picture of Jason; it had passed in front of me a few times on the sides of city buses. This photo and the others like it were nothing in themselves—they left the pornographic part to our adult imaginations—but I didn't like these kids being used this way. The fact that I'd looked made me feel complicit.

I heard a strange, sad whine from down the hallway.

Jenks came toward us stepping almost sideways, his eyes glassy. He made it to Callie's feet and collapsed, rolling on his back with his tongue lolling out and his paws in the air. He looked like he should have two black X's across his eyes.

I poked him to try to elicit a reaction.

"Jenks?" Callie said. "My God, he's dead."

"No, he's not." I could feel his pulse: fast by our standards but fairly relaxed for a dog. "He's just out."

"Maria?"

Maria stepped into the room looking troubled, as if she knew she had done something wrong. "Yes, Mrs. Blassingame?"

"You gave Jenks only half a pill, didn't you?"

"I'm sorry, Mrs. Blassingame. I couldn't find the Ritalin, so I gave him half a Valium. Is he all right?"

Callie looked to me.

"I don't know," I said. "I'm not a vet. If I were you, I'd call one. Ritalin's a stimulant, Valium's a depressant."

"What happened to the Ritalin?" Callie asked.

"I don't know," Maria said.

"Is the prescription just for the dog?" I asked.

"Yes," Callie said. "Well, it's in my name. They don't make a canine pill. My vet talked to my doctor, and he prescribed it to me, but I don't take it. It's for Jenks only."

"Jason doesn't have attention deficit disorder, does he?"

"He certainly does not," Callie said, as if I were casting aspersions on her genetic legacy.

"How many pills were in the bottle?"

"It was nearly full last time I saw it," Maria said. "That was this morning."

"But Ritalin is harmless," Callie said. "Isn't it?"

"No drug is completely harmless," I said. "Some kids abuse Ritalin, grinding it up and snorting it like cocaine. They don't try to control their dosage."

"But Jason wouldn't be so stupid—"

"How sure are you anymore of what he would or wouldn't do?"

She looked at me as if I'd said something particularly low. But then her face relaxed; she seemed to realize that my concern was well placed.

"You don't look surprised that he might have taken the bottle," I said.

"Do you think he's in any immediate danger?"

"No. It might mean he's getting involved with other drugs, though. Or just about to. Fourteen's a rough age."

"Mr. Quaintance," she said, "I guess I do want you to talk to him. But I think you'll have to go out there yourself, to Raritan. For Jason's sake I should try to stay out of it."

"Do you think your husband will let me see him?"

"Sure, he'll let you," she said. "As long as you don't tell him you came from me."

"What do you suggest I say?"

"Tell him the truth. Tell him you're working for David Loeb, on behalf of Jimmy Gilbert. He'll let you right in."

Four

The red carpet took me back out to the sidewalk. The doorman smiled at me like we were old comrades and gave me a last wink. Either he thought I'd gone up to Callie's for a quickie or he had a thing for bald guys. He asked if he could hail me a cab. I told him no thanks and dashed back across the street. A delivery truck accelerated and tried to clip me, but it missed. Nothing nefarious; for a pedestrian in Manhattan, it was all in the game—like running from the bulls of Pamplona, only every day.

I put a quarter in the pay phone and turned around to keep an eye on Callie's building. I dug out the unlisted phone number David Loeb had given me, but I hesitated before pressing the final digit. I wasn't ready to tell Loeb everything I knew, and I didn't want him telling me what I should do next.

"Hello," Loeb said after the fourth ring.

"David, it's Greg Quaintance. I saw Callie Blassingame."

"Callie? How is she?" He sounded as if I'd run into an old friend of his on the street quite by accident.

"I found her a little unstable."

"Sorry to hear it. What about the evidence?"

"If she's got anything, she's not sharing."

"You must have formed some kind of impression about it. Do you think there is any?"

"She was pretty cagey on that."

"What about Jason?"

"What about him?"

"How did he seem to you?"

"He wasn't there. Neither was the father. There's a chance we could bring Jason in for a Q and A, though. Callie didn't rule it out, anyway. Had she made you an offer yet?"

"We hadn't gotten that far. She may have said something to Ferrante."

"Well, now she's made one. She wants twenty million."

Loeb paused, and I imagined him taking a big toke on one of his cigars. "That cocksucking—"

"Otherwise, she'll be perfectly happy to see Jimmy Gilbert carted off to prison to reap his reward."

Loeb laughed curtly, like he didn't find me funny at all, and said, "That's a bluff."

"Maybe. But if you hired me for my honest opinion—"

"Yes, go ahead."

"This is looking like a big tar baby. You're sure you don't want to just settle and put the whole thing behind you?"

There was another pause, and this time no response.

"David?" I said. "I mean, even without evidence, she might be able to make enough waves to ruin Jimmy Gilbert's career."

"You think I don't know that? What do you think this is all about?"

"Are you going to let me speak to Jimmy?"

"I don't think you'll need to."

"It might be worthwhile to hear what he has to say."

"I told you," Loeb said, growing impatient, "whether the charges are true has no bearing on any of this."

"But we may get to hear Jason Blassingame's version. You don't want to compare what each of them has to say?"

"I don't particularly care."

"Now's your only chance. If you show Jimmy a transcript of Jason's story, he'll modify his own. We should get Jimmy's side of it while we can keep the stories separate."

"Give me a break, Greg. What do you think Jimmy's going to say? That he fucked a fourteen-year-old boy? Do you think he'll admit it to you?"

"If he did it, you mean."

"Okay," Loeb said, sighing a couple of times like he was deliberately calming himself down. "Maybe you should talk to him, but not now. I want to hear what Jason has to say first. When can we have him?"

"I'm working on that."

"What do you mean you're working on it?"

"You may have to put in a call to Dr. Blassingame and vouch for me. We'll need his permission to talk to Jason."

"Callie's dragging Troy into her scheme?"

"No, I don't think so. It's just a necessity. She doesn't have Jason right now." I felt like I was telling him too much. "He's with his father at their estate."

"So what? You can go out there and get him, can't you?"

"We'll need Dr. Blassingame's permission. He's got sole custody while they work out their divorce."

This elicited another pause.

"I'll call him right now and try to set it up so you can see Jason tonight. The sooner the better. I don't care how late we have to keep them up."

"Okay," I said. "If you think it can't wait till tomorrow."

"No, I don't think so. I'm going to call Troy right now. I'll call you back and give you the details. Where are you?"

I saw Callie Blassingame emerging from the entrance, under the awning. She was distracted, looking down into her purse, putting something away and snapping the clasp shut. She must have left Jenks in Maria's capable hands.

"David, I'm at a pay phone," I said. "Across the street from Callie's building. I can't hang around here. You can call my home number and leave a message on my machine."

"Why don't you call me when you get back to your apartment?"

I told him I would, and we hung up.

Callie looked annoyed at the doorman as he asked her a question. She shook her head no and went on, turning onto the sidewalk and heading toward East Seventy-eighth Street, slinging her purse over her shoulder. She kept looking down, preoccupied. If I were a purse-snatcher, I'd have her pegged as an easy mark.

I moved away from the phones, pacing her on my side of the avenue. At the corner, she turned onto East Seventy-eighth, heading east. I crossed and followed her at a discreet distance until she reached a parking garage. She waited near the entrance while the attendant went for her car. I waited up the block in the shadow of a tree. Two minutes passed, during which she looked at her watch six times. A metallic green Lexus emerged from the mouth of the garage onto the lip of the sidewalk. The attendant got out. Callie got in and turned out onto East Seventy-eighth, cutting in front of a cab.

The cab came to a stop. It was available. The driver, a middle-aged man in a turban and handlebar mustache, was cursing Callie in his mother tongue as I opened the back door and got in. He didn't notice me until I said, "See that car?"

"Yes, my friend?" The driver spoke in a singsong. He switched the fare on and took off, speeding down the street and staying not far behind Callie. "Where to this lovely evening?"

The hack license on the dashboard said he was MAHMOUD HAMIDULLAH. I hoped he understood me.

"Follow that car," I said, feeling embarrassed.

Mahmoud Hamidullah said, "Pardon me, my friend, but are you kidding me?" His smiling face turned fully around to face me, though he kept his hands on the wheel. "Follow that car?"

"That's what I said. Follow that car."

"That car?" He turned back around just in time to brake behind Callie, who was stopped at the red light. My right foot was pressing firmly against the seat in front of me.

"That's right. *That* one. Follow it." I was forceful, trying to be the ugly American.

"Follow that car!" Now that he knew I meant it, he started laughing and couldn't stop. "Follow that car!"

"Keep it down, will you?"

"Okay, Kojak!"

Mahmoud proved to be a quick and slippery hack, maneuvering in and out of lanes to jockey into the best position. We followed Callie down half of Manhattan. She drove fairly well herself, considering she had who knew how many double Scotches in her. We kept up with her all the way to the west end of Canal Street, where she got into the lane for the Holland Tunnel.

"You want me still to follow, boss?" Mahmoud asked. If he was leaving the city, he'd want to know where we were going, and I had no idea other than Jersey. If we followed Callie to the other side of the tunnel, the New York City cab would be too conspicuous to maintain a tail. For all I knew, Callie could be heading to Atlantic City to see Tony Bennett.

I didn't have time for it.

"No," I said. "Skip it."

"Okay by me, my friend," Mahmoud said.

He ducked out of the lane and back onto Canal Street.

"Where to now?"

I gave him my address in Chelsea. The next thing I knew, we were going up Hudson Street at a full head of steam.

I leaned against the headrest and took a five-minute nap.

Five

The Barney's suit had served its purpose and went back into my closet. I could do with less for Troy Blassingame, and if I got to talk to Jason, I didn't want to be wearing anything too intimidating, so I pulled on a black T-shirt, black Calvin Klein briefs, black jeans, and black boots. I doused my head in cold spray at the kitchenette sink and let it drip-dry while I listened to my messages. There were three.

The first was Juan, wondering where I was and sounding hopeful that I was just unexpectedly delayed. The second was David Loeb, telling me I'd been squared away with Blassingame and that I should call him before I left for Jersey. The third was Juan again, telling me that he hadn't been stood up by anyone in a long time. He called me a *pendejo*, and this time he meant it.

I switched the machine to Erase.

I felt like wringing the neck of the twerp I'd spoken with on the phone. It was pitiable to think that a young male receptionist at a full-service hair salon in the Chelsea gay ghetto had already risen to his level of incompetence.

I tried the salon, but they were closed. A recorded message encouraged me to try their new UV beds for that all-over tan.

I called Loeb and got him on the second ring: "Yes?"

"It's Greg. I got your message. I'm ready to head out."

"Troy's willing to see you as soon as you can get there."

"I'm about an hour away. Do I need to call him first?"

"No, that won't be necessary."

"Did he agree to let us have Jason for a Q and A?"

"Not exactly. Listen, Troy is a friend of mine, and we agreed not to make it so official right now. Troy would rather simply let you talk to Jason and see what comes of it. You play it by ear, Greg. If there's any meat to Jason's story, we could set up the Q and A for tomorrow, as long as Troy agrees."

"Okay, if that's the way he wants it. But David, tell me one thing. You've known the Blassingames for a long time."

"That's right, so?"

"You must know Jason, too."

"I do, as a matter of fact."

"Is he credible?"

"As much as any kid. I wouldn't say I've ever paid much attention to him." He sounded bored with the subject. "Listen, Greg, I have some other business to attend to before I turn in. If anything unexpected happens tonight, call me, no matter how late. Otherwise, I'll expect to hear from you tomorrow."

We said good-bye and hung up.

I checked out my watch: 11:10 p.m. Juan might still be at the coffee joint. It was only a couple of blocks away but in the opposite direction from Kotby's garage. I was anxious to get my car out of dry dock and get to Jersey, but the slim chance that I might catch Juan won out.

I pulled on my shoulder holster and checked to make sure I had a full clip in my Glock and a round in the chamber. I didn't have to check the safety, because on Glocks it's not on a switch but built trickily into the trigger. Too hot for a jacket, but I put one on to keep the gun hidden. It was lightweight and, like everything else in my ensemble, flat dead black.

I locked up my place and went over to Eighth Avenue, then up a few blocks, and looked in through the glass at the coffee joint. The place was a smorgasbord of twenty- to forty-year-old men who wore tiny shirts to show off their muscle mass. All the seats were taken. Some guys simply stood against the walls, holding their coffee freezes and chatting amiably. Some spilled out onto the sidewalk, while others spilled out of their clothes.

I stepped inside and glanced around but saw no sign of Juan. I wondered if he'd gone home or headed out to a club or found someone else to get to know.

Fuck it, I thought. I'd just wasted a good ten minutes.

Ahmed Kotby's garage was reconstructed out of an old meat warehouse on West Sixteenth Street between Tenth Avenue and the West Side Highway, just down from the Chelsea Piers along the Hudson River. The attendants in the small office keep a rusty meat hook at the ready in case of trouble. I seldom see Ahmed. He employs young mestizo men to park and watch the cars, particularly during the night shift. Tonight it was Alejandro, who was about twenty. His thick black hair stood straight up on top like a hedgehog's quills, was shorn half an inch long over his ears, and hung long and straight down to his shoulder blades. Alejandro wore a sleeveless T-shirt and had fine shoulders and a nose like Juan's but without the nosering. He was always friendly, but I couldn't tell whether he looked forward to seeing me or to driving my car.

"Hey," he said, smiling and running his hand over the top of his head, staring at my naked scalp. "Nice do, man."

"Your turn next, Alejandro."

"Me?" The thought of it made him blush. "No way, man!"

Alejandro locked up the office and hurried to get my car, a black '70

Plymouth Barracuda with a V-8 engine too big to be street legal in New York State. I'd bought it in El Paso during my training days at Fort Bliss, before I was transferred to Fort Bragg. I used to dream about the 'Cuda while I was stuck in Saudi, and it was with the 'Cuda that I had my sweetest reunion on returning. Ever since we'd moved to New York, it was feeling ignored; it sometimes ran like it was in a fit of pique.

It rumbled like a kitten tonight, though, as Alejandro rolled it up to my feet. Reluctantly, he turned over the keys.

"I'll think about it," he said.

"Hmm?" I'd closed my door and was ready to go.

He touched the top of his head again, ruffling his stiff spines, and said, "Maybe I will, man. Summer, you know?"

"Yeah, go for it. I'd like to see it."

Alejandro laughed heartily, without malice. "I bet you would, man. I know all about you."

Traffic was light through the dirty tiled tube of the Holland Tunnel. I skipped the New Jersey Turnpike, choosing instead to brave the brittle old ironworks of the General Pułaski Skyway, an endless high-level bridge over the Hackensack and Passaic Rivers that always gave me a feeling of foreboding. I didn't care if they did give it regular inspections; if someone would have only given the thing a coat of paint, it would have made me feel much safer. Once I was off the skyway and onto US 22, I was free to throttle up to a cruising speed of 75 mph. The 'Cuda thanked me; for a big-engined car like this, some good quality time on the highway was the closest I could come to giving it a massage.

The headlight beams caressed the road while Mayflies and June bugs committed ritual suicide against the windshield.

An hour out of Manhattan, I turned off US 22 onto US 202 and came into Raritan. I stopped at a 7-Eleven, filled the gluttunous 'Cuda with high-test, checked the oil, and washed the tiny victims' dismembered legs and wings and egg-yolk entrails off the curved glass. I went inside to pay.

The clerk was in his early twenties, with a wispy mustache that hadn't done any growing since he was sixteen, sunken eyes and cheeks that said he hadn't had a decent meal in weeks, and hair that was stringy and mussed and hadn't been washed in days.

"Gas on pump three and a pack of Luckies."

"Uh, okay." The clerk stared at the readouts on the gas pump panel, looking baffled like they were the main controls to a nuclear power station. "Which pump was that?"

"Three." It was the only one that had been put into use since I'd pulled up.

He flipped a switch he'd forgotten to flip. "Oh, yeah, there it is. Oh, that must be your Barracuda, then."

I said that was right. He told me how much I owed, but it was just the gas total, so I reminded him about the cigarettes.

"Oh, yeah. Lucky Strikes, right? Filters or regular?"

"Regular." The bills in my wallet were damp with sweat. I took some out and paid him. I thought he probably wouldn't be any help to me, but I went ahead and asked: "You wouldn't know where I'd find the Blassingame estate, would you?"

"Oh, sure," he said. "Somerset Hills Estates."

"Some kind of development?"

"Uh-huh. That's where the rich folks live."

"Who all do you know lives out there?"

"Oh, President Reston, of course, and Jimmy Gilbert, Dr. Blassingame, and . . ." He named a few names of people I'd never heard of and didn't care about.

"How do I get there from here?"

He gave me verbal directions, which I had him sketch out on a napkin. He had a shaky hand, but the map was legible enough.

"They won't let you in, though. It's all fenced off with a guard. You don't get in unless you're some kind of big shot."

I thanked him for the compliment and went back to the 'Cuda.

*   *   *

The guardhouse was a well-lighted beige structure on a concrete island in between the Somerset Hills exit and entrance. The road was blocked on either side by tall, symmetrical gates of black wrought iron. Off the road, the gates were continued as silvery chain-link fencing with coils of razor wire strung along the top. No estates could be seen from here—only dense black forest that stood motionless in the still night air. It seemed like the entrance to a prison compound or a top-secret military facility.

I pulled up to the open guardhouse window, smiled my best dopey smile, and said, "Evening."

"Evening," the guard repeated, skeptically.

The military motif was echoed by his uniform. He wore an intimidating Special Forces–style beret, a creased black shirt with epaulets, and a patent leather Sam Browne with a silver buckle in the middle. The shoulder patch said SOMERSET HILLS SECURITY. The black plastic nameplate on his left breast said FERRIGNO. He was about my age, with fine olive skin, thick black eyebrows, and a look of deep suspicion. He seemed determined not to let me in and was ready to challenge anything I had to say.

It was becoming on him. He was cuter than any guy I'd seen tonight at the Chelsea coffee joint. Under other circumstances, I might have asked for his phone number.

"What do you want?"

"I'm here to see Dr. Troy Blassingame."

"Pretty late for visitors."

"I didn't pick the time." I shrugged, feigning innocence.

Ferrigno decided to get out of the guardhouse and stand right up next to my window. He wore a black gunbelt that holstered a nine-millimeter semi-automatic pistol. The legs of his pants were tucked into high-laced boots, and the fly had an open, exposed silvery zipper that was sewn upside down for easy access. Somerset Hills Security really went in for the paramilitary look. I had to agree with them, if only because it looked awfully sexy on Ferrigno. He bent over and set his forearm against my door, sticking his face right up into mine.

"What's your name?" He smelled of cinnamon breath mints. Black stubble poked out of his jaw, and his face was coated with a thin layer of sweat.

"Greg Quaintance."

"Let's see some ID."

I pulled out my New York State driver's license, my private investigator's license, and my business card.

Ferrigno took them and said, "Be right back."

He went back to his booth and glanced at his clipboard. He grabbed a phone and spoke a few words over the receiver.

From behind me, headlights flared across the guardhouse, and a noisy engine came zooming up. Ferrigno squinted into the light. When he shielded his eyes and saw whose car it was, he frowned. The driver leaned on the horn. I hoped it wasn't Callie Blassingame. I saw in the rearview mirror, though, that it wasn't a metallic green Lexus but a canary yellow Ferrari.

"Shit," Ferrigno muttered, storming out of the booth. As he passed my window, he said, "Wait here, bud."

Casually he approached the Ferrari. The driver honked twice more and called, "Get off your ass, Bert!"

It was a woman. I turned to get a look at her.

"I can't let you in, Ms. Gilbert. You know that."

"You damn well better let me in, Bert. I've got to see my brother."

All I could see was a big pile of wavy brunette hair and a pair of glasses with large black frames. The only sister of Jimmy Gilbert's that I knew of was Julianna. Jimmy had hosted a variety show in the late 1970s, when he was in his mid-teens, and Julianna had been a frequent guest, singing precocious songs and acting like a smart-ass in their insipid comedy routines. She was about three years younger than Jimmy.

She still had a singing career and was a minor diva, but she had never had any hit songs in America. She was popular in Europe and among a handful of gay DJs at a few Manhattan clubs. She was a bad singer, and her songs were worse, but she had a powerful celebrity persona that kept her in the limelight. I'd seen her recently on late-night TV in a thirty-minute infomercial promoting long-distance tarot card readings given over a pricey 1-900 number. It was a great scheme, and only someone like her could get away with it. It had to be making her a scad of money.

"No way, Julianna," Ferrigno said. "I've got my orders."

"It's important, you asshole! Who do you think you are! You can't keep me from my own brother, goddammit!" She hit at his forearm ineffectually with a closed fist.

Ferrigno snapped his hand up and clutched her wrist like a vise. "I sure can, and you're at the top of my keep-out list."

"This is insane! You're nothing more than a glorified bouncer, Bert! You have no idea how you're hurting Jimmy by keeping me from seeing him."

"Nothing I can do about it. Not until they call and take your name off."

"*They!*" Julianna said. "Who are *they?* Just who the hell are *they* to tell Jimmy who he can and can't trust? If I had my way they'd all be history."

"Including your mother?"

"Oh, I do hate you, Bert."

"Just doing my job." Ferrigno was still smiling, unfazed. "Now you be a good girl and go back wherever you came from."

"First tell me who's that!" Julianna said, pointing at me.

"None of your business."

"Just who are you letting in instead of me?"

"He's not interested in your brother, Julianna."

She threw her Ferrari into reverse and backed up with a spinning of tires and a burning of rubber. She turned around in two more maneuvers and went driving off, disappearing around the edge of the forest.

"Sorry about that," Ferrigno said to me, grinning now.

"No prob."

"By the way, I like your car. Ever think of selling it?"

"Nope."

Ferrigno handed back my identification, keeping the business card: "Private eye. You make good money doing that?"

"That depends."

"On what?"

"On whether you're thinking of going into it yourself."

Ferrigno smirked and made a check mark on his clipboard. "Okay, you're good. You know how to find the estate?"

"Actually, you mind if I ask you a few questions first?"

Ferrigno shrugged. He didn't mind, but he was a mite wary.

I got out, stepped up onto the concrete barrier, and leaned across the guardhouse window, getting a good whiff of the coffee he had brewing. The booth contained a small table, an IBM-style computer, color Sony video monitors showing several different alternating outdoor views of the darkened estates, and a Mr. Coffee machine in the back corner next to a stack of Dixie cups.

Ferrigno offered me a cup of coffee. I took him up on it.

"You have a map of the estates you could show me?"

"Sure." He pulled one up and flattened it out to reveal a close-up look at Somerset Hills. It was a topographic quadrangle map of the U.S. Geological Survey that had been modified with various demarcations in red felt-tip marker. I set my coffee down, accidentally leaving a ring over the Raritan River.

Ferrigno pointed out the Blassingame estate—several hundred acres of hilly land extending from the central road to the river. In all, there were seven estates within the broadly outlined security perimeter. The four on the north side of the road were labeled with names I did not recognize. The three on the south side all adjoined the river: BLASSINGAME, GILBERT, and RESTON. Gilbert's estate was the largest in acreage, sandwiched between the other two. Of them all, the Restons' lay in the most secluded spot, farthest away from the entrance.

"The road seems to stop at the Restons'."

"It's the only way in or out. Secret Service likes it that way. Do you mind telling me who you're working for?"

"Jimmy Gilbert. But my business tonight is only with Blassingame."

"Oh, I see."

"I do some security consulting work, so I've got a kind of personal interest in your layout here. I assume each estate has its own separate security system."

"Sure. The Secret Service runs the Restons' security, and they have their own private gate up there and a number of video cameras and laser trip wires."

"What about Gilbert and the Blassingames?"

"Oh, they rely a little more on the video cameras. It's a pretty secure fence. Haven't had any major problems."

"What are your criteria for letting people in?" I thumbed over my shoulder in reference to the departed Julianna Gilbert.

"People who live here or have regular business here are issued photo IDs. Guests have to either be on my list or confirmed by video by someone at the estate."

Ferrigno pointed out a video camera bolted to the wall behind him and switched a button on one of his monitors to show me a wide-angled view of myself putting my coffee cup to my distorted fish lips. It wasn't very flattering.

"You log everyone in and out?"

"Yeah."

"Including the ones with permanent passes?"

"That's right."

"Could you tell me the last time Callie Blassingame came?" I asked, casually putting a cigarette in my mouth.

Ferrigno drew himself up like a porcupine about to launch its quills.

"Don't worry, I'll blow the smoke away from your window."

It wasn't the smoke he was worried about. "Comings and goings are confidential," he said.

"I heard that Callie hasn't been here for the last week." I was improvising, but I suspected it was true.

"I can't give out that information." Ferrigno was eyeing my cup of coffee as if he wanted to take it back.

"Come on. What could it hurt to tell me?"

"My job, for one." Ferrigno grabbed the first stray pencil and scrap of paper at hand and pretended to do some work.

"Who's going to know?" I said, playing the devil on the shoulder. I wasn't very good at it.

"Sorry, can't help you." He would no longer look at me.

I didn't think he would go for a palm-greasing, and it would probably be a waste of Loeb's money, anyway. I ought to be able to find out from Blassingame himself whether Callie had shown up here tonight after she'd bailed from New York.

"Forget about it, Bert," I said. "No hard feelings?" Ferrigno stared at me wide-eyed like a cat. I'd overstayed whatever welcome I might have had. "You keep a list of people who are to be kept out?"

"We have a regular list from Secret Service. Of course we also honor requests from the other estates."

"It wasn't Secret Service that wanted Julianna kept out."

"No. Julianna's still good friends with Natalie Reston."

"Then who did make the request?"

"Jimmy Gilbert. Your client."

"Jimmy made the request personally?"

"I took the phone call myself."

"Do you have any idea why?"

"Because she's Julianna." Ferrigno rolled his eyes as if it ought to be obvious. "She's a fucking fruitcake. Other than that, who knows? It's not my business to ask. Why don't you ask Jimmy yourself?"

"You don't think Jimmy's a bit of a fruitcake?"

Ferrigno held up his hands and spread them wide as if I'd drawn my gun on him. "Hey, he pays part of my salary. What do you think I'm going to say?"

"Okay," I said. I wasn't going to get any more out of him tonight. "Thanks for the kaffeeklatsch. Now would you be so kind?" I pointed toward the gate.

I got back in the 'Cuda and got the engine rumbling. With a look of reluctance, Ferrigno threw the switch or whatever he had to do in the booth. A loud buzzer sounded as the entrance gate rolled aside to stop on the right shoulder. I drove through the breach, and Ferrigno closed the gate behind me with another long buzzing and a dull clang as the gate met the post.

I was past the drawbridge now and heading toward the palaces of kings and trying my level best to feel humble.

Six

I turned off the main road into a shadowy mouth and went delving through the overhanging foliage of the nightwoods along a paved drive that switched back and forth until the trees faded to black in my rearview and the 'Cuda's headlights landed on a rising lawn capped by a colonial-style mansion of classical pretensions. I took a peripheral artery, trailing along a leafy ornamental hedge, to the lighted and colonnaded portico.

I rang the doorbell and waited, finishing a cigarette and gazing up at the faux lantern with yellow electric bulb that dangled above my head by an iron chain from the second-floor balcony. It took longer than I thought for my call to be answered. I assumed I'd be met by another Maria or by some stuffy old bald butler from *Masterpiece Theater*. I was wrong.

The door was opened by Jason Blassingame, tossing his golden locks back off his tanned face and smiling up at me. He was a full head shorter than I—though a head taller than in his photos. He wore a pair of black jeans shorts and a snug white T-shirt that advertised Dolce & Gabbana and revealed the slender shape of his unformed body. His jewelry consisted of gold hoop earrings, a gold choker, a couple of gold bracelets, and several gold rings, some set with stones. He smelled subtly of some earthy cologne.

"Who are you?" Jason sounded uncertain but eager to know.

"Greg Quaintance. I'm here to see your father." I threw down my cigarette butt and smothered it with my toe.

I had been unprepared to meet Jason so abruptly. His beauty was strong and had not been adequately captured in any of the photos I'd seen. Yuri Zetlin's lens had made him look tawdry, and the Macy's ads showed someone wholly clean-cut, plastic, and nonoffensive. Justice could only be done by a Herbert List or anyone willing to put him in his element, standing against the white rocks of a Greek island or sunbathing on the sand in an Aegean cove. He was a genuine golden lad, and he had no business degrading himself in magazine advertisements.

"Is he expecting you?" Eyes narrowing, puzzled, skeptical.

"Sort of." I half-swallowed my words, feeling tongue-tied, embarrassed at being unable to take my eyes off him.

Jason was far, far too young, but it didn't take much imagination to realize what he would look like five years hence. I was disarmed by the thought. I looked away from his face and found myself staring at his toes, which were wiggling nervously in his sandals. Looking back up again, I noticed that he had the nicest pair of patellas I'd ever seen.

"*Dad* doesn't usually have visitors so late. Must be something special about you." Jason spoke with a lilt, standing casually now with one arm draped along the door, his other hand on his hips.

"Um," I said, "I wouldn't know."

"*Dad*'s out in the stables." Every time Jason said *Dad*, it sounded ironic or disrespectful. "You can talk to me, though."

Pop music wafted down from an upstairs stereo—a catchy tune with an eminently danceable beat and lyrics devoid of all meaning. It could have been the work of any contemporary artist and completely unrecognizable to me, if it weren't for the spectacular falsetto pyrotechnics that were so characteristic of Jimmy Gilbert. No matter how forgettable his songs were, his voice was as distinctive as Pavarotti's and, by now, twice as famous. Jimmy Gilbert's music was ubiquitous, as likely to be heard over the speakers in a Monaco disco as it was to pour forth from boom boxes in the Jakarta slums or the Fez medina.

"Maybe you could tell your father I'm here," I said, allowing my eyes to leave Jason and dart around the foyer, which was not half as interesting.

Bright red Persian rugs bled down the central staircase and across the floors, bordered by dark-stained wood. The long balustrade, as white as the walls, was capped by a dark, heavy arm that ended in a neat scroll-like fist. The wall that hugged the stairs was hung with Hudson River landscapes. The crystal chandelier hung by a chain from the second-floor ceiling above Jason's head, the shiny twin of the dull lantern above my own.

"Why don't you come on in," Jason said.

"I guess I was expecting a housekeeper or someone," I said, still searching for my sea legs. I stepped inside.

"It's her night off, lucky for me." Jason shut the door.

"Don't you have any other help?"

"I don't need any help. I can do things for myself."

I had no doubt of that, and I nearly said as much, but I had the good sense to hold my tongue.

"Come into the front room, and I'll try calling *Dad.*"

I followed him into a deep, high-ceilinged space lighted by lamps on small rosewood tables, furnished with conservative sofas and chairs and vases overflowing with flowers. The red brick fireplace was made a centerpiece by the arrangement of carefully chosen pieces of firewood and a hanging copper kettle that looked as if it had never felt the lick of flames. The lighted oil painting above the mantel was another nineteenth-century American landscape, with brooding, windswept trees dwarfing a farmhouse and a woman doing her wash in the shallow of a dark stream, all illumined by the last, dramatic shaft of sunlight eking out through the approaching storm clouds.

"What do you want to see my dad about?"

"Stuff," I said, admiring the gloomy painting.

"I bet it has to do with my mom, doesn't it?"

"Maybe." I turned around.

"She's crazy." Jason said this like he meant it—not like *crazy, man, crazy*, but as if Callie Blassingame belonged in a straightjacket and a padded cell in some terror-filled Bedlam. He reached toward the ceiling, stretching his arms, and his T-shirt rose up to expose his midriff and belly button.

"That's too bad," I said.

"You don't know what it's like." He lowered his arms, and his shirt relaxed. "She treats me like a baby. Do I look like a baby to you?"

I made a production out of looking at my watch and gave out a deliberate sigh.

"Jason, don't you think this coy boy act is a bit much?"

He looked startled for a second, then grinned wide to show me his perfect teeth, which were probably caps already. I wondered whether his father had ever done any work on his face.

"Okay, so you know my name. Must have got it from *her*. You win, I'll call *Dad*. He always carries his cel phone with him."

Jason picked up the receiver of the cordless phone on the coffee table and punched out a few digits.

"*Dad?* . . . Yeah, I know . . . *Dad*, I know, all right? . . . There's some guy here. . . . Uh-huh, that's him. . . . Standing right here, all in black." Jason turned to look at me, and even in the mellow lamplight I saw him grow red in the face. "No, I haven't! . . . *Dad*, Jesus! . . . Yeah, okay . . . *Dad*, I said okay, all right? . . . I know . . . Yeah, I will. 'Bye."

He hung up, and I raised an interrogative eyebrow.

"Guess what *Dad* wanted to know?" Jason was grinning widely.

"I have no idea."

"He asked if I was flirting with you."

"That doesn't sound like a dad kind of question."

"You won't tell him I was, will you?"

"Why should I?" This was my opportunity to gain Jason's trust. "The funny thing is, I've never met your father before, so why would he think I was worth flirting over?"

"Maybe he heard you were hot." Jason acted nonchalant. "Because you are, in case you didn't know. But don't worry, I'm not flirting with you for real. I've already got a boyfriend."

"And who would that be?"

"That's a secret."

Not for long, I thought, thinking of next week's *Enquirer.* I wondered whether Ferrante had managed to strike it rich with this, a simple case of celebrity pederasty.

"Do you ride?" Jason asked.

"Horses, you mean?"

"Yeah. *Dad* won't respect you unless you know how."

"He's not going to take me riding at one in the morning."

"No, but he'll ask if you ride, anyway. He asks everybody."

"I used to, out in Wyoming."

"Oh, you're a cowboy?" Jason's smile turned wicked, twisting up at the corners. Apparently, he didn't know how to stop being fresh. He also didn't know how easily an older guy could see through it. I was embarrassed for him and wondering why he was acting this way; I'd never met anyone like this who was younger than eighteen. It was the kind of guy who, when he came out of the closet, burst out with a vengeance.

"Maybe I was," I said, and shrugged. "When I was a boy. A pal of mine had a couple of horses. I used to go out to his place, and we'd ride together. I must have been about your age."

"Two cowboys together. Sounds romantic." Jason spoke full of innocent meaning and without the slightest hint of sarcasm.

It *had* been romantic, actually. The boy I'd ridden horses with had also been the first boy I'd ever kissed, which, I now recalled, had indeed been when I was fourteen. I couldn't help thinking about it now, and suddenly it was my turn to blush. But I wasn't about to share this story with Jason.

I was taken aback by his forwardness, but perhaps he wasn't acting all that much different from other kids his age. Most of them tried to provoke their elders with cigarettes or alcohol or drugs or music or hairstyles or short skirts or facial piercings. I admired Jason's self-knowledge and self-confidence, but only if innocently acquired. Kissing another boy in a barn, as I'd done at his age, was one thing. Being raped by a man of thirty-five—if that was what had occurred—was another.

"Come on," Jason said. "I'll take you out to meet *Dad.*"

He reached for my hand.

I gave it to him, but only for a moment, to squeeze his in solidarity. Then I let go. It was easy.

I followed Jason through dim corridors and past darkened rooms, sometimes losing sight of him though he was a few feet ahead, and wondering at one point where exactly he was taking me, until at last we emerged out the back of the house, onto a vast tiled patio encircling a swimming pool glowing with blue fluorescence. The patio and pool were built on a terraced shelf on a downward-sloping lawn. Dark outbuildings stood in silhouette against the starry sky. The Blassingame land encompassed the valley below and the far hills and all the surrounding woods. A white-fenced riding area stood out against the darkness some distance away.

"Maybe when you're finished with *Dad* you can come back up here for a swim," Jason said.

"No, thanks."

"Oh, come on. I'm not going to *do* anything to you."

"I would," I lied, "but I don't have the time."

"You're just scared."

"I don't think so."

Jason took me down side steps to a path lighted by lampposts following close to a greenhouse still radiating mild heat.

"What kind of man is your father?" I asked.

"Well, he's very busy, for one thing."

"What kind of a relationship do you have with him? You guys get along okay?"

"Oh, sure. He's a pretty good guy. I like to think of him more as a friend than a father, though. He lets me do what I want, as long as I'm responsible and don't lie about it."

"Like what—do you drink?"

"I've tried beer. No big deal. Oh, and I had a sip of a martini once. Didn't like it."

"What about drugs?"

"Me, do drugs? I'd never get away with it."

"Why not?"

"Because I was in this TV commercial where this other kid comes up to me and offers me drugs, and I tell him, 'No way,' and he asks me why not, and I say, "Cause I don't do drugs, dummy,' and then he goes away."

"A public service announcement?"

"Yeah, the kind they only run at this time of night. You probably never saw it. It was a long time ago, anyway."

"How long ago?"

"When I was twelve. It was part of that whole 'Just Don't Do Drugs' campaign."

"You must be proud of it."

"I don't know," Jason said. "The whole thing was kind of lame, and I only got the part because of Natalie Reston, anyway. She's our neighbor. *Dad* did her face."

"Yeah, I know." *With some of my money*, I thought.

"She thought I'd be perfect as their poster boy."

"So you don't do drugs, then."

"No, of course not."

"But your dad lets you do pretty much anything else, right?"

"Yeah."

"You must love him, then."

"Sure, I guess so. He's kind of boring, just into his horses and stuff. That's why I asked you if you ride."

"What about your mom?"

"She pretends to be a horse person, but she isn't, really."

"No, I mean, do you love her?"

"I told you, she's crazy. She wants me to stay her precious little angel forever."

"Most moms are like that," I said. "They can't help it."

"She doesn't understand anything," Jason said, shaking his head in contempt. "I fucking hate her."

Warm light came from the open doors of the stables. As we approached, I caught a glimpse of a neatly ordered wall hung with saddles, straps, bits, bridles, crops, and other gear. Through the doors was a long central way strewn with hay, with stalls on either side. Seven horse heads poked up over the stalls—and one man's head.

"There he is," Jason said. "He's in there with Helen."

"Ah, Mr. Quaintance?" came a man's voice. "Is that you? Be through in a moment, just brushing her down."

"Don't you have stablehands for that?"

"One," he said, "and I let him do most of this, but these are my horses, and I believe your horse never gets to know you well enough unless you spend some quality time with them like this, grooming them and talking to them a little. Do you ride?"

"See?" Jason whispered.

"Sure, I mean, I used to quite a lot. I grew up in Wyoming, and some of my friends had horses."

"You ever ride English saddle or do any jumping?"

Jason and I stood near the stall. Troy Blassingame's head ducked down and disappeared entirely from view.

"No, I can't say that I have."

"Well, then! I should take you out sometime!"

"Sure," I agreed, assuming that this was just one more of those things people say without meaning it.

The horse next to Helen lifted its head over the gate and made a snuffling noise. Jason reached over to stroke its nose.

"This is Dido," Jason said. "She and Helen are sisters, from the same mother and the same stud."

I stood on my toes to get a closer look and saw that both Dido and Helen were Arabians—beautiful young mares of a fine chestnut color, with exquisite, proud tails and newly brushed manes. Troy Blassingame was finishing with Helen's.

"There we are," he said, unlatching the stall door and swinging it open. He emerged with horse brush in one hand, reaching out to shake my hand with the other. "Troy Blassingame. It's good to meet you."

He had the squarish face and thrusting jaw of a TV news anchorman and the tan of a Hollywood has-been, with a big head of blow-dried hair to match. He blinded me with his smile and made constant direct eye contact in the manner of politicians and salesmen and other people after your money.

"I'm glad you had the time, especially at such an hour."

"Nonsense," he said. "Anything for David Loeb."

Jason shot me a wondering glance.

"You've met Jason, obviously."

"Yes, I've had the pleasure." I glanced at Jason, curious to know what he knew of why I was here so late.

"Jason, you can go back up to the house now."

"Come on, *Dad*, I want to spend some more time with Dido." Jason continued stroking Dido's nose and didn't so much as look at his father.

"No, run along now. The horses have to sleep, and so do you. Mr. Quaintance and I have business to discuss."

"Like it has nothing to do with me," Jason muttered.

"Jason," his father warned. "Go back up and go to bed."

Jason turned back to look at me one more time—imploringly it seemed, though I had no idea what he was trying to convey.

Without another word, Jason whirled around and went running out of the stables, back up the path toward the house.

"This divorce isn't going to be easy on him," Blassingame said, standing at the stable door and watching his son until he had vanished inside the house. "I remember what it was like for me when my parents split. We adults can be such shits."

"He told me he hates his mother."

"Then that makes two of us." Troy Blassingame laughed with a bluster, as if this were the most offhand remark imaginable and not to be taken too seriously. I assumed he was talking about Callie, but maybe he meant his own mother. "You know, I would have preferred to talk with you in the morning, but our mutual friend David Loeb was insistent."

"He's only my employer. Sorry if the time's inconvenient."

"Time's nothing to a surgeon. I've done some of my best work at four in the morning. It's just that if you'd come out tomorrow, by daylight, we could have gotten in a ride together."

"I think David felt this was important."

"I could have introduced you to an English saddle."

"Some other time."

"You ever ridden an Arabian?"

"I'd like to. Your Helen and Dido are beautiful animals."

"A surprise gift from a grateful patient." This was said all in a rush, with a certain modesty.

"Must be some patient," I said, but then his clientele had probably all been profiled on *Lifestyles of the Rich and Famous.*

"I don't normally accept such large gifts, but how could I ever give up these two girls?" He patted Helen's neck. She raised her head, whinnying, chocolate eyes wide with apprehension.

Blassingame led me back to the stable entrance and shut off the lights. I helped him swing shut the heavy metal doors. He locked the door latch, then brought down a long steel bar and secured it with a giant padlock.

"I suppose you could say this is all a gift of my patients," he said, leading me back up the lighted path toward the house.

"I'm sorry, what is?"

"All of this." He motioned broadly. "I had some patients over for an open house, and Natalie Reston joked that she paid for my greenhouse."

"With her own money or some of mine?" Tactlessly, I dredged up Facegate.

"Now, now," Blassingame chided, patting me on the back. "That's not what you came here for. You're working for David, and Callie's got this crazy idea that she's going to press charges against Jimmy Gilbert, and you were hired to make sure it never happens. You want my cooperation. Well, you've got it."

"All I want right now is to be able to talk to Jason."

"You have already."

"Not about Jimmy Gilbert. Look, it won't be a delicate talk. I wouldn't broach these subjects without your permission."

"As long as David trusts you, I have no problem with it."

"You know what I plan to ask him?"

"I have a fair idea."

"In a case like this, it'll be best if I get to speak with him alone, one on one. You have any objections to that?"

"No. Be my guest. The sooner you do, the sooner this will all be cleared up."

"Listen, I don't want to shoot myself in the foot here, but I don't exactly think I've ever run into a parent who didn't want to be present when their kid was being interrogated."

"That's because those other parents are afraid of what their child is going to say. They coach their kids and give them hidden signals to make them say, 'Daddy touched me here,' or 'Mommy's boyfriend locked me in the linen closet for a week and fed me nothing but Meow Mix.' Hell, I've got no stake in this."

"Other than making sure Jason's all right."

"Well, of course! But Jason can be counted on to tell the truth, and no question you're prepared to ask is likely to harm him. He may not look it on the outside, but he's a tough one."

I had long since grown suspicious of the idea of toughness in guys. I'd learned firsthand in the chaos of the Gulf War and afterward, with my undesirable discharge, just how quickly a tough exterior can turn into a brittle eggshell. Some guys can be put back together again. Some can't.

"How much has Jason actually told you about Jimmy Gilbert?"

"Enough. Frankly, I don't want to know any more than I do."

"Are you afraid of finding out more?"

"One thing I *don't* need is psychoanalysis."

"Sorry. I didn't mean to touch a nerve."

"No, *I'm* sorry for snapping like that. It's just that Callie is so *wrong*—I can tell you right now that she's fabricating most of this. I'm not sure she knows that she's doing it, but it doesn't make her any less wrong."

"What are you saying, that she's out of touch with reality?"

"Callie is out of touch with a lot of things. Has been for a long time. It hasn't exactly been happy for me, but I've tried to stay with her and be supportive. I always thought if I were to divorce her, she would do something drastic."

"Suicide?"

"It's not as if she hasn't tried before. And now, will you look at this? *She's* divorcing *me*. Of all the—"

"You know, Dr. Blassingame—"

"Troy, please. Even my patients call me Troy. For Christ's sake, I don't enjoy formality. I didn't grow up with a silver spoon. I had to earn all of this."

"It might be useful for me and David if you'd tell me what you think

Callie's up to, the way you see it."

What I really wanted to ask was whether she was doing it for the money—but I had to assume that Blassingame knew nothing about her extortion attempts, and tipping my hand seemed unwise.

"Simple," Blassingame said. "She wants custody of Jason. She knows she can't have him short of doing something drastic. Well, what do you know, out of thin air, she spins this up."

"Why can't she have Jason?"

"First, because I won't let her." Blassingame counted off points his fingertips. "Secondly, Jason doesn't want it. Then there's the courts, who would never allow it. She's addicted to booze and pills, which makes her an unfit mother."

"She has that bad a problem?"

"Betty Ford wouldn't take her back. Even a good word from Natalie didn't help. Callie's been granted several second chances, and she's blown them all. I want to see Jason safely make it to adulthood before she drags him down with her."

"You're think he's safe hanging around Jimmy Gilbert?"

"I couldn't think of any place safer." Blassingame smiled at me smugly, begging me to ask him why he thought so.

I waited for him to tell me.

"I've known Jimmy all his life. I couldn't think of a better friend for a boy like Jason—especially now, when he needs a friend most."

"Because of your divorce?"

"Yes," he said. "I was an only child myself, and when my parents split, I had no one to turn to. Better that Jason spend time with Jimmy Gilbert than get messed up with drinking and drugs and the wrong friends. Jimmy's not going to harm him."

"How do you know?"

Blassingame was silent as we climbed the steps up the side of the patio. The gentle waves on the pool cast shifting patterns of light and shadow across the back of the house. Only one second-story window was alight. I wondered if it was Jason's room, the one the Jimmy Gilbert music had been coming from.

"Greg, you a fan of single-malt Scotches?"

"Never tried one."

"Come with me into my study, then, and we'll finish our discussion amid the accoutrements of civilized men."

Whatever, I thought.

It was a dark and overstuffed study with a window overlooking the front lawn. I breathed in book dust, leather upholstery, cigar smoke, and stale beer—the kinds of manly odors women detested because they could never be gotten rid of. It smelled as if Blassingame had cultivated them over the years, with a blanket injunction against his wife or any housekeeper spraying them away with air fresheners or corrupting them with sachet.

Blassingame stood at the wet bar and selected a bottle, pouring out two small glasses of rich, darker-than-amber liquid.

"Here, have a taste of this."

I took the proffered glass and tried a tentative sip.

"Be bold, Greg," he said. "This isn't sherry."

It was much stronger than I expected, but my tongue responded to it like a kitten with a bowl of warm milk.

"Very nice," I said, my voice a little hoarse.

"You looked like a man who might appreciate it."

"I'm not here for a tasting."

"I understand. Just want you to be comfortable. Go ahead, have a seat. Care for a cigar?"

"No, thanks." I sat in one of the tall-backed leather chairs. I had a Lucky Strike lit and in my mouth before Blassingame had finished preparing his stogie. "You've got to help me out here, Troy. I'm a little confused."

"Oh?" Blassingame held up a tall flame and drew it in several times, deftly twisting the cigar as it crackled to life.

"You obviously know your son is gay."

"Yes, go on."

"Yet you're not worried about his spending time alone with a man who's twenty years older. Jason's a good-looking kid. You're not worried that he'll be taken advantage of?"

"Jason is mature for his age, both physically and intellectually. I've tried to provide Jason an environment in which he could find himself without having to struggle through some of the baggage the rest of us were saddled with, if you follow me. Did your parents ever talk to you about sex?"

"Just the bare bones," I said. "And by the time they got around to it, I already knew more than they were willing to tell me. I think my mother was relieved. I kept telling her I knew everything already."

"How old were you?"

"Twelve, I think, maybe thirteen."

"And how old were you when you realized you were gay?"

"Excuse me?"

"It's all right. David Loeb told me all about you on the phone. You're not in the closet, are you?"

"No," I said, "I'm not, but I try to keep my business life separate from my personal life. My sexual orientation usually isn't very relevant to my job."

"Not in this case it isn't. If David had wanted to send over some straight macho shithead to interrogate Jason, I would have said no. We need someone who isn't going to judge him, who isn't going to be coarse or upsetting or judgmental."

"I don't understand. Did David know before he hired me that you felt this way?"

"Probably."

"You're unusually accepting of Jason's sexuality."

"What's so unusual? Callie's the one who can't accept it. At least I understand that it's nothing to do with the way we raised him. Callie is worried that she coddled him too much, which is preposterous. If anything, she was too cold. Listen, I'm a surgeon, and everything I do in my practice is based on evidence. I've read up on it and seen enough scientific proof to convince me that a person's sexuality is a matter of biology—whether it's genetics or the influence of certain hormones during gestation or something else altogether. Why should I persecute my own son over something over which he had no control? I'd rather he grow up healthy and happy."

"That's a very impressive point of view for a father to take," I said. "Even so, I wouldn't think you'd want your fourteen-year-old boy running around and having sex."

"Who says that he is?"

"Callie."

"And there you have our problem. My wife is so incapable of coming to grips with Jason that she's willing to put him on trial for it and drag down Jimmy in the process. Jimmy is innocent, and Jason is innocent. Do you understand what would happen if Callie were to file her charges and bring this to trial?"

"Why don't you spell it out for me."

"It would be a virtual rehash of the Oscar Wilde trial. When his long-standing affair with Lord Alfred Douglas was discovered by Douglas's family, they had Wilde tried on counts of sodomy and corrupting a young man's morals. Isn't that what Callie is threatening to do?"

"Lord Alfred Douglas wasn't a minor, though, I don't think."

"He was nineteen when Wilde met him," Blassingame said, puffing on his cigar and rolling it nimbly. "You tell me who was more innocent: a nineteen-year-old Victorian Englishman, or a modern-day American boy of fourteen?"

"Ask twelve different people and you'll get twelve different answers on that one," I said.

"That's why it would be so dangerous if this were to go to trial. It would be all too easy for a jury to find Jimmy guilty, even in the absence of conclusive evidence. The result would be the same as in the Wilde trial. Two young lives ruined."

"You've apparently thought a lot about this."

"I only want what's best for Jason. Jimmy is a patient of mine, but I also count him as a friend. I would hate to see his career go up in smoke because of my wife's wrath."

"Is that what this is?"

"Yes," he said decisively. "Callie wants a jury to tell her that her son was seduced into homosexuality by a predatory older man. She wants them to tell her it wasn't her fault. She wants Jimmy punished, and she thinks the process will cure Jason of his gayness. You've got to admit that's pretty crazy."

"Can I speak with Jason now? It's getting late."

"Yes, of course, you're right."

"You don't think we ought to wait till tomorrow?"

"No, David's right. The longer we wait, the worse off we'll be. Callie's got to be stopped. I'll take you up to Jason's room. He's a night person and usually stays up late on weekends. He'll be listening to music or watching some old movie."

I followed Blassingame up the soft, blood-red stairs and down the second-floor hallway to a door at the far end. A shaft of light shone at the base. Blassingame knocked.

"Jason?"

There was no answer.

"Jason? I'd like you to have a few more words with Greg Quaintance here. Can we come in?"

There was still no response.

"He's probably got his headphones on," Blassingame said, turning the knob and swinging the door open.

Jason's bedroom was mammoth in size and better ordered than most boys' bedrooms. The walls were covered with posters of Jimmy Gilbert from various different phases of his career. A life-size cardboard cut-out of Jimmy Gilbert in his *Provocateur* pose stood in the far corner. Jimmy Gilbert action figures stood posed in myriad ways on Jason's dresser.

The lights in the room had been left on, but there was no sign of Jason.

"Maybe he went down to the kitchen or to the bathroom or something," Blassingame said. "He must be around."

"What's that?" I asked, pointing at a fluorescent piece of paper laid prominently on Jason's pillow.

Blassingame went over and picked it up. "It's from Jason."

"May I have a look?"

Blassingame let me look over his shoulder. The note had been generated on the laser printer that sat alongside Jason's Power Macintosh, and it said, in bold, bumped-up type:

DEAR DAD,

    SORRY TO DISAPPOINT YOU, BUT I'M GOING WITH JIMMY TO BUENOS AIRES NO MATTER WHAT. HE NEEDS ME. I CAN'T LET HIM DOWN. I'LL BE O.K. THE TOUR'S OVER IN AUGUST AND I'LL BE BACK IN TIME FOR SCHOOL. SORRY TO GO AGAINST YOUR WISHES, BUT I JUST CAN'T LET THIS SHIT BETWEEN YOU AND MOM KEEP ME FROM THIS TOUR. YOU KNOW WHAT IT MEANS TO ME. HOPE YOU UNDERSTAND. I'LL CALL FROM ARGENTINA.

    LOVE,
    JASON

Seven

Blassingame stood there glassy-eyed, slack-jawed, and dumb.

"Troy, talk to me. What's this about?"

"Goddamn it! I thought he understood me! I told him he couldn't go this time, and damn it, I meant it!"

"A South American tour?"

Blassingame nodded nervously. "But just the first leg of a longer tour. Jason would be away for two months. I told him he couldn't go!"

I wondered why David Loeb hadn't bothered to tell me. The *Enquirer* story was set to coincide with the beginning of Jimmy Gilbert's tour. Callie Blassingame had to be dealt with before Jimmy left, or the scandal would balloon out of control and jeopardize the tour, the album, and everyone connected to it.

Matters, obviously, that Loeb had decided were irrelevant as far as I was concerned.

"He can't have gone far. What did he do, walk over to Gilbert's?"

"No, he probably drove."

"Drove? Isn't he too young for that?"

"I've already taught him how to drive. He's not supposed to leave Somerset Hills Estates, though."

"What would he do, take one of your cars?"

"No, he has his own."

I glowered at him. I felt like giving him a good shake.

"I didn't give it to him," Blassingame said.

"Callie, then?"

"No." He swallowed hard, and a trickle of sweat appeared on his brow. He was worried I might hit him for being such a putz. "It was a gift of Jimmy Gilbert. A black Eagle Talon."

"An Eagle Talon. For a fourteen-year-old."

"He's almost fifteen."

"So most likely he drove over to Jimmy's, and he's there right now."

"I want you to go get him."

"I suppose I'll have to. Otherwise, I don't get to talk to him, do I? Care to come along?"

"I want to, but I can't." Blassingame looked at his watch.

"You got something more important on your agenda?"

"If Jason's set on defying me, it'll only make things worse if I'm there."

"Callie said something along those lines. What are you afraid of? You're his father. All you have to do is grab his arm and take him home."

Blassingame shook his head violently. "I've never handled Jason that way before. Sometimes he aggravates me so much I feel like strangling him—but I could never lay a hand on him. I don't think I could make him come. You, Greg—he's already met you, and you seem to have hit it off—you might be able to talk some sense into him."

"I'll try."

"Thank you."

I considered asking him for a fee, but it would be double dipping. I was already working for Loeb, and my immediate concern was speaking with Jason. I had to go get him regardless.

"I need to know a few things first," I said. "What do you know about this tour? They're not leaving right now, are they?"

"No, I thought they were scheduled to leave on Sunday."

"Good. Tell me something else. That Eagle Talon, is that the only thing Jimmy's given Jason?"

"Not on your life. Look around you. Almost everything in this room is something Jason got from Jimmy. All this Jimmy Gilbert paraphernalia, and these clothes . . ."

Blassingame lifted a pair of jeans from off the floor and handed it to me.

"Paul Smith," I said. "Expensive pair of jeans."

"You're telling me. I'd never buy Jason this stuff. Levi's ought to be good enough. He's still growing, and he's going to outgrow all of this. But these are the only things he'll wear."

Blassingame opened a door, and we stepped into a walk-in closet hung with more clothes than I could ever imagine owning. I pulled down representative shirts, jeans, and trousers.

"Mossimo," I said, "Armani, Dolce and Gabbana, Jean-Paul Gaulthier, DKNY, Calvin Klein, Versace."

"Not exactly to my taste, most of this. I'd rather dress him in Brooks Brothers."

"But you let him accept all these gifts."

"Hey, Jimmy Gilbert is a patient of mine. What can I do?"

"You could say thanks, but no thanks."

"I don't see the point, as long as no one's getting hurt."

He turned off the closet light, forcing us out.

"Is Jimmy the one who got Jason into modeling, too?"

"No, that came about after he met Yuri Zetlin."

"Who introduced him to Zetlin?"

"Natalie Reston. Zetlin directed a public service announcement for her antidrug campaign. Jason starred in it."

"Troy, that reminds me, when I was at Callie's tonight, she discovered that Jenks's supply of Ritalin was missing."

"What does that have to do with anything?"

My eyes scanned the walls and the multiple images of Jimmy Gilbert, who seemed practically a different person in each, and who was almost always hiding behind a pair of sunglasses.

"You didn't take the bottle, did you?"

"Why would I do that?"

"Then that leaves Jason. You don't look worried about it. Don't you know that kids his age like to get Ritalin from other kids, grind it up, and snort it? They think it's safe. The kids with attention deficit disorder get better grades when they take it, so the other kids think it's a smart pill. They think the more they take, the smarter they'll get. It's the brightest students who abuse it. Jason's a perfect candidate. I'm worried that if he's doing this, he might be doing other drugs, too. Do you happen to know whether Jimmy Gilbert does drugs?"

"I wouldn't know about illicit use," he said, blustering. "But I do, of course, prescribe painkillers for him when he's in recovery from an operation."

"You haven't ever overprescribed for him, have you?"

"No, never. I'd rather keep my license."

"Troy, do you really think you have any idea of what Jason does when he's out of your sight? He seems like a smart kid. He could be one of those who's too smart for his own good."

"How would you know?"

"Maybe I was one of those myself."

Blassingame checked his watch again. "Greg, don't waste any more time. I want Jason back in this house within the hour."

"I'll do my best."

"You'll have him back here, or I'll have serious doubts as to whether you're up to the job David's cut out for you."

"Aye, aye," I said, wondering why he refused to be forceful like this with his own son. "Can you show me your garage? I'd like to make sure he didn't go off in one of your other cars."

Blassingame seemed to think this was unnecessary, but I insisted. We didn't have time to search the house, and I didn't want to be sent off on a wild goose chase only to discover later that the goose—or the gander, or whatever—had never left.

I stepped into the darkness. Blassingame threw on the switch behind me. Fluorescent lights flickered to life, illuminating a vast, well-ordered garage. Tools hung from hooks in the pressboard walls, and the painted concrete floor was remarkably free of oil and grit. The eight roomy stalls were occupied by six vehicles clean and glimmering from constant polishing: a camel tan Rolls-Royce coupé, a burgundy Jaguar sedan, a cherry red Porsche Targa, a baby blue '63 Corvette, a vintage red-orange '37 Cord, and the black Lincoln limousine I'd seen earlier in front of Callie's apartment building.

"Two empty slots," I observed.

"Jason's Eagle Talon and Callie's Lexus," Blassingame explained. "I guess now I'll have to buy another car."

"What for?"

"To fill Callie's spot."

I borrowed Blassingame's phone and took a certain pleasure in waking up David Loeb. I told him what had happened and what I was doing and asked him to clear me with Gilbert's people. He said that he would. I asked him why he neglected to tell me that Jimmy was leaving on a big tour. He said he didn't think it was important. He was confident Jimmy's problems would be solved before then, and he didn't want to put any additional pressure on me. He was doing me a favor, he figured. I told him it was hard to do my job when I had less than a hundred percent cooperation from my employer. He understood and said he'd share more with me in the future. Yawning, he asked if that was all.

I said that it was.

Eight

Halfway up the road to Gilbert's house, I saw in my rearview a pair of headlights creeping closely up behind, egging me on to greater speed. I gave the driver a reflected scowl, sped up a little, and tried to get a make on the car, but the lights switched rudely to brights. I was blinded by the glare before flipping my mirror from Day to Night. The car became a ghost.

In the darkness, all I could make out of the Gilbert house was a broad, low slab with Frank Lloyd Wrightish half-step tiers and overhangs and hints of flagstone and regularly spaced horizontal windows. Some of the windows were alight. I drove up into a cul-de-sac before the front entrance and parked the 'Cuda alongside a navy blue BMW Z3 roadster.

The car that had been tailing me, a cream-colored Infiniti coupé, swerved up alongside and stopped short, parking with a screech of tires as I was emerging from the 'Cuda. When the driver got out, the first things I noticed were her cream-colored pumps and tight cream-colored slacks that hugged legs and hips so slender they were close to anorexic. Her top was a sleeveless knit orange thing stretched across small breasts and showing the clear demarcations of her nipples. Draped across her shoulders was a white silk scarf. She clutched a white leather handbag. Her hair was cut boyishly short, greased down, and parted on one side. She had pencilled-in eyebrows. Her purple lipstick seemed not to go at all with her ensemble.

I recognized her at once and said, "Madeleine Downey?"

She squinted at me. "Um, do I know you?" She had a deep, manly voice like Bacall or Garbo. Very pleasant on the ears.

"Um, no. I recognize you from your *Vogue* covers. Greg Quaintance. I'm a private investigator." I offered my card, which she ignored, maintaining a tight grip on the handbag. "David Loeb hired me on Jimmy's behalf."

"Happy to hear it," she said morosely. "Have you taken care of Callie Blassingame yet?"

"Taken care of?"

Madeleine rolled her eyes and slouched. "I told David to pay her off, but no. He's so cheap."

I wondered if she knew how much Callie wanted.

"You don't think Jimmy ought to fight her?"

"I don't think anyone ought to know about it, period."

"They will anyway. You know about the *Enquirer* piece?"

She nodded, closing her eyes, and said, "Don't remind me."

"Don't you think Jimmy ought to defend himself in public?"

Madeleine stared at me coldly and drew out her words: "I don't see the point. Jimmy will be ruined either way. The only way out is to shut her up now and make her recant. I *told* David, but he's such a *wuss*."

Wuss didn't fit the image in my mind of Loeb telling off reporters after the outcome of the Hugo Wallis trial.

"Can't *you* do something about Callie?" Madeleine asked.

"It's not really up to me. I'm just following orders."

"But whose orders? David works for Jimmy, but Jimmy doesn't always make his own decisions. Could be one of his advisers."

"Aren't you one of his advisers?"

"Nobody listens to me. I'm out of the loop."

"That's what Ralph Reston said about Facegate."

"Fuck Ralph Reston. If you're not doing anything about Callie, what are you doing here?"

"I'm here to pick up Jason and take him back to his father."

"Jason's here?"

"I believe so, yes."

Madeleine's face betrayed no emotion, but she turned at once and hurried up the flagstone walk, taking her electronic key from out of the handbag and holding it at the ready.

I followed on her heels. "Mind if I come in with you?"

"Not at all, if you promise to get rid of that little shit."

"Scout's honor," I said and held up two tight fingers.

Once we were through the door, I was stopped by a security guy in broad pinstripes with a blond crewcut and a bodybuilder's build. The taut skin on his face revealed the exaggerated bone structure of a guy who takes a regular regimen of steroids. He asked Madeleine not very politely who the hell I was. She told him and continued clip-clopping down the tiled hall, leaving me behind.

"Did you check his ID?" the security guy yelled after her.

"That's *not* my job," Madeleine intoned over her shoulder. "He could be Charles Manson for all I care."

I handed him my private eye's license and my business card. He handed them back, patted me down lightly, and found my gun.

"I'll have to keep this," he said, reaching into my jacket and removing my Glock. "What's your business here?"

"Peter, is that Mr. Quaintance?" said a man's voice from down the hall, too strident to be Jimmy Gilbert's.

"Yeah," Peter said.

"It's okay, we're expecting him." To the voice was added more clip-clopping, coming toward me now, and finally a face. He looked youthful but in a plastic surgical way and was probably at least in his forties. He had a gym body, a tan, an unnaturally delineated jawline, and a trendy, close-cropped haircut. As he neared, I saw his eyes widen and narrow again as he got a good look at me. He seemed to be smirking, like I was the punch line to a lengthy joke someone had just been telling.

"Good to make your acquaintance, Mr. Quaintance. I bet you've heard that before! I'm Todd Curwen, Jimmy's manager. David called and told me all about you." He had a significant look in his eye. "Come this way."

"I'll give you back your gun on your way out," Peter said.   I told him I hoped so and followed Curwen down the hall.

The home was modern in ways that homes hadn't been modern in years. If it wasn't Wright, it was one of his acolytes. All the intersecting lines of the furniture, fixtures, walls, and ceiling fit together somehow into a coherent whole. Chair backs stood upright. Wood was dark-stained and polished. Some walls were made of formed concrete blocks with a bas relief chevron pattern. Most of the illumination appeared to come out of nowhere, from just under the eaves or out from behind corners. Upholstery and rugs and stained glass shared a stylized midwestern motif hinting at grass fields and corn stalks and amber waves of grain.

"I heard you did some work for Tay Farrell," Curwen said.

"Maybe I did."

"In fact, I believe you and I met some weeks ago at one of Tay's boy-parties at his place in Southampton."

"Could be," I said. "I don't remember."

"Oh, come! He introduced us."

"I doubt it. If I was there, I wasn't mingling. I would have been doing security."

"I'm sure it was you. I have an eye for faces."

"There were a lot of bald guys there. We all look alike."

"Are you kidding? Most of *them* were hopelessly forgettable. I'm surprised I didn't try to pick you up. Were you in uniform?"

"Plainclothes." I tried to veer Curwen off the subject: "Did David tell you why I was coming?"

"Not really, as it turns out."

"What do you mean?"

"He said you wanted to talk to me," Curwen said, like he was disappointed. "Then Maddy comes in looking for little Jason Blassingame and says you're here to retrieve him."

"That's right."

"Problem is, Jason's not here."

"Why is that a problem?"

"Maddy doesn't believe us. In other words, you're causing us some trouble. Not that I'm the least bit surprised. The tarot told me this was going to be one of those days."

"The tarot? You don't happen to call Julianna Gilbert's one nine hundred number, do you?"

"Julianna?" Curwen was apalled. "Who do you think introduced her to the tarot in the first place? The only idea she ever had that made her any money, and who did she get it from? Me. And what thanks do I get?"

He meant this rhetorically, but I had no idea what he was talking about, so I said, "Don't know. What thanks *do* you get?"

"What's the matter with you? Don't you watch *Hard Copy*? Julianna left me for another manager."

"When did this happen?"

"A few months ago."

"Was there some kind of precipitating event?"

"The only thing that's precipitating is me," Curwen said, laughing at his own clever turn. "I bust my ass for my clients. If they just up and desert me for no reason, what am I supposed to do? I can't lock a chain around their ankles. I only hope Julianna isn't starting a trend. What kind of job security do I have if my clients have no qualms about stabbing me in the back?"

"Beats me," I said.

"Here we are." Curwen led me around the corner, into a large open space with people in it who were arguing. He folded his arms and stood back, as if we were regarding a diorama at the American Museum of Natural History. "Now see what you've done?"

Madeleine Downey was standing over an obese older woman with magenta hair who lay on a beige chaise longue looking persecuted.

"Where is he?" Madeleine was demanding.

"For the last time," the older woman said through gritted teeth, "I have not seen hide nor hair of Jimmy's playmate. If he were here, I'm sure you'd find them together, playing video games in the rec room or games of another kind in Jimmy's bedroom."

"How can you speak that way about your own son?"

"I have the right to do as I please. A right you haven't earned yet, Maddy. Anyway, I've never seen *you* coming out of Jimmy's bedroom. No wonder he has to look elsewhere."

"Jason was there first," Madeleine said. "Which none of you bothered to tell me before Jimmy and I got married. As far as I understood it, Jason was *not* a part of our deal. I've told Jimmy to get rid of him, but he refuses. Now he'd better do it. Once the *Enquirer* comes out, I'm going to be a laughingstock. If he doesn't dump Jason now, so help me, I'll divorce him."

"No, you won't," Jimmy's mother said. "We'll sue you for breach of contract."

Curwen cleared his throat theatrically to let them know we were there. They looked over at us, then back at each other.

"Jason *is* here, isn't he?" Madeleine said. "I'm going to go see for myself."

"Go ahead, go look, but stop hammering at me!" Jimmy's mother said. "You're giving me one of my migraines!"

"Oh, sure I am."

"I'm experiencing an aura already!" Jimmy's mother flopped the back of her hand against her forehead like a dead carp.

"Stand back, guys, she's having an aura." Madeleine turned to us with one hand on her hip, like a dissipated flapper.

"Maddy," Curwen said warningly, brushing past her on his way to the stricken mother. He knelt down beside her and clasped her free hand, the one that was lolling off the edge of the chaise like Socrates' after he drank his hemlock.

"Oh, Todd, thank goodness. Why couldn't my boy have married someone sweet like you?"

"A Hawaiian marriage?" Curwen said wryly.

"See? I can always count on you to make me laugh. My daughter-in-law, on the other hand . . ." She lowered her hand from her face and drilled Madeleine with laser-beam eyes.

"Jesus Christ," Madeleine said. "After all I've done for you people!"

"She didn't mean it, Maddy," Curwen said. "It's just the aura talking."

"Like hell it is," Jimmy's mother mumbled.

"I'm going to find Jimmy," Madeleine said. "Anyone want to stop me?"

This was met with blank stares.

Madeleine stormed out of the room.

Curwen stood up and motioned me over. "I'd like you to meet Marcia Gilbert." He pronounced it *mar-SEE-uh*. "Jimmy's mother."

"Pleased to meet you," I said, shaking her clammy hand. I remembered from the days of Jimmy Gilbert's prime-time TV variety show that Jimmy and Julianna had had a classic stage mother—the kind who had worked crappy jobs for long hours to raise her kids all on her own, without any man's help. She had hired teachers to train their talents so they would grow up and take over the world. Jimmy had practically succeeded in doing so, and he still had plenty of opportunity to finish the job. Julianna must have been a disappointment. Long-distance tarot readings over a 900 phone line could never earn her anything close to

Jimmy's income, which was generated by royalties from twenty-five years of hit singles and platinum albums, not to mention his current $100 million recording contract.

"Marcia, honey," Curwen said, "this is Greg Quaintance, the man David told us about."

"Oh, yes, the detective. Maddy says you're looking for little Jason Blassingame. Well, he's not here."

"So I gathered," I said. "All I know is, he left a note with his father saying he was going to accompany Jimmy on the South American tour."

"That's not very likely, unless he's planning on stowing away in one of our trunks." She shared a glance with Curwen.

"Didn't he go along last year to Asia?"

"Yes, but we've made no provision for him this time."

"We'd take him, though," Curwen interpolated, "as long as we had his father's permission."

"It doesn't seem that you do," I said. "And Jason left in a manner that would be considered running away from home, in any other family."

Running away to join the circus was more like it, I thought.

"Troy *does* want him back, doesn't he?" Curwen asked.

"That's what he said. That's why I'm here."

"But he's not here, dear, so you can go," Marcia said, flitting her hand in the air dismissively.

"Jason could have at least called here," I said. "Isn't it possible Jimmy knows something about it?"

"I doubt it," Curwen said, "but I'll go ask."

"I'd rather have a word with Jimmy myself."

"That's out of the question," Curwen said. "Jimmy's been resting up, getting ready for the tour. It might be upsetting for him, what with your being a perfect stranger."

"It's late, I know."

"It's not even that. Jimmy's probably up, and under other circumstances he might be willing to talk, but he's a little keyed up now because of the tour. Some of what Jimmy wants to bring along is in New York. We're just waiting for him to get ready, and then we're heading into the city."

"In case you've forgotten, Jason's still just a kid," I said. "And I'm growing concerned about his welfare."

"So am I," Curwen said. "That's part of the point I'm trying to make. What if it takes you a few days to find Jason? If you tell Jimmy that Jason's run away from home, he'll be so worried that he might cancel his tour."

"I don't give a damn about your tour," I said. "And I'm sure Madeleine's already told him by now."

"Todd, why don't you go look in on Jimmy?" Marcia suggested. "Maddy's probably making a scene. You know how she can be."

Curwen looked annoyed at her. Marcia's hand went back up to her forehead; now it was Curwen giving her a migraine.

"All right, Marcia," he said, resigned.

"Ask if he's heard from Jason," she added, with a nod at me.

Curwen went down the hall, his footfalls resounding off the tile floor with increasing speed until they fell out of earshot.

"You're a very attractive young man," Marcia said, smiling up at me as she brought her hand down. "Please, have a seat."

I took a chair close to the chaise longue. "This is a big house. Do you live here with Jimmy?"

"Heavens, no! Jimmy's given me some rooms here, but I have my own house in East Hampton."

"Oh."

"What do you mean, oh?"

"Because I asked an idiotic question. My mind must be going." I tried but could not stifle a yawn. "You're a grown woman—why should I assume you'd be living here with Jimmy?"

"Because you assume he's a mama's boy. Everybody does. But it isn't so. We're just very good friends. We enjoy each other's company. I don't tell him what to do. We have fun."

"You're accompanying him on the tour?"

"Yes, but I don't follow him around or stick my nose into his life. I think I can manage to entertain myself suitably in Buenos Aires and Rio de Janiero." Her smile crept up on one side. "Maybe I'll hire a Latin gigolo," she added.

"I hear Rio isn't what it used to be."

"One has to be careful of AIDS, of course."

"That's even more true in New York and New Jersey."

"I've been careful since the beginning. One of the first five cases in New York was a close personal friend of mine."

"They didn't know what it was then or how not to get it," I pointed out. "You couldn't have been that careful until later."

"That's true, but once they started talking about safe sex, I must have been the first to try it! And I told Jimmy to always wear a condom. Always. No exceptions. Does that sound like a mama's boy kind of mother to you?"

Marcia grabbed the sides of the chaise longue and inched her way to a higher sitting position.

"Maybe I should go see what's keeping them," I said.

"No, you stay right where you are." She reached out and touched my knee. She squeezed it a few times and didn't let go. She stared into my eyes. "Greg, tell me something . . ."

"Yes?" I was expecting a proposition of some kind, I guess.

"What does Callie want?" She removed her hand from my knee.

"I don't know. Maybe you could tell me what you think."

"I can't understand why she wants to ruin Jimmy's career with all these stories. I'm sure she wants money, but what on earth would possess her to go about it this way? That's not the Callie I know."

"How long have you known her?"

"I must have met her about a year before she married Troy."

"How long ago was that?"

"I guess it would have been, what, twenty-five years ago. Jimmy would have been ten. He was already a star, of course."

"How do you feel about Callie and Troy separating?"

"It'll be good for Troy."

"How do you think it'll be for Jason?"

"Jason will be better off without Callie in his life."

"Isn't that a harsh thing to say about the boy's mother?"

"Life's harsh. You won't see me crying for Callie."

My ears perked up to the sound of hurried footsteps.

"Out!" came a high-pitched voice. "All of you, out!"

I stood up.

Marcia inched herself up and looked over her shoulder.

Madeleine Downey emerged first from down the hall, her fists clenched at her sides, striding as fast as her toothpick legs could carry her. Her face was a ball of anger. She didn't bother to stop. She dug around in her handbag, took out her car keys, and continued on down the hall.

Curwen's voice was saying, "Please, Jimmy, be reasonable!"

A moment later, Curwen appeared, walking half backward, motioning wildly with his arms as he spoke. "You can't do this!"

Jimmy Gilbert was right behind him, giving him a shove.

"Go on, get out of here!" Jimmy sounded like a small child who was about ready to burst into tears.

"Jimmy!" Marcia said. "What's gotten into you?"

"You, too, mother!" Jimmy said. "I want all of you out!"

I was surprised at how well he could project his small voice without the assistance of microphones. He really had a gift.

"You're acting irrationally, Jimmy," Curwen said. "You haven't had enough rest. You're not thinking straight."

"Is this the guy who's looking for Jason?" Jimmy said, turning toward me.

"That's me," I said. "Greg Quaintance."

"You can stay," he said. "The rest of you, out!"

"But Jimmy," Marcia pleaded.

"Now, mother!"

"But I was going to ride into the city with you!"

"Todd can take you."

"Sure, Jimmy, I can take her," Curwen said. He went over to the chaise and helped Marcia to her feet.

"Thank you, Todd," she said. "At least someone around here has some consideration. I just have to go to my room and get my things."

"Leave them here," Jimmy said, shutting his eyes. "I can't stand to have any of you in my house another second!"

"And me with a migraine!"

"Come on, Marcia, let's go," Curwen said. "I'll send Angel by tomorrow for your things."

"Todd, you're such a dear." She began to sniffle.

"Marcia, please."

Jimmy and I stood on opposite sides of the room while Todd Curwen grabbed Marcia's hand and led her down the hall. Jimmy waited until they were far away before he approached me.

"You're Greg Quaintance," he said. "Working for David Loeb?"

"That's right," I said.

Jimmy looked different from his album covers and music videos, mostly because he wasn't wearing his usual sunglasses. His irises were a sharp green, so striking I figured they were probably colored contact lenses. His shoulder-length hair had been a number of shades over the years but was currently a sandy blond. It looked natural and was slightly messy, as if he'd been sleeping on it and hadn't bothered to comb it out. His face was not exactly a man's but not exactly a woman's, either. It was a manmade face of fair skin, aquiline nose, chiseled cheekbones, and elfin eyebrows. I wasn't exactly sure what kind of a look he had been going for all these years. The many operations had turned him into something that looked not of this earth.

"How long has Jason been missing?" Jimmy spoke in what must have been his natural speaking voice, as falsetto as his singing voice and with a breathy quality not unlike Marilyn Monroe's.

"Close to an hour," I said. "He left a note saying that he was coming over here."

"No, he didn't," Jimmy said with a smile. "I just called Troy Blassingame to offer my help. He read me Jason's note. Jason only said he was coming with me on my tour. He didn't say anything about coming over to my house."

"Jason isn't here, then?"

"No, he's not. You can come with me to my bedroom and search the whole rest of the house if you don't believe me."

"This is a huge house. It would take me all day to search it. I guess I'll have to take your word for it. Do you have any idea where he might have gone?"

"All I can think is that maybe he went on into New York. Jason knew I was planning to be in the city Saturday and Sunday before my flight left."

"Did you invite him to go along?"

"Yes, but it was some time ago. Troy wouldn't let him."

"Do you still want him along?"

"Yes." Jimmy couldn't help but smile at the thought. "I'd like to take him out of the country for the rest of the summer."

"Why?"

Jimmy shrugged. "Keep him out of trouble."

"What kind of trouble?"

"The usual trouble kids his age get into. You know."

"Look, Jimmy, I know all about the story that Ferrante sold to the *Enquirer*. David hired me to talk to Callie and try to keep her from filing a criminal complaint. Jason is the key to this whole thing. David thinks that if we can talk to him and find out his side of the story, we can use it to get Callie to come to her senses. You're positive you don't know where he is?"

"I'm not lying to you, Greg," Jimmy said. "I haven't got the slightest idea where you can find him."

"Okay. You leave for Buenos Aires when, Sunday night?"

"That's right."

"You still planning to go?"

"Of course. Why do you ask?"

"Todd Curwen seemed to think you'd be so distraught at the thought of Jason being missing that you'd cancel your tour."

"I've had just about enough of Todd."

"You thinking of dropping him, like Julianna did?"

"I wouldn't go that far," Jimmy said. "I just think I've given him too much control over my life for too long. I need to stand up for myself a little bit more."

"You did a good job of it tonight."

"Thanks." Jimmy blushed. "I was a little worked up."

"Over Jason?"

"Well, yes, but I'm sure he'll turn up."

"Almost everyone turns up. What I'm worried about is what condition he'll be in. The sooner I can find him, the better."

"I wouldn't worry too much. He can take care of himself."

"The world can be pretty rough on a fourteen-year-old boy out on his own. If he did go to New York, would you have any idea where he might be staying? Does he have friends there?"

"I'm sure he does, but I wouldn't know where to begin."

"And you're going into the city when?"

"A little later today, sometime this morning, probably."

"If you see Jason, if you hear from him, or if you have any other ideas about where he might be, will you call my beeper?"

"Sure."

I handed him one of my business cards.

Jimmy yawned, and I got a look at his exquisite vocal cords.

"Sorry I couldn't be any more help to you, Greg," he said.

"You did your best," I said, though I wasn't so sure.

"Could you excuse me now? I need to go back to bed."

"All right," I said. "Nice to meet you, Jimmy."

"Same here." Jimmy shook my hand. "Good luck. Oh, and if you see Jason before I do, you'll give me a call, won't you?"

"Just give me your number."

I took out my notepad and a pen and had him write it down.

"That's my private line," he said. "Please don't give it out to anyone. But feel free to call anytime, day or night. I don't care if you wake me up. I want to know Jason's all right."

"Will do," I said.

"Do you mind showing yourself out?"

I told him I didn't.

On my way out, Peter the security guard handed me back my pistol.

"Are you security for the house?" I asked as I made a quick inspection of my Glock and its clip.

"No," he said. "Bodyguard."

"You get to go along on the tour?"

"If I wanted to, but I don't."

I put the gun back in my shoulder holster.

"You haven't seen a young kid around here, have you? About fourteen, looks a year or two older? Cute kid about yea high?"

"You mean Jason?" A warmth entered Peter's eyes.

"Yeah, Jason."

"I've seen him around here, sure."

"You have?"

"He's around here a lot. There was that party last weekend, and a couple nights since. Oh, you mean tonight?"

"Yeah, I mean tonight."

"Nope, not tonight. Haven't seen him. Sorry."

"Thanks a lot," I said and went out the door.

Both Madeleine's Infiniti coupé and what I assumed was Curwen's BMW roadster were gone from the cul-de-sac. As I got in behind the wheel of the 'Cuda, my thoughts turned to a hot cup of coffee. I hoped Bert Ferrigno had made himself a fresh pot and wouldn't mind sharing.

Nine

"Here you go," Ferrigno said, handing me the Dixie cup. He had overcome the funk I'd put him in earlier and seemed eager now to share a cup of joe with me. "You take it black?"

"You got milk?"

"Nondairy creamer."

"Black's fine, then."

I was outside of the 'Cuda and leaning against the shelf of the gatehouse window, on the inner side of the Somerset Hills Estates exit gate. I lit a cigarette and took in deep puffs in between sips while Ferrigno regarded my car covetously.

"How fast you taken her up?" he asked. I could smell his cinnamon breath mints again. I wondered what his mouth would taste like if I were to lean over and kiss him.

"A hundred twenty, once," I said, exhaling smoke.

"Where'd you do that?"

"A stretch of highway between El Paso, Texas, and Carlsbad, New Mexico. Smooth as a hovercraft."

"I'm still serious about wanting to buy it."

"I don't know if I want to sell, but I'll consider it if you'll answer me one thing."

"What's that?"

"Did you let Jason Blassingame out through this gate tonight?"

"I'm not supposed to give out that kind of info, but I guess it wouldn't hurt anyone if I told you I didn't see him. Not since he came in earlier with his dad and their chauffeur."

"In the Lincoln stretch?"

"That's the one."

"You didn't let anyone else out this evening who might have been driving an Eagle Talon?"

"I know the car you mean, but I haven't seen it tonight."

"That's the truth?"

"Why shouldn't it be?"

"I don't know. You wouldn't be the kind of guy who'd cover up for Jason if he were to give you some money or promise you favors, would you?"

"Favors?" Ferrigno grinned sheepishly. "What kind of favors?"

"Come on Bert, you know as well as I do. You know what Jason's like, don't you?"

"He's a little foof. Everybody around here knows that."

"And you're kind of cute in that beret. Don't tell me Jason's never flirted with you."

"Sure, he has." Ferrigno grinned proudly.

"You didn't go for it?"

"Hey, he's just a kid, for Christ's sake."

"You don't care that he's a guy?"

"Why should I care?" Ferrigno leaned closer, his eyes drifting all over me. "You're a guy, and you're not so bad."

"You don't like girls?"

"Nothing wrong with them. Some of my best friends are girls. I just don't want to see them with their clothes off."

"I hear you," I said.

"I know you do," Ferrigno said huskily. "I was looking forward to you coming back through the gate. I've been sitting here looking at your card. You live in Chelsea?"

"Me and a few hundred thousand other people."

"You know, sometimes I go into the city myself."

"Congratulations."

"Maybe I could meet you there sometime."

"In uniform or civvies?"

Ferrigno grinned: "I guess that's up to you."

"I guess it'll depend on what mood I'm in. I can't even think about it now, though. I'm in the middle of this damned case. You got a day off coming up or something?"

"Tuesday."

"I hope to be finished by then." I thought about Juan; after the last message he'd left, I had no idea whether we would ever hook up. I saw no reason why I couldn't leave my options open—and besides, Ferrigno was hot. "Give me a call, okay?"

"I will, Greg."

"And if you do let Jason Blassingame out tonight—whether alone or with someone else—call my beeper, will you?"

"Sure thing. You want me to let you out now?"

"If you don't mind. And Bert?"

"Yeah?"

"Thanks for the joe."

Ten

As I was heading down US 202 on my way back toward the city, I spotted what looked like Julianna Gilbert's yellow Ferrari in the parking lot of a nightclub with a neon sign flashing REX. Loud dance music blared from within. Flanking the entrance were four freestanding Doric columns with gas-fueled Olympic flames burning madly atop. I entered Rex's parking lot.

The valet was a lanky, freckle-faced redhead of about twenty who wore his black slacks a couple sizes too big so they bunched up around his ankles and barely hugged his pelvis, giving him the appearance of an unnaturally elongated torso. The tail of his white tuxedo shirt was about to come out, and the comparatively small black vest looked comical in the extreme.

"Park this for me, will you?" I asked.

The valet approached the 'Cuda with reluctance. All around me was the sparklingly polished evidence of what he'd parked tonight: Lexuses, Mercedeses, Jaguars, BMWs, a second Ferrari, a white Lotus, a couple of Rolls-Royces. There was at least one car he hadn't parked—a Bentley whose driver still sat in the front seat, close to the entrance. Useful as the 'Cuda might have been in landing me a date with Bert Ferrigno, it wasn't going to help me win any friends or influence any people at Rex.

The valet took my keys, gave me a claim, and took my car around back, out of sight—by the service entrance, I supposed.

The bouncer, an unshaven neolithic man, grunted at me and blocked my path. "Twenty-five-dollar cover," he said, sounding like he'd divined the number miraculously out of the ether.

I paid him without a grumble. It was David Loeb's money.

The bouncer eyeballed me top to bottom like I was an unsolved mystery. I must have lacked the Rex look, and he'd never seen me before; I was shorting out his primitive circuitry.

"Do I get to go in now?"

He snorted his assent, huge nostrils flaring, and stood aside magnanimously. "Go on," he mumbled.

I went in and found nothing more than a dance club for young, wasted, rich singles with nothing else to do but drink, do ecstasy, and fuck. It would be the same people here night after night, only in different permutations. There were more blond heads here than I'd seen in any one place since Tay Farrell's Southampton job. The place was as dark as any other, with the usual swirling and flashing lights that bathed the faces in comic-book colors. Everyone had a deep tan and impeccable teeth. The crowd was mixed—mostly straight guys and girls, though several of the guys appeared to be cruising me as I made may way through, and I spotted a few other guys in tight cliques who looked as if they'd feel right at home in the Chelsea gay ghetto. It must have been the only bar for rich kids for miles around.

I saw no sign of Julianna on the dance floor, so I went to where it was less crowded. There were tables one could sit at, and some of them spilled out from the front room to an open garden in back. I spotted Julianna seated alone there, half hidden by the weeping leaves of a dangling branch.

I tried to enter the garden but was stopped by another bouncer type. This one was as bald as I was, except that he had no eyebrows or eyelashes. Either he was afflicted with alopecia, or he was into something kinky and painful during his off-time. The large gold hoop earring in his left ear made him look like Mr. Clean—only with a constipated look on his face.

"Sorry, pally, V.I.P.'s only," he said.

"My mother thinks I'm a V.I.P."

"Do I look like your mother to you?"

"I'll take that as a rhetorical question," I said and tried to go around him, but he stuck out an arm as gnarled as an old tree limb and put his hand firmly against my left pectoral.

"I can't let you in," he said robotically.

"You don't have to feel me up," I said.

He folded his arms against his chest, spreading his legs apart like he was expecting me to try a battering ram.

"I'm meeting Julianna Gilbert," I said.

Mr. Clean was unmoved.

"You don't believe me?"

"No."

"Would you let me send her a drink with a note?"

"Free country." He shrugged. "Have it your way."

"Great, two clichés for the price of one," I said. "I'll be right back. Don't go away."

I went to the bar. There I obtained the specialty of the house, called a Firefighter, some kind of insane red concoction in a frosted zombie glass with a brandied cherry and a small red paper umbrella on top. At the bar, I composed a message on a napkin: *Invite me over. It's about your brother.* I signed it *Angelo Ferrante.* I folded the napkin in half and handed it to Mr. Clean along with the drink and a twenty-dollar bill. He pocketed the bill and told me to wait.

He took the Firefighter out to Julianna and served it to her clumsily, pointing out the napkin and thumbing over his shoulder, toward me. Julianna read the note, and her gaze snapped up. She looked my way and nodded to Mr. Clean. He shuffled his way back.

"Go ahead," he said, sounding repentant. "Guess I was wrong about you. Can't blame a guy for doing his job, can you?" He laughed to show that he had no hard feelings and patted me on the back chummily, launching me into the V.I.P. garden.

Julianna watched me through her glasses, poker-faced. When I reached the small café-style table, she offered me her lazy hand and said: "Angelo Ferrante. Nice to meet you at last."

"Likewise, Ms. Gilbert, likewise." I touched her hand and sat in the iron chair. A fountain or birdbath gurgled behind me.

"The drink's cute, but I'm starving for a cigarette."

I gave her a Lucky Strike, took one for myself, and was reaching for my lighter when she beat me to the draw. Her flame shot up several inches but somehow managed not to singe her hair. She closed the lighter and replaced it in her purse.

"Oh," she said. "You wanted me to do yours for you?" She took it back out, sighing like I was causing her *so* much trouble.

"If you don't mind," I said. I felt the strong heat of the flame as it scorched the tip of my cig. She blew her first drag into my face. I sucked it up and blew it back.

"Now who the fuck are you?" Julianna removed the umbrella and twirled it upside down on the tabletop while she sipped at her Firefighter through the straw. Behind the glasses, she batted her eyelashes like Betty Boop.

"You never heard of Angelo Ferrante? I work for Jimmy. I'm a private investigator."

She weighed this for about half a second. "I've heard of Angelo Ferrante. I've also seen him. In fact, he's a good personal friend of mine. So who the fuck are you, really?"

"Would you believe an adoring fan?"

She didn't believe me. "If I hear any more bullshit out of you," she said, "I'll have them throw you out of here with this umbrella shoved up your dick."

"And I'm supposed to take it and like it—yeah, I know. I'd like to see you try, frankly."

"Try this," she said, and planted the sole of her shoe in my crotch, the stiletto heel landing between my testicles.

"I see you've never outgrown that precious little kid act from your brother's TV show."

"Don't think of getting up. My knee's only half extended, and I've got a mean kick I picked up from Jean-Claude van Damme."

"Another personal friend of yours?"

"I'm about to puncture your scrotum, bucko."

"Promise?"

"Don't provoke me." She dug her heel into me more firmly.

I kind of dug it, but I pretended to wince.

"That's just a taste," she said, feeling superior.

"Quite a pleasant one, too."

"What's pleasant is you think I'm joking. You're not Angelo Ferrante. You know it, I know it—"

"The American people know it—"

This time she hurt me quite a bit. I didn't dig it anymore.

"Tell me who you are. And don't lie to me, or you'll be sorry you didn't believe me about the umbrella."

"Okay. Uncle. You know what that means, don't you?"

Julianna smiled but didn't let up the pressure.

"Here." I took out one of my business cards and presented it to her between two fingers. She took it and asked to see my P.I. license. I showed her the frayed thing, thinking I ought to start carrying around a copy before the original disintegrated.

"Greg Quaintance, huh?"

"That's me."

"What happened to your hair?"

"Didn't like it. Shaved it off."

"You're cute," she said, removing her foot from my groin and handing me back my license. She kept the business card. "Cuter than Ferrante, anyway. Why were you trying to get into Somerset Hills Estates? Bert said you weren't interested in Jimmy."

"Actually, I'm interested in Bert."

"I'd believe that. You two fucks are made for each other."

"We made a date. Tuesday. His day off. I might ask him to wear his uniform. I'm going to show him off all over Chelsea. Assuming I'm through with this case by then."

"You're not kidding, are you?" Julianna appeared to relax a little. She liked me now. "So who were you trying to see?"

"Nobody. I wanted to check out the area. I had no idea it was a demilitarized zone. If you knew I wasn't Ferrante, why did you invite me over?"

"I want to know what's what. Who are you working for?"

"Your brother."

"Okay, maybe you are. But who recruited you? Todd Curwen?"

"Until tonight, I had no idea who Todd Curwen was."

Julianna smiled like she got some kind of private pleasure out of the fact. "Maybe my mother?"

"Marcia? God, no!"

She smiled at that, too. "You've met her, then."

"Just a bit ago. But she didn't hire me, either."

"Then that leaves David Loeb."

"You are correct," I said. I took out a business card Loeb had given me with his signature on it and showed it to her.

"You're Ferrante's replacement." She regarded the card.

"As if anyone could replace Ferrante." I retrieved it.

"That's not like David, fucking up like that."

"It wasn't his fault Ferrante ditched him."

"It sure was. David should have talked to Callie himself. He should have known better than to trust Ferrante with this."

"You know about Callie?"

"We both know, or we wouldn't be here now, would we?" she said. She had a point. "I canceled a booking in Atlantic City so I could come up and see Jimmy. I didn't think they'd bar me during a family crisis."

"Well, Julianna, as long as we're both in on it, why don't you tell me what you know? Starting with Jason Blassingame."

"Why should I tell you anything?"

"I overheard you screaming at my buddy Bert. It sounded to me like you wanted to help your brother."

"How is my talking to you going to help Jimmy?"

"David's trying to cut Callie off at the knees, in a manner of speaking. I'm gathering information for him. It might help to know if there's any truth to her claims."

"You mean about Jimmy and Jason. Whether they're lovers."

"Callie wouldn't exactly phrase it that way, but yeah."

"I could tell you what I told Ferrante."

"You spoke to him?"

Julianna nodded. "At David's request. But I'm not sure it's safe anymore. I'm not sure I ought to tell you anything."

"I'm not going to sell it to the *Enquirer*, if that's what you're worried about."

"The *Enquirer*? That's the least of my worries." She blew out a thick fog of smoke that swirled around her wavy hair like it was a part of her. "I can't believe Callie would do this."

"Do what?"

"Ruin Jason Blassingame's life, that's what."

"How's she ruining it?"

"She wants money out of Jimmy, fine—but she should find a way to leave Jason out of it."

"You think she's making the whole thing up?"

"I don't know what she made up. It's just that she makes it seem so dirty. Jimmy and Jason are like best friends."

"You don't think it's odd for a thirty-five-year-old man to have a fourteen-year-old boy as his best friend?"

"Jimmy took Jason with him on his Asian tour last summer. So what? It's not as if he kidnapped the boy. Troy and Callie allowed Jason to go. Jimmy and Jason spent a lot of time together and got photographed all the time and all that. Jimmy relates to Jason on a deep, spiritual level. Callie's trying to misconstrue it into something it's not."

"She doesn't have any evidence."

"But there are all those photographs of Jimmy and Jason together. Videotape of Jimmy taking Jason through toy stores, theme parks, walking the streets of Tokyo, Bangkok, and Singapore. They went skiing together last winter on Jason's school break. A jury's going to wonder why."

"Any ideas?"

"You've got to understand, Jimmy's like a child. He never had a brother, and I wouldn't exactly call what we went through a childhood. His friendship with Jason must be filling some kind of need. Jason's mature for his age. Jimmy is not the kind of person who uses people. But how can you prove that to a jury?"

"The burden of proof will be on Callie. If she has nothing more than photos and video, it should be a cakewalk for David. And David could call you as a character witness."

"My mother wouldn't allow it."

"Why should she have anything to say about it?"

"That's what I've been wondering my whole life."

Julianna was more than halfway through her Firefighter. It looked like a stiff drink, and I doubted whether it was her first for the evening. Maybe I should have bought her a Pellegrino.

"Does Jimmy have any idea how concerned you are about him?"

"No, how could he?"

"How long have they been turning you away from the gate?"

"The last three months. Ever since he married Madeleine Downey. It's not Maddy's fault, though. She and I are great friends. It's just that when things start going badly in our family, I always get blamed. They're circling the wagons, but they've left me outside to fend for myself."

"Why do you think that is?"

"I don't know. Ever since I can remember, I've been the black sheep. It's because I talk back to the queen bee."

"Marcia, you mean? Like what do you say to her?"

"That she's destroying Jimmy. Of course they don't want to hear it. They don't trust me around him. They say I'm a bad influence. I thought marrying Maddy would be good for him and he'd be able to break away a little, but it seems only to have gotten worse. They've got Maddy under their spell."

Julianna made a rubbing motion with her thumb and fingers.

"Who do you mean by *they*?"

"Mom and Todd. You're sure you never heard the name Todd Curwen until tonight?"

"Positive," I said. "Should I have?"

"He's a top manager. Handles lots of top celebrities. Actors, singers, models."

"He used to be your manager, didn't he?"

Julianna looked at me warily. "How would you know?"

"Curwen told me you stole the tarot phone line idea from him and then ditched him for another manager."

"That's a lie. The tarot thing wasn't Todd's idea. I don't deny ditching him. He was skimming royalties off me."

"Is this a regular practice of his?"

"One can only assume so. I don't know how many times I've told Jimmy that he ought to get rid of Todd."

"Why won't he?"

"He doesn't believe me. Or he just doesn't care. The money Jimmy makes doesn't mean a lot to him. He's probably talked himself into thinking that Todd somehow deserves what he skims. Jimmy would never confront him on it, though. Too passive."

"Did you ever confront Curwen over Jimmy?"

"I sure did."

"And?"

"He told me to mind my own business. He tries to take all the credit for turning Jimmy into a superstar. He says I've ridden Jimmy's coattails and ought to be grateful to him. I told him he could ram it up his ass. Then I got a new manager."

"Tell me about David Loeb."

"David's the third part of the triangle. The difference is, David's a mensch. He doesn't try to micromanage Jimmy's life. He's very conscious of territory—I guess because he doesn't want Mom or Todd telling him how to handle the legal matters. He never tries to tell Todd how to shape Jimmy's career, and he never tells Mom how to mother him. Sometimes I wish he would."

"David's taking Callie very seriously," I said. "He wants to squash her."

"Good for him. I hope he does." She sucked up the rest of the Firefighter. "All I want is a chance to speak to Jimmy."

"Would it help if I asked David about it?"

"I doubt it. David thinks I'm a flake, and if Todd and Mom are keeping me away, he'd be stepping on their toes. He won't."

"Do you think Jimmy wants to see you?"

"I know he does."

"Why doesn't he do anything about it?"

"Because of the way they control him. If he took the initiative to see me, they would lay the biggest guilt trip on him, telling him how much they've done for him and then he goes behind their back. You beginning to get the picture?"

"Sounds pretty bad. For Jimmy, I mean."

"The problem is, he's gullible. He'll believe anything anybody tells him. He's easy to manipulate."

"You haven't ever done it yourself, have you?"

"I like getting my way as much as the next person—and I wouldn't be where I am today without bullying people—but I won't bully Jimmy. I wouldn't be able to live with myself. I don't ever want to hurt him. I guess that's why I'm not against his spending time with Jason Blassingame."

"How so?"

"Jason's the only nice person he has left."

"What about Madeleine Downey?"

"Oh, Maddy's just a front. Todd Curwen arranged it to try to give Jimmy a more macho image, if you can believe that."

"Why now?"

"Excuse me?"

"I thought Jimmy's whole appeal was in being androgynous. Why wait all these years to decide that he's really a man?"

"I told you, it was Todd's idea." She looked at her watch but seemed to have trouble focusing on the dial.

I looked at mine: 3:55 a.m. I was wondering whether I'd be able to stay awake enough to drive back to New York without flying over the edge of the General Pułaski Skyway.

"I'm sorry," Julianna said, pulling her purse strap up over her shoulder. "I've got to go. I didn't mean to stay so long."

"Why did you stop here in the first place?"

"I needed a drink. Bert made me so mad. I know he turns you on, but he really can be a son of a bitch." She stood up, and her hair got tangled in the overhanging branch. She flailed against it like it was a vampire bat.

"I may want to talk to you again," I said, getting up.

"David knows where you can reach me." She fixed her hair.

"And you have my number," I reminded her. "If you think of anything else that might help Jimmy, you let me know, okay?"

"I will, Greg. Sorry again."

"I'll escort you outside."

I reached for her arm, but she shrank away, saying, "Thanks, but I can take care of myself."

I stayed by the table and watched her go. As she passed by Mr. Clean, he glanced over at me glumly.

I smiled back, keeping my eyes on him as I walked out of the V.I.P. garden. I wished him a pleasant morning.

"Same to you, pally," he said, yawning.

I stood on a short queue for the Rex men's room. There were still four guys between me and the door when someone came up behind me and poked something hard into my ribs, on the right.

"Don't make a move," a man's voice said breathily in my ear.

"Okay," I whispered back. "What's the plan, Stan?"

"Come with me outside, and keep your mouth shut, dipstick."

I did as he said, and no one was apparently the wiser.

He maneuvered me out the back exit, past the restrooms. We came out in the dingy back lot, where my 'Cuda was parked.

I saw no one. We had the whole lot to ourselves.

"Don't turn around," he said, "and keep your hands away from your sides."

He patted me down with his left hand and wasn't polite about it. No guy had explored me this thoroughly since my last one-night stand. He found my Glock at once and removed it. He must have put it away somewhere on his person, because his left hand was free again and patting down my pants legs.

I tried to find a spot on the 'Cuda's black finish where I could catch a glimpse of my assailant's face, but the images were rounded and distorted like in a funhouse mirror. He was either tall or short, fat or thin, and wearing black like me.

"You know what this is," he said, standing up again.

"A stick-up?"

I felt the tip of his gun pry into my ribs: Wrong answer.

"I told you to keep quiet, fuckhead. I'm giving you a message, that's what this is. You don't need to know who it's from, so don't ask."

"Okay, I won't."

I sensed an itchy trigger finger or, worse, an inexperienced one, and wondered whether it was worth losing my life over a case of alleged man-boy love.

"Now you listen—" he began.

I cut him off by bringing my arm down and grabbing his thick wrist in a tight grip, turning my trunk away from his gun and hooking my leg behind him. He fell flat on his back while I yanked up on his arm. I heard his shoulder pop, and in the same moment his hand let go of the gun. It clattered onto the asphalt at his feet. I leaned over and landed a punch on the underside of his jaw for good measure. I found my Glock in his coat pocket and stood up, training it on him. I kicked his own gun away, and it went skittering under the 'Cuda.

He lay writhing on his back, his left hand clutching his shoulder. He was breathing noisily in and out through gritted teeth—the closest his manliness would allow him to come to a scream. His clean-shaven face was drenched in sweat.

It was Peter, the security guy from Gilbert's. I reached inside his coat and found his wallet. His New Jersey driver's license and various credit cards said his name was Peter Denneny.

"Okay, Peter," I said. "What's the message?"

"You . . . you dislocated my fucking shoulder, you asshole."

"I'll pop it back into place in a minute. First, I want to hear the message."

He nodded, grimacing.

"The message," I said, prodding his shoulder with my boot.

"Ow! I was supposed to tell you to disappear, like . . . like Ferrante. No more talking to . . . to Julianna Gilbert. And don't go selling anybody any . . . any stories, like Ferrante did. You happy now, asswipe?"

"Hey, dummy, I've got seventeen rounds of hollow-point bullets in this gun, and I'm already pretty pissed off at you, so if I were you, I'd be careful about calling me asswipe, got it?"

He nodded again. "I got it."

"Good. You know, you're not very good. If you were a real professional, that little Army maneuver I pulled on you wouldn't have gotten me very far, and I probably would have got a bullet in my thigh. You're new at this kind of thing, aren't you?"

Denneny grunted a yes.

"Who's the idiot who made the mistake of sending you instead of a real man? Was it Jimmy Gilbert?" I waggled the gun in his face to keep him from stalling.

"Curwen," he said, still gritting his teeth. "Todd Curwen."

"Todd Curwen? How did he know where to find me?"

"He didn't. Asked me to . . . to follow you. I saw you come . . . come and join Julianna, so I . . . so I called Todd, and he . . . and he told me to give you the . . . the message. I wasn't going to hurt you, just . . . just supposed to scare you."

"Do you know where I can find Angelo Ferrante?"

"I don't know," he said. "Honest."

"Okay, good enough. Now let's have a look at that arm."

I holstered my Glock and knelt alongside Denneny, felt my way carefully around his shoulder, asked him if he was ready, and jammed his arm back into its socket.

This time he really did scream.

Mr. Clean came running out, made a quick assessment, and asked, "What the fuck is going on?"

"Nothing much," I said.

"Sorry, pally." He was addressing me. "Ms. Gilbert asked me to keep an eye on you, but I must have lost you somehow."

"Yeah, nice try."

"You all right?"

"I'm okay, but my friend Pete here seems to have dislocated his shoulder."

"Aw, the poor baby," Mr. Clean said.

Denneny looked up at him with wolfish eyes like he wanted to tear Mr. Clean's throat out. He was in too much pain to speak.

"I think I've just relocated it for him," I said. "His name's Peter Denneny. You ever seen him before?"

"Yeah, I seen him at the gym at the SAC."

"What's that?"

"Somerset Athletic Club."

"Oh, so he's a local boy. Look, Mister—" I had to bite my tongue to keep from uttering the horrible appellation. "Be a chum and call him an ambulance, will you?"

"Sure, pally." He went back inside.

I went to the other side of the 'Cuda and found Denneny's gun. I dumped the bullets out, put them in my pocket, and shoved his gun into the waist of his pants. Even though I'd popped his arm back into place, he wouldn't be able to use it for a while.

"No hard feelings?" I said.

Denneny stared up at me with bulging eyes like I was a nut.

"Tell Todd Curwen this was all a misunderstanding and that I'll be speaking with him tomorrow. You got that?"

"Got it."

"Good. And when you see the doctor, ask for some codeine."

I searched my pockets for the keys to the 'Cuda, but then I realized I had given them to the redheaded valet. I walked all the way around to the front entrance and handed him my claim.

He stared at the claim and looked confusedly at the lot.

"It's the Barracuda," I said. "You parked it in Siberia."

"Huh?" he said, his mouth hanging open. "Oh, yeah."

While I waited for him to return, I scanned the lot and saw that Julianna's canary yellow Ferrari was still parked where the valet had left it.

When the valet came back with my car, I pointed this out to him, and he confirmed that it was indeed hers. I passed him a twenty and asked if he had seen her leave with anyone else.

He took the money eagerly and said, "Didn't see her, sorry."

I went back in and searched the crowd. I paid a girl to look in the ladies' room. There was no sign of Julianna.

I went back out front and gave the valet my business card. I asked him to call my beeper if Julianna came back for her car—or if anyone else did. He stared at me for a while.

I had to pay him another twenty bucks before he would agree.

Eleven

The taillights in my rearview were a slow-moving river of magma leaving the Rex parking lot—a drunken stream heading east to engulf Raritan and Somerville and New York. I was going west, back to the estates, sober and steady and pissed off. I throttled up to eighty.

I had a burning pain in my stomach. I switched on the dome light and rifled through the over-the-counter pill collection I kept in the glove compartment. I spilled a few packets on the floor until I came up with a Pepcid. I popped it into my mouth—but I doubted I had heartburn.

The burn I felt came from the fact that I was working for David Loeb and being dicked around by his people. I'd felt it before and didn't like it.

It was the feeling of not being picked by the captains of either squad until the P.E. teacher made one of them take you. It was being led into the woods by a gang of pals and being ditched. It was growing a little older and blaming your father for going missing in Vietnam before you ever got a chance to see him as anything more than a photo of an Army man in dress duds. It was falling in love with your best friend in high school and watching him go out with some girl and forget all about you. It was looking to the future and seeing no place in it for you.

I thought I'd left that feeling behind me for good once I got through basic training. I was adept at soldiering, part of a sacred brotherhood. I came back from Saudi triumphant, looking forward to a career in the service—only they didn't want me anymore. My name was on a list. They interrogated me like I was a traitor. They asked me to name names of other queers, promising to go easy on me if I did. But I didn't—I *wouldn't*—because I wasn't a rat. It was only after they gave me my undesirable discharge that I learned who the rat was who named me. He was a guy I never thought of as a rat, one I thought I could trust, who was closer to me than a brother—exciting and tender and charming and a great soldier. I'd loved and admired him. After Desert Storm, we'd gone and gotten identical bald eagle tattoos in Fayetteville—a tattoo that once seemed an unbreakable bond between us but was now there forever to remind me that I could never trust him or the Army or anyone else.

This feeling was like being hollowed out from inside, and no amount of Pepcid was going to get rid of it.

I was going back, and I was going to wake up Jimmy and take him up on his offer. I was going to search every square foot of his damned house until I came up with Jason Blassingame.

The texture of the asphalt came up through my Michelins to the floor of the 'Cuda. The painted lines on the road streaked past in my bright beams, stained an inky red in spots from recent roadkill. It was a long, straight stretch before I reached the Somerset Hills Estates turnoff. I took it too fast, and one side lost contact with the road for a moment. When the 'Cuda settled back down on the pavement, I patted its dashboard placatingly.

I pulled up to a screeching stop before the guardhouse.

The entrance gate was closed, but the exit gate had been left wide open. I saw no other cars ahead or behind or parked anywhere along the shoulder. The light was on in the guardhouse, but no one was inside. A dark form lay half in and half out of the guardhouse, one arm splayed out in a pool of dark blood.

I got out of my car, my Glock drawn ahead of me. I listened carefully but could hear no sound of movement. I scanned the trees and thickets on either side of the road and tried to penetrate the foliage, but I could see no one hiding.

"Bert?" I asked.

Still no sound as I approached the body.

It was Ferrigno, though barely recognizable. He was in his uniform, though his beret had fallen off. His service weapon remained holstered at his side. He had been shot twice in the face at point-blank range. His face was covered in blood. The entrance wounds were highly disfiguring, made by large-caliber shells. He lay on top of the exit wounds, but that didn't keep me from noticing the bits of brain lying around.

I hurried over to the side of the road, far away from the crime scene, and experienced a painful series of dry heaves that failed to bring up anything but the half-dissolved Pepcid.

I stood there bent over with my hands on my knees.

"Jesus," I muttered.

Ferrigno's legs held open the door to the guardhouse. I managed to step around, avoiding the blood, to reach inside and grab the phone. I phoned 911 and told them a murder had been committed. I told them where. I hung up without giving them my name.

I made a quick inventory of the guardhouse, noting the maps and the video screens and the Mr. Coffee machine and the Dixie cups. At least one thing was missing: Ferrigno's log book.

I went back to the 'Cuda and put it in gear. Going wide around the crime scene, I drove through the open gate. Once inside, I held the steering wheel low with my left hand while I kept my Glock in my right and watched out the windows.

Ferrigno lying back there dead was probably just somebody's footnote or afterthought to something else that had happened.

Twelve

I came to a gap in the foliage and a gray tongue of road that was the Blassingame turnoff. I idled for a moment, my foot tense on the clutch. I only had time to check out one estate before the police arrived. My hunch favored Jimmy Gilbert's.

I let my foot off the clutch and sped up, keeping a lookout, wishing I'd equipped the 'Cuda with a rotatable searchlight so I could scan the darkness on all sides. I took the Gilbert turnoff and made it up to the house without noting anything out of the ordinary. All the lights were out. The cars that had been parked out front earlier were gone. I rolled up the windows, got out, and locked the doors. The big engine ticked as it cooled.

The doorbell elicited no response. The front door was locked. I leapt up a couple of times and tried to see inside through the high windows. Nothing obscured my view, but inside all was dark. If I broke in, I was sure to set off alarms.

I began checking the grounds, keeping close to the house for cover and directing my Glock up at the stars. The sides of the house fell back in steps, giving me corners to take without knowing what I might find. The dread I felt was like nothing I'd known since nightly patrol duty around our base camp perimeter, when we were within spitting distance of the Kuwaiti border, just before Desert Shield became Desert Storm.

Not a light was to be seen anywhere on the grounds, but my eyes were growing accustomed to the darkness. In back of the main house were several outbuildings, some a considerable distance away. One tall structure on a far distant hill was visible because a single window was alight, way up at the top.

Gilbert's swimming pool was larger than Blassingame's, but the poolside chairs and tables were in disarray, as if a scuffle or other disturbance had occurred.

I stepped down the path to the pool to have a closer look.

Dimly, I made out a portrait of sorts at the bottom of the pool—a mosaic of small tiles adding up to Jimmy Gilbert's face as it appeared about ten years ago, wearing the requisite wraparound sunglasses. In the light of sun it was probably luminous and colorful, but in the dark it was gray and vague, the image distorted by the still rippling water.

A body, clothed in a dark skirt and light blouse, was floating facedown at the deep end, under the shadow of the diving board. Wet hair lay flat against the skull, fanning out all around the head like seaweed.

I stepped carefully out on the diving board and knelt, reaching for the body but falling short. I holstered my Glock and got onto my belly, grasping the side of the board with one hand and stretching out my arm. I grasped a few tendrils of hair and pulled, bringing the body closer. I balanced my body across the board, reaching with both hands, and brought the head out of the water. The scalp fell back in a large flap that was still attached at the neck. There was a superficial gash and bruising at the left temple. The forehead had been shattered by the entry of a large-caliber shell that created a star-shaped wound.

The face was recognizable. It was Callie Blassingame.

I let go of her, and water splashed into my face. I was spitting some of it out of my mouth when I felt a jarring of the diving board from heavy footfalls behind me. I was cocking my head to see who it was when the mass of a body fell on top of me, and with it the weight of a blunt object against the back of my skull. I struck out at my assailant but was pushed off the board, grazing Callie's body as I fell in and made my splash.

I gasped for air and took in water. I fought my way up to the surface and coughed, trying to keep afloat, my vision blurred and veiled by the darkness. The arm hanging off the diving board swung at me again with the object, clocking me across the left temple. I went under again. My diaphragm spasmed, and I was breathing in water again and gagging on it. I kicked and flailed but seemed to go nowhere. I couldn't break the surface. It felt like someone had grabbed onto my boots and was dragging me down.

My hand found Callie's skirt and grabbed on. I pulled myself up, draping my arms over her floating thighs. Out of the corner of my eye, I saw the arm swing at me again from the diving board. I felt the swish of the object near my head, but there was no contact. I was out of reach. I was trying to cough up the water, trying to get a decent breath of air, trying to get my vision clear, and trying to stay afloat by hanging onto Callie.

The diving board made a sudden *sproing*. My assailant jumped back to the edge of the pool. The footsteps went hurrying off into the grass—I was unsure which direction.

Callie's body was steadily sinking, and I had taken on water. I lunged for the edge of the pool but came nowhere near. I attempted a few strokes but ran into the wall. I reached up to grab the tiled lip and managed to pull myself out, though my arms felt like lead weights.

I lay there on my stomach, coughing and choking and trying to breathe. Water oozed out of my clothes. My vision cleared enough for me to see the cool water mingling with the warm black ink that was streaming down off my head. The ink bubbled up into a murky gas cloud and obliterated everything. I was dead.

Thirteen

Someone was sitting on my back, trying to bust my ribs. I was expelling water out of my mouth and nose. I breathed in with a rattle when the weight let up. This was repeated a few times. I was helpless to do much else but lie there, and I felt oddly detached from what was happening to me, as if I were outside my own body and standing there with my arms folded.

When no more water emerged from my lungs, I was grabbed by the arm and turned over onto my back, flopping over wetly like a fish. My eyelids were heavy. The person who'd been pumping me tilted my head back, put one hand under my neck, stuck a finger down my throat, and poked around to check that my airway was clear. My nose was pinched shut. A pair of warm lips formed a tight seal over my mouth. My lungs were filled with air. The lips left mine and allowed the air to escape, then settled back to do the procedure again. It was oddly soothing.

My eyelids fluttered open like a butterfly's wings. In the darkness, I saw a face staring down at me looking anxious and concerned. It was the same face as that done in mosaic on the bottom of the pool, without the sunglasses.

"Jimmy?" I said, feeling woozy.

"Don't try to talk." He laid a hand on my forehead.

"But, but—" I was trying to tell him about Callie.

"Shh," Jimmy Gilbert said. "Help is on its way."

I was about to thank him when my eyelids grew heavy again and the murky gas cloud came back to finish me off.

Fourteen

I found myself lying on a not very comfortable white paper sheet on a padded table in the subdued light of a hospital emergency department. My clothing had been removed, and I had been dressed in a not very tasteful turquoise gown. My allotted space was cordoned off with a matching curtain. I didn't see any doctors or nurses around. What I did see was a cop—a young pockmarked sheriff's deputy in beige uniform who was leaning forward in his chair with his cap far back on his head, chewing gum and reading a *People* magazine with wide-eyed intent. Hugo Wallis's gorgeous mug took up most of the cover, alongside big block letters that spelled out WALLIS CONFESSES – 'I'M BROKE!' I was surprised they hadn't gone for SEXIEST KILLER ALIVE.

"Excuse me," I said.

The deputy jumped and dropped the *People*.

"Shit," he said, staring at me like I was a corpse come to life. The equipment on his belt clattered as he got to his feet. He poked his head around the curtain and called, "Detective!"

A white middle-aged woman wearing a man's blazer, a polo shirt, and a detective's badge came in chatting amiably with a black man in bleached blond hair, a turquoise nurse's frock, and two gold hoop earrings. The detective leaned against the wall, sipping her coffee and whispering with the deputy, while the male nurse stepped up smiling to have a look at me.

"Let's have a look at you, Mr. Quaintance," he said. "My name's Carlton. I'm a nurse." This was confirmed by his name tag: CARLTON HEDGES, P.N.

"Where am I, Carlton?"

"Somerset Medical Center, in Somerville. How does that head of yours feel?"

"Not great, now that you mention it." I reached up to touch it, but Hedges gently grabbed my hand and set it back down.

"Don't want you disturbing those stitches," he said. "You got a couple of nasty bumps and some broken skin. We took you in for x-rays and a CT scan. You looked okay, considering."

"People tell me I've got a hard head."

"And I didn't even have to shave it," Hedges added cheerily. "We x-rayed your lungs, too, since you took on some water. But you must have coughed everything out. I want to hear how you're breathing now."

Hedges checked me out with his stethoscope, examined the dilation of my eyes, and replaced the bandages over my stitches.

"Soon as the doctor has one last look at you, we'll be able to let you go."

"Not till I'm through with him," said the detective. She had a deep, arrogant voice. Her gray hair was wiry and unkempt, like an old poodle who'd been allowed to go too long without a trip to the groomer's.

"He's all yours, Paula," Hedges said.

I thanked him before he vanished through the curtain.

"Mr. Quaintance," the detective said, coming up from the wall and staring at me with kindly black eyes. "I've been nosing around in your wallet, which has revealed to me that you're a private detective hailing from the wilds of New York City."

"That's right."

"I'm Detective Paula Ozwick of the Somerset County Sheriff's Department. I'm glad you took so long to come around. I wanted to be here when you did, but I've been a little preoccupied this morning, what with fishing a corpse out of a swimming pool and seeing what the M.E. tentatively has to say about her."

"It's Callie Blassingame."

"We know that. I've confiscated your clothes as evidence, by the way. You'll get your personal effects back."

"Fair enough, but what do I wear out of here?"

"Carlton will be happy to give you pants and a smock."

"I'll need a ride back to my car."

"Either that or a ride into the station. Would you like to tell me what happened?"

"I don't know."

"You don't know," Detective Ozwick repeated.

"Not if you mean what happened to Callie, I don't."

"Then why don't we start with what you do know. What you were doing there, for example."

"Something was bugging me, and I had to go back," I said, still too groggy to realize I wasn't making any sense to her.

"You were there on business?"

"I was. I'm working for Jimmy Gilbert."

"That was going to be my next question."

I had a vague, dreamlike memory that Jimmy Gilbert had come down from his house like an angel to revive me. But I wasn't ready to share this with Detective Ozwick. I had no idea whether he had stuck around the pool to meet the police and E.M.S.

"I was hired by his attorney, David Loeb," I added.

"This is the same bozo who got Hugo Wallis off scot-free?"

"That's the one."

"What was the nature of your business with David Loeb slash Jimmy

Gilbert?"

"I'm not sure I'm at liberty to discuss it. I was helping Loeb on a legal matter related to Gilbert. You'd have to take it up with them."

"You were up at the Gilbert house earlier last night."

"How do you know?"

"You said you had to go back. Something was bugging you. Anything you might be *at liberty* to share with me?"

"Nothing I could put my finger on." I had gone back to Gilbert's to find Jason Blassingame, but mentioning this might open the can of worms I'd been hired to squash. "I went back to the gate of Somerset Hills, and I found Bert lying there dead."

"By Bert you mean Alberto Ferrigno, the guard?"

"I knew him as Bert," I said defensively. "Nice guy."

"You wouldn't happen to be the man who phoned 911 and reported his murder, would you?"

"That was I."

"Why didn't you give your name or stick around to meet us?"

"I was worried that something else might have happened."

"What made you think that?"

"The exit gate was open. I figured that something had happened at one of the estates, and whoever did it had to kill Bert to keep from being identified later."

"How did you know which estate to go to?"

"I didn't. But I'm being paid by Jimmy Gilbert."

"For what kind of work? Security? Investigations?"

"Yes."

Detective Ozwick sighed in frustration and said, "Okay." She downed the last of her coffee and crushed the styrofoam cup, throwing it angrily into the wastebasket.

All this time, the young deputy kept staring, as if his orders were not to take his eyes off mine. I gave him a smile, and he gulped nervously. I hoped he didn't swallow his gum.

"Were you acquainted with Callie Blassingame?"

"I met her for the first time last night."

"At Jimmy Gilbert's?"

"No, at her apartment in New York."

"Do you have any idea what she was doing at Gilbert's?"

"I don't think she went over there to use the pool. She was dead and fully dressed when I found her."

Detective Ozwick's mandible ground against her maxilla. "Stop being facetious," she said. "Just tell me how you found her. If I don't like what I hear, I'm going to hold you in the county jail for forty-eight hours while I decide whether or not to charge you with murder."

By this point, I figured that Jimmy Gilbert hadn't stuck around. If he had witnessed my attack and seen the attacker running off, he would have said so to police, and they wouldn't be trying to scare me with the suggestion that I was a suspect.   I agreed to tell her what I could. I asked for some coffee first. She sent the deputy out through the curtain to get it.

I gave her just the facts of finding Bert Ferrigno and Callie Blassingame. My account of what happened on the diving board and in the pool came out confused. I never saw more than a glimpse of a blurry arm. I had been saved from being bludgeoned and drowned to death when my attacker inexplicably fled. I could only assume that this person heard a noise and feared discovery.

"How did you manage to get out of the pool?"

"I don't know. All I knew was I had to get out or I'd die."

"That can be a good motivator," Detective Ozwick agreed. This would have been a good moment for her to bring up the fact that Jimmy Gilbert had found me lying half-drowned outside the pool and set about reviving me. But all she continued with was, "And you have no idea who this attacker could have been?"

"I couldn't even guess."

"Was it a man or a woman?"

"I have no idea. I do figure it was an adult, from the way the body fell on me and pushed me off the diving board."

"Good, that rules out children." She was sarcastic. "Your meeting with Callie Blassingame last night was purely business?"

"That's right, business."

"Then I take it that Callie Blassingame is somehow connected to the work you're doing for Mr. Loeb and Mr. Gilbert, right?"

"The Blassingames and Gilberts have been neighbors for years. That's the only connection I'm aware of."

"If Callie was in New York last night, what was she doing in Somerset Hills later?"

"I have no idea. She does have a house next door."

"She didn't tell you she'd be going back to New Jersey?"

"No, she didn't."

"You weren't planning to meet her at Gilbert's, were you?"

"No, nothing like that. I went back to Gilbert's because I had some unanswered questions to ask Jimmy. But by the time I got back, the house was dark."

"How long were you away from the Gilbert house before you went back?"

"A little more than an hour."

"What were you doing during that time?"

"I was at Rex."

"The nightclub? Doing what, dancing?"

"Talking," I said, "with Julianna Gilbert." I didn't want to bring Julianna into the discussion, but it would be all too easy for Ozwick to confirm my whereabouts during that hour, and any number of people could have seen me speaking with Julianna.

"Jimmy's sister, right?"

"Right."

"And it was after talking with her that you went back."

"That's right."

"What did she say to you?"

"Nothing important. Like I told you, I went back to the house because something was nagging at me. You must get like that yourself sometimes. When things just don't gel."

"I wish you'd tell me what wasn't gelling."

"As soon as I figure it out, I'll let you know."

"How good of you. I guess I'm finished for now."

"You running me in?"

"Just don't go on any vacation, all right? I want you sticking around the New York–New Jersey area so I can reach you. I took the liberty of removing one of your business cards from your wallet. I assume these phone numbers are all still valid?"

"That's right," I said. "As long as my beeper still works after falling in the drink."

"Oh, it still works."

"How do you know?"

"It's been beeping for you."

"Probably my mother."

"And some other people. I've been writing down all the phone numbers it's recorded since you last cleared it."

"You sound like a very thorough detective, Ozwick."

"Oh, I am," she said modestly. "And I always get my man. Or my woman." She gave me a wink. "Speaking of cards, here's mine. I'll be in touch, but if you think of anything else you'd like to add to your statement, you give me a buzz, okay?"

The interview ended. Ozwick was already pulling out a pack of cigarettes from the inside breast pocket of her blazer as she made her exit through the curtain. The deputy gave me a nervous, birdlike nod as he followed her out.

The doctor on duty eventually came and saw and gave me a thumbs-up, scribbling his flourish at the base of my release forms. I summoned Carlton Hedges with the push of my nurse button and asked him if he'd be a pal and bring me some temporary clothes. He said he would, and he did.

"Oh, and Carlton?" I asked. "Where does a guy go around here to get decent clothes?"

Dimples punctuated his smile like parentheses. "Well, honey, *I* go to Saks Fifth Avenue, at Somerset Shopping Center."

"Saks? Thanks, Carlton. That'll do. That'll do nicely."

Fifteen

I took a taxi to Somerset Shopping Center and had the driver drop me at Saks. I asked him to wait and not to let anyone else in the car. He said okay. I checked my Glock and noticed that a slug was missing; Ozwick must have taken one for ballistics comparisons. In my temporary duds, I could never conceal my weapon, so I left Glock and holster under the back seat. I did, however, bring along my wallet and credit cards. I was happy to be alive and felt like splurging. It was all going down as expenses; if David Loeb didn't like it, he could kiss my ass.

I received my share of looks from store clerks and loss prevention officers as I made my way from Mossimo to Armani to Calvin Klein to Donna Karan to Joseph Abboud to Gianni Versace to Jean-Paul Gaulthier. In my thin orderly's pants and smock and with my bandaged, bruised, and shaved head, I must have looked like an escapee from a mental institution.

The clerk hovering around the section gradually made his way toward me while he pretended to straighten clothes that were hanging just fine to begin with. His eyes kept darting up at me from under black eyebrows plucked into an archfiendish shape à la Vincent Price. He was about twenty-two, tall and skinny, with sucked-in cheeks, a black Vandyke, and black hair in a decadent Roman cut. He was wearing a five-button jacket and matching trousers in maroon with orange pinstripes, a tangerine shirt, and a vermilion tie. It made my eyes ache.

"My name's Michael Anthony." He was wary of me. "Can I be of any assistance?"

I'm usually the type who says no, I'm just looking, thanks, but this time I said, "Yes, you can." I went on to add that I was looking for a shirt, a jacket, trousers, a belt, and shoes.

Michael Anthony looked down at my hospital slippers and seemed quite appalled. "Nothing on this floor is on sale."

"I don't want anything that's on sale," I said, and pulled out my American Express Gold Card. "I want expensive stuff."

"Of course."

Obsequiousness, I decided, was an underrated virtue.

"I don't normally look like this," I said. "An accident."

"I understand, sir. Please forgive me."

"You're forgiven. Can we make it snappy, Michael Anthony?"

He of coursed me a few more times as we went around plucking things off the racks. I liked the leather Gaulthier pants he showed me, but they wouldn't be great for conducting my business, and they would be murder in the sun. The only other pants I could get without waiting for alterations were jeans; I selected a pair of snug, straight-legged Gaulthiers in stark white with orange double-stitching. To this we added a lime green rayon shirt, a white single-button jacket, an orange patent leather belt, and a pair of black ankle-high snakeskin boots.

"Jesus Christ," I said, admiring myself grinningly from five different angles in the mirrors. "I'll take it."

"I'd be happy to box everything up for you." Five images of Michael Anthony wrung their hands greedily behind me.

"That's all right. I'm just going to wear them. But you can cut off all these tags for me."

"Absolutely, sir."

"Oh, and I left my old clothes in the dressing room, but I won't be needing them anymore. You can just throw them away."

"Yes, sir."

"I guess I'll need some underwear and socks, too."

Michael Anthony eyed me up and down, giving me one of those smirks like he hadn't seen a customer like me in quite a while. "I'll direct you to Men's Accessories, sir."

I picked up some black socks and white Versace briefs that cost me a bundle, as socks and briefs go, and went back to the dressing room to put them on.

I nudged the taxi driver and asked him to take me out to Somerset Hills Estates. He closed up the Atlantic City newspaper he was reading, which had Hugo Wallis on the cover sitting alone at a roulette table.

"I thought Wallis was broke," I said.

"He's trying to win back his fortune," the cabbie said, as if this were a perfectly reasonable explanation.

Settling into the back seat, I took off my jacket, strapped on the shoulder holster, and put the jacket back on. I made a quick check of my Glock, which was completely dry by now but would be unreliable without a thorough cleaning.

The taxi whisked me out through the countryside, and I noticed what had been invisible by night: the low stone fences, the forested hills and grass-swept dales, the whitewashed wooden corrals of the lesser estates along the way. Shadows of cumulus clouds skimmed across the greenery. People were out riding their horses, some in red coats practicing jumps. The horses made me think of Wyoming—where there were no stone fences but only barbed wire, where the grass was ever a dusty palomino tan, where the cowboy and the Minuteman missile could still be friends.

The taxi pulled up to the guardhouse with both sun visors down against the brutal gaze of the sun god. The security fencing with razor wire was unsightly, marring New Jersey's natural serenity. Anyone who needed such fixtures to protect themselves simply had way too much money.

"Morning," said the day guard, a chubby guy of perhaps fifty with a facial scar he'd tried to obscure by growing a kinky black-and-gray beard. The beret that had been so sexy on poor Bert Ferrigno only made this guy look like a Navy S.E.A.L. at his thirtieth reunion. The plastic nameplate, slightly askew on his left breast, said ENNIS. He stayed inside the guardhouse.

I asked the driver to wait while I got out to speak with Ennis. The driver agreed happily, putting his feet on the dashboard. He grabbed his *Racing Form*, licked the tip of his mechanical pencil, and started handicapping.

I handed Ennis a business card, squinting as I removed my sunglasses. "Greg Quaintance," I announced, leaning an elbow against the window shelf. "I'm a private investigator out here from New York on police business."

"I figured from your clothes that you were from New York. I don't know about the police business." He gave me back my card.

"You know Paula Ozwick of the Sheriff's Department?"

Ennis snorted. "That dyke dick?"

"I wouldn't know. I've never been to bed with her."

Ennis eyed me with suspicion while his tongue tried to work a piece of food out of his teeth. He had nothing to add.

"I'm working with her on the investigation into the murders of Callie Blassingame and Bert Ferrigno."

"You knew Bert?"

"Slightly," I said sadly. "I met him last night just a few hours before he was killed."

"Whoever did that, I'd like to kill them myself," Ennis said, showing me thick, meaty hands suitable for strangling.

"Have you ever had any violence out here before?"

"Nothing since I started here, and that's been ten years."

"The killer took your log book, is that right?"

"Yes."

"How far back did that go? A week?"

"More like two weeks."

"You have any other way of knowing who came in or out last night?"

"Not without the videotape."

"And they took that, too," I guessed. "What's your system, you recycle your tapes weekly? Daily?"

"I already went over this with that bull dyke bitch."

"You have something personal against Detective Ozwick?"

"I got something personal against a lot of nosy questions."

"No need to get defensive. What's the matter? You embarrassed? You guys are running the security for seven different estates, including pre-security clearance for Ralph Reston's Secret Service agents, and you're reusing a couple of lousy videotapes daily, without even a backup, I bet."

"Now wait a minute—"

"You only save the tapes if something occurred, only last night, whoever killed Bert and took the log book also took the tapes, am I right? And you call this security?"

"That's not fair. The system worked fine till last night."

"Well, it might be fine for New Jersey—"

"You can't blame me for what happened to Bert."

"Oh, so it's your system? I'm not trying to blame you or anybody. If anyone made a mistake, it was Bert. If he hadn't stepped out of the guardhouse, he probably wouldn't be dead, and the log book and videotape couldn't have been stolen. Isn't this bulletproof glass you have here?"

I rapped on it with my knuckles.

"It is. I don't know why Bert would do that. It's against procedure."

I shrugged. "He trusted the person enough, and he was probably asked to step out for a moment and help with something."

"He shouldn't have done it," Ennis said bitterly. He was angry at Ferrigno for going and getting himself killed.

"It had nothing to do with your security system, Mr. Ennis. The same thing would have happened to Bert even if you had a backup recorder somewhere and a duplicate tape. It would have just been easier for us to catch the killer, that's all."

"Why?" Ennis wanted to know. "Why would he be so stupid?"

"I have no idea. Of all the people you work for, who do you think Bert would have trusted the most?"

"I couldn't say."

"Did he maintain strictly professional relations with everyone, or did he do any fraternizing?"

"Bert was always a true professional. He never saw any of the women. Not that there are any single women living here."

"I didn't know they had to be single," I said.

Ennis smiled lecherously at that. "That's true. Still, I don't know much about Bert's private life."

"Did he have a girlfriend?"

"Not that I know of."

"And he didn't do any other socializing inside the estates?"

"Socializing, yes. I thought you said fraternizing. In the Navy, they always used fraternizing to describe guys having contact with native women or prostitutes . . ."

"I only meant to ask if Bert had any personal contact."

"Sure, he was up at Jimmy Gilbert's a few times. Big parties up at his place every now and then."

"When was the last one?"

"Last Saturday night."

"Why are you so sure it was Saturday?"

"I filled in for Bert, worked two shifts straight through."

"And Bert was up there in an unofficial capacity, not doing private security or anything?"

"I'd say it was unofficial," Ennis said with a laugh. "He was wearing something like what you got on. But if you're thinking Jimmy Gilbert killed Bert, you're thinking too hard. I bet it was a woman. You know how they are, pretending like they need help all the time. 'Come tell me if I'm reading my gas gauge correctly,' shit like that. I bet that's what happened."

"You think Bert would get out of his guardhouse just for a woman?"

"Who else?" Ennis was being rhetorical.

"I could think of twice as many alternatives."

I left Ennis there scratching his head.

The 'Cuda remained where I'd left it in front of Gilbert's house, joined by several marked and unmarked sheriff's cars. I shelled out a wad of bills and a hefty tip for the driver, making sure to get a receipt. He said he was taking the rest of the day off.

The door handles of the 'Cuda were dusty with fingerprint powder. It was a good thing I'd locked it up, or they might have gone ahead and entered. As it was, the interior looked untouched. I got in and grabbed my silver Oakley sunglasses from the glove compartment and locked the 'Cuda up again.

I was prevented from going much further by a chubby female deputy who came up to my chin and wouldn't have met the weight requirements back in the days when police departments had such things.

"Sorry, restricted," she said with her mouth full, licking the last of a glazed doughnut off her fingers.

"I know this is shit duty, and you're just doing your job," I said. "I may not look like it, but I'm a private detective cooperating with your Detective Ozwick on this investigation."

"Issat so?" she asked, unimpressed.

"My license and identification." I handed them over.

"Take off your sunglasses."

I did, and she checked my face against my photo ID a few times.

"What's with the hair?"

"Had it shaved off yesterday."

"And the bandages—somebody bang you up?"

"Ask Ozwick," I said. "She can tell you all about it."

"I believe I'll do just that, mister," she said, and opened a hailing frequency on her portable radio. She got Ozwick on the other end and had a few words before putting her radio back on her belt. "Okay, you're clear. Paula's—Detective Ozwick's out back." She thumbed over her shoulder.

I thanked her and went around the house the way I'd done last night. It was far less minatory in the noonday sun.

Most of the pool area was marked off with yellow crime tape. Callie's body was long since removed. The only visible blood around the pool had dried in irregular splotches near the diving board and was probably my own. Special investigators were down on the tiles and in the nearby grass, combing with combs and placing samples in dime bags. Detective Ozwick was standing, java in hand, thinking.

"Mr. Quaintance, my goodness," she said, regarding my new duds. "I'm sorry now we appropriated your clothes."

"I like my new look."

"To each his or her own. I could tell from your driver's license that you live in Chelsea, but I didn't realize you were a Chelsea boy. My own taste runs to tweed, if you hadn't guessed."

"And leather elbow patches, no doubt." I was playful.

"What brings you out to the scene of the crime?"

"Curiosity."

"That's what almost killed you last night."

"Did you take a slug from my Glock?"

"Sure did. I checked your gun while you were sleeping. It hasn't been fired. Tested your fingers for powder burns, and they were negative. Ballistics cleared you, too. You're firing nine-millimeter hollow-points. The shooter used forty-five Magnums. We haven't located the offending weapon."

"What are your special investigators looking for?"

"Anything," she said. "Blood from Callie or anything else that might show what happened. So far, they've found a blood trail from the parking circle to the edge of the pool. I don't think they're going to turn up anything else. I'm just making them look out of sheer sadism."

"You're saying Callie was shot elsewhere, dragged over here, and dumped in the pool?"

"Looks like it. Would have been somewhere nearby, because she continued to lose blood while in the pool. That's why we had to confiscate your clothes. They're soaked through with chlorine and blood."

"You can keep them."

"You have any idea where she might have been shot?"

"None yet, but if I do, I'll let you know."

"Anything else you'd like to share with me?"

"Nothing much. I'll have to do some asking around first."

"I think we're going to be asking the same people."

"Then we'll just have to stay in touch and compare notes. I don't intend to obstruct your investigation, but my first duty is to my client."

"Humph," Ozwick said.

"Don't suppose you can let me into the crime scene?"

"Nope. Not until my boys are through with it."

"You're almost done?"

"We're almost done."

"Then I think I'll go for a little walk."

"You do that, Quaintance. Break in those dancing shoes."

Dancing wasn't what I had in mind. I wanted to find the outbuilding from which I'd seen the light glowing before my attack. The daylight was disorienting, but the outbuilding couldn't be that difficult to find. It had to be somewhere on the grounds, and on a hill. I vaguely recalled the light as having come from the west. I took that hill first and discovered that my snazzy boots were not great for hiking.

*   *   *

I stopped every now and then to take a look at the pool area as I went further up the rise, trying to gauge whether anyone would be able to make out anything from whatever distance I was at. By night, they probably couldn't have seen a thing.

I headed on up into a grove of oaks that obscured any view of the pool. When I emerged from the woods, I saw ahead of me a towerlike structure attached to what was probably a large house, not a mere outbuilding, standing at the top of the hill. A picture window near the top of the tower looked like my window.

A chain-link fence prevented me from getting any closer. A sign riveted to one of the steel posts warned me that any trespassers would be shot, on authority of the United States Secret Service. The ten-foot-tall fencing was looped around with razor wire along the top and looked as if it extended deep into the earth. Just on the other side of the fencing was a series of concrete walking paths and a meticulously tended garden.

I was curious to see the rest of the house and the grounds and to speak with the Restons, but I would have to try the front entrance, and it would have to be some other time.

"Nurse!" someone called.

I ducked behind a tree.

What I saw was the decrepit body of an impossibly old man who had once been President Ralph M. Reston, former governor of the State of New Jersey and former quarterback for the Cleveland Browns, known to football fans as "the Tiger." He was sunk deep into an electric wheelchair, a crocheted afghan draped across his lap, and he was maneuvering himself speedily down the concrete path, heading straight for the fence. I didn't see any nurse around, not to mention Natalie Reston or any Secret Servicemen.

"Nurse!" he called again, in the ghostly echo of that voice I'd grown so familiar with over the TV for eight years. Under Ralph Reston, it had been "A New Dawn in God's America," made possible by a herculean military build-up that had led to his sending me to fight his bloody battle to liberate the oil fields of Kuwait and save the shirts of the billionaire shieks. "You there, nurse! Why the hell are you hiding? Afraid to give ol' Tiger his enema? I'll be a good boy this time!"

"Sir?" I said meekly, stepping out from behind the tree to look on the withered face of my former Commander-in-Chief.

"What are you doing on the other side of that fence? Get over here!"

"Sir, it's restricted, and I'm actually not your nurse—"

"Of course you are, don't be ridiculous! In those white clothes, what else could you be? You're just trying to get away from the ol' Tiger. Causing so much trouble for you last time, making all that mess."

"Sir—"

"It's not an easy job, but somebody's got to do it. Now get over here. Oh, now what's that?"

"Sir?"

But Ralph Reston had lost interest in me for the moment. From underneath his afghan, he pulled a pair of binoculars and held them shakily up to his eyes. He leaned one elbow on the arm of his wheelchair to steady himself. His shriveled fingers worked deftly at the focus ring.

"Will you look at that! They must have found them."

I looked behind me. Reston was aiming his sights on the special investigators checking out the crime scene.

"Found who, sir?"

"The Martians. Shh! I'm concentrating."

I waited until he'd found a focus he was satisifed with. Then I asked, "What Martians?"

"The ones in Jimmy Gilbert's pool. Don't you remember? I told you all about them. The little green men."

"You mean from last night?"

"You haven't been paying attention!" Reston lowered his binoculars unsteadily into his lap. "I don't know where Natalie found you. Were you from the agency? I like a nurse who pays attention when I'm talking!"

"Of course, sir."

"Jimmy Gilbert must be one of them, because he invited them into his pool. Only it wasn't just little green men. There are big ones, too. That's the thing we never told the American people. My hands were tied, those damned Joint Chiefs!"

"I have no idea what you're talking about."

"Roswell."

"No, sir, please, don't." I was not a fan of the *X-Files*, and I did not enjoy listening to UFO conspiracy theories.

"It's real. It really did happen. I had the Army show me all the evidence they're keeping out at Area Fifty-One. Green men from Mars. You'd better believe it!"

"Sir, there's no life on Mars except a couple of fossilized bacteria from four billion years ago."

"That's what we told the American people. But the truth is, they're here. Little green men and big ones. Martians, among us, here, now! You think I'm mad, but I'm not mad."

"No, sir."

"Just because I have senile dementia. What have they been telling you? That I have old-timer's disease?"

"You mean Alzheimer's?"

"I knew it! It's Natalie, isn't it? She's been telling lies about me again! It's senile dementia! Senile dementia! I don't now nor have I ever had old-timer's!"

"Nobody said anything to me, sir. Certainly not Natalie."

"I shouldn't even be talking to you. You're probably not even a nurse at all."

"Actually, sir—"

"You're probably one of them yourself."

"One of who?"

"The green men."

"Do I look green to you?"

"A-ha!" he said, as if he'd caught me. "That's how you fool the people all of the time. Lincoln warned us about you. Of course you're not green! Not in the sunlight!"

"You mean you only see the green men at night?"

"You know I do." Reston narrowed his eyes at me. "I'm onto you people—you Martians—whatever-you-are."

"Tell me, do you ever look over at Jimmy Gilbert's pool at night with your binoculars?"

"With these?" Reston turned his lips down in disgust. "Funniest damn thing. These things don't work at night. Secret Service gave me another pair, but wouldn't you know? They only work at night, not during the day. I think they're trying to drive me crazy, like Ingrid Bergman. Natalie must think she's Charles damn Boyer. Never should have married the bitch."

"Forget about Natlie for a moment, sir," I said. "I have a question for you that's very important."

"National security?" His head rose up.

"Yes, sir. Top secret. You can't repeat this to another soul, you understand?"

"Roger," he affirmed.

"This second pair of binoculars—let's call them night vision goggles—were you wearing them last night, or very eary this morning, looking for little green men in Gilbert's pool?"

Reston shook his head. "Negative. I wasn't looking out my window last night. I was watching American Movie Classics with my imaginary friend. Only he's not imaginary, I tell you!"

This was no good. As pathetic a witness as Ralph Reston might have made at this stage of his decline, I was hoping he might have seen something I could decipher. I thought I might try rephrasing the question.

"I believe you, Sir. But can you tell me the last time you saw the green men in Jimmy Gilbert's pool?"

"I'm sorry, I can't remember. My memory's not what it used to be."

This was said with such cogent self-knowledge, I couldn't help but pity the bastard. Then he started counting on his fingers. He held them up. "How many fingers is that?"

"Seven," I said.

"Then it was seven enemas ago. Exactly."

"You receive a daily enema?"

"One a day, like a damn vitamin." Reston grinned wickedly. "Tell you a secret, I don't think I need them. It's all part of this scheme of Natalie's to humiliate me in front of the nurses. Sometimes they bring in the Secret Service boys to hold me down while they shove the tube up. High colonic, sometimes."

"I'm not interested in that, sir," I said. "Remember, this is for the sake of national security. Can you tell me what the little green men and the big green men were doing at the pool?"

Reston shuddered. "To you and me, it may have looked like they were playing leapfrog. It was more like they were consorting with demons. All these green bodies pressing together in unholy unions. They're going to bring on Armageddon!"

"Green bodies pressing together in unholy unions? Was it big green men with little green men?"

"Yes, yes, but sometimes little green men together while the big green men stood around and watched."

"Did you recognize any of them?"

"How could I recognize them? Haven't you been listening? They're damn Martians! You're not paying attention!" Reston put his day binoculars back up to his face and started fussing again with the focus. "Ooh, lookie! They're leaving empty-handed!"

I looked over my shoulder and saw that in the distance, the investigators had packed up and were quitting the crime scene. When I turned around again, I saw several people hurrying toward Ralph Reston down the concrete path: a Secret Service agent in a charcoal-gray business suit, the plastic surgically reconstructed former First Lady, and a female nurse in a white uniform who looked nothing at all like me.

"Hold it right there!" shouted the Secret Service agent as he came up to the fence. "What are you doing here?"

"I was on a walk," I said. "I didn't know I was so close to the property. Before I knew it, President Reston was down here talking to me. He thought I was his nurse."

The nurse stood protectively behind Ralph Reston, grabbing the handles of his wheelchair. Natalie Reston grabbed Ralph's hand, but he pulled it away spitefully and scowled up at her.

"Who are you?" asked the Secret Service guy.

"Greg Quaintance," I said, handing over my P.I. license, driver's license, and a business card through the fencing. "I'm assisting in the murder investigations down there. Bert Ferrigno and Callie Blassingame."

Natalie Reston stiffened noticeably and clutched her pearl choker. In these rarified circles, murder was a distasteful thing that could never happen far enough from one's doorstep.

"What were you doing on a walk?" The Secret Service agent examined my IDs minutely.

"I wanted to know if anybody could have seen anything from up here, but now I realize that's impossible."

After determining that the President was unharmed, they handed me back my IDs and told me I was free to go.

As they were turning him away, Ralph Reston shouted, "I'm not sick! My wife's pumping me full of drugs and locking me up in the tower! Help me!"

"Don't mind Ralph," Natalie told me serenely, in a honey-soft voice. "Reading's difficult for him now, but he's fond of audiobooks, and I recently got him *Jane Eyre*. He's been hard to control ever since. The only drugs we give him are to keep him from seeing his imaginary people who walk through the walls of our house to have conversations with him. Not to mention his little green men. Come, Ralph, it's time for your cleansing."

"Get away from me!" Reston shoved at Natalie. The nurse turned his wheelchair around and started to push him up the hill, but he engaged the motor himself and went speeding off.

The nurse, Natalie Reston, and the Secret Service agent hurried along after him.

Sixteen

When I got back to the Gilbert house, Detective Ozwick and the special investigators were gone, and all that remained were a couple of rookies standing guard. I took a quick look around the crime scene but saw nothing interesting. The rookies told me I had no business there. I told them I'd seen everything already.

I went back around to the front of the house and tweaked the buzzer. The door was answered by a well-built black security guard with a down-turned mouth and a look that told me I was an instant enemy. I produced various identifications, told him I was working for Jimmy Gilbert, and asked to speak with same.

"Mr. Gilbert is not at home," he said with finality.

"Maybe Jimmy went on into the city," I said.

"Maybe he did." He attempted to close the door in my face.

I stopped it. "You mind if I ask you a few questions?"

"Make it quick."

"Were you on duty here at all last night?"

He shook his head no. "My shift started at nine this morning. I'm like just back after two days off."

"Have you seen anyone else around."

"You mean, like, besides cops?"

"I mean Todd Curwen, Marcia Gilbert, and Madeleine Downey."

He shook his head again. "Nope. Sorry."

"I suppose they're all in the city."

"Maybe they are. I wouldn't know. It's not like I'm their fucking keeper. Now maybe you can answer a question for me."

"Shoot," I said.

"Do you, like, have any idea who's the asshole parked that piece of shit out front?" He nodded toward the 'Cuda.

"I'm the asshole."

"Figured as much. I want it like the hell out of here. Now." With that, he slammed the door.

I went back to the 'Cuda, turned on the engine, and ran the AC. I took out a notepad and a pen and wrote down the phone numbers from off my beeper—the ones Ozwick had stolen. I had to call all these people as soon as I could get to a pay phone. I didn't carry a cellular phone, for a variety of persnickety reasons: it was expensive, transmissions were not secure, and I could always find a working pay phone, even in Manhattan. The beeper was a necessary evil, but I tolerated it because it could be conveniently ignored.

I drove down the road to Blassingame's, parked in the front circle, and stood under the lantern while I rang the bell.

"Jase?" asked the Hispanic domestic woman who opened the door, wearing a gray dress and a white apron and holding a feather duster. Her Indian features were not unlike Juan's—earth-red skin, bony prominences, and a beak like Quetzalcóatl's—but something about her told me she wasn't Mexican but likely Salvadoran or Nicaraguan. The lines in her face had been etched by a considerable grief. "Whad you wan?"

"Is Dr. Blassingame at home?" I asked, wondering at the irony. Here

she was, employed by a man who had smoothed out the lines on the face
of the wife of the man whose meddling in Central America had turned her
into a refugee in the first place.

The housekeeper shook her head. "Doctor no is at home."

"Do you know where he is?"

"No, I no know where he is."

"Have the police been by here today?"

"*Policías? Sí?*"

"*Muchas policías?*" I prompted.

Taking this to mean that I spoke Spanish, she embarked on an
animated tirade. Something about coming back after her day off and
having a lot of work to do and suffering multiple interruptions and being
terrorized by the police. The word *policías* came up frequently. If she was
from El Salvador, she probably didn't feel very kindly toward men in
uniform.

"*Inglés?*" I requested, wanting to hear the dirt.

"No," she demurred. "My *inglés* no good, is lousy."

"Okay. What about, um—" I tried to think of a suitable Spanish
word. "*El niño?*"

"*El niño?*" She was confused at first. Then, suspecting what I meant,
she looked at me like I was an idiot.

"*El muchacho?*" I tried. "Jason Blassingame?"

"*Señor* Hason? No, no, no." She threw up her arms in frustration and
pointed at her watch.

"Sorry for bothering you."

"Sí, sí, sí." She'd heard enough sorries for one lifetime.

I wished her good day. She slammed the door on me.

I was heading back down US 202, thinking that I'd stop off again at the
Somerset Shopping Center to use one of their pay phones, when I saw
ahead of me two Sheriff's Department squads with full lights and siren
and an unmarked Crown Vic with magnetic red light on top and a wiry-

haired female detective behind the wheel. They took the turnoff for Duke
Island County Park. I followed.

The police cars came to a halt in a paved parking lot on a lushly green
hill above the Raritan River. Tall trees provided ample shade all around,
their leaves rustling in the breeze and hiding small twittering birds. One
squad car had already been on the scene before the others, and a couple
of uniformed deputies were guarding a parking space that was cordoned
off by yellow tape and contained a metallic green Lexus.

I slowed a little and parked a certain distance away, alongside a Chevy
Suburban that was off-loading a young couple with three children, two
dogs, a picnic blanket, and a Coleman cooler. I rolled down my window,
letting in the hot, humid air, and took a moment to watch the policework.

Detective Ozwick got out of the unmarked Crown Vic and tramped
over to the scene, stepping not very nimbly over the crime tape. A
sheriff's van pulled up, and a few uniformed deputies got out who I
recognized as the special investigators from Gilbert's pool. One of the SIs
took out a camera and started snapping photos. They dusted the handles
and removed prints before they allowed Ozwick inside.

I got out of the 'Cuda and wandered over.

The diminutive female deputy I'd run into at Gilbert's reached out a
halting arm—the practiced motion of a traffic cop. Having no whistle
handy, she said, "Whoa!"

"Whoa yourself. Let me see Detective Ozwick."

"If it isn't the fashion plate." She was chewing gum in a circular
motion like a cow her cud. "Take a number. Ozwick's busy, case you can't
tell."

"Let him through," Ozwick said from the door of the Lexus.

"Oh, okay." The female deputy stood aside. "Never mind."

I stepped over the crime tape with more grace than Ozwick.

"Why do I get the feeling I'm sharing more with you than you are
with me?" Ozwick was blocking my view of the car's interior.

"I shared all those phone numbers with you," I said.

"That doesn't count. You know whose car this is?"

"Callie Blassingame's."

"That is correct. What do you think it's doing here?"

I peered over Ozwick's shoulder and caught a glimpse of brown leather upholstery darkly stained with blood.

"I'd say this is where Callie met her killer."

"Does look like a likely rendezvous point, doesn't it?" Ozwick stared around appreciatively at the park's scenery.

"The killer got in the car with her?"

"Looks that way."

"Then it was someone she trusted," I said, "unless she was being incredibly stupid."

"Or unless the killer was holding the gun on her. She had a gash on her forehead unrelated to the entry wound. There were traces of gun oil along the gash. Looks like the killer pistol-whipped her. She said something the killer didn't like."

"He tried to get information from her before he killed her?"

"I try to be gender neutral in my speculations, Quaintance. But yes, that's what I would assume. What kind of information is anybody's guess at this point, unless you're willing to start sharing with me."

"You're giving me too much credit. The further I get in this case, the more I realize I don't know anything." I wanted to get her off the subject of what I knew. "So the killer met Callie here, got in her Lexus, talked with her, struck her, and shot her. He had to transport the body somehow. If you're still worried about me, you're welcome to search my car."

"That old Barracuda? Please! That won't be necessary."

"Don't tell me you trust me."

"Of course not. We already checked out your car visually when it was parked in front of Gilbert's. Looked clean."

"What if I put her in the trunk?"

"Your trunk's clean, too. I jimmied it open myself." She pulled out a pocketknife and showed me the blade.

The SIs continued their meticulous work. Ozwick directed them to obtain tire prints from the empty parking spaces in the vicinity of Callie's Lexus. Ozwick and I strolled around the perimeter of the crime scene. She hung her head down and moved it slightly from one side to the other like a hound sniffing out a fox—only Ozwick sniffed with her eyes.

"Do you have any suspects?" I asked.

"I have a few in mind," she said.

"Was Jimmy Gilbert at his house when police showed up?"

"He was, indeed. He was the only one. There weren't even any security personnel, which seemed strange. It took us a while to raise Jimmy. He claimed he'd been sleeping."

"You don't believe him?"

"I'm not sure I'm *at liberty* to discuss what I believe of Jimmy Gilbert's statement, considering that you work for him."

"Ah, touché," I said. Ozwick snorted in amusement. "What if I give you a little dollop of information?"

"No one's going to stop you," she said.

"I assume you've searched Gilbert's house."

"We effected a warrant early this morning. Jimmy apologized for making us get a warrant, if you can believe that. He said he would have given his consent, but he called his lawyer first—your friend Loeb. I had to wake up Judge Maxfield at five this morning, and she wasn't very happy. Jimmy was very gracious, took us all over the house. It took several hours."

"You didn't find anyone else in the house?"

"I already told you he was the only one there." Ozwick raised her head up to examine me quizzically. "Should there have been anyone else?"

"Not necessarily," I said.

"Come on, Quaintance, I've given you what you want. Now what's this damned dollop of information?"

"Last night, I was searching for a missing juvenile. I thought he was over at Jimmy Gilbert's, but Jimmy denied it. Later I decided I didn't believe him. That's when I went back and found Ferrigno at the guardhouse. I was concerned about the welfare of my missing juvenile, among other things, so I went up to Gilbert's without sticking around to meet police. Jimmy didn't answer. I searched the grounds. You know the rest."

"Who's this damned missing juvey?"

"Jason Blassingame. Callie and Troy's son."

"When did he go missing?"

"He left the Blassingame house around midnight."

"Has Dr. Blassingame reported Jason's disappearance to us?"

"I doubt it. He thought I could take care of it."

"I'm confused," Ozwick said. "I thought you were working for Jimmy Gilbert, yet you thought he was harboring your juvey?"

"It's a long story. I've given you all I can."

"Well, thanks. You heading back to New York now?"

"Is that a hint?"

"No, an educated guess. That's where everybody on your beeper was calling from. Some of them are people I very much want to talk to. Like the good doctor and the big bad lawyer."

"Then I guess you'll be joining me soon enough."

"Not as soon as I'd like." She looked at the SIs and at her watch and let out a frustrated sigh.

"Look, Ozwick, if you find Jason, you'll call me, right?"

"Sure I will. And you can return the favor by catching Callie's killer for me. You'll get a lousy commendation from the sheriff, and I'll collect your fee. How's that sound?"

Seventeen

After I left Duke Island County Park, the highway took me past Rex. It was even tackier by day, with its columns extinguished. I ducked briefly into the mostly empty parking lot to confirm what I'd seen from above: Julianna's Ferrari was still there.

Somerset Shopping Center was teeming with teens. The girls were made up like whores and wearing shorts two sizes too small for their ample, heart-shaped behinds. Some of them had to reach back every now and then to pull their shorts down to keep them from riding too far up. The boys were still affecting the look of a street gangster, wearing skewed baseball caps and gigantic T-shirts tucked into their underwear, the elastic band of which advertised TOMMY HILFIGER or BOSS above baggy jeans with no belts held up just barely by the slight, underdeveloped curves of their boyish asses. A few of the boys reached down surreptitiously every so often to yank up their pants a couple of centimeters while still trying to maintain their cool.

I tried to find a phone away from any kids—especially the girls, who were speaking at a thousand decibels and cackling with high-pitched laughter that was more disagreeable than the shriek of a squirrel monkey. I lucked out with a bank of phones in front of Felicia's Big & Tall Store. One phone was free, the others occupied by middle-aged women who were grossly obese. I smelled a mélange of hairspray, sweat, talcum, and polyester.

I squeezed in between two of the women and picked up the phone, dialing the first number on my list. I didn't recognize any of them except for David Loeb's. I wanted to call him last.

"Hello?" said a woman on the third ring.

"Greg Quaintance," I said. "You beeped me?"

"Oh, yes, Mr. Quaintance. This is Maria Arcos. Callie Blassingame's housekeeper. We met last night, if you recall."

"Yes, Maria. What can I do for you?"

"I must speak with you. You know what has happened?"

"You're talking about Callie?"

"Yes."

"I was out here in Jersey all last night. I know what there is to know. Which isn't much."

"I'd like very much to see you," Maria said.

"Why?"

"I don't mean to sound cynical, Mr. Quaintance, but now that Callie's dead, isn't your work for David Loeb finished?"

"Yes and no. Why do you ask?"

"I'd like to hire you."

"What for?"

"To bring Callie's killer to justice."

"If I took your money it would be stealing, Maria. The police ought to be able to find Callie's killer on their own."

"I would not bet on it. There are things I know that I do not wish to share with the authorities. But I would share them with you if you promised to apprehend the killer."

"Why would you do that?"

"I believe I can trust you."

"You don't trust the police?"

"It's not that. Would you please come up here? I'm at the apartment where you saw us last night. After what happened to Callie, I would rather speak with you in person. What I have to tell you makes me fear for my own safety. I am uncomfortable speaking about it over the phone."

"Okay, Maria, I'll see you. I'm still in Jersey right now, and I have a few other phone calls to make. I can see you in about an hour and a half. Is that all right?"

"Yes, that will be fine."

"Do you think you're in any imminent danger?"

"Not as long as you don't tell anyone you're seeing me. I feel safe as long as I stay in this apartment. It is a very secure building. I don't think anyone would dare."

I wasn't so sure about that. In a world where people were willing to shoot innocent security guards, I doubted very much whether kindly doormen would be spared.

"I won't tell a soul. I'll be there as soon as I can."

A friendly female voice said, "Blassingame Cosmetic Surgery Associates. How may I help you?"

"Uh, yeah, this is Greg Quaintance," I said. "I believe Dr. Blassingame beeped me this morning. I'm returning his call."

"The doctor's in surgery at the moment, but I'll be happy to take a message."

"You do have other plastic surgeons there, don't you?"

"We have two other board-certified plastic surgeons," she said, "but I'm afraid that they're both away this weekend to a conference in Palm Springs. If you'd like to leave a message for one of them—"

"No, no, that's not what I mean. I'm just surprised that Dr. Blassingame would still want to work today, in light of what's happened."

"In light of—" she said confusedly. "Oh, you mean his wife. I'm afraid I can't speak for the doctor."

"I would have thought he'd turn his caseload over to one of his associates, under the circumstances. Or cancel."

"Are you the police?"

"Private detective," I said. "Board certified."

"Well, all I can say is that Dr. Blassingame has a number of clients who refuse to be treated by anyone else. And sometimes it's not so easy to reschedule."

"I understand. Please ask Dr. Blassingame to give me a call back." I rattled off my office number and beeper number and added, "I may be hard to reach this afternoon. I'll probably just stop by later and speak with him myself."

"I'll let the doctor know," she said mildly. "But I'm afraid he'll be in surgery for the next several hours. I can't say for sure when he might be free."

"That's all right. I have plenty of other things to do this afternoon. I'll stop by later and take my chances."

"Do you know where we're located?"

I told her I didn't, and she gave me the address, in the upper nineties just off Fifth Avenue, a block or two from Mt. Sinai Medical Center. I asked her for her name.

"Rita," she said. "Rita Hedgepeth."

"Thank you, Rita. I'll see you later."

I called the next number and found myself listening to Juan's voice on his home answering machine. I wanted to talk to Juan, but I didn't care to leave an impersonal message, so I hung up.

The next two numbers, no one picked up, and no machines kicked in. They were probably unlisted. I didn't know who I was trying to call. I decided to try them again later.

At last, I called David Loeb, and he said, "I've been trying to reach you all morning, Greg. What's going on?"

"Well, I'm in New Jersey," I said. "And Callie's dead."

"I know. The police called. Have you found Jason yet?"

"No, David, I haven't. I would have been working on it all morning if I hadn't been in the hospital."

"The hospital?"

"I'm the one who found Callie's body. I was hanging over the pool to get a good look at her. Somebody dumped me in the deep end and tried to knock me unconscious. I came close to drowning. The next thing I knew, I was lying on a bed in the emergency room, being grilled by a detective."

"Greg, I'm sorry. Did you see who knocked you in?"

"No, it was too dark, and I was taken by surprise, and then I was just trying to stay afloat. Whoever it was must have heard a noise or got scared and went running off."

I didn't mention Jimmy Gilbert's role in my rescue. Until I could explain it to myself, it would have to remain my secret.

"Greg," Loeb said, collecting himself. "This is a tragedy. You realize, though, that even with Callie gone, our problems aren't over."

"Why not? Callie was the one threatening to file charges. Troy certainly isn't interested, and I don't think Jason has any intention of causing any trouble."

"There's still the *Enquirer* story."

"You said that could be minimized through public relations."

"That depended on getting Callie to tell the press she'd made everything up. Since that is no longer possible, there remains only one solution. You have to find Jason."

"You want to use him the way you were going to use Callie?"

"Why not?" Loeb sounded smugly superior.

"You'd be asking him to humiliate himself in front of the world press. At least with Callie doing it, he could have remained somewhat anonymous. He's still just a kid, David."

"You have to find him, Greg. It's the only way."

"I think Jimmy knows where Jason is, but he's not telling. Why don't you try asking him?"

"I did. Jimmy hasn't seen Jason since Callie removed him to New York a few days ago. He never saw Jason last night."

"You're sure he's not hiding Jason somewhere?"

"Why would he do that?"

"You tell me," I said.

Loeb said nothing in reply.

I asked, "Where's Jimmy now?"

"Here in New York, at his apartment."

"I need to talk to him."

"You won't be able to for a few hours, at least. I'm meeting him in a few minutes. We're driving out to where you are. The sheriff's department isn't satisfied with Jimmy's statement. They want him back for more questioning."

"I'm coming into the city. Are you going to be in later?"

"What? Sure. Absolutely." Loeb sounded distracted. "But Greg . . ."

"Yeah?"

"Be careful, will you? Callie and Bert aren't the only ones who've been killed."

"What are you talking about?"

"About two hours ago, I was contacted by a Detective Don McGarrity, a homicide detective with the Atlantic City police. He told me that a maid at the Trump Castle found Angelo Ferrante dead in his room this morning. Murdered, I should say."

"Angelo Ferrante?" I repeated. "Did this McGarrity say how long Ferrante's been dead?"

"He wouldn't tell me. Ferrante checked in Thursday evening, and there was a 'Do Not Disturb' sign hanging on the doorknob the entire time. They can't tell whether he ever left his room. This morning the maid smelled something funny and decided to knock. No one answered. She had a bad feeling about it and called security. They went in and found Ferrante lying on the bed, dead of multiple stab wounds. The sheets were drenched with blood. The detective said it was an unreasonably savage attack."

"Any idea what Ferrante was doing in Atlantic City?"

"None."

"Why'd the detectives call you?"

"They found my card in Ferrante's wallet. My answering service connected them to my home number."

"What did you tell them?"

"That Ferrante had been working for me but that I'd let him go. They wanted to know what it was about, but I cited attorney-client privilege. That had them shitting bricks. But I can't hold them off forever. Once the *Enquirer* story hits, they'll know what I was trying to keep from them."

"Did Ferrante ever need any money in a hurry before?"

"No. I've employed him on an as-needed basis for nearly two years, and he was always well paid. I was shocked when he went to the *Enquirer.*"

"How much did he make from them?"

"A measly fifty grand, according to my sources."

"Maybe it wasn't enough," I conjectured. "Why else would he go to Atlantic City but to gamble it?"

"I never thought Ferrante was that stupid." Loeb sounded genuinely angry. "Didn't think he was stupid at all, or I never would have relied on the son of a bitch."

"Sounds more like desperation than stupidity. You don't ruin your career for a hop down to the Boardwalk."

"It doesn't sound like Ferrante to me. Still, you never know. Maybe he owed money to a loan shark. Maybe his murder is totally unrelated to our case." Loeb sounded hopeful.

"Maybe," I said dubiously. "For now, we'd better go on the assumption that it is related."

"That's why I said to be careful. I assume you have a gun?"

"Yeah," I said. "Though it got a little waterlogged last night. I'd better clean it when I get back to my place. You're sure you have no idea who might have done this?"

"Haven't the faintest, Greg."

"You'd better watch yourself, too, then."

"Thanks, Greg. I intend to. Absolutely. Bye."

Eighteen

I walked around the outside of the mall, hoping I would spot some marker that would reveal where I'd left the 'Cuda. The lots had been largely full when I came, and I'd parked somewhere far from the entrance. Now the 'Cuda's low-slung blackness was swallowed up by a blinding sea of windshield reflections from late-model minivans and sport utility vehicles, and I was without a clue.

Four teenage boys were standing off in a group by themselves to one side of the multiplex cinema, smoking. The three shorter ones seemed to be congregating around the tall one, who had long, bleached-blond hair, tanned flesh, and something pretty about his features that reminded me of Jason. He was laughing with his buddies, but when his eyes met mine, he stopped and set his jaw. His friends turned to see what was up.

"Hey, Gaulthier!" the blond boy said. "You eyeballing me?"

"Are you talking to me?" I said.

"Yeah, fag. What do you think you're looking at?"

"Not much, obviously." I began walking toward them.

"Oh, yeah?" the blond said.

I realized now why he reminded me of Jason. It wasn't because of any overt physical resemblance, it was because this boy had also modeled for those same jeans ads. His was one of the six or seven faces I'd seen plastered all over New York City buses, bus stops, subway tunnels, and a Times Square billboard before the campaign had been shelved.

"How do you know I'm wearing Jean-Paul Gaulthier?"

The blond shrugged. "I seen a lot of fags wear that shit."

"In New Jersey? I find that hard to believe. Do you mind if I ask you some questions?"

The blond looked momentarily frightened. He braced himself by sucking up the last of his cigarette. He got rid of it hastily and tossed his head back, running his fingers through his hair. "Like what kind of questions?"

"Like do any of you guys know Jason Blassingame?"

The three shorter boys shook their heads and looked up to the blond, who was staring stoically at me. The shortest one, who wore a couple of silver rings through his left eyebrow, said, "You know him, don't you, Derek?"

"Shut up, Vince!" the blond said, his tanned face turning bright persimmon.

"Derek, is it?" I asked. "Mind if I speak with you alone?"

Derek turned to his friends: "It's cool, guys. Go on in. Somebody get me a large popcorn with butter. I want to sit up close. It's a small fucking screen. I'll be there in a minute."

"Come on, Derek," Vince whined. "You'll miss the start of the movie."

"I don't give a fuck," Derek said, sneering. "I've seen it three times already. I won't be long with this joker, anyway. I'll be in my seat before the fucking Coke commercial's over."

Looking dejected, Derek's three friends dug their tickets out of their pockets, threw their cigarette butts on the sidewalk, and trudged on into the theater like would-be hoods.

"Looks like you got Vince and the other two wrapped around your finger," I said.

"They're ninth graders next year." Derek was dismissive. "I'm going into tenth. I guess they kind of look up to me."

"Is Jason in your grade?"

"I think so, but he doesn't go to our school. His folks send him off to private school somewhere."

"Then how do you know him?"

"He used to hang around here the first part of last summer. We palled around a little."

"You and he friends anymore?"

"Friends?" Derek said coolly. "No. Why?"

"I'm trying to find Jason."

"Find him for what?"

"I'm a private detective. Jason left his house late last night, and his father asked me to find him. He may be in trouble. You haven't seen him around here today, have you?"

Derek shook his head no, looking apprehensive.

"Or driving around in a black Eagle Talon?"

"No, man, I haven't seen him or his car."

"So you know that's his car?"

"Yeah," Derek admitted. "I've been in it."

"Jason's father told me he's only allowed to drive it within the estates. You've been up to his house, then?"

"Yeah, some. So?" Derek was defensive. "What's Jason in trouble for? Does it have something to do with his mom?"

"What about his mom?"

"The double murder at Somerset Hills. I saw it on TV. Mrs. Blassingame in the pool, Bert Ferrigno at the gate."

"You know—knew Bert Ferrigno?"

Derek's mouth opened, and he started to say something, but then he clammed up. He wasn't sure how to answer.

"You didn't just pick his name up off the TV," I prompted.

"No, I knew him, I guess."

"Just from going in and out of the gate?"

"Yeah, so?"

"You know, kid, when you called me a fag I wasn't going to bother with you, but—"

"Sorry about that, man," Derek said, looking embarrassed. "You know how it is, in front of the guys and shit."

"Never mind. This isn't about me. I wouldn't have even come over and talked to you except I recognized you."

"Shit, from the ads?" The persimmon drained from his face. "Man, I wish I never done those fucking ads. Dude, I got to go—I'm going to be late for my movie."

Derek made a move to go, but I placed a hand on his shoulder and stopped him. "You've already seen it three times."

"I don't want to answer any more of your fucking questions!"

"Look, I'm not the police. Nothing you say is going to get you into any trouble. I'm just trying to help out Jason. Whatever you can tell me could turn out to be very important."

Derek shrugged off my hand and said, "Okay, mister. I'll talk. You got a cigarette?"

"I shouldn't be contributing to the delinquency of a minor," I said, pulling out my pack of Lucky Strikes. "But in your case, I guess it's already too late."

"You got that right, mister."

I lit his cigarette for him and one for myself.

"Where are the cigarettes you were smoking before?" I asked.

"In there," he said. "I just bum off my friends."

"That figures. So why did it scare you so much when I brought up those ads?"

"Scare me? I wasn't scared." Derek tried to laugh. He was a bad actor. "What I told you is the truth. I met Jason here at the mall last summer, and we did stuff together. One day I'm hanging out here and up comes this black limo. The window rolls down, and Jason pokes his head out and asks me into the limo."

"Was this a Lincoln limo?"

"I don't know, man. A limo's a limo."

"Did you get in?"

"Yeah, why not? The next thing I know, we're in New York, and there's this big photo shoot going on with all these models, girls and boys, all about my age. This fashion designer's there, and this bigshot photographer."

"Yuri Zetlin?"

"That's him. Big fat pig, I'm telling you. Anyway, Jason drags me over, and Yuri takes one look at me and his eyes get all wide and he says, 'Ooh, he's *perrrfect*!' Which kind of surprises me, because I never thought I looked like no model or anything. But it turns out they want this kind of 'wasted youth' look."

"Is that what they called it?"

"No, that's what *I* call it. Your basic druggie washout, and then the clothes they put us in were kind of seventies, jeans jackets and cut-offs and shit."

"So they just took your picture, right there?"

"Lots of them."

"Didn't you need your parents' permission?"

"There's only my mom, and what they did was develop the pictures and show them to her first, kind of like a surprise."

"Must have been some surprise."

"Oh, yeah, she didn't like them one bit. But when they told her how much they were willing to pay, she was all for it."

"Uh-huh."

"Hey, it's not like we've got money. I mean, we would if my dad paid his fucking child support. But he doesn't, and my mom figured this would make a good down payment on my college."

"She swallowed her pride?"

"I guess, something like that."

"How'd she like it when the ads came out?"

"She didn't want to see them. I didn't either, and that's a fact. I mean, it was kind of fun taking the pictures, but then to be exposed like that in front of the whole world . . ."

"I forget what your picture looked like."

"Oh, the one they used had me slipping out of a jeans jacket so it was coming off one shoulder, and my mouth's hanging open like I'm a moron, and I've got no shirt on, and the top button of my cut-offs is undone, and they had me kind of standing on one leg with the other propped up on a staircase in my bare feet—"

"Okay, I remember it now." I remembered it, all right, and poor Derek had reason to be embarrassed. The picture had made him look like a fourteen-year-old boy slut. Which was the whole concept behind the ads. Photos of little boy and girl Lolitas were supposed to sell jeans. Madison Avenue at its finest.

"I wish I'd never done it," Derek said.

"Derek, was this all strictly professional?"

"Sure, there were all these people around. Make-up people, lighting people, prop people, all these assistants standing around. Nothing fishy."

"Did you ever go back for other shoots? Private shoots?"

"I didn't," Derek said, looking down at the ground. "But a friend of mine did."

"A friend of yours? You mean Jason?"

"No, someone else."

"What's his name?"

"I don't know, just some guy, all right? A friend of mine. Some other kid I met. He told me he went over to Yuri's apartment. He thought it was for another professional shoot, but it turned out . . ." Derek couldn't go on.

"It turned out to be what?"

"I don't know, man, my friend wouldn't tell me the rest." Derek's eyes were yellow and watery, and I wondered whether it was just from the cigarette smoke. He wouldn't look at me.

"That's okay. I'm not asking out of any prurient interest. I'm only trying to help Jason. You're telling me that Zetlin took more photos of your friend. He made your friend get naked?"

"More than that." Derek's mouth turned down in a bitter frown. "A lot more than that."

"Forget about it, Derek, you don't need to go on."

"Can I go inside now? I want to see my movie."

"In a minute. You're sure you haven't seen Jason today?"

"No, man, not since last week."

"What happened last week?"

"Just some party," Derek said. Finally, he looked up at me, and he looked a lot younger and a lot less tough than when I'd first laid eyes on him. "Can you let me go now, man?"

"If you'll give me your full name and an address where I can contact you again in the future."

"Derek Peterson," he said, giving an address in Somerville, his home phone number, and his beeper number.

"Okay, you can go. And thanks, Derek. You've been a big help to me. And to Jason."

"Yeah, okay, see ya."

Derek got away from me as fast as he could.

I didn't blame him one bit.

Nineteen

I made it as fast as I could over the decrepit General Pułaski Skyway, through the filthy Holland Tunnel, back to the decaying streets of New York. I stopped off at my apartment and removed the bandages from my head. The stitches looked pretty gross. While I cleaned my Glock, I turned on my answering machine and listened to my messages. The first was from Juan:

"Hey, *gringo*, sorry about last night. I shouldn't have left such an abusive message on your machine. Our little numbnuts receptionist here gave me a message from you this morning. I guess you meant him to give it to me last night, but he fucked up. It don't surprise me a bit. *Well*, the upshot from me is, I spent the night curled up in bed with John Grisham. Hope you're not mad at me for being such a jerk. Call me, okay?"

The other messages turned out to be from ghosts, lasting for only a couple of seconds of deep silence before beeping off. The last message was a series of NYNEX tones and a man's voice saying, "We're sorry— your call did not go through as dialed. Please hang up and try your call again."

I put my Glock back together carefully, reloaded the clip, put a round in the chamber, and reholstered it under my arm.

I called Juan at the salon.

"Hey, Gregory," he said. "Thanks for calling me back."

"Listen, I'm the jerk. I should have tried harder to get hold of you last night. Something came up, and I'm sorry."

"*No problema.* You working on a case?"

"I'll tell you all about it when it's over. I won't have time to see you until then."

"When's that?"

"I don't know. I'll keep you posted."

"I'll wait for you," he said.

"That's sweet. No one's ever waited for me before. Say, you know anything about Yuri Zetlin?"

"The fashion photographer? Why should I?"

"No reason." I felt like an idiot. I was expecting Juan to know something about Yuri Zetlin merely because I guessed Zetlin was gay and because Juan wore fashionable clothing. It was like people who, when they found out you lived in New York, asked if you knew their one friend there. Besides, from what I knew of Zetlin, he wasn't so much gay as an honest-to-god pederast. From what Derek Peterson described, Zetlin sounded like a card-carrying member of the North American Man-Boy Love Association.

"I saw him once," Juan said suddenly, "having drinks in the lobby of the Royalton."

"Oh yeah? With whom?"

"Madeleine Downey. She was stoned out of her gourd."

"How did you know it was Zetlin?"

"I know what he looks like. They run his picture in *Vanity Fair* whenever he does a spread. Anyway, you can't miss him."

"Why's that?"

"'Cause he's a big fat *puerco*."

*   *   *

The old doorman was working hard to keep smiling. When he saw me, the entire structure collapsed. He no longer wanted to wink at me. The last time he'd seen me had been a few minutes before Callie had turned down his offer of a cab and gone skipping off into the night. He stared at my stitched-up head wound.

"I'm here to see Maria Arcos," I said.

"That would be the Blassingame apartment," he said, stumbling a moment on *Blassingame*. He fingers trembled as he grabbed the white phone. "Your name again?"

"Quaintance," I said distinctly. "Greg Quaintance."

"Oh," the doorman said, realizing he'd got it wrong last night. He probably already told police that Callie's mysterious lothario refused to identify himself, saying only that he was an acquaintance. And he was probably kicking himself all morning for not getting my real name.

I showed him my P.I. license, hoping to ease his guilt. My wallet was still damp from my dunking, and it gave off a strong chlorine smell. The doorman appeared to notice.

I was glad there was no smell of blood.

Maria seemed happy to see me. I stepped onto the parquet floor I associated with Jenks's clicking claws. I saw no sign of the Scottie; I hoped he was all right.

"Please have a seat, Mr. Quaintance," Maria said, and we took our places where I'd sat with Callie last night. Maria's strong features drew a kind of nobility from the key light. They morphed into a cringe as she asked, "What happened to your head?"

"I was the one who found Callie. Found her too soon for somebody. I got bashed on the head and knocked in the pool. I'm all right, though. How are you doing?"

My concern was genuine; I tried to make it come across.

"Not terribly well," Maria said, taking in a deep breath through her nose. Her skirt came just to her knees, and she wore sleek dark hose that showed off legs as fine as a dancer's. A brown leather Gucci suitcase stood in between her and the coffee table. Her knee touched the corner of it and shrank back away as if touching the cold hand of a corpse. "As difficult as it was cleaning up after Callie—and I'm not talking about housecleaning—I did genuinely care for the woman."

"I'm sorry," I said.

"Yes, well, aside from that, I've been fired. Troy Blassingame wants me out of the apartment by seven tonight."

"Thus the suitcase?"

"That's not my suitcase," she said, shifting uncomfortably.

"Oh. Why do you have to be out by seven?"

"Why not? A sadistic whim."

"Is Troy prone to sadistic whims?"

"That question's a little too loaded, Mr. Quaintance."

"I'm just asking."

She gave the semblance of a smile, but it soon vanished. "I may have struck you as cold last night."

"More like protective."

"Yes, that's probably an accurate description. Callie was never good at doing anything for herself. Once she decided to divorce Troy, I knew she was headed for disaster."

"How long have you worked for the Blassingames?"

"Two years. It seems like longer."

"In what capacity, exactly?"

"I began as head housekeeper. That soon changed to unofficial nursemaid. But you saw yourself last night, I'm no nurse. I almost killed that dog."

"How is Jenks?"

"He's recuperating at the animal hospital. They say he'll be all right. I don't know who's going to take care of him when he comes out of it, though. Troy only cares for his horses."

"What about Jason?"

"Jason's too irresponsible to care for a dog."

"What I meant was, does Troy care about Jason?"

"I'll get to that," she said. "I'm sorry, would you like anything to drink? Soda, Pellegrino, whiskey, anything?"

"No, thanks. If you played nursemaid to Callie, why were you handing her all those drinks last night? I understand she had a problem."

"She did. She needed those drinks to maintain her sobriety. It was one of the more distasteful aspects of the job. Sometimes I felt like I was handing her poison. Only a few weeks ago, I was considering quitting. I couldn't take it anymore."

"Couldn't take what?"

"The quarreling. The tension in the house. But when Callie gave Troy her ultimatum, I knew I couldn't leave her. Not yet, anyway. So I took her side and came here to the city with her. And I resented her for it, of course. Now all I wish is that I might have been able to keep her from going out last night."

I waited for tears of self-recrimination, but they didn't come. Maria was reserved, keeping her chin and her eyebrows up.

"Why did she go out?"

"There was a phone call."

"Do you know who it was?"

"No. We have two lines, and I was on the other one talking to the vet. I didn't catch Callie until she was heading out the door. I asked her where she was going, and it was clear she did not want to tell. All I could get out of her was that she had to go meet someone. I asked her who, and she said it was no one important. She asked me to make sure Jenks was taken care of. I never saw her again."

Maria was tough; even this didn't bring on the tears.

"You said you wanted to hire me to catch her killer."

"Yes, that's right."

"I'll do my best, but I can't take your money. The police are far more likely to find the killer than I am. What I don't understand is why you'd ask me. I was here last night as Callie's adversary."

"No you weren't." Maria shook her head vehemently. "Not really. I listened to nearly every word of your conversation. Aside from whatever David Loeb sent you up here to do, I know for a fact that you were trying to talk some sense into her. I know, because I was constantly trying the same thing myself—with far less success. For Callie to have proceeded with a criminal complaint would have been folly. Against Jimmy Gilbert? With his money and his lawyers? And with what? She'd cut herself off from Troy and his money. No one would have represented her."

"She seemed awfully convinced of Jimmy's guilt."

"That's because she was a witness."

"A witness?" I repeated. "Witness to what?"

"That," Maria said enigmatically, "is what I could not tell you over the phone. If you would like to smoke a cigarette, be my guest. I no longer live here as of seven o'clock."

I lit up a Lucky Strike and offered her one, which she refused, choosing one of Callie's Dunhills from the Russian lacquered box. She allowed me to light it with my Zippo.

"Are you sure you want to hear it?" she asked. "I strongly believe that the things Callie saw last week led to her murder. If they knew Callie told me, they would try to kill me, too."

I thought she was being overly dramatic.

"Go on, Maria," I said. "But if it's that serious, maybe after you tell me you should go to the police."

"Are you saying you're not up to handling the case?" She drew deeply on her cigarette, making it crackle.

"No, I'm saying if you have an idea who killed Callie, you should have shared it with the police already. Especially if it's going to put you at risk."

"This is not the kind of thing that one just brings to the police," Maria said haughtily. "It's rather delicate."

"I'm not," I said. "Try me."

Twenty

"We were at the house last Saturday," Maria began. "Callie drank most of the day, a little more than her usual. She seemed very depressed, but this was not uncommon, and I was in no mood to keep watch. Rosario and I were undertaking a thorough cleaning of the house. Callie kept finding us and offering to help. Now, I had no intention of letting the mistress of the house get down on her knees and scrub out the toilets. Perhaps I might have given her some small task, just to make her feel better, but I knew she would do a sloppy job and I would only have to do it all over again. I didn't have the time for any nonsense, so I turned her down. I was very firm with her, told her to go away."

"How did she react?"

"Slightly hurt, sulky, like a child. She finally left us alone, and I was glad, because Rosario and I had plenty of work."

"Was Dr. Blassingame around?"

"He was out riding one of his new horses. Helen or Dido."

"Callie didn't ride?"

"She used to, until her accident a few years ago. It was before I started working for them. Callie was out riding with her husband one day and fell off one of the horses. I suppose she was intoxicated. She suffered some head injuries and went to the hospital. Troy was disgusted with her for falling."

"Disgusted? Why?"

"Because the fall ruined some work he had done on her face, and he had to redo it. Callie said he did twice as many operations as before, trying to restore her to the way she'd looked before. But he was never satisfied with the results."

"She didn't look bad to me," I said. "For fiftysomething."

"Nor to me, but I never knew her before the fall. I've seen old pictures, but all they show is a younger Callie. I'm not sure what Troy thought was missing."

"You were talking about last Saturday. Troy was out riding Helen or Dido. Where was Jason?"

"Over at Jimmy Gilbert's, as usual."

"How often is he over there?"

"Seems like all the time. Jason started spending a lot of time with Jimmy last summer, and then Troy allowed him to go with Jimmy on the Asian tour. Callie was against it."

"Why?"

"She's his mother—she didn't like him being away from her all the time. Jason was going to be with Jimmy for a month, and then when he returned, he'd be going back to school. Callie thought she'd never see him. She was right. Jason's school gives him a long Christmas break, and Callie was looking forward to spending the time with him. Then Jimmy invited Jason on a ski trip to the Swiss Alps. Callie said no, but Troy overrode it. He told her she was being overly protective."

"Do you think she was?"

"No. She loved Jason and wanted to spend some time with him, that's all. For all her faults, Callie was not a clinging person. She told me her philosophy was to 'mother, not smother.' She probably got that from one of her self-help books."

"You make it sound as though Callie wasn't very smart."

"Well, I hate to speak ill of the dead," Maria said, "but anyone who would marry Troy Blassingame couldn't have been all that bright. Still, she was an RN."

"Callie was a registered nurse?"

"That's how they met. She used to work for him, but after they got married, Troy made her give it up, for the usual reasons. He wanted his wife at home to take care of him."

"When did they marry?"

"They were set to mark their silver anniversary next month."

"Callie gave up nursing twenty-five years ago?"

"Yes."

"How long was she Blassingame's nurse before they married?"

"I have no idea. A year or two, I'd guess."

"Why did it take them so long to have a child?"

"According to Callie, they tried. After many years, she finally went to see a fertility doctor. She thought she was barren. Turned out she was fine. The problem was Troy. He had a low sperm count. The fertility doctor suggested that Troy switch from bikini briefs to boxer shorts so his body heat wouldn't kill so much sperm. Jason was born nine months later."

"That's all it took?"

Maria reached for another cigarette, and I lit it for her.

"I'm sorry," she said. "I'm taking up far too much of your time. I'm only trying to tell you what Callie saw."

"You're doing fine."

"Rosario and I were quite busy, so I had no idea what Callie was doing. I confess I didn't much care. Sometime after sundown, I went up to Jason's room to hang up some things of his I'd gotten back from the dry cleaners. Jason's room is normally a mess. When I started my employment with the Blassingames, Troy told me Jason's room was off limits as far as cleaning. He wanted Jason to clean it himself, to keep him from becoming too spoiled. Apparently, when Jason was younger, this was fine, and he very dutifully cleaned up his room. But for the last year, he has neglected it. It was all I could do to keep my hands off it, but I was not about to disobey Troy's directions.

"When I entered Jason's room that night, I found everything neatly ordered. Callie had been in it all afternoon, putting things away, dusting, picking up dirty clothes off the floor. The carpet had been vacuumed. The bed was made up with fresh sheets. Books were put back on their shelves. Jason's desk was no longer cluttered with junk. His closet was just as neat as the room. The shoes had all been matched and placed in rows along the floor. Usually they're all in a pile."

"Callie was going through his stuff all day?" I said, appalled. When I was fourteen, I hated it when my mother cleaned my room. My life had already become my own private property.

"My guess is, she'd been wanting to do it for a long time," Maria said. "So had I, but I would have been fired."

"What did Callie find?"

"Well, I didn't know at first. When I was hanging up Jason's dry cleaning, I heard Callie's voice carrying through the house. She was screaming at Troy, who had just come back from the stables. They were downstairs, in his study."

"What was she saying?"

"I couldn't tell. I certainly wanted to know, but I did not wish to face the consequences of being caught eavesdropping. Rosario felt the same way and went running to the farthest corner of the house to escape them. Troy and Callie engaged in a shouting match, that is true, but I could make out nothing."

"Callie was confronting Troy over something?"

"Yes, definitely a confrontation. She told him she wanted a divorce. I learned that later. It was when I came back to New York with her the next day that she told me the rest."

I lit myself another Lucky and said, "Go on."

"When Callie was cleaning Jason's closet, she tried to move a suitcase and found that it was very heavy. It was one of the Gucci suitcases Jimmy Gilbert had given Jason for the Asian tour. In fact, there in the closet, Callie was surrounded by expensive designer clothing Jason had received as gifts from Jimmy—which she never entirely approved of, since she and Troy were perfectly capable of buying Jason clothes, even from big-name designers."

"Dr. Blassingame told me he thinks designer clothes an extravagance. Would Callie have been able to buy them anyway?"

"Sure," Maria said. "She did, sometimes. But she gave up after a while, because Jason never wore any of the things she gave him. He only wore Jimmy's. Anyway, she couldn't understand why this suitcase should be so heavy, and she wanted to open it to find out what was inside. It was locked. She went looking for the keys and found them among the clutter of Jason's top desk drawer. Then she sat on the floor of the closet and opened up the suitcase. What she found was a collection of pornography."

"It's not unusual for fourteen-year-old boys to have *Playboy* or *Penthouse* lying around," I said, not letting on that I was sure Jason's collection was different. "They either shoplift them or get older boys to buy them."

"Jason was not interested in *Playboy*," Maria said knowingly. Her hand fell on the suitcase and stroked the fine leather. "What's in here is homosexual pornography. Magazines, videos—"

"Let's see it," I said.

Maria looked taken aback.

"That's the suitcase, isn't it?" I asked.

"Well, yes, but I thought I'd just tell you what's inside. I looked it over with Callie when she brought it here. I don't much feel like seeing it again. I don't want to keep it around here, either. I'd rather you took it for safekeeping. It might be relevant to Callie's murder. It might be evidence.

You can take it home and look at it all you like."

"If it's evidence, it may have to go to the police," I said. "I think I'd better have a look at it now. You can go into another room if you want. I'll call you when I'm done."

"All right," she said, handing me a small key ring with two golden keys. "I'll go finish my packing."

Some of the magazines were relatively tame—things like *Torso*, *Advocate Men*, *Playguy*, and *Honcho*, which basically ran a lot of pictures of naked men and some pornographic short stories. Other magazines were more hard-core, featuring pictures of men in couples and groups engaging in oral and anal sex. Jason owned some magazines in a series featuring guys with dildos, called *Anal Masturbation*, and several issues of the SM magazines *Drummer*, *International Leatherman*, and *Bound & Gagged*.

I wondered where Jason had managed to get the stuff. I'd developed a similar collection of porno myself, starting when I was sixteen, back in Wyoming. I'd been able to pass for eighteen and enter the adult bookstores without being carded. I'd also kept my collection hidden away under lock and key in my closet—but my mother never discovered it. Jason was up to the same thing, only at a younger age. Mature as he was, I didn't believe he could pass for eighteen. Maybe the store clerks didn't care.

The magazines took up about half the space of the suitcase. Taking up the other half were five VHS videotapes, a couple of latex dildos, and a stash of Gold Circle condoms. The videotapes had home video labels and were merely marked TAPE 1, TAPE 2, TAPE 3, TAPE 4, and TAPE 5. It didn't tell me anything about the content. They could be home movies, or they could be duplicates of professional films. One couldn't tell without watching them, but I'd have to do it later.

"Did you find the pictures?" Maria came back into the room.

"What pictures?"

"A set of Polaroids." She looked apprehensive.

"Polaroids of whom?"

"Of Jason, of course." She came over behind me and looked over my shoulder at the contents of the suitcase. "I don't get it. They should be right there, tied up with rubberbands."

"I haven't seen them. These were pornographic photos?"

Maria nodded, looking pale. "They were quite distasteful."

"You and Callie both saw them?"

"Yes. I saw them when she brought the suitcase back here. Callie first saw them originally in Jason's closet. Everything else was bad enough, but I believe it was the Polaroids that sent Callie downstairs to talk to Troy."

"Could you or Callie tell whether someone else had taken the pictures? Or had Jason taken them himself?"

"I don't think we ever considered the possibility that Jason would have taken them himself. As hard as it was for Callie to look, she did check each one to see if there was ever anyone else with him. But they were all only of Jason."

"He could have used a Polaroid with a timer," I said, recalling how much time I'd spent as a teen doing erotic things to myself in front of a mirror.

"I doubt it," Maria said. "Anyway, Jason looked as if he was doing things to please the person behind the camera."

"Did he look frightened?"

"No, he was smiling, relaxed." Maria's lip turned up.

"At least Jason had them in his possession. Though that doesn't mean others don't exist. Whoever took them could have also scanned them and put them on a computer. Did you or Callie have any idea when or where they were taken?"

"I'd say sometime this summer. Callie recognized it as Jimmy Gilbert's bedroom."

"So she did have evidence, but now it's gone." I closed the case and locked it back up. "You still want me to take this?"

"Yes." Maria sat down again.

I put the keys in my pocket.

"When was the last time you saw the pictures?"

"A few days ago."

"Who else was in the apartment during that time?"

"Only myself, Callie, and Jason. Troy briefly, last night."

"And you didn't remove the pictures from the suitcase."

"No, I didn't. Callie kept the keys, but I suppose Jason could have found a way to sneak them from her."

"What was it about them that made Callie confront Troy?"

"She told me she didn't go down intending to confront him. She merely wanted to bring it all to his attention. Troy didn't know anything about the suitcase, but he said he knew Jason was gay. He didn't seem bothered by anything Callie said, and that made her angry. She started blaming him for Jason's association with Jimmy Gilbert. She accused him of allowing Jason to be corrupted. Then she said she wanted a divorce."

"How did Troy take it?"

"He tried to shout her down. He called her ignorant and intolerant. He didn't understand why she was so stupid, she hadn't been able to figure any of this out on her own. He said they would be better off letting Jason discover himself, and there were worse persons he could do it with than Jimmy Gilbert."

"What did Callie think of Jimmy?"

"Up until last year, she always thought the world of him. She disliked him from the time Jason started spending more time with him than with her. But that was just natural jealousy."

"How did she feel about Jimmy after she found the photos?"

"She hated him. She was quite upset. I was coming downstairs when she and Troy were finishing. I saw her storm out of his study and slam the door behind her. Troy came out a moment later demanding that she come back. She simply ignored him. She didn't say another word. She went out the front door."

"Back to New York?"

"No. That's what Troy thought, or he might have got on the phone and warned them."

"Warned who?"

"Jimmy Gilbert and the others. Callie was going over there to retrieve Jason."

"What others?"

"Callie didn't know about it, and I certainly didn't, but I suspect Troy did. I think he knew everything all along but just didn't care. He has probably made more money off Jimmy Gilbert than any other patient. Then there are all the gifts."

"You mean the gifts to Jason, like the clothes and the car?"

"Not only the gifts to Jason," Maria said. "Over the years, Jimmy has given Troy various things to add to his collections. Rare books and early American landscape paintings, mostly. Then just a few weeks ago, he gave Troy those Arabian mares."

"Helen and Dido?"

"I've never seen Troy happier than when he saw them."

"That's a generous gift. Did Jimmy give a reason for it?"

"Like all the other gifts, it was *ostensibly* to express his gratitude for all the work Troy has done remaking his face."

"What happened when Callie went over to Jimmy's?"

"She knew if she used the front door, she would never learn what was going on. She wasn't thinking entirely rationally at this point, perhaps. She didn't even take the car. She decided to cross over the stone fence between the properties and sneak up on Jimmy's house. She knew where his bedroom was, and she was going to peek through the windows. But she didn't get that far."

"There was a party going on, right? A pool party?"

"How do you know?" Maria eyed me suspiciously.

"I spoke with Ralph Reston today. He witnessed it."

"Ralph Reston?"

"Not that he had any idea what he was looking at. He likes to watch over the valley through binoculars. By night, he uses a pair of night vision goggles the Secret Service gave him. Everything's green in night vision goggles, and his brain isn't what it used to be—if it ever was—so he thinks he's looking at green men from Mars. He told me about little and big green men he'd seen last Saturday down at Jimmy's pool, and what he described sounded like an orgy."

"Well, that's precisely what Callie found," Maria said. "Orgies are one thing, but this was more than that. Jason was there, and so were a lot of other underage boys."

"How young was the youngest?"

"Jason was probably the youngest. Callie said some looked as old as seventeen or eighteen. All the other men were adults, and Callie knew them all."

"Did she tell you who they were?"

"Absolutely. Would you care to guess at any?"

"Bert Ferrigno, for one," I said. "The guard named Ennis told me Bert had been up to Jimmy's house for a party last week. He didn't know what kind of party, though."

"Yes, Callie mentioned Bert was there. But that's only the beginning. The other men included Yuri Zetlin—"

"Not terribly surprising."

"Also Hugo Wallis."

"Now that's *very* surprising."

"Are you ready to guess who else?"

"Don't tell me David Loeb," I said.

"Yes," Maria said. "David Loeb. In the flesh. In fact, he was the one who was paired off with Jason at the moment Callie surprised them. Which was particularly unfortunate for David."

"Why is that?"

"Callie didn't want to say anything to David in front of everybody—especially in front of Jason. She made Jason put on his clothes and dragged him back home with her. Once we were back in New York, Callie delivered a letter to David's office."

"What about?"

"After what she'd seen, she felt he had to know. She'd kept it a secret from him for close to fifteen years. The truth is, David Loeb is Jason's father. According to Callie, anyway."

"David never had any idea?"

"He probably should have suspected."

"Did Troy know?"

"I don't think Troy knows even now who Jason's father is. Callie never told him, and I doubt David did. Troy certainly always knew Jason wasn't his."

"But he still acted like he was Jason's father, didn't he?"

"Yes, nominally. I don't think Jason ever suspected a thing. Not until last week."

"Callie told him?"

"Yes, she told him who his father was."

"Why?"

"She wanted him to feel bad about what he'd done. She never wanted him doing it again."

"What, having sex with David Loeb?"

"No, having sex with men, period. Callie had a violent hatred toward homosexuals."

"You said 'they' would kill you if they knew Callie had told you all of this. Who exactly were you talking about?"

"I don't know," Maria said. "All of them, I suppose."

"By them, you mean the men at the pool party?"

"Yes, that's what I think."

"You think they got together and plotted Callie's murder?"

"They must be involved somehow."

"Bert Ferrigno was one of them," I pointed out, "and he was killed, too, by whoever killed Callie."

"I'm just telling you what I believe."

"Why would all of them want to kill Callie?"

"To keep it secret that they're gay. All of them are in the closet, publicly, for business reasons."

"Staying in the closet is the least of their worries if they've been engaging in sex with minors," I said. "Just being gay isn't the same thing as being a pederast. I'm gay myself—"

"I figured you were," Maria said mildly. "That's one reason I wanted to talk to you. I thought you might understand better than a straight detective."

"My point is, I've never even considered preying on a kid. The proportion of child molesters among gay men is probably the same as it is among straight men."

"Yes, I'm sure of that. I'm also sure there are far too many child molesters, whatever their stripe."

"Was Callie threatening to go to the police about them?"

"Not that I know of, but with Callie, the threat would always be there."

"Did you see the contents of her letter to David Loeb?"

"No, I didn't."

"And you think this group of men would want to kill you, too, just for knowing what Callie told you?"

"If they killed Callie, why not?"

"We don't know that they did."

"That's why I hired you. To find proof."

"Troy isn't letting you stay here. Where are you going?"

"I'll be with relatives. I have your phone numbers, Mr. Quaintance, and I'll be in touch."

I rose to go and said, "Stay safe," though I suspected Maria had nothing to worry about. A murderous cabal was the least likely scenario I could imagine. If these men had plotted together, it would have probably come unraveled by now. If any were involved, it was more likely that one had acted alone.

"Don't forget the suitcase," Maria said. She seemed quite eager to be rid of it, as if it brought with it a death-curse.

I hefted it with a grunt and took it with me out the door. There might be clues on the videotapes, but I had too many other leads to follow and no time to watch them. I wondered who I could enlist to help and immediately thought of Juan.

Twenty-One

I walked into the ground-floor entrance of Blassingame Cosmetic Surgery Associates and thought I'd taken a wrong turn into a hall of mirrors—or into Bloomingdale's. Every wall in the lobby was covered with mirrored glass tiles. The furniture was made of chromium-plated tubing. End tables and coffee tables were topped with beveled glass. Couches and chairs were upholstered in shiny black leather that smelled of recent oiling. The light came from fluorescent tubes in the ceiling and was reflected glaringly off a black marble floor. My own reflection reverberated in all directions in a succession of identical rooms, to infinity.

The receptionist was about twenty-five, with the face and teeth of a beauty queen and long auburn hair. I couldn't tell whether she was twenty feet away or two hundred yards. A diminutive elderly woman was standing at the desk speaking to her. She had a big head of sprayed hair that looked like a pile of canary feathers.

I approached the reception desk with caution, hoping it was not an optical illusion. I was relieved when my knee touched the edge of the desk. Up close, the two women looked real enough.

"I should wait till September for a breast reduction?" the elderly woman said. "I'll be dead by then."

"That's the best we can do, Mrs. Gelb."

"Let me talk to Dr. Blassingame, honey. I'm sure he can make room for me in July. I'm one of his best customers."

"He's been in surgery all day. I can't disturb him."

"It'll only take a second."

"Sorry. We can set a date here, or you can come back next week and discuss it with the doctor. That's the best I can do."

"Fine." Mrs. Gelb fixed the strap of her purse over her shoulder and straightened her skirt. She turned to me and motioned toward her ample bosom. "Do these look like they can wait till September? Meanwhile, my back is killing me. Twenty years I've been coming here, I don't even matter. The little missy's been here six months, they let her run the place. What are you having done? No, don't tell me. A hair transplant?"

"No," I said. "Just here on business."

"See you next week, Mrs. Gelb," said the receptionist.

"I'm going to tell Dr. Blassingame all about you," Mrs. Gelb said, putting on her sunglasses. She tromped through the lobby and out the door.

"Tough customer," I said.

The receptionist rolled her eyes.

"Are you Rita Hedgepeth?"

"Yes. How may I help you?"

I told her who I was and handed her my card. "We spoke a little while ago on the phone. Is Dr. Blassingame really unavailable or were you just trying to get rid of her?"

"He's still in surgery."

"He's been with the same patient all day?"

"Yes, though I don't even know who it is. I came in this morning, and he was already here in the operating room."

"Has he come out at all?"

"No. He left strict orders that he wasn't to be disturbed under any circumstances. I haven't seen him myself."

"Have you seen any of the nurses?"

"I haven't seen anybody," Rita said. "I've been alone here all day. The whole staff was supposed to be off today. I just came in to catch up on paperwork."

"This operation Blassingame's doing," I said. "It wasn't on his schedule?"

"No, must be something urgent."

"Isn't that unusual?"

"Not terribly. Dr. Blassingame deals with a lot of celebrity clients, and sometimes they demand total secrecy. There've been a number of operations I haven't been let in on."

"I see," I said. "You're sure there's no way I could speak with Dr. Blassingame, even for a second?"

"No, sorry," Rita said. "I can't give you any different answer than I gave Mrs. Gelb. You're welcome to wait around until the doctor's finished."

"How long will that be?"

"I have no idea. Could be the rest of the afternoon."

"Just tell him I came by to see him, and ask him to give me a call, will you?"

"I sure will, just as soon as he comes out."

"You're sure he's okay in there," I said.

Rita Hedgepeth shrugged. "Far as I know."

"After what happened to his wife, I'm growing a little concerned. You wouldn't want to risk taking a look, would you?"

"No, I wouldn't. He'd fire me on the spot. When a customer wants secrecy, they get it. I'm content to wait."

"I'm not. What if I just went around your desk and through that door and down that hall and had a look for myself?"

"I'd have no choice but to call the police," Rita said.

"It was worth a shot. I'll call again later."

I turned to go, thinking that Mrs. Gelb was right about Rita Hedgepeth. She had been given too much power, and it was getting in the way of her common sense. I wondered which one of the doctors Rita was fucking. I decided not to turn around and ask.

I drove back down to Chelsea and went up to my apartment to get my canvas book bag. I drove over to the yellow-brick Manhattan Mini-Storage building across the street from Kotby's garage. I rented a small locker for a short term and went back to put the suitcase away in privacy. I removed the videotapes and placed them in my book bag. I locked the suitcase, slid it into the locker, locked the locker, and carried the book bag out with me into the daylight. I did not notice anyone spying on me.

I managed to grab a parking space on Eighth Avenue right in front of the salon. Past me went the usual Saturday crowd of huggable guys, showing off their pecs and abs, their shirts tucked into a back pocket or tied around the waist, or wearing slutty things like tight T-shirts, spaghetti-string tank tops, jeans, cutoffs, and spandex shorts with rugged workboots or in-line skates. The neighborhood boys greeted their friends and ex-boyfriends (who might be both) with a smile and an "Oh, hi!" and sometimes a sweet kiss before they introduced new friends and caught up on what happened last week.

Every seat in the salon's waiting room was taken. Several guys were standing around the receptionist's desk. I went in carrying the book bag with me. The receptionist was a toothpick of a guy, about nineteen, with pale skin and bleached-blond hair, laughing it up with the standing men. They had perfect hair already, so I supposed they had appointments for tanning booths or massages or manicures or full body waxes or what-have-you.

I noticed Juan in back finishing up with a customer.

The receptionist stopped laughing long enough to bat his eyes at me and ask, "May I help you?"

"Yeah, I'd like to speak to Juan," I said. "Could I just go on back there?"

"You wouldn't be Greg, would you?" he asked.

"I would."

"I am so sorry," he said. "I totally choked on your message to Juan. I was just so swamped. All these people kept calling and rescheduling and I never seemed to have time to—"

"Forget about it," I said, yawning. "Okay if I go back?"

"Oh, sure. Sorry. It's all right. Go on."

As soon as I left his desk, he was laughing again.

Juan's customer gave Juan a tip and smiled proudly at himself a few times in the mirror before leaving. Juan pocketed the money and rollerbladed over, throwing an arm around my waist and dragging me back to his chair. I refused to sit, though.

"Hey, Gregory, what's with the clothes, man? Looks like you raided my closet!"

"Could you do me a favor, Juan? It would mean taking off the rest of the day."

"I don't know, I've got a lot of appointments."

"I'll pay you whatever your time is worth. More, even."

"Hmm, I suppose I could rope someone else into doing them." Juan stroked his chin. "Depends on what you want me for."

"I have some evidence that may or may not be important. Five videotapes. I haven't seen them, but I may need to know by tomorrow what's on them. It could be nothing. Or something."

"You want me to watch some movies?"

"They could be half an hour long, or six hours each. I don't have the time to spare. I'll pay you, like I said."

"Sure, Gregory, I can do that for you."

"You can use the VCR at my place, if you want," I said.

"I got a VCR." Juan sounded defensive. "And I live right around here. What's wrong with my place?"

"Actually, you're right. Your place would be safer."

"Safer? You asking me to do something dangerous?"

"I don't think so. Nobody's going to know you have these tapes. And you're not going to tell anyone, okay?"

"Okay by me. When do you want me to start?"

"Now."

Juan lived in a third-floor walk-up on Fifteenth Street. It was a studio apartment like mine, though it was larger by a couple of square feet and got more sun. He had a futon couch, too, neatly folded up, just opposite his television set. I set the book bag on his coffee table and pulled out the tapes.

"Keep the door locked and the chain on," I said. "Don't open it for anyone but me. If anyone tries to get in, you might want to protect yourself with something. You got any weapons?"

"I got a baseball bat. Why would anyone want to come in?"

"The tapes might be important. I don't know. I don't think anyone knows I have them. I've been keeping an eye out, and I haven't seen anyone watching me. No one ought to know you're helping me. I think the woman who gave them to me was a little paranoid. Don't worry about it. Trust me."

"What makes these tapes so important?"

"All I can say is, they're related to the case I'm working on. They were kept in a box with a bunch of gay porn magazines, so I guess they might be porn, too. They might be home movies. There might be minors involved. Is that going to disgust you?"

"Disgust me? I don't know. Depends on what they're doing."

"Try to watch whatever you can. Use Fast-Forward only with the Play on to make sure you don't miss anything."

"Gotcha."

"Make a note of everything you see on each tape. I'll call or come back later to see what you've found. Whatever you see, don't discuss it with anyone. This has to remain confidential."

"No problem, Gregory."

"And one more thing."

I leaned into him and gave him a kiss. His nose-ring was cold against my upper lip. Juan grabbed the back of my neck and held me tight against him.

I broke the kiss and said, "Sorry, Juan. I've got to go."

"Later, then." Juan licked his lips. He reached into his pants and readjusted himself. "Hey, while I'm watching, what are you going to be doing?"

"Looking for a lost boy."

Juan followed me to the door and started to close it.

"Do you have work tomorrow?" I asked, holding it open.

"No, tomorrow's Sunday. I'm free all day."

"If I'm finished with this case, we could go have brunch."

"Mmm," he said. "Sounds delicious. And Gregory?"

"Yes?"

"After brunch, I want you."

With that, Juan closed the door.

I waited until I heard him throw the chain.

Twenty-Two

I went back to my office and called David Loeb's office, hoping that Alex Clements was enough of a workaholic to be there on a Saturday. He was: "Bulkeley, Stearn. David Loeb's office."

"It's Greg Quaintance. Is David in?" I knew he wasn't.

"He can't be reached at the moment. He'll be checking in later, if you'd like to leave a message."

"Just have him call me as soon as he's free," I said. "So Alex, what are you doing there on a Saturday?"

"Please! This is my catch-up day, the only time I can get any work done. Too many phone calls during the week."

"Like this one, I guess."

"Oh, I don't mind."

"Really? Come to think of it, Alex, you could be a doll and help me out with something."

"Yes, what?" Clements sounded anxious to get back to his transcribing or filing or whatever he did on Saturdays.

"I need to see Yuri Zetlin, the fashion photographer."

"I know who he is." Clements was insulted. "He's to be a client of David's."

"Then can you give me a number where I can reach him?"

"I can call and try to arrange a meeting."

"Great."

"This is related to the Gilbert case?"

"Yes, it is."

"Just when did you want to see Yuri?"

"Immediately. If that's possible."

"I'll see what I can do."

"You're a peach, Alex."

"Of course I am," Clements said, sounding as queeny as the receptionist at Juan's salon. "I'll call you right back, Greg."

Yuri Zetlin agreed to see me as soon as I could get over. I was given an address on Greene Street in SoHo. I found a parking space a few blocks away and walked the rest of the distance, weaving in and out of packs of tourists. I checked out all the parked cars, hoping to spot a black Eagle Talon with Garden State plates. I struck out. But that didn't mean it wasn't around.

Zetlin's address proved to be one of the old cast-iron buildings, with row upon row of columns and Italian arches stacked one atop the other and painted off-white. I pressed the buzzer. A male voice answered and asked who I was. I told him.

"Oh, yes," the voice said. "Come in and go on back, way back, and take the freight elevator to the top floor—unless you'd prefer eight flights of torture on the knees."

I was buzzed in and took the freight elevator up to the top floor. I emerged into a tiny corridor lighted only by a single low-wattage bulb. I knocked on the only door. As I waited, the elevator suddenly was engaged and went slowly back down to a lower floor. I felt momentarily trapped.

"Hello?" I said, knocking again.

Several undone deadbolts and chain locks later, the door opened to reveal a tall, obese man draped in yards and yards of silky red embroidered fabric. I didn't take it as a kimono at first; the only fat Japanese I'd ever seen were sumo wrestlers, and I'd never seen one of them in anything but a giant thong. Yuri Zetlin belonged in neither a thong nor a kimono; he wasn't Japanese, and the costume seemed a great affectation.

"Ah, Mr. Quaintance! And what a pleasure it is to make yours—if I may say so." Zetlin pursed his lips and narrowed his gaze. His wavy brown hair was slightly pomaded, and he wore a thin mustache and a chinstrap beard that gave him the semblance of a jawline amid all that doughy flesh. "Do come in."

I crossed the threshold into a residential loft with the approximate square footage of the Mammoth Caves. It was an open space divided into rooms by well-placed screens. Windows sloped up to meet the high ceiling, on which was painted a celestial fresco featured naked, Raphaelesque cherubs. I craned my neck to get a better look. The angels were fleeing from the day—blue sky, downy clouds, and warm sun—into the starry cold of night and the embrace of a leering moon.

Zetlin slammed the door behind me. The locks were turned and the chains refastened, and he replaced an iron bar that reached from a notch in the floor to just under the doorknob.

I sensed Zetlin's gaze following me as I went deeper into the loft. I felt trapped in the lion's den. I was grateful for once that my meat was no longer so young, tender, and easy.

"Are you afraid of someone getting in?"

"Habit," Zetlin replied, testing the bar to make sure it held. "One can never be too careful in this town. Here, now, follow me to the bar and let me fix you a little cocktail."

"I could use one," I said.

Zetlin took me past a "room" decorated in a Moroccan motif, covered in rugs, with oversized pillows strewn about, walls hung with wine-dark draperies. In the middle of a low table was an elaborate Arabian water pipe from which ten tubes protruded like the writhing snakes of Medusa's wicked hairdo.

I turned a corner and met a long teakwood bar bathed in the mid-afternoon sun from the studio windows. I sat on a stool while Zetlin took his place among the liquor bottles.

"Ah, yes, what'll it be, what'll it be?" he said, stretching his fingers and trying out a bad W. C. Fields impersonation.

"Tequila."

"Oh? Hmm!" he said, as if my choice offered a window into the decrepitude of my soul. He found a good bottle and poured a shot nimbly. "Don't mind me while I mix up a Singapore Sling."

"Go for it," I said.

"Just like Raffles used to make." Zetlin winked at me, squeezed a lemon into his shaker, dropped in a little ice and a lot of gin, and shook it up over one shoulder and then the other, like Carmen Miranda with a pair of maracas. "I once saw a man in a sling in Singapore—but that's another story."

"I'll bet."

"Our young comrade Alex Clements was rather obtuse with me on the phone," Zetlin said. "I'm not sure exactly what it was you wished to see me about. Something to do with Jimmy Gilbert?" He waggled his fingers in the air vaguely, as if he couldn't be expected to keep straight whatever Clements had told him. Maybe the phone call had woken him up. He looked like he'd slept late. I entertained the possibility he had no idea Callie was dead.

"It's something to do with Gilbert, all right," I said.

Zetlin strained the contents of the shaker into a collins glass, poured in a layer of cherry brandy, and dropped in a slice of papaya from a jar. He slid another slice of papaya into his mouth and swallowed it down like a frat boy sucking down a live goldfish. "Now. I take it you're one of David's men."

"I work for him, if that's what you mean." Unconsciously, I threw my voice deeper. "I'm a private detective."

"Yes, yes. We all know that. Alex gave me all the dish. David hired you to look out for Jimmy's interests, and you're a queer private dick. I'm sure your mother is quite proud of you."

"Not since I got myself kicked out of the Army."

"Oh, do tell!" Zetlin's first chin disappeared into his second as he sipped his drink through a red straw. He folded his arms onto the bar and leaned against it. The old teak creaked.

I hoped to gain his trust further by sharing a confidence. I allowed him to play bartender-confessor to my alcoholic sinner.   "All I wanted was a career in the Army," I said. "When I was a fourteen, I wrote away for their free posters and put them up all over my room. I used to wake up staring at the face of this blue-eyed soldier, his face all smeared in camouflage greasepaint. I don't know if it was all those raging teenage hormones or what, but I always thought the Army was pretty sexy."

"The *uniforms* are sexy," Zetlin said. "The killing isn't. They tried to draft me, but I was 4-F. What ever got you interested in the first place?"

"My dad."

"Oh?" Zetlin's eyes grew wider.

"I grew up thinking of him as a hero. I kept a picture of him in his dress uniform on my wall. He enlisted in the Army during Vietnam. He survived his first tour, came home for a bit, and helped my mom conceive me. He went off on his second tour before I was born and went missing in action. I was a year old."

"Oh, dear," Zetlin said, looking genuinely pained. He looked old enough to be a part of that generation. Some of the boys he grew up with must have died in the war. Maybe in a weird way he was still searching for all the pals he had lost.

"After high school, I signed up. My recruiter encouraged me to go to a junior college. They took care of my tuition. I never quite finished my associate's degree, though. I went to Fort Bliss to complete my Army training, then got transferred to Fort Bragg. Sometime after that, Saddam Hussein invaded Kuwait, and we got sent to Saudi."

"Sent to Saudi!" Zetlin's heart was going pitter-pat. "Like Lawrence of Arabia!"

"Not quite," I said. "I was there from the beginning. Desert Shield became Desert Storm, and we went in and mixed it up with the Iraqis. A buddy of mine died right alongside me."

"A lover?"

"Just a friend. But I did have a lover there and at every other step of my Army career. Beginning with my recruiter."

"No!"

"I was discreet. My conduct was never a problem. I wasn't raping guys in the showers. I came to know a whole group of queers in the service, and you can bet we were careful in that environment. But when I was in Saudi, I fell hard for this guy Steve. He was a great soldier and a great lover. I thought he was a great guy, too, but once the war was over and we were back in North Carolina, and the investigations started—"

"Witch hunts," Zetlin interrupted sympathetically.

"I should have said the investigations resumed. It was all put on hold during Desert Shield and Desert Storm, but once the war was over, it all started back up with a vengeance. Steve got snared. They threatened him. They said they could see to it that his parents lost their house. They told Steve that just for being gay in the Army, he could be sent to Ft. Leavenworth for a life sentence at hard labor—which isn't true, but he didn't know that. They promised they'd go easy on him if he cooperated. They asked him to name names of other queer soldiers, and he did. He named every one of our friends, including me. They didn't go easy on him, of course. They gave him the same undesirable discharge that I got later, even though I never ratted on anybody."

"Bravo for you," Zetlin said. "What about Steve?"

"I never saw him again. Don't care to, either."

"So you came to New York."

"Eventually."

"I don't quite see the jump from soldier to detective."

"I didn't work at all for a while. Had black depressions. Drank a lot of tequila. Finally picked up work as a security guard. Made a few connections, started doing security consulting, and wound up expanding. Got a private eye license eight months ago. It's starting to pay off. I've had some success tracking down missing teens, and I lucked out earlier this summer with some security work for Tay Farrell."

"Oh, I know Tay!" Zetlin said brightly.

"What a coincidence."

"Not really. *Everyone* knows Tay."

"Except his fans," I said. "They see him on *E.T.* going to premieres with young supermodels on his arm. Females."

"Well, you can't expect him to come *out*."

"Why not? You're well known, and you're out, aren't you?"

"I am *not* out. Just obvious. And I'm not that well known."

"Your photos are," I said. "And you've directed television commercials and music videos, haven't you? You're a part of the culture, whether they know you or not."

"That's very flattering," he said. "But I prefer staying in the background, out of the public scrutiny."

"Then why would you take such risks with your photography?"

"I'm sorry," he said, frowning all of the sudden. "Perhaps you could tell me what risks you're talking about."

"That ad campaign last year for those jeans. The pictures everyone accused of being child pornography."

"Aren't we getting off the subject here? I thought you came to see me about Jimmy Gilbert."

"You don't see any relation between those ads and Jimmy?"

"You don't mean his little boyfriend?" Zetlin rolled his eyes toward the starry ceiling. "Ugh!"

"I'm sorry if the subject bores you," I said, working up some anger. I got up from the stool and paced a little before the bar. "Jason Blassingame is missing and could be in trouble."

"Missing?"

"He could even be in danger, unless he's somewhere very safe. His mother was murdered last night."

Zetlin's jaw dropped. His pasty face went even whiter. "Murdered? Callie?"

"You didn't know?"

"I had no idea. How would I?" Zetlin set down his Singapore Sling with a sudden look of distaste.

"You mind if I ask what you were doing last night?"

"I was with a friend. We were here all night. You don't mean to imply that I had anything to do with Callie's murder?"

"Stop looking so horrified. You had plenty of reason."

Zetlin let out an outraged laugh. "Such as?"

"Weren't you at some sort of party last Saturday night?"

"How do you know about that?"

"Maybe David told me."

"David would never have told you."

"So he was there, then, wasn't he?"

"I'm unsure what it is you think you know, Mr. Quaintance." "Callie caught you, didn't she?"

"Doing what?"

"You want me to spell it out for you? I spoke with a young man today"—I took out my notepad and checked my notes—"a Derek Peterson of Somerville, New Jersey."

Zetlin stared at me as if he didn't comprehend a word.

"He's one of your models," I went on. "About fifteen, with long blond hair and an attitude."

"Yes, yes, of course I know Derek. Nice boy, but a chronic liar. What crazy story did he tell you?"

"He didn't tell me much. I got the rest from another source. But

Derek was there last Saturday night, along with Jason and you and a bunch of other people, including David Loeb, apparently, over at Jimmy Gilbert's house. A pool party."

"What other source? Who told you this?" Zetlin's face was taking on the color of the cherry brandy in his drink.

It was a good thing he and I were separated by the bar. He looked about ready to leap over it and throttle me.

"Maybe I heard it from Bert Ferrigno," I said.

"Who?"

"You saying you don't know who he is?"

"There was somebody there I'd never met before," Zetlin said, concentrating. "I remember now. Younger guy?"

"Not young enough for you, I'm sure."

"No," Zetlin said, annoyed. "I mean, about your age? Built? Very hairy chest?"

"Could be," I said. "I never got to see his chest. He was killed before I got the chance."

"He too? But why?"

"I was hoping you might shed some light on that. You're telling me you never met Bert Ferrigno before that night?"

"That's right."

"He was a security guard at Somerset Hills."

"Now I remember! Funny I didn't realize it at the time."

"I suppose you were too busy."

"It seems you know everything."

"Everything except what I need to know. Like who killed Callie and Bert and where I can find Jason."

"I can't help you with any of that. I wish I could."

"It could make a difference to Jason. Anything you can tell me might be of some help."

Zetlin thought for a moment. "You are really just a private detective, right? You're not like a regular policeman?"

"Look, Yuri, I'm not going to run you in," I said. "Unless you tell me you killed Callie and Bert or kidnapped Jason. I'm working for David Loeb, who's also your lawyer, so anything you tell me will fall under attorney-client privilege. Under the circumstances, I don't have any authority to take you down to the precinct house and book you for statutory rape. If I did, I'd have to bring David along, too. Not to mention Hugo Wallis. I could do it, but then I'd be out a chunk of dough. But I wouldn't have any proof to offer the cops, anyway. The prime witness is dead. Unless, of course, they could get one of the kids to talk—which shouldn't be too difficult."

"All right, all right," Zetlin said, clutching his temples between thumb and forefinger. "What do you want from me?"

"I was hoping I might find Jason Blassingame here."

"He's not here. I'll give you a guided tour and prove it."

"Later. You swear you know nothing about where he is?"

"I haven't seen Jason since last week."

"When Callie appeared during the party and took him away?"

"That's right." Zetlin turned his eyes away. "If anyone should know where Jason is, it's Jimmy. I suggest you ask him."

"He claims he doesn't know," I said. "Jason was planning on going with Jimmy on his South American tour. I suspect Jimmy is hiding Jason out somewhere until they can get safely on board his jet. They were supposed to leave tomorrow. I hope to find Jason before then. I was hoping maybe Jimmy might have asked you to hide Jason here for a while."

"No, sorry. I hope you find him. He's a good kid."

"No thanks to you," I said.

"Don't blame me for his corruption."

"You did take those photos of him."

"Which photos?"

"For the jeans ads. What other photos did you think I was talking about?"

"I've taken other pictures of Jason. Don't get any funny ideas. They were all fashion photos. All fairly chaste."

"I'm not sure I believe you. Derek Peterson told me about the other photos you took of him, and what else you did. And I'm not talking about the pool party. I'm talking about in private. Nude photos. And sex between you and Derek, here in this loft. Derek tried to pretend it had happened to someone else."

"I told you Derek's a liar. You can't prove anything."

"I don't care to. What I'm worried about is that the same pattern may have been followed for all of the boys you used in the jeans ads. I take it you're not interested in the girls."

"No, I'm not."

Zetlin wasn't proud of himself. Instead of a bartender-confessor, he now looked like a prisoner in the dock.

"You should be glad you're not in prison," I said.

"Those boys instigated it themselves," Zetlin insisted.

"No one's going to buy that. I certainly don't. Child molesters are always trying to say that the kid wanted it."

"Kids these days are more mature than they used to be."

"That's the other thing child molesters say."

"Aren't you wasting time here? I thought you were looking for Jason Blassingame."

"Do you understand now why I came here? How am I to know that whatever you're doing with Derek and who knows how many other boys you aren't also doing with Jason?"

"I can't touch Jason anymore. Jimmy would kill me."

"Is that so?" I said. "Then how come he let all of you onto his property for your pool party?"

"He didn't know about it. He was in the city all last weekend. He had no idea we were there."

"Then who let you in?"

"Maddy."

"Madeleine Downey? Why would she want to do that?"

Zetlin smiled and said, "Ours is not to reason why."

"She knew what you guys were up to?"

"She didn't ask questions, but she probably had a fair idea. She's known me for years. And my proclivities."

"How many underage boys were there?"

"Jason and Derek were the youngest. There were also two seventeen-year-olds and one Asian boy who's nineteen but looks about five years younger."

"Madeleine knew all about it?"

"She knew we'd been wanting to have a party. She knew we didn't have a suitable place. She invited us to use her house."

"Jimmy's house."

"Well, it's hers, too. She knew who was coming. She didn't ask what we planned to do, and she didn't stick around to watch."

"Doesn't it seem a little convenient to you?"

"What's convenient?" Zetlin said. "In what way?"

"That Callie should have snuck up on your little pool party at just the right hour on just the right night. Especially if you weren't doing this sort of thing all the time."

"No, that was the only night we ever did it at Jimmy's."

"I won't ask you how many other times you did it at other places. That's for the police to investigate. It's safe to say you were shocked when Callie appeared from out of nowhere?"

"Yes, of course. We all were."

"How did she know to sneak across the grounds?" I asked him. "If all she thought was that Jason was over at Jimmy's, why wouldn't she use the front entrance and demand to see her son? How did she know she should check out what was going on at the pool? How could she possibly have known?"

"You're not suggesting that Maddy tipped her off—"

"Your words, not mine. I can't think of any other way."

"But she couldn't have! She's one of my dearest friends!"

"It has nothing to do with you. From her perspective, it has to do with Jimmy and Jason. Maybe David. And maybe Bert."

"Jesus," Zetlin said. "I need another drink."

"Make it something simple," I said. "And give me another shot of tequila while you're at it."

Zetlin poured out two shots of tequila, downing one for himself before I even had a crack at mine.

"I'd still like that tour, if you don't mind," I said. "Just to make sure you don't have Jason hidden away somewhere."

"Jason, no," Zetlin said enigmatically. His voice was hoarse from the shot. "But I'll show you what I *have* got."

"As long as it's nothing illegal."

"Oh, no, it's a consenting adult. Come and see."

Zetlin took me all around his loft, showing off the huge kitchen, the living areas, and the two bathrooms. One sunlit corner was set up as a private photographic studio, though he told me he kept a professional studio in another SoHo building, with more space and better lighting. He had a private darkroom, which he kept spotlessly clean.

He led me into the bedroom, where I found the alleged consenting adult lying facedown on the four-poster, one foot tangled up in the rumpled sheets. The rest of him was naked. His skin was bronzed and hairless, with no tan-lines. His limbs were splayed in all directions. He didn't stir. He was asleep.

"Wake up, boy," Zetlin said, tickling his free foot.

The youth jerked his foot away and rolled onto his back. He was a young Asian man, perhaps Vietnamese, with sharp cheekbones and a boyish body. If he wasn't underage, he was borderline. I wondered what Zetlin had promised him to get him to come up here: money? a modeling career? dinner for two at Le Cirque 2000?

He looked up at Zetlin groggily. Then he looked at me. "Who's that?" He sat up against the pillows but did nothing to cover his nakedness. He blinked the sleep from his eyes.

"This man is a private detective," Zetlin said. "He thought you might be someone else. I had to bring him in here to prove that you weren't."

"Sorry," I said. "I didn't know we'd find you like this."

"I don't care," the youth said through a yawn.

"Satisfied?" Zetlin asked me. He showed me his bedroom closets, in which no one was hiding. Zetlin grabbed a pair of black jeans from a chair and removed the wallet from the back pocket. "Here's my boy's driver's license. Here, see? He's nineteen. He's also the young man I took with me to the pool party last week, if you'd care to interrogate him about that."

"Nhat Nguyen?" I said. "What's your phone number, Nhat?"

Nguyen recited his number with a sigh of boredom.

"You can answer a couple of questions for me, Nhat," I said. "How long have you been here with Mr. Zetlin?"

"I don't know," Nguyen said. "What time is it? I met Yuri at ten last night. We hung out at The Web, had a few drinks, then came up here."

"And Mr. Zetlin's been with you all night?"

"Yes." Nguyen tossed Zetlin a hard stare. "You might say he hasn't left me alone."

"You're absolutely sure?"

"How could I not be?" Nguyen rolled his eyes.

"Couldn't he have left while you were asleep?"

"No. We didn't even go to sleep till six. Was it six?"

"Roughly," Zetlin said.

"I'd like to go back to sleep now," Nguyen said. "Are you through?"

"For now. Okay if I call you later?"

"Yeah, sure," Nguyen said, smiling condescendingly.

Zetlin showed me out of the bedroom, saying to Nguyen, "I'll be back in a minute, boy. Don't go anywhere." He led me back through the maze of screens until we were back at the front door.

"That alibi he's got for you," I said, "how do you think that could be presented in court, in front of a jury?"

"All the boy has to say is that he was with me all night," Zetlin said confidently. "He doesn't have to tell them what we were *doing* together."

"Let's hope it doesn't come to that. By the way, you might be questioned later by a Detective Ozwick from the Somerset County Sheriff's Department. I recommend you don't meet her in a kimono, offer her a drink, or introduce her to your boy."

"Oh, I agree," he said. "That wouldn't be prudent."

"Then why were you so lax with me?"

"I knew I could trust you. You *are* working for David."

"What do you mean by that?"

"Nothing. You yourself pointed out that everything I've told you falls under attorney-client privilege. You can't even take it to the police."

"I wish I could," I said. "Don't be surprised if one day one of these boys goes running to the police on his own. If that happens, your career will be finished. If I were you, I wouldn't press my luck."

Zetlin nodded solemnly, as if he appreciated my point. Maybe he did, but that didn't mean he was going to change. They never change. Zetlin wouldn't stay repentant for long.

"For Christ's sake, Yuri, stay away from the boys. Let them discover themselves in their own way, in their own time."

"I'll take that under advisement," Zetlin said, and locked the door after me, chuckling to himself.

Twenty-Three

I drove up to Midtown and found a parking space close to the Sony Building. I called Alex Clements from the nearest pay phone.

"Alex," I said, "it's Greg Quaintance."

"David still isn't back yet," Clements said.

"Good," I said. "Listen, I'm coming up. I'm just outside the building. Call down and square it with the guard, will you?"

"I'm not sure that I ought to—"

"Alex, listen to me. I'm not going to have time to do my job the way David wants me to do it. I need to come up there and get some information, whether David likes it or not. Are you going to let me come up?"

"You can come up, but I'm not sure I can help you."

"I'm sure that you can, Alex," I said, and hung up.

I went inside the atrium and wandered in and out of the central sculpture for a few minutes like a tourist. The mocha security guard with the Brillo mustache sat at his desk, poring over a magazine and glancing up at me every now and then without raising his head. I gave him a nod and stared at the ceiling, a Gothic vault of bricks dipped in gold paint—the same kind as in the ceiling at the Metropolitan Opera House. Twenty more years, and these bricks would start looking as dull and crumbly as those at the Met, and their Japanese owners would have to fork over a fortune restoring them or else let the whole building go to seed.

The security guard's white phone rang, and he nodded as he spoke into the receiver, jotting down a note and glancing up at me again. That was my cue.

I wandered over. "I'm Greg Quaintance. I should have an appointment with Bulkeley, Stearn."

"They just called down," he said, scribbling on a little red slip of paper and tearing it from his book. "This is your pass."

"Thanks," I said. "Who am I supposed to give this to?"

"Nobody," he said. "You can give it back to me if you want, but I'd rather you held onto it."

"Then what good is it?"

"Weekend procedure. I know it don't make a lot of sense."

"Say, I'm supposed to be seeing David Loeb," I said. "You wouldn't know if he's in?"

"I can't tell you that," he said dyspeptically. He turned his attention back to his magazine and glared up at me.

I took the hint. I went on past his desk, into a waiting elevator car that gleamed all clean and brassy inside and pressed the button for the thirtieth floor.

Bulkeley, Stearn looked deserted again. I buzzed from outside, and Alex Clements came out to the reception area and let me in. He was wearing dressy slacks, white shirt, suspenders, and tie. So much for weekend casual.

"Hi, Greg." He smiled mechanically. "Come on back."

Clements led me down the hall. The grip of his fingers appeared slightly looser than yesterday. With the suspenders hiking his trousers up, his butt appeared perkier, too.

"What's the weather like out there?" he asked.

"Sunny and hot. You should be in it."

"Too much work to do," he chanted.

"Like keeping track of David?"

"That's not that difficult. He lets me know where he is."

"Do you know where he is now?"

"As a matter of fact, he just called. Here, have a seat."

We arrived at Clements's desk. He sat behind it, and I pulled up a chair. His in box was piled high, his desktop hidden under a sea of bleached-white documents and pink Post-it Notes.

"Have they arrested Jimmy?" I asked.

"No. David sat in and counseled Jimmy while he answered their questions. They seem to suspect Jimmy killed Callie Blassingame and the security guard, but they don't seem to have enough evidence to charge him. David's presence probably intimidated them a little on that score. They made David promise that Jimmy would leave himself available for further questions and that he wouldn't leave the country until he's cleared."

"When did you hear from David?"

"A little while ago. He was calling from a cel phone in his car. He and Jimmy were on their way back into the city."

"When do you expect them back?"

"Hard to say. Maybe another half hour." Clements grabbed a paper clip from his desktop and began twisting it in his fingers. Now, what was so urgent you had to come up here and see me?"

"I can't afford to waste any more time," I said. "I have to find Jason Blassingame. I need you to give me as much information as you possibly can."

"I'd like to, but I don't know how much I can say without David's consent. I mean, we're talking about my job here."

"And I'm talking about Jason's life, Alex. After what happened to his mother, I believe he's in danger. If you help me save him, I think I can guarantee that David won't fire you."

Clements gave an astonished laugh. "Yeah, right!"

"Alex, I'm going to tell you something about David, but you have to promise me you'll keep it to yourself."

"There isn't anything you can tell me about David that I don't already know," he said. "You're welcome to try."

"You know Callie and David are old friends."

"That's no secret."

"They apparently had an affair some fifteen years ago. Callie was sure that Troy was not Jason's father. David was."

Clements dropped his pretzelized paper clip. "That's impossible!" He leaned over his desk and spoke in a whisper: "Don't you know?"

"Know what?" I whispered back.

"David's gay!" Once he got to the word *gay*, Clements's lips were moving but no sound was coming out.

"So are you," I said, returning to a perfectly natural tone of voice. "And so am I."

"I know that," he whispered, looking around as if the walls had ears, "but David's deep in the closet. And I mean deep."

"Stop whispering. No one's listening. How old are you?"

"Twenty-two."

"And I'm twenty-nine. How old is David, fiftysomething? He's from a totally different generation. Pre-Stonewall. He wouldn't have had it so easy, especially as a lawyer. He probably went through psychoanalysis. Maybe he had phases when he considered himself bisexual. Or maybe he *is* bisexual. You and me, we look at his wife and we figure she's a beard, right? But maybe when he married her, he was genuinely trying to give it a shot. He probably gave Callie a shot, too. It didn't work out. David didn't expect to get a son out of it. And she never told him."

"You mean he doesn't know?"

"He does now. Ever since last week."

"Do you think it's true, or was it just Callie being crazy?"

"I don't know. Alex, tell me. You know David well enough."

"Well enough?" he repeated. "I've been sleeping with him."

"Uh, okay, so you know him very well. Even if there's only a slight chance Callie was right, don't you think David would want to do everything in his power to see that Jason is safe?"

"Yes, of course, if he thinks Jason's his son."

"Then trust me. He isn't going to fire you for helping me."

"I guess not," Clements agreed. "What do you need to know?"

"Anything you can dish about Jimmy's entourage. Starting with Madeleine Downey. Julianna Gilbert told me she's a front."

"You needed Julianna to tell you that?"

"My hairstylist told me first."

"Your hairstylist," he repeated, staring at my baldness.

"Never mind," I said, wondering how Juan was doing with the videotapes.

"So your hairstylist knows it," Clements said, "and Julianna knows it, and you know it, and I know it. So how come it's not universally assumed to be true? Because the American public is pretty dim. Todd Curwen knows that, and he exploits it for all it's worth. That's what makes him a good manager. God knows it's not because Todd has any great intelligence! I mean, we live in a country where all these housewives out there honestly believe all their favorite soap opera hunks are straight."

"Perhaps a couple of them are," I said.

"Well, I for one can't understand how any of those people could possibly be fooled by the likes of Tay Farrell and Hugo Wallis. I'm amazed that we made it all the way through the Wallis trial, through that barrage of negative publicity, without anyone ever once questioning Wallis's sexuality. Who knows? It might even have been germane to the case."

"Oh?" I said, sitting forward.

"But that's another story!" Clements said. "My point is, Todd Curwen is a master of this. He arranged Wallis's marriage and Jimmy Gilbert's. He makes sure Tay Farrell's always seen in public with a different girl on his arm, and he makes sure the footage gets on *E.T.* and *Hard Copy* and into Liz Smith's gossip column. Thanks to Todd, Tay Farrell is considered a real lady's man—an eligible bachelor! Meanwhile, Tay has three or four musclebound Chelsea boys shipped out to the island every weekend. If you told those housewives about it, they'd never believe it. Todd's brainwashed them. He knows how to build a front."

"I know all about that," I said. "But what I don't get is Madeleine Downey. I always thought the whole point to Jimmy Gilbert was that he was androgynous, even as a boy. When did Todd Curwen decide Jimmy Gilbert needed a wife?"

"When he and Marcia started selling Jimmy to Hollywood. The film studios are more desperate than ever about having big-name stars in their movies to make sure the opening weekend grosses are huge. All they care about anymore is name recognition. That's why you're getting all these basketball stars in the movies. They can't act, but the film execs couldn't care less. They're willing to pay them five or ten million for the use of their name. Jimmy Gilbert's one of the biggest names there is, and he photographs well, too. But he's never been in a movie before because he's not anyone's idea of a leading man. Adrogynous heroes went out with Rudolph Valentino."

"You're saying that Todd Curwen married Jimmy off to one of the world's most beautiful supermodels and tried to turn him into a macho man just to make him bankable," I said.

"Bankable is the word. It's my understanding that the studios couldn't even get insurance on Jimmy until he married Madeleine Downey. Plus, the studios are insisting that his voice be digitally enhanced and lowered, like Disney did with Robby Benson's voice in *Beauty and the Beast.*"

"That's just plain stupid," I said. "What is Jimmy Gilbert without his voice?"

"You know that," Clements said, "and I know that. But these Hollywood execs are not much smarter than those housewives."

"Has Jimmy been signed onto any projects?"

"He's got a two-picture deal worth twenty million."

"How much does Todd get out of the deal?"

"Directly? Plenty. I'm not sure how much, but both Todd Curwen and Marcia Gilbert will get executive producer credits on the pictures. They have their own company, Curgil Productions. They've been cut in for some cash, plus points."

"Is David Loeb involved in this?"

"Only insofar as he brokered Jimmy's part of the deal. He doesn't have any direct association with the film projects. Todd and Marcia wouldn't want to work that closely with him. They seem to think he gets in the way."

"Why's that?"

"David tends to counsel Jimmy conservatively. He doesn't think it's good for Jimmy's career for him to branch out into untried areas. He thinks Jimmy should stick with his music."

"How did he feel about the marriage?"

"He was against it," Clements said, "and he told Jimmy so, but David is uncomfortable when he gets into other people's territory, and he saw this as Todd and Marcia's purview."

"I see," I said. "But while all this has been going on, Jimmy's been hanging out with Jason Blassingame. I'd think that would throw a wrench into everything Todd was trying to do."

"Todd doesn't see it that way. He has supreme confidence in his ability to sculpt his clients' public personas. As far as I know, neither he nor Marcia ever considered Jason a liability."

"What about Madeleine?"

"I'm not sure what she thinks. You'd have to ask her."

"But Jason did become a liability when Callie started trying to blackmail Jimmy. Do you have any idea what set Callie off?"

"No, you're getting into areas I know nothing about."

"Did you know Jimmy is Jason's godfather?"

"No, I didn't know that."

"Callie apparently never suspected that anything was going on between Jimmy and Jason," I said. "Not until a week ago. Can you tell me at least how her contact with David began?"

"I'm afraid I don't know."

"When did you first get wind of the case?"

"David called in Angelo Ferrante for a briefing. I sat in."

"What day was this?"

"Wednesday."

"Did David seem to have the case well in hand by then?"

"Sure."

"What did he ask Ferrante to do?"

"Same thing he asked you to do. Explain to Callie that she had to be insane to pursue a criminal complaint against Jimmy."

"Why do you think Ferrante sold out to the *Enquirer*?"

"He needed the money, is my guess," Clements said.

"David's rich," I pointed out. "Why not go to him and ask him to match it?"

"I have no idea. Ferrante wasn't my kind of guy."

"What kind of guy was he?"

"A real type A personality, and violently heterosexual."

"Who do you think killed him?"

"I wouldn't know. Same person who killed Callie, I assume."

"I can't figure what anyone had to gain by killing Ferrante," I said. "Other than revenge."

"Security," Clements suggested. "Ferrante's been working for David longer than I have. He's done investigative work on all of David's high-profile cases."

"Are you suggesting he was going to start parceling out secrets to the tabloid press?"

"It's just an idea," Clements said. "He didn't stand to make all that much off the Jimmy Gilbert story. Not enough to set him up for life, anyway. David's clients are all famous. Maybe Ferrante intended to start selling off their secrets."

"The kind of secrets Todd Curwen tries to keep shut in the closet," I said.

"Exactly. I could go into that business myself, if I wanted to be stupid."

"If what happened to Ferrante is any indication, you're better off where you are."

"Yeah, this is a pretty good gig."

"If you get fired for helping me out, maybe you should come and work for me."

"You couldn't afford me. Anyway, David will never know I told you a thing, right?"

"You can trust me," I said. "But there's one more thing I want to ask of you. I'll understand if you refuse."

"What is it?"

"I'd very much like to have a look at a certain blue file folder of David's."

"What blue file folder?" Clements raised one eyebrow.

"The one he keeps locked in the top drawer of his desk."

"Let's have a look." Clements rose from his desk, grabbed a set of jangling keys from his pocket, went around me, and unlocked the door to David's office.

"How much time do we have?"

Clements checked his watch. "We'll have to hurry."

"We'll be in and out, I promise."

"Don't sweat it." Clements flicked on the lights.

He went in, and I followed, feeling guilty at having instigated him. I certainly had no way of knowing that Loeb wouldn't fire him if he found out what we were up to—even if the two of them were sleeping together. For that matter, I had no way of knowing Loeb wouldn't fire me.

And what was I in this for, anyway, if not my fee?

Twenty-Four

"I have a key to this desk, but I've never used it before," Clements said, sliding it in and giving it a twist. The latch made a nice clean clicking noise, and the drawer seemed to leap out into his hand. "I don't see it."

It was a cluttered jumble of pens and pencils, rubber bands, paper clips, old phone messages, and other meaningless scraps of paper. No folder.

"He took it with him?" I suggested.

"No, wait." Clements stuck his hand under the lip of the desk and felt around. "Something's caught here." He pulled out what looked like the same blue file folder David Loeb had been referring to on my first visit. "Is this it?"

"Looks like it," I said. "Let me have a look."

Clements handed it over, and I set it down atop Loeb's immaculate desk. It wasn't very thick. I opened it up and began leafing through the contents: papers mostly, and a manila envelope containing some 8×10 glossy black-and-white photos.

Naturally, my curiosity turned to the photos first. They were grainy shots—either taken on fast film or blown up from a small portion of the negative—but the naked men in the photos could all easily be identified.

Yuri Zetlin was easy enough to spot from his sheer corpulence and the chinstrap beard. In the first picture, he could be seen dangling his legs over the edge of the pool. A dark-haired youth (revealed in later photos to be Nhat Nguyen) rose up in between the legs, clutching on to the humongous thighs and burying his face in Zetlin's crotch while Zetlin ran his fingers through Nguyen's hair.

Bert Ferrigno was there, his face recognizable to me at least, with a leanly muscled frame and a thick carpet of black hair from his neck to his toes. A waiflike youth was on his knees before him, worshiping his godhead.

The face of Hugo Wallis, already so famous from his soap opera, had been etched so firmly into the public consciousness that few would be able to look at these photos without picking him out, leaning into the prostrate figure of Derek Peterson.

Thanks to the Wallis case, David Loeb's face was now equally as well known—and here Loeb was, looking not at all bad for fiftysomething, lying on his back in an outdoor lounge chair. Jason Blassingame had his feet planted on the arms of the lounge chair and was squatting down squarely onto Loeb's lap.

"My God!" Clements said, looking at them. "What are these?"

"Looks like Callie brought a camera to the pool party," I said, without offering to explain further. "Are you shocked?"

"They're only kids!"

"Do you recognize that one?" I asked. "The one with David?"

"No, why should I?"

"That's Jason."

"But . . . but you said David was Jason's father."

"Neither of them knew that when this photo was taken."

"Still!" Clements said. "I mean, Jesus Christ, Greg!"

I replaced the photos back in the manila envelope.

At the front of the blue file folder were several pages from a yellow legal pad that had been scribbled all over in flowing black ink from a fountain pen.

"Whose handwriting is this?" I asked.

"Those look like David's notes," Clements said.

"What about this?" I turned to a personal letter several pages in length, composed on pale beige stationery in blue ballpoint pen. The writing started fairly neat and cramped, but as the pages went on, the lines began sloping down to the right. The letters became larger. The cursive loops grew wider. Some words appeared to scream from the page. The tip of the pen had cut deeply into the stationery at times, especially where certain words had been underlined. The ink was smeared in spots from what may have been tears. It was signed simply, CALLIE. "Would you know if this is Callie's handwriting?"

"No, I wouldn't," Clements said. "I've never had any dealings with her. David's coming back any minute. Why don't you let me copy everything up for you?"

"Make sure it's everything—including each of the photos."

I closed up the file and handed it to Clements.

"I'll be right back," he said. "I'm just down the hall."

I went out to Clements's desk while he was gone and rifled through his rolodex. I copied down the addresses and unlisted phone numbers of Madeleine Downey, Todd Curwen, Marcia Gilbert, Julianna Gilbert, Hugo Wallis, and Ralph and Natalie Reston.

I was just closing my notepad and putting away my pen when Clements came back from down the hall bearing a plain manila file folder, which he handed to me, saying, "Here you are."

"Thanks," I said and riffled through the photocopies. It looked like a complete set, and the photos came out as clear as the originals. "I owe you one, Alex."

"It's nothing. Now I have to put these back."

Clements dashed back into Loeb's office, put the blue folder back in the top desk drawer, and locked it. He turned off the lights, came back out, and made sure the knob was locked. When he sat again at his desk, his forehead was beaded with sweat.

"You don't think this means David had anything to do with Callie's murder, do you?" Clements looked suitably horrified.

"I don't know," I said. "But if I were you, I wouldn't let David know you showed me the folder or that you know it exists."

"Believe me, I won't." He snatched a tissue from the box on his desk and wiped the moisture away from his face.

I heard the distant ding of an elevator, followed by the echoing footfalls of somebody's leather-soled shoes on the marble floors of Bulkeley, Stearn.

Hastily, I tucked my copy of the file behind me, snug in the waist of my jeans, hidden behind by jacket.

Loeb appeared, briefcase in hand, looking weary. Jimmy Gilbert was not with him. He stopped in his tracks.

"What are you doing here?" Loeb said, looking at me.

"I was hoping I could get Jimmy to tell me where Jason was," I said. "Alex said you were bringing him in with you."

"I was. Originally, they weren't going to charge him. On our way back into the city, they changed their minds for some reason. They caught up with us at Plainfield, pulled us over, and placed Jimmy under arrest, right there at the roadside. Traffic slowed to a standstill. Everyone was driving by gaping at the scene. It's going to be all over the six o'clock news. Not to mention *Hard Copy* on Monday."

"Jesus," Clements said.

"There goes Jimmy's tour. There goes everything!"

Loeb hefted his briefcase and hurled it across the room. It sailed past me and struck his office door, sending chips of wood flying. The briefcase sprung open at the hinges and landed on the floor, spilling papers everywhere. There were no illicit photos among them, from what I could tell.

"I'm sorry," Loeb said. "Forgive me, gentlemen."

Clements was already crouched down over the briefcase, gathering papers and putting them back in.

"No, Alex, that's okay, I'll take care of it," Loeb said, going over and joining him. He didn't bother to put anything in order but merely stuffed everything in and shut up the case.

"You didn't go back to the jail with Jimmy?" I asked.

"No need to," he said, standing up. He took his keys out of his pocket and unlocked the door to his office. "We'd already been through their questioning. They have what they want for now, and they can't question him further without me or one of my associates present."

"Is Jimmy all right?"

"As far as I can tell." Loeb flicked on his office lights.

I followed him into his office but stayed near the door so I could turn and go easily without him spotting the obvious outline of the file folder behind me.

Loeb set his briefcase on his desk and turned to face me: "I want you out there finding that kid."

"Did you try asking Jimmy?"

"I did," Loeb said. "He claims he has no idea. He's not a very good liar, but I didn't want to lean on him too hard. Jimmy tends to grow uncooperative when pressed. And he's very protective of Jason. We'll never get it out of him. You'll have to come up with it some other way."

"Any suggestions?"

"If I knew where Jason was, I wouldn't need you, would I?"

"I suppose not." I couldn't help wondering what was going to happen to Jason once I did find him.

"Now go on, go," Loeb said, grabbing a cigar from his box. "I've got work to do. We'll talk later, whatever you find."

"Yeah, I'll want to talk to you, too," I said. "*After* I find him. Which I will."

"How can you be so sure?"

"If I don't, he may end up like his mother. I don't intend to let that happen."

Loeb turned toward his view, staring out at the GE Building while he lit his cigar. "You can't save the world, Greg."

"I'm not trying to," I said. "I'm just trying to save one kid who needs saving—from a lot of things."

Loeb had nothing to say to that. Puffs of smoke wafted up around his head. I could already smell it from the doorway.

I left while his back was still turned.

Twenty-Five

In the safety of the 'Cuda, I opened up the file and read Callie Blassin-game's letter to David Loeb:

David,

It's been a few days since I caught you, but I'm still so angry I can hardly write. You call yourselves MEN? I wouldn't say that I'm an "innocent" or even a "prude," but I don't think I've ever even thought of such a thing as I saw with my own two eyes the other night. Never mind the fact that one of the boys was MY OWN JASON! I would have been just as DISGUSTED if Jason hadn't been among them. How in the world could you get these poor boys to do those things? How can you even look yourself in the mirror and think you're such a GOOD GODDAMNED PERSON? That's what everyone always says about you—what a GOOD MAN you are—HA! I'll be sure to set the record straight with everybody, including Lydia.

I've always pitied Lydia—even though I'm sure you spelled it all out to her long before she signed the prenup. Didn't Todd find her for you? Matchmaking is one of his specialties—scouting out beauties like Madeleine and Lydia who might benefit from becoming the show-wife of some rich fag. I'd say there but for the grace of God go I, but then I wasn't much of a beauty when I met you, before Troy started carving my flaws away. What was I to you, anyway? Were you trying to find a CURE for your DEPRAVITY?

Where do you go to find your DATE for the evening—the malls, the video arcades, F.A.O. fucking Schwarz? How many of your clients do you think you'd be able to KEEP if it became known that you're a SEXUAL PREDATOR with a taste for ninth-grade boys? You probably think it's all ONE BIG JOKE, don't you? I wouldn't be surprised if you're sitting there LAUGHING right now. NO ONE is going to believe the word of Callie Hewitt Blassingame, the well-known ALCOHOLIC and PILL ADDICT, over that of David Loeb, everybody's favorite lawyer and fucking BEST FRIEND!!!

If that's what you think, you're making a big mistake, David. Why? Because I've got PHOTOS of what you were doing to Jason. If that doesn't bother you, maybe you should contact all your BUDDIES, because I've got shots of every one of them SODOMIZING teenaged boys! Hugo Wallis apparently doesn't mind that the WHOLE WORLD (except for one misguided jury) thinks he MURDERED the beauteous Fiona (another of Todd's successful matches!) and that he GOT AWAY WITH IT (thanks to your fucking brilliance, David—no matter what you are, you're one hell of a lawyer!), but how do you think Hugo would like it if they learned he and his lawyer belonged to some bigshot BOY-RAPING CLUB????

By now, you're probably asking yourself what I want. Money? Sure, I'd love some money, especially now that I'm divorcing Troy. Of course, Troy has one of the best lawyers in the world handling his side of the divorce. You and I can work out what I'm going to get from you, but it's going to be some combination of REMUNERATION and REPRESENTATION.

In case you didn't REALIZE, what you did to Jason is going to SCAR him for the rest of his life!! Even if Troy is made to pay some hefty child support, I wouldn't be the least bit surprised if he became a DEADBEAT DAD. But actually, it would be UNFAIR to call him a DEADBEAT or even a DAD. You probably haven't even guessed at the reason why, even after ALL THESE YEARS!!

You know WHY? Because Troy is NOT JASON'S FATHER! Hard as we tried, we couldn't conceive. That was when I turned to YOU as a RESOURCE I could USE.

Yes, I used you. Yes, I always knew Jason was your son. Troy knew that he wasn't Jason's father, but we never discussed JUST WHERE EXACTLY the baby came from. Well, IT CAME FROM YOU. Happy now? Are you SATISFIED, you PERVERT!!! You were MOLESTING your own SON!!

Which brings me back to REPRESENTATION. There are only two things I want out of the divorce with Troy: (1) CUSTODY OF JASON and (2) HALF OF TROY'S ASSETS. I can see only one way of getting what I want: YOU HAVE TO REPRESENT ME.

Of course, you'll have to take it on PRO BONO, and depending on what kind of SETTLEMENT you negotiate for me, YOU may end up having to PAY ME!! That would be a FIRST, wouldn't it!!! A lawyer getting POORER off a divorce!!!

And if you don't BELIEVE that you're really Jason's FATHER, I'd be more than happy to SUBMIT him to a BLOOD test. After all the fucking DNA experts you heard from during the WALLIS TRIAL, I'm sure you know better than anyone how COMPELLING such evidence can be!!! If we were to run DNA tests on YOU and on JASON, I'm sure we'd discover within a statistical probability of about ONE in ONE BILLION that you are indeed Jason's father. Are you willing to see such PROOF? Or are you afraid?

I know I'm not good for much, David. I can't do anything for myself, and I'm worried about how I'll manage to survive. With enough money, I can finally get the treatment I've been needing. I'll clean up my life, get sober, and finish the job of raising Jason.

Maybe you don't give a damn. If you'd like to see the chips fall where they may, all you have to do is let me know that you've REFUSED. Then you can take your chances with the press, and if the VIGILANTE MOB doesn't get you, your BUDDIES will probably MURDER you for allowing them to be EXPOSED. (I know you got him ACQUITTED, but do you really TRUST Hugo?)

Who's to say what the COST would be to you if you were to IGNORE this letter. In addition to the PUBLICITY, I would very likely press CRIMINAL charges against you. This means I have nothing more to offer you than PUBLIC HUMILIATION, DISBARMENT, a PRISON sentence, and very likely

CONSTANT RAPE by your new friends at the penitentiary!!! After that, if you ever SURVIVE, and if you ever get RELEASED, you can look forward to being tagged as a SEX OFFENDER having to report your whereabouts at ALL TIMES to your parole officer. By then, you'll be an old man, anyway, and you won't have any more money, so you won't be able even to BUY sex from men of LEGAL age!!

Think about it, David. It's your life. Instead of ruining it for yourself, why not help out me and Jason? It will give you a warm and fuzzy feeling inside.

In remembrance of that one magical evening,

I remain,

Yours,

CALLIE

P.S.—I've already told Jason the truth about you. He's counting on you to help us. Don't let our boy down.—C.B.

When I finished Callie's letter, I felt like Alice emerging from Wonderland. I could hardly believe that I was sitting on the hot vinyl front seat of the 'Cuda deep in the heart of Midtown.

The Saturday afternoon crowd passed this way and that, carrying shopping bags from Saks Fifth Avenue (the real one), Barney's, Bergdorf Goodman, Salvatore Ferragamo, and Richart Design et Chocolat. I was jealous of all the guys carrying shopping bags. Here I'd been thinking that I was going to join their ranks as soon as this case was over. Now I was worried that if I took a wrong step, everything was going to blow up in my face and I'd never see a dime from David Loeb.

Worst-case scenario, I might get what Ferrante got.

I turned back to the file folder, hoping I'd be able to decipher Loeb's notes to himself. Somehow, the situation had changed greatly from the time he'd received Callie's letter to the time he called me. He had still appeared to be somewhat in control of the situation when I first met with him, and I wanted to know how he had managed to maintain whatever edge he had.

His notes showed that I was continuing to underestimate him. One page appeared to be his initial thoughts on reading Callie's letter. I would have expected him to be emotional, even panicky, but there was no evidence of that. Loeb seemed to go about solving his predicament the same way he would in defending a client whose case seemed desperate. He made a point-by-point analysis, beginning with the two things Callie seemed to want the most: (1) a great deal of money and (2) custody of Jason.

Loeb asked himself whether Callie was entitled to both of these things, and he decided she was. However, he wanted to come up with alternative solutions to the ones she had proposed. It was his desire to remove himself as far as possible from these affairs of hers. He did not want her to have any of *his* money if he could help it, nor did he wish to represent her. He outlined the reasons he would give to Callie. First, he agreed that he owed her what was essentially back child support for Jason; however, the way he saw it, he could use his expertise to *obtain* the money—from whatever source—and still be fulfilling his paternal obligations. Second, he would try to convince her that merely signing him on as her divorce attorney would not guarantee that she would gain custody of Jason. Custody would be an uphill battle that was doomed to failure unless Callie had evidence that Troy Blassingame was somehow less fit as a parent than she was.

After several pages in which Loeb outlined several possible scenarios for achieving Callie's goals, he landed on what seemed the best possible solution for all concerned—that is, for him and for Callie. It was clear from her letter that she believed Jimmy Gilbert had been having a sexual relationship with Jason and that Troy appeared to have full knowledge of it. All Callie needed to do was threaten to expose Jimmy and Troy by means of a criminal proceeding. The mere threat of it should be sufficient to obtain cash settlements from both Jimmy and Troy and to get Troy to give in on custody of Jason. Loeb's sole condition for helping Callie achieve these outcomes was that he remain in the background. She would receive no money from him, and he would not take her on as a client. She could go to him for unofficial advice, but she would have to proceed using her own counsel. He would help her find suitable representation for the custody case, but she could not divulge his role to anyone.

Loeb would tell her she could take this plan or leave it—but if she did, she was more likely to get custody of Jason.

Loeb's notes showed that once he had his arguments all in order, he spoke with Callie by phone on Tuesday afternoon. He began speaking with her at 3:51 P.M. and finished at 4:12 P.M. His notes of the conversation seemed to indicate that Callie was reluctant at first, but she quickly came around and "agreed to the wisdom of my plan," as Loeb put it. His final note to himself at the conclusion of the phone call was that he had agreed to send Angelo Ferrante over to Callie's on Wednesday. In addition to going over the plan with Callie in more detail, Ferrante's mission was to gather any information she had about Jimmy and Jason. He would bring the information back to Loeb, who would analyze it and offer Callie advice on how to proceed with her threats of a criminal complaint.

By Wednesday evening, things had changed considerably. Loeb received a phone call from Callie at 6:42 P.M. Ferrante had been with her much of the afternoon and was supposed to return to Loeb's office. Loeb notes that Ferrante never showed up. Callie is angry about this. Loeb tries to calm her down and asks her why she is so upset. She says that she turned over to Ferrante the only evidence she had that Jimmy had been molesting Jason. Loeb asks her what sort of evidence. His next notation reads, "Polaroids: Jason, naked, JG's bedroom. JG in photos? No." Callie says she trusted Ferrante, since he was acting on Loeb's behalf. Loeb tries to play it cool, telling her he's certain Ferrante will show up and explain himself. End of call.

Loeb's notes from Thursday indicated a frantic attempt to locate Ferrante. Callie calls several times, but he puts her off. Finally, he speaks with her, and she tells him she has taken Jason from the house in New

Jersey and brought him back with her to New York. She wants Loeb to come over to the Fifth Avenue apartment and "try and knock some sense into Jason." It seems Jason isn't ready to go along with their scheme. "Callie thinks some words from his father (!) might help," Loeb notes. He tells her he thinks now is the wrong time for him to see Jason, in light of all that has happened. She is anxious about Ferrante, and Loeb admits he hasn't heard from him.

Friday's notes revealed little that I didn't already know. Loeb learned that Ferrante had sold the story of Jimmy and Jason to the *Enquirer*, who planned to publish it in next week's issue. They planned on using one of the tamer Polaroids (tastefully censored and masking the identity of the juvenile), along with another photo that had once appeared in a *People* magazine profile of Jimmy, showing him lying on his bed surrounded by photographs of himself (to authenticate the location of the Jason photo).

The last of Loeb's notes summed up my meeting with him and subsequent developments, without anything that might indicate he was acting duplicitously toward me. Likewise, I felt I could take at face value what Callie had told me. Clearly, Ferrante's defection had thrown a wrench into their plans. Callie had trusted Loeb and felt betrayed. By last night, all bets were off. Callie had chosen the dangerous route of going it alone.

Twenty-Six

I went to a pay phone and called Rita Hedgepeth, who informed me that Dr. Blassingame was still in surgery. She assumed he would be finished in an hour or two at the most, provided there were no complications. I told Rita I hoped for an uncomplicated operation and would stop by in an hour or so. She told me to ring the buzzer; she was leaving soon and would be locking up. I asked her if she wasn't having second thoughts about checking in on her boss before she left. She said that she wasn't.

I tried Julianna Gilbert's phone numbers, but no one answered, neither person nor machine.

I retried the two numbers from my beeper that I'd been unable to reach before. The first number went unanswered. A deep, manly female voice answered the other: "Hello?"

"Greg Quaintance," I said. "You beeped me this morning?"

"Yes, Greg. It's Madeleine Downey. Where are you?"

"Here in Manhattan, in Midtown."

"Can you come up and see me?"

"Right now?"

"Yes, now."

"I'll be right over. Where are you?"

"I'm at Jimmy's—at our apartment. You have the address?"

"I believe so, let me check." I looked at my notepad. "One West Seventy-Second Street—is that right?"

"Yes," she said. "You can't miss it."

"Why's that?"

"It's the Dakota."

I knew of the Dakota Apartments long before I moved to New York. It played the role of the Bramford in Roman Polanski's *Rosemary's Baby*, in which it was eerily photographed with a wide-angle lens perched above its ornate Victorian gables. John Lennon lived in the Dakota and was shot outside it when I was thirteen. I was sorry he was shot, but I didn't care any more about him than I did for V. I. Lenin. Whatever the appeal of the Beatles was for the baby boomers, it was lost on me. Yoko Ono still lived in the Dakota. I was happy for her. They were arguably the most desirable co-ops to be had in the city. No matter how rich and well-connected you were, you had to get on a waiting list.

I managed to find a parking space near the American Museum of Natural History and walked the few blocks down to the Dakota along Central Park West. From West Seventy-second, I entered under an archway into a courtyard and up some steps to enter the mahogany-paneled domain of the doorman. He was a large, jolly Hispanic man with a neatly trimmed black mustache, dressed in a uniform that outdid itself for spiffiness. He stood behind a chest-high counter alongside a row of mail slots carved of the same dark mahogany, looking like the front desk of an Old West hotel. A solid door beyond the counter was firmly shut and locked against undesirables.

"Yes, sir?" The doorman gave me a cheerful smile.

"I'm here to see Madeleine Downey. I'm Greg Quaintance."

He called up and checked on me, signing off with a "Very good, ma'am." He hung up the phone and said, "You can go on up, Mr. Quaintance. It's the Gilbert apartment, third floor. Elevators are through the door, to your left."

He smiled and pressed the door release button.

I thanked him and went on through, breathing wood polish.

Madeleine led me down a wide hallway into the front sitting room. A cross hallway extended endlessly in both directions, opening up onto numerous additional rooms that I'd never see. I couldn't help but gape at the dark paneling and high ceilings. The windows in the sitting room overlooked Central Park, where thousands of people were spending a relaxing Saturday afternoon. The apartment was decorated in a neo-Victorian fashion, with deep red and purple fabrics, thick velvet drapes, Persian rugs with intricate patterns, and overstuffed sofas, settees, and chairs. The fireplace mantel was lined with porcelain figurines and pieces of china. Tiffany lamps sat around, and I was curious to know whether they were original. One very non-Victorian item in the room was a framed photographic print of Madeleine herself, tastefully nude on a sandy beach. It looked like a Zetlin.

"Please, have a seat," Madeleine said.

She directed me to the sofa before the coffee table, where a silver tea service was set. Steam spun out of the teapot's spout like a genie. Madeleine sat on the sofa with me, close but without crowding. Her bobbed hair was plastered again to her head. It took me a while to realize that the dark rings around her eyes were make-up, put on with intent.

"Tea?" she asked.

I said yes, please.

"David called me," she said, pouring a cup for me over a strainer. "Jimmy's been charged with Callie's murder. You must know that already. It's ridiculous, of course. Lemon?"

I dropped a slice into my tea. "Why is it ridiculous?"

"Don't you believe Jimmy's innocent?" she said.

"I do. I also want to know why *you* think it's ridiculous."

"To think that Jimmy would be capable of killing anybody. He won't even kill cockroaches. Won't let *me* kill them, either."

"Is he a Buddhist?"

"No. My father, who hunts, would say that Jimmy lacks backbone. As if that were such a great thing to have! Jimmy doesn't believe in harming other creatures if they aren't trying to harm you, and in that sense he's more of a man than my father. I don't know where he got it. Certainly not from Marcia."

"What about Jimmy's father?"

"What father?" Madeleine said. "Jimmy doesn't have one. Technically he does, sure. James Gilbert Senior abandoned Marcia and the kids shortly after Julianna was born. One of those 'going out to get some milk' deals. He just vanished and was never heard from again. Marcia worked extra hard to raise Jimmy and Julianna on her own. She was more of a surrogate father to them than a mother. Not a lot of loving kindness in that house. Jimmy won't say much about his childhood, but I've heard earfuls from Julianna."

"Julianna got the short end of the stick, didn't she?"

"That's right," Madeleine said. "Julianna says that Marcia blamed her for James Gilbert's abandoning them. Little Jimmy was given all the advantages, but Julianna had to fight for hers."

"And no one has any idea what became of James Gilbert?"

"Who knows? Jimmy has this fantasy that his father went off into the Army and died in Vietnam. That's too romantic for me."

"It happened to me," I said. "My father died over there the year I was born. It could have happened to Jimmy, too."

"Somehow I doubt it," Madeleine said, cultivating a vicious look in her eyes. "I like to think that he's still alive somewhere—some slob in a run-down trailer, watching his son's music videos on MTV, too scared or embarrassed to come out of hiding. That's what *I* call a lack of backbone."

"So where do you think this gentleness in Jimmy comes from?"

"It's just Jimmy," she said. "There's no changing him. I watched him get bit by a mosquito once. He sat there and watched the blood being sucked out of his arm. I wanted to swat it, but he wouldn't let me. I saw this mosquito filling up until it was ready to burst. When it was finished, it flew away, and Jimmy just watched it go, like he was wishing it well. He likes to say that animals and insects are incapable of malice."

"But human beings are," I said. "What if a man or woman were intentionally trying to harm Jimmy? Would Jimmy feel like it was okay to strike back?"

"Absolutely not. Jimmy is disturbed by senseless acts of violence. I don't think he could hurt anyone for any reason."

"Sounds like a nice man to have for a husband."

"You can have him if you like," she said lightly. "Though I don't think you're his type. He goes for young buns."

"You're talking about Jason Blassingame. There wouldn't be any chance that you're keeping Jason here, would there?"

"What? Looking after Jason? For Jimmy? Are you crazy?"

"You can cut the jealous wife routine, Madeleine," I said. "You and Jimmy got married at the behest of Todd Curwen to better your careers. Jimmy was supposed to gain his manhood and you, even greater fame. Don't try to tell me there was ever any love. It's a good old marriage of convenience."

Madeleine took a sip of her tea and stared out the window.

"You don't deny it," I said.

Madeleine turned back to me and set her teacup down on the coffee table. "It may be a marriage of convenience," she said, "but that doesn't mean I don't love Jimmy. He's supremely talented and one of the kindest, most giving men I've ever met."

"Then why this animosity toward Jason Blassingame?" I said. "It can't matter to you."

"It does matter."

"Julianna told me she thinks Jimmy's friendship with Jason is the only positive influence over his life right now."

"Julianna, Julianna." Madeleine shook her head as if there was simply nothing to be done about Julianna. Her cheeks colored slightly. "She and I are opposites in almost every respect. She is highly colorful and romantic. I have a darker, more realistic frame of mind. Julianna looks on Jimmy and Jason as some kind of classical romantic friendship—Achilles and Patroclus, Alexander and Hephaistion. That's a load of bull."

"You disapprove because of Jason's age?"

"Are you kidding?" Madeleine stared at me through her raccoon eyes like she wanted me to get serious. "I was screwing older boys when I was thirteen, and I turned out all right. Jason knows what he's doing. For me, that's the problem. I told you Jimmy is the most giving person—he's also the most gullible. I disapprove of Jason because I don't believe for an instant that he gives a flying fuck about Jimmy. There's nothing innocent about Jason. He's voracious, and I'm not talking about sex. Every time I turn around, he's asking Jimmy for something. Jason Blassingame is nothing more than a cheap gold digger."

"Jimmy can afford it, can't he?" I said. "It's his money."

"I'm not concerned about the money," Madeleine said. "Well, I am and I'm not. No, it's not going to bankrupt him, but I *do* think it's a waste. My concern is for Jimmy's well-being. He's under the delusion that Jason is his long-lost other half. What happens to Jimmy one day when he realizes all Jason's after is his loot? Jimmy's heart would be shattered. He's too delicate to survive such a shock."

"What do you want for Jimmy, then?"

"I wish he could have a mature relationship with someone his own age—someone who loves him for himself, not his image."

"How do you know Jason doesn't truly love him?"

"I can spot a fake when I see one."

"I take it you have no idea where I can find Jason?"

"That is correct. I was surprised he wasn't with Jimmy."

"So was I," I said. "I believe Jimmy knows where Jason is but won't tell anybody."

Madeleine nodded her head vigorously. "Oh, that's quite possible. Jimmy can be childishly stubborn. If he doesn't want to cooperate, you're going to be out of luck."

"Do you have any idea where Jason might be?"

"I'm sorry, I can't help you."

"Can't or won't?"

"If I knew where Jason was, I would tell you. I may not like the kid, but I don't want him getting hurt. I find Callie's murder truly frightening. Not to mention poor Bert."

"But Madeleine," I said, "wasn't it you who put them into jeopardy in the first place?"

"I don't know what you mean."

"You let Yuri Zetlin use Jimmy's estate for a pool party last Saturday, didn't you?"

Madeleine's eyes widened within their black mask.

"Didn't you?" I repeated.

"Yes," she said.

"Zetlin told me all about it," I said. "According to him, Jimmy was in the city all weekend and knew nothing about it, is that right?"

"Yes. But I am his wife. It's my house, too. What's wrong with me letting one of my friends use the place? I'm not responsible for what Yuri does or for who he brings over."

"Oh, so you know the kind of people Zetlin brought over?"

"Yuri's gay. I figured he'd bring over some guys. So?"

"You're evading me," I said. "You and Zetlin are close friends, you must know he likes what Jimmy likes—young buns, as you put it. And you made sure Zetlin brought Jason, too."

"Why should I do that?" Madeleine took my cup and replaced it on the silver tray. She started rearranging the tea service, absently, to keep her fingers occupied.

"You wanted to put an end to Jimmy and Jason once and for all," I said. "No matter how noble your reasons, that's what you wanted. That's why you phoned Callie Blassingame."

"I what?"

"You phoned Callie and tipped her off to what was going on. You told her what really goes on between Jimmy and Jason. You told her she'd better come over to the house and have a look for herself. You told her to cross the grounds and arrive at the pool, and you told her the best time to come. After the fact, you even provided her with photographs of the pool party."

"You're crazy."

"Would you like to see the photos?" I said. "I have photocopies of them right here."

I pulled my copy of David Loeb's blue file out from the waist of my jeans, behind my back. I pulled out only the copies of the photographs and laid them out on the coffee table.

"I find it hard to believe that Callie would stop to take these," I said. "Her only thought would be to grab her son and go, which is what she did. She may have been grateful to have them afterward, but she never would have taken them. Looks like dim lighting, too. Did you use some special film? Infrared?"

"You bastard," Madeleine said. "What are you trying to do, blackmail me?"

"I'm trying to find my way out of a labyrinth," I said. "Mostly, I'm trying to locate Jason. I'm not interested in blackmailing anybody. But you do admit, don't you, that what you did last week started this whole chain of events?"

Madeleine's eyes grew watery. Tears spilled down, bringing the silent-movie makeup with them.

"I never meant for any of this to happen," she confessed. "Yes, I took those photos. I'm not proud of it. I hid in the bushes with some high-speed film. I turned the negatives over to Callie for her to use as she saw fit. And you're right about what I wanted to do. Jimmy was going to take Jason with him on his South American tour. I wasn't going—I've got my work. It was time to put an end to it before it became too embarrassing. I also thought I could spare Jimmy the heartbreak that's sure to come down the road. He could blame Callie for the breakup. That would have been the end of it. How was I to know what Callie was going to do from there?"

"You couldn't have," I said. "But you might have guessed. What mother is going to sit idly by? Callie wanted justice."

"I'm not responsible for what Callie did," Madeleine said, sniffling. I handed her a tissue. She blew her nose. "Nor am I responsible for what happened to her."

"That remains to be proved."

"You think *I* killed her?"

"I have no evidence to the contrary. Where did you go last night after you left Jimmy's estate?"

"I'll tell you the truth."

"I hope you will." I gathered up my photocopies and put them back in my file.

"I—"

"She went looking for me," said a woman's voice at my back.

I craned my neck to see who had joined us.

Julianna Gilbert walked into the room from one of the long hallways. She was cradling a calico cat in her arms and stroking its fur. The cat's eyes were closed. I could hear it purring from ten feet away.

"Hello, Greg." Julianna couldn't suppress a smile.

"You've been listening?" I asked.

"Wouldn't you?" Julianna said. She sat across from us. The cat took this as its cue to leap from her arms onto the floor. It lifted its curious head over the coffee table and sniffed around the tea service, turning up its nose at the lemon slices.

I asked Madeleine: "How did you know Julianna was in Somerset

County last night?"

"We planned it that way," Madeleine said. "We were going to meet at Jimmy's. I didn't realize Marcia was going to insist on turning Julianna away even when Jimmy was facing a crisis."

"Maddy found me at Rex," Julianna said. "After you did. I saw her standing there just outside of the garden. Your back was to her, Greg. She motioned at me, got my attention, and vanished. I guess she didn't want you to see her."

"Why would that be?" I turned to Madeleine.

"Maybe I didn't want you seeing the two of us together," Madeleine said. "You're awfully nosy, even for a detective."

"The cat's coming out of the bag," Julianna said, reaching down to stroke the calico's tail. "Greg's going to need a little help, dear. He may be nosy, but he's also slow, like most men."

"The two of you?" I said.

Julianna laughed. Madeleine looked like she might, but she was still too distraught over what I knew of her recent acts.

"Men are always the last to suspect," Julianna said.

"You two planning to move in together? What about Jimmy?"

"What about Jimmy indeed!" Julianna said. "Jimmy is very supportive of us. That's partly why he agreed to marry Maddy, to give her shelter from all the scrutiny around her. She and I are both in the public eye. You won't ever see us moving in together. You'll hardly even see us together in public. The only thorn in our side has been my mother. I haven't been able to see Maddy at her own house because of my mother's dictums."

"Madeleine's just been telling me how different the two of you are," I said.

"I said we were opposites," Madeleine said. "You know what they say about opposites. I may disagree with Julianna, but I love her for who she is. I can't make her more like me."

"What was the plan last night, then?" I looked from one to the other. I didn't care who was going to explain.

"Shall I?" Julianna said.

Madeleine nodded. The cat jumped up into her lap.

"We wanted to see Jimmy in private and present a united front. Maybe I should have met Maddy beforehand and tried to sneak in with her in her car. But that's hindsight."

"What kind of united front?" I said. "You totally approve of Jimmy and Jason. Madeleine's against it. I don't get it."

"We both agreed on one thing," Julianna said. "Callie had to be paid off. As long as we got her off Jimmy's back, he could make up his own mind what to do about Jason. We knew the only way we could get Jimmy to pay her would be to talk to him in private, without Todd or Marcia or David around. We wanted to convey to Jimmy the gravity of the situation. Even after all these years, Jimmy's an innocent. I don't think he could fully comprehend the kind of damage the *Enquirer* story was going to do to him. The only way to save his career was to pay Callie whatever she wanted and get her to cooperate. Maddy had already talked with David. She told him to pay Callie off. He said, what, 'Over my dead body' or something like that?"

"It seemed like David had his own score to settle with Callie," Madeleine said. "He refused to budge."

"Jimmy might have paid her, if only we could have presented our case to him. He might have listened to us. He certainly doesn't care about the money. I'm not sure what Callie wanted, but—"

"Twenty million," I said.

"I know that sounds like a lot to you, Greg," Julianna said, "but Jimmy wouldn't even miss it. If we had prevailed, maybe Callie wouldn't be dead now."

"Are you saying Jimmy had something to do with it?" I said.

"No," Julianna said. "Not at all. I have no idea who did it. But it had to be someone who thought they were looking out for Jimmy's interests. I don't know anything about it."

"Okay," I said. "Let me get this straight, for the record. Madeleine, you picked Julianna up from Rex last night—early this morning—just after I finished talking with her, right?"

"That's right. Sometime around four in the morning."

"And you left together in your Infiniti coupe, leaving Julianna's Ferrari in the Rex parking lot."

"Oh, you noticed my car," Julianna said. "Yes, we left it."

"Where did the two of you go from there?"

"We came into the city," Madeleine said. She had wiped the tears from her cheeks, spreading dark makeup and mascara. "Back to this apartment. We haven't left. I called you this morning once I heard the news about Callie."

"Who told you about Callie?"

"Jimmy. He was here for a few hours today. I called you to see if you knew anything that might be of help to him."

"I tried calling earlier," I said. "No one picked up."

"Jimmy was catching up on his sleep," Julianna said. "Maddy and I must have been in the shower."

Madeleine glared at her and gave her a kick under the table.   The cat had dozed off in her lap and was disturbed by the sudden movement. It changed positions and went back to sleep.

"I should be going," I said.

"Now we've embarrassed him," Julianna said.

"No, you haven't. I've still got a boy to find."

"Poor Jason. I wish I could help you, Greg."

"You don't know what Jimmy might have done with him?"

"No, sorry."

"Would Jimmy tell you if you asked him?"

"I doubt it. And maybe he doesn't know."

"All the worse for Jason if he doesn't. Good day, ladies."

Twenty-Seven

Todd Curwen lived on West Eleventh Street between Fifth and Sixth, in what a lifelong New Yorker once described to me as "ruling-class territory." Some owners of red-brick townhouses here went to great trouble to have a facade of faux brownstone slapped up, but even I could tell which ones were fake. Curwen's house, however, was a genuine brownstone with a discreet brass plaque quietly announcing the year of its birth: 1848. Some of these town houses were divided into high-priced apartments, but many were single-family dwellings. I'd walked past plenty of times at twilight, when the owners turned the interior lights on and parted the drapes so passersby could peep in and drool over the original ceilings, plaster moldings, antique chandeliers, crowded bookcases, and working fireplaces. Short of winning the New York lottery, I had no hope of ever owning one. They had asking prices in the several millions.

Finding a parking space on the street wasn't difficult; people who lived here tended to go away to their country houses on weekends, especially in the summer. I locked my copy of Loeb's blue file in the glove compartment, then locked up the 'Cuda.

The steep stone steps felt gritty and solid beneath my boots. The original brownstone balustrade was chipped in a few spots, weathered only slightly in the last hundred-fifty years.

I pressed the buzzer. Mounted on the wall within the foyer was a video surveillance camera aimed directly at me. Curwen might see me coming, but he would have no time to prepare a story to put me off. The voice that came back at me over the intercom was at once bitchy and lackadaisical:

"Oh, it's you. Hold on, I'll send someone to get the door."

Curwen's response was anticlimactic. I'd been expecting surprise. Perhaps he was doing a good job of masking it.

The door was opened for me by a young Puerto Rican man, probably no more than twenty-two, with a slim dark face and eyes that were waiting to be discovered. His hair was pomaded flat against his skull, and he was dressed in black trousers and a white Nehru jacket. I gathered he was the houseboy. If he played his cards right with Curwen and put a little more meat on his bones, he could end up as the newest lifeguard on *Baywatch* next season.

"You're Mr. Quaintance?" he said, almost inaudibly. He would need some lessons in projection as well. "I'm Angel. Please come in. Mr. Curwen will see you upstairs in his office."

Angel went up the stairs with a slight swaying of his hips. That would have to be corrected if he wanted the job on *Baywatch*, but I liked it the way it was. As a matter of fact, I would have liked to see an effeminate queer lifeguard on *Baywatch*.

I followed Angel into Curwen's office and entered a twilight zone between tacky and tasteful. The walls were painted a deadly shade of pumpkin, the trim and moldings yellow squash. Pale marble statues stood on pedestals in corners and in the nook by the fireplace: the disembodied head of a beautiful Greek youth; a bust of some Roman emperor with a beard and a chipped nose; and the headless, limbless torso of a Roman centurion in a cuirass.

In the sunlight of the south-facing bay window was a wide marble-topped desk cluttered with color snapshots in cheap frames standing at various angles like sailboats crammed into a marina. Each showed Curwen snuggling up with some famous celebrity. I assumed these were his clients. Several pictures were of him with Jimmy Gilbert. In one, a drunken Curwen with his mouth hanging half open was throwing one arm around Jimmy and the other around Jason Blassingame, both of whom wore dark sunglasses and appeared completely oblivious to the world.

Curwen was nowhere to be seen. I asked Angel about this.

"He was down in the gym," Angel muttered, drilling me with his doelike eyes. "I'll go find out what's keeping him."

Angel turned around and undulated back down the stairs.

I stood there and waited, admiring the cuirass.

I was idly pinching the cold nipple on the centurion's left breastplate when Curwen entered. Angel pulled the door softly closed behind him, leaving us alone.

"Forgive me, Greg," Curwen said, scratching behind his ears with a towel. His bristly, close-cropped hair was damp with sweat. "I was just finishing my workout."

Curwen was wearing a slight spaghetti-strap tank top that revealed ample chest hair carefully landscaped by electrolysis. The tank top failed to meet the waistband of a miniature pair of shimmering blue spandex workout shorts that were tight enough to tell me he didn't believe in jockstraps. He had a flat tummy and tight abs that made me begin to revise downward my previous estimate of his age. Curwen wiped the towel across his chest and along the insides of his thighs before grabbing a seat on one of the two leather sofas flanking the marble-topped coffee table.

"You're forgiven," I said.

"I wasn't expecting you. You should have called first."

"After what happened to me last night, I wasn't so sure you'd see me. I believe you know what I'm talking about."

Curwen motioned me over. "Sit down and let's discuss it."

I crossed the Persian rug (a complementary butternut squash). The thin wood flooring creaked beneath my feet. I wondered whether Curwen had bothered to get the old floor slats reinforced before he had all this marble dragged up here.

I claimed the sofa opposite him and bumped my knee against the rough-hewn edge of the coffee table. The marble was about four inches thick and slightly weatherbeaten, its surface nicked and gouged. The scratches were caked with a dark substance.

"This looks fairly old," I said, digging up flakes with my fingernail that were rusty like dried blood. "A Roman altar?"

"Not that old," Curwen said, rubbing his palms across it lovingly. "But it is a treasure. My decorator discovered it for me. It was once a work table in the kitchen of the old Delmonico's, about a hundred years ago. A number of turtles must have lost their heads on it on their way to becoming soup."

"Is that so?" I pretended to be impressed. I was skeptical of Curwen's decorator. More likely it had been a cold hard slab in the dissection room at Bellevue, not quite a century ago.

"I admire the way you handled my boy." Curwen wound his towel into a tight snake and threw it across his shoulders, leaning back against the upholstery. He spread his thighs; his basket fell into the breach as if loaded with ball bearings.

"Your houseboy?" I said, playing stupid. "Angel?"

"No." Curwen was both confused and annoyed. "I'm talking about Pete Denneny. The boy meant you no harm, of course."

"Of course not. That was you."

"I only wanted him to scare you." Curwen folded his hands behind his head, exposing neat tufts of dark hair in his armpits. "I certainly didn't expect that you'd send poor Pete to the E.R."

"Life's full of dislocated shoulders," I said.

"Pete didn't give you that bump on the head, did he?" Curwen stared with mock concern at my stitched-up pate.

"No," I said, "but he left a nice little bruise where he tickled me with his pistol, between my tenth and eleventh ribs. Care to see it?"

"Thanks, no. It must take nerve to disarm a man who's got a loaded gun at your back."

"Not nerve, just dumb luck."

"Don't sell yourself short," he said like an inspirational guru. "Where'd you learn those moves, anyway?"

"Fort Bliss. Just basic steps. Wouldn't have done me much good against a real killer. Where'd you dig up Pistol Pete?"

"Oh, he was good enough for my purposes. I told you, I didn't want him to harm you. I didn't think it would require a Green Beret. If it looked like Amateur Hour to you, that's because it was. I'm not in the business of threatening people."

"Then what was that? Shits and grins?"

Curwen laughed.

I sat there and waited for him to explain himself.

"I didn't know how far I could trust you," he said. "Look what happened when David got Angelo Ferrante mixed up in this. How was I to know you wouldn't jerk us around like Ferrante? I didn't even see why David needed you. I wanted you to get lost and let us handle our own problems."

"Happy families are all alike, I guess."

That threw him. "Anyway, the point is now moot."

"Why's that?"

"Because of what happened to Callie Blassingame."

"You look almost gleeful," I told him.

He shook his head in protest. "Not at all."

"But you're suggesting that Callie's murder solved all of Jimmy's problems."

"Oh, sure, I'd say so, yes—and I don't mean to imply that I had any hand in it—but it does make things a lot easier for all concerned."

"Not for Callie," I pointed out. "And whoever killed her."

"I'd put my money on Troy," he said a little too quickly.

"You have something against Troy?"

"No, nothing per se."

"If you do, I'd like to hear it."

"Come, Greg, isn't it always the husband?"

"Yeah," I said. "In England it's the butler. Here it's the husband. Just like your client Hugo Wallis."

"Who happened to be acquitted." Curwen was smug.

"That's a rousing defense if ever I heard one."

"I still say you should look into Troy."

"I'm sure the police are taking care of it," I said. "I'm concerned about finding Jason. It could be a matter of life or death for the boy. Whoever killed Callie might not stop there."

Curwen shrugged. "Then Jason will live or die no matter what I say, because I know nothing."

"You don't have any idea where he is?"

"I certainly don't, but I'm sure Jimmy does."

"Last night he claimed he didn't."

"Then he was lying," Curwen said knowingly. "Trust me."

"Trust you? That's a good one. You're sure that Jason was never at Jimmy's house last night?"

"Not to my knowledge, and I would have known."

"How about Jimmy's apartment, here in the city?" I asked. I'd already proved to my satisfaction that Jason wasn't there, but I wanted to know what Curwen thought of the idea. "Jimmy could have given him the key, couldn't he?"

"Sure, but I doubt you'll find Jason there."

"Why not?"

"Because Madeleine Downey should be there now, and that penthouse isn't big enough for the two of them."

"Oil and water?"

"Think of the cat fights between Krystle and Alexis on *Dynasty*," Curwen said. "Name-calling and mud-slinging."

"Madeleine's jealous of a teenage boy?" I acted incredulous.

"Why not? Jimmy *is* her husband."

"Look, Curwen, even my hairdresser knows that marriage is a sham. You arranged it, you should know better than anyone."

"I assure you, they married out of love. Didn't you see their public kiss at the Oscars?"

"Nicely staged," I said. "I'm not buying it. Madeleine was already a client of yours before she married Jimmy, and she married him to further her career. So why should Madeleine be jealous if Jimmy chooses to place his affection elsewhere?"

"All I can say is that Maddy truly loves Jimmy. I will admit she's had a difficult time adjusting to living with him."

"Why is that?"

"They're both used to getting their way, but Jimmy is like an immovable object. For the first time in her life, Maddy's been the one who has to give in to someone else, and she doesn't like it very much. It's gotten worse the last month or so."

"Ever since Jason came home from school?"

"Yes," Curwen acknowledged. "Jimmy's been spending a lot of, shall we say, quality time with Jason. He's the kid's godfather, you know. He really enjoys their time together."

"I'll bet he does," I said.

"It does Jimmy a world of good. I've tried to get Maddy to see how happy it makes Jimmy to be with Jason. Whatever Jimmy and Jason do together shouldn't make any difference to her, as long as all the public sees is Jimmy and Maddy as a couple."

"Madeleine doesn't agree with you, obviously."

"No."

"Maybe it makes a difference to her that her husband has been fucking a fourteen-year-old boy every chance he can get."

"I have no knowledge of what Jimmy and Jason do or don't do when they're behind closed doors."

"From a legal perspective, you don't. If any statutory rape has been committed, I'm sure you won't be held culpable. Don't you think perhaps Madeleine's upset because she's being used?"

"Models are used to being used," Curwen said. "It's their job. They're paid for their image. Their image sells the product. In this case, the product is Jimmy. We're using her to sell him. She shouldn't be bothered by that."

"You hired her to be Jimmy's wife."

"That is *not* what I'm saying."

"Jimmy's been fine at selling himself all these years. Why did you suddenly think you needed to attach a woman's face to him? To make him seem masculine by comparison? My hairdresser pointed out to me that the macho image Jimmy projects in his newest video doesn't even fit the song."

"Every artist goes through phases," Curwen said. "Look at David Bowie, Elton John, Madonna. Jimmy's no different. Madonna had a baby, for Christ's sake!"

"I'm sure it wasn't for His sake."

"If Jimmy wants to be more of a man and act macho for a while and get himself a wife, why shouldn't he?"

"You're trying to pass it all off as Jimmy's idea?"

"It was. As Jimmy's manager, I'm working for him. It's not the other way around. Jimmy wants to get married, I try to find a suitable match. No celebrity marriage is ever going to be like *Ozzie and Harriet*. They're always going to be thinking of their careers first. Robert Taylor and Barbara Stanwyck had a marriage of convenience. He was a flaming queen, and she was king of the bull dykes. They both got what they wanted out of it."

"Are you trying to say Madeleine Downey's a lesbian?"

"You're missing my point." Curwen shook his head as if cleaning out cobwebs. He'd nearly said too much. "I'm saying you shouldn't be so shocked. It's the way it's always been in show business. I guess it's easy for you to act high and mighty. Not everybody can afford to be out of the closet like you, Greg."

"You're pretty far out yourself, aren't you?" I asked.

"Yes, but my situation's no different from yours. Nobody outside of show business knows who I am. They could care less."

"So you managers and agents and other hangers-on—all you people who make a cottage industry out of a celebrity's career—you can live your lives however you want, but the stars you're leeching off of have to keep their real selves hidden, on the assumption that their fans will turn on them and their careers will be over. That's what you mean by the way it's always been in show business."

"I'm not sure what point you're trying to make," Curwen said. "Are you suggesting that Jimmy should make it known to the world that he has a taste for young boys?"

"Does he?"

"You'd have to ask him. I didn't say that he does."

"You *were* worried that it was going to get out, weren't you? And you thought that getting him married to one of the most beautiful women in the world would be an adequate counterweight."

"A precautionary measure only."

"But all you were worried about was some kind of leak to the press. You weren't prepared for Callie Blassingame's threats. Not even a real marriage would have protected Jimmy from a criminal complaint of statutory rape."

"Well, we no longer have to worry about that, do we!"

"You know, for a guy who's already seen one client go through an entire murder trial, you seem to be taking Jimmy Gilbert's current predicament in stride."

"What predicament?" Curwen sat forward. "What are you talking about?"

"I can't believe nobody told you."

"Told me what?"

"Jimmy's been charged with Callie's murder."

"That's insane! When did this happen?"

"Earlier this afternoon. David Loeb was with Jimmy when they arrested him. You mean David didn't call you?"

"No, he didn't, damn it! And I take it you weren't sent over here to tell me, either!"

"No, I wasn't. I came over because I'm looking for Jason."

"This really burns me up! David's been acting strangely all week, and now this!"

"When did David start acting strangely?"

"When Hugo Wallis dropped him. There's still the civil trial coming up, and David could have made a second fortune off that. Hugo dropped him like a hot potato."

"I thought Hugo Wallis was out of cash."

"Well, yes and no," Curwen said. "There are book deals, speaking engagements, a few other projects pending. Hugo may be having a cash flow problem right now, but he's got money coming."

"Why exactly did Wallis drop him?"

"That I don't know. It happened out of the blue, Tuesday.

David was upset not to be cut in on the civil trial, but I'm surprised he would let it cloud his judgment on other matters."

"What makes you say his judgment has been clouded?"

"The way he's handled this thing with Callie. I've never experienced a breakdown in communication like the one David and I have had over this. We've got Jimmy's South American tour coming up. After that he's shooting his first feature film out in L.A. He's already cut a few tracks for his next CD, but it's far from being completed. If Callie made good her threats, Jimmy would have been tied up in a criminal proceeding for months—maybe a full year—and the outcome was anything but assured. Jimmy has commitments. He's booked. David's bungling has hurt us badly."

"Now it looks like Jimmy will be facing another kind of criminal proceeding. I'm sure none of you want that."

"Jimmy facing murder charges? Of course not! That's the worst thing that could happen! Jimmy didn't tell the police about Callie's threats, did he?"

"I wouldn't know. I'm sure David wouldn't have allowed him to discuss it. That would be Jimmy's only motive, wouldn't it?"

"Motive?" Curwen was appalled. "Jimmy couldn't possibly have any motive to commit any crime of violence against anybody! You don't understand what kind of a man he is."

"Everyone keeps telling me that. None of you people seem to think that Jimmy is capable of doing anything for himself."

Curwen stood up. He went over and looked out the bay window and closed the venetian blinds, cutting out the sunlight. The room was made considerably darker, with only one floor lamp alight. Curwen stared at me over the sea of framed snapshots.

"Come over here," he said.

"What for?"

"Indulge me."

"Okay." I got up and came around the desk, but I kept a certain distance between us.

"I like you despite myself," Curwen said.

"Is that a come-on?"

"Make of it whatever you like. I admire your style, Greg. You've really grabbed this case by the horns. David hired you to talk to Callie, to try to get her to drop her threats. Now he's got you looking for Jason. Ostensibly, that's why you came to see me. You say it's a life or death situation, but I don't see you engaged in any frantic search for the boy. Instead, you're doing all you can to dig up dirt on Jimmy Gilbert."

"You're eminently unqualified to tell me how to do my job."

"Don't get me wrong." Curwen took a step closer. "I told you I admire your style. You're good at what you do. I'm sure much better than what David thought when he hired you."

"What do you mean by that?"

"I've known David a long time. I know him much better than you do. He compartmentalizes everything. I'm sure all he wants you to do is find Jason Blassingame. Nothing more, nothing less. He doesn't want you digging into Jimmy's marriage. He doesn't want you talking with Julianna or nosing around in my affairs. He certainly doesn't want you solving Callie's murder. In fact, I'm sure David has no idea of all this extra work you've been doing for him while you're on his payroll. I have half a mind to call him up right now and tell him."

"Everything I've done has been to help me find Jason," I said. "I'm sure David would approve."

Curwen shook his head. "No, he wouldn't. I know him. He expects you to go out there, find Jason, and bring him in. You're too inquisitive. You already know too much for your own good. David trusted Ferrante because he always knew where to draw the line. For some reason, he suddenly went bad and turned on us. David would be surprised to find out that you're going the same route. All he was hoping for was that you'd fulfill your mission. Then, when you're through, he was probably hoping for a good fuck, a little taste of what Tay got."

"I doubt that. David's been strictly professional."

"Would you like to make a bet on that? David told me himself that he hired you on the recommendation of Tay Farrell. Not that you did anything so extraordinary for Tay. All you ever did for Tay was act as bodyguard and bouncer for a couple of parties, consult with him about his home security arrangements, and get in a few wild fucks with him on the side."

"You spoke with Tay?" I felt my face grow warm with blood.

"I know all about you and Tay, straight from the horsecock's mouth. I know what you like, how you like it, how long and hard you want it. Tay said you're a real slut—talented, too."

Curwen was catching me off guard. Before I could see it coming, he had reached out and grabbed my crotch in his fist. He squeezed tighter, looking up at me with a wide smile.

"Let go," I said, grabbing his wrist.

He did as I said, frowning at my resistance.

"What I did with Tay I did on my own time, off duty, because I liked him. He didn't pay me for it. Right now I'm working. I don't have time for this shit."

"What if I paid you to drop the case? Then you'd be off duty, and I could take you upstairs and see what you're like."

"You couldn't pay me to drop the case, Curwen."

"I'll double whatever David's paying you. I'll take my checkbook out of my desk right now and cut you a check for all your trouble. The least you can do is reward me with a fuck."

"I'm not interested in your money," I said. "Or your cock."

"It's only sex."

"No means no."

"It was worth a shot."

"You're confusing the issue, Curwen. This isn't about sex. You want me off the case. I'd like to know why."

"I'll tell you what, I'll write you the check, plus I'll set you up with all my best clients. You can be their security consultant. It could make your career."

"That sounds okay except for what I'd have to do for it."

"You don't have to go to bed with me if you don't want."

"I'm talking about Jason Blassingame. You want me to forget about his well-being and whore myself out to your clients."

"These are some of the top names in show business. You'd become very rich, very fast. Soon, you'd start doing work for other celebrities who aren't my clients. You can't lose."

Curwen sat down at his desk and pulled a ledger out of a drawer. He opened it up and armed himself with a fountain pen. He dated a check and signed it, leaving the amount blank.

"Just tell me how much," he said.

"And the only condition is that I drop the case?"

"That's right. Come on, Greg, how much is it worth?"

I was more interested in how much it was worth to him. The money was tempting. I don't know of anyone who wouldn't be tempted by the money. The guarantee of steady, lucrative work wasn't bad, either. I wasn't sure how far I could trust Curwen's word, but the idea of it was certainly appealing.

"Give me the check," I said. "Let me look at it."

Curwen ripped out the blank check and handed it over.

I tore the check in half, then again, and handed it back.

"I don't think I could live with myself," I said. "Sorry."

"I'm sorry, too, Greg," Curwen said glumly. He pressed a button on his speaker phone but didn't say anything into it.

The door squeaked as it opened behind me. I hadn't realized I had my back to the door. I turned around quickly.

"Slowly, Mr. Quaintance," said Angel, who was standing just inside the doorway holding a .45 Magnum revolver on me. He held it expertly, with a steady hand and dead aim. His voice was just as soft as ever. "Hands in the air."

I did as I was told—slowly.

Curwen stood up behind me and said, "You got a gun on you?"

"In my shoulder holster," I said, keeping my eyes on Angel.

"Good boy, Angel," Curwen said, reaching around the left side of my chest and pulling my Glock from its holster. "You keep that gun on him until I tell you to stop. You got that?"

"Yes, boss," Angel said.

Curwen held my Glock in his right hand and patted me down with his left. I could tell he'd never done it before. He was more inexpert at it than Peter Denneny. Rather than briskly patting my flesh, he groped at it. When he came to my crotch, he grabbed the whole bundle in his fist again and squeezed hard.

If it weren't for Angel, I could have easily taken Curwen. I wasn't entirely sure Angel was ready to follow through and shoot me, but I wasn't willing to take the chance.

"Okay," Curwen said. He shoved me in the middle of the back. "Go stand on the other side of the coffee table. Slowly!"

I went and stood in the clearest spot, near the edge of the Persian rug, in between the emperor and the headless centurion. Curwen stayed close behind, and Angel carefully followed me with the .45 Magnum.

"Now turn around," Curwen said.

I turned to face him. He wasn't far away, and he had my Glock trained steadily, aimed directly at my chest.

"Now take off your clothes," he said.

"What have you got to hide, Curwen?" I said. "What could be so important that you'd resort to this?"

"This isn't the time for you to talk, Greg. You wouldn't play ball. Now you're going to do what I say. I told you to take off all that Gaulthier shit. Now move!"

I'd cleaned that gun and loaded the bullets myself, and I wasn't eager to be on the receiving end of a hollow-point slug. I removed the one-button jacket and let it fall to the floor. I slithered out of my shoulder holster. I unbuttoned the shirt and took it off, and the undershirt as well.

"So far so good. Now the rest." Curwen wiggled the muzzle of the Glock in the direction of my crotch. He was smiling.

I slipped out of the boots and socks and pulled off the jeans, naturally hesitating before proceeding further.

"Don't be shy. Show me what you showed Tay."

I pulled off the briefs and added them to the pile of clothes on the floor.

"Disappointing," Curwen said, *ts*king. "Maybe it's just gun shy. Now spread your legs. Hands behind your head."

I did all that. It was easy enough. I was more worried about what was going to come next. I found out soon enough.

"Angel, honey," Curwen said.

"Yes, boss?"

"Go upstairs and get the bag."

"The bag, sure," Angel said. "And some clothesline?"

"No, no, the coarse stuff, the hemp."

"Right, boss, the hemp!" Angel laughed. He turned the .45 over to Curwen and looked me over with a leer of anticipation.

Twenty-Eight

I tried to talk them out of it. Before I got very far, Angel stuffed one of my own socks in my mouth and secured it with a few wraps of rope. He pulled it painfully tight and secured it in back with a complex knot, then set about expertly tying my wrists behind my back. The rough hemp bit tight enough to screw with my circulation. My protests came out as animalistic grunts. Curwen didn't let that go on for long; once my hands were fixed behind me, Angel held me up while Curwen pistol-whipped me across the face with my Glock. When I recovered from the blow and met Curwen's eyes, I saw on his face the rapturous grin of the true sadist.

The bag Curwen had asked for lay in a lump on the floor where Angel had dumped it alongside my piled clothes. It was made of gray canvas like a postal bag but was reinforced along the bottom, sides, and collar with wide strips of black leather. The canvas was pierced in spots by metal grommets. The collar had a drawstring and a short leather belt that could be secured around it with a padlock. This was no regular postal bag; mail doesn't need to breathe or be locked in to keep it from getting out.

"You should have taken the check," Curwen said.

He pushed down on my shoulders while Angel kicked me behind the knee. I would have fallen to the floor, but Angel caught me by the arms and lowered me carefully. He looped more hemp tightly around my ankles and tied it off, leaving a length of it free. He made me sit with my knees up against my chest, took the end of the rope from my ankles, and tied it around my neck, pulling my head forward as far as it would go. One last length of hemp was used to tie my shins together just below my knees.

Angel double-checked all his knots to make sure they held, pinching and prodding my flesh while he was at it. Finally, he pushed me over onto my back. Curwen pulled open the collar of the bag and threw it over my feet. Together, he and Angel worked it partway around me. They sat me up again, pulled the bag the rest of the way up over my head, cinched the drawstring, and locked the belt tightly around it, leaving a hole at the top about the size of my wrist. The grommets were at too inconvenient a height for me to see out of them, and they let in little light. The inside of the bag was musky with leather and sweat.

"Careful now, Greg," Curwen said. "Struggle too much and that rope at your neck will cut off your air. We're going to take you out and deliver you somewhere like a load of laundry."

With a bit of a struggle, they lifted me up, out of Curwen's office, and down the stairs. They stopped in the foyer.

"Once we're outside, don't move," Curwen said. "You don't want to draw attention to yourself. We could just as easily dump you in the East River as deliver you to our friend. Got that?"

They carried me outside. I heard them open a car door that sounded suspiciously familiar. They deposited me in the front passenger seat and shut the door. Curwen and Angel got in on the driver's side. Angel sat in back, directly behind me, and stuck the muzzle of his .45 into my ribs.

Curwen turned the ignition key, and the big engine roared to life. They were taking me in the 'Cuda. I wanted to kill them.

*   *   *

My sense of direction was always keen. Even out in the Saudi desert, when I was on patrol duty and got caught in a sudden dust storm, I never grew confused about my location. I hardly ever had to use a compass. Once I moved to Manhattan, I found it slightly disorienting because the streets didn't run directly north-south and east-west. The sun would skim across the sky and show up in places where it didn't seem to belong. After about a month, I grew to where I could navigate through any neighborhood, even in lower Manhattan where everything fell off the grid.

I could tell that after leaving West Eleventh Street, we crossed Fifth Avenue to University Place. Curwen made a left, taking us to Fourteenth Street, where he went right. We went around Union Square and onto Park Avenue South, heading uptown. This was confirmed when I felt us riding up the ramp at Pershing Square and taking the loop around Grand Central Terminal. From there, it was a straight shot north on Park Avenue. After that, I got lost; it was impossible to know how fast we were moving, and the constant stopping for traffic made me dizzy.

All I knew was we were moving on up to the East Side.

Curwen turned into what seemed like an alley or loading area; the rumble of the 'Cuda's engine echoed closely off the walls. We came to a stop. Curwen shut off the engine and pressed the ratchety emergency brake.

"I'm going inside to talk with our friend," Curwen said. "Angel's staying here to keep you company, so don't you move."

Curwen got out and pounded loudly on a metal door—what I presumed was some kind of service entrance. I couldn't hear what he said to the person who let him in. The door slammed shut.

"You like it in the bag, Mr. Quaintance?" Angel whispered to me. The muzzle of his gun turned loving, caressing the canvas up and down my flank.

I wouldn't be baited into making a noise. It was more than likely Angel would take after his boss and pistol-whip me for it.

"You're hot." Angel poked the tip of the revolver through one of the grommets and stroked my flesh with the cold steel. "I don't know why the boss don't want to keep you for himself. We could have brought you up to his playroom and hung you from a hook until he was ready to use you. I bet you never seen anything like his layout, man. He got enough toys to keep you entertained for a long time, maybe leave some tasty whip marks down that nice back of yours. It's a real shame. I bet you would have liked it, too. Boss told me all about you and Tay Farrell. Tay told him you're a slut, and I bet he's right. You take it up the ass? You like it rough? I bet you do, yeah. Boss says loaded guns turn you on. That's wild, man. Guns get me hot, too. I saw that cock of yours twitch when Todd hit you. Yeah, I bet you're ready for a real adventure. I don't get why Todd wants to hand you over to someone else. But it's his show."

I worried that Angel's gun lust might lead to an itchy trigger finger and a premature firing. But I was spared.

Curwen returned and asked Angel to help him carry me inside.

The light that filtered in from my new surroundings was stark white, fluorescent. The air smelled of bleach and antiseptic.

I was taken into a room. The collar of the bag was unlocked and widened. They grabbed the bottom of the bag and dumped me out on the floor of a medical examination room.

"Hey, boss," Angel said, "this guy into medical trips?"

"Shut up!" Curwen said.

"I was just asking." Angel was hurt.

"I said shut up. Now help me get him on the table."

Angel took out a pocketknife and cut the rope tying my neck to my ankles. He cut loose the ropes binding my wrists, and at first I thought of making some desperate move. I couldn't. My hands were numb, and the strain on my shoulders left my arms too stiff to move. My arms would be okay in a few minutes.

I didn't have a few minutes. Curwen and Angel lifted me up onto the examination table and cinched my wrists into brown leather straps on either side. Angel cut the ropes at my knees and ankles but quickly rebound my ankles with leather straps at the end of the table. A strap was tightened around my waist and another at my neck. They left the uncomfortable gag in place.

"We're finished now, Greg," Curwen said. "And I'm washing my hands of you. I'm going to turn out these lights and give you some time to rest and build up your strength. You may need it."

Angel went out the door smiling wickedly, fantasizing already about the wild sexual trip he thought I was embarking on.

Curwen knew better, and his face was grimmer. He shut off the lights and became a silhouette as he shut the door.

After that, dead silence.

Twenty-Nine

I tried to get free, but the straps held fast. I managed to rock the table. I had an idea where I was, and I didn't like it. I almost nodded off and had to force myself to stay awake; falling asleep with a sock tied in your mouth was an excellent way of choking to death. I had little idea how much time was passing.

The door opened and the lights came on, momentarily blinding me. The door closed. By the time my eyes adjusted, I found myself staring into the puffy, tired eyes of a man in a surgical cap and mask. He wore a blue smock that was smeared with blood, as if he'd just been engaged in butchering a large animal.

I grunted into my gag, hoping he'd get the message that I wanted him to remove it. He paid no attention. He was staring down at me, examining my face. His mask alternately puffed out and drew back against his lips. His breathing was rapid, almost to the point of hyperventilating. He did not appear calm.

I smelled a strong odor of alcohol on his breath.

"Hugo, Hugo," he whispered. It was Troy Blassingame.

He brought his right hand out from behind his back. He wore a latex glove streaked with blood, some of it dried, some fresh. He held an unclean scalpel in a wildly trembling hand.

"Thought I was finished with you, Hugo," Blassingame said.

I made the loudest noise I could. Blassingame ignored me and brought the blade up to my face. My eyes followed it as it hovered over me, wavering. The scalpel halted above my nose.

"Wait," Blassingame said, seeming to recognize me. "You?"

I made another noise and nodded my head encouragingly.

Blassingame seemed to come back to himself for a moment. The scalpel withdrew from my face. He surveyed me like I was a thorny problem. The blood on his smock smelled noxious.

"Misunderstood, maybe I—" Blassingame said, but his voice seemed remote. I got the impression he was not talking to me. "She told him to. Told Todd to have me—"

I shook at my bonds and rattled the table.

"Take care of you," Blassingame said. "Todd, yes. He spoke to her. So tired. Should do what he says, and yet—"

I shook my head to indicate that he shouldn't.

"No sleep," he muttered. "And Callie. Christ, Callie—"

A drop of blood fell from his scalpel onto my neck.

"Hugo, Hugo, we all scream for Hugo." Blassingame's languid eyes crinkled at the corners. Behind the mask, he was smiling. He began to giggle. "Killed his wife. Too recognizable. Can't stand it anymore. We're giving him a new face, she says—"

His right hand came back up, holding the blade over my eyes. He laid his left hand on top of my head. It was wet and sticky.

"So easy," he said. "New face for the wife killer."

The scalpel shook back and forth in his hand.

"Do this, do that," Blassingame said disgustedly. "Story of my life. Give him a new face! Like it's that easy! She says I have no choice. Because of Jimmy. So I give him a new face—"

Blassingame snatched his hands away from me.

"Anesthesic! Almost forgot. Nurse! Nurse!"

Blassingame darted his gaze around the examination room. He set the scalpel down on the formica countertop near the door.

I made another noisy attempt to get his attention.

Blassingame looked at me again and seemed to come back to awareness. He pulled the mask down from his face, smearing blood on his cheek. He blinked his bloodshot eyes. He looked weary.

"Someone playing a joke? You? You're not him, you're that detective. . . . Todd talked to her, yes, she asked me to take care of you. I won't! Who does he think he is, asking me to do *that*? Aren't you that fellow who wanted to find my son?"

I nodded adamantly.

"Where is he?" Blassingame stepped forward threateningly. "Where is Jason? What have you done to my boy, you, you . . ."

He shook his head violently and took a step back.

"Oh, Christ." His voice was faltering. He stared down at his shaking hands and tore off the filthy gloves. He stepped on the pedal of the garbage can and dropped them in, shuddering. He stood at the sink and scrubbed his hands thoroughly, then worked the lather up his forearms. He went about it for three minutes.

When he turned around, he was holding his hands up in the air as if expecting somebody to dry them for him.

"Where is my nurse? Nurse! Nurse!"

Blassingame grabbed a towel for himself and dried his arms.

"Day off, that's right," he muttered. "No wonder. Patient wasn't prepped. Have to go ahead without her. No more time!"

I was losing him again. If I lost him, I lost me.

"Oh, Christ, what the devil time is it? Where's my watch?"

He opened drawers aimlessly, pulling out packages of swabs and bandages and syringes. Finally, he looked up at the clock on the wall. It was 7:30.

"Must be wearing off by now. Hugo must be coming out of it. He's going to feel it. Want to see the look on his face!"

Blassingame looked at me and began cackling.

"Face?" He turned to the mirror and smiled. *"What face!"*

From another room, I heard glass shattering and a man screaming. The scream became a roar. Objects hit the walls.

"What have I done?" Blassingame said, looking at his hands.

I bucked against the table, trying to get his attention.

But Blassingame was far gone.

He stared at the door and backed up against the wall.

"He's coming," Blassingame said. "Hide, hide!"

Something banged against the door.

The knob turned, and the door swung open.

A man came in. He had no skin from his collarbone up. The entire structure of the face and neck was exposed—red striated muscles, white tendons, the cartilage of the nasal cavity. There were no lips to hide the grinning teeth. The eye sockets were fully open with no eyelids. He had no hair, no scalp—just a mass of flesh above the neck of a bloodstained gown.

"Troy, what have you done to me?" It was a practiced voice. A trained voice. An actor's voice. I knew it from the soap opera he was in before he went on trial for murdering his wife. It was Hugo Wallis. *"What have you done to me?"*

Blassingame shrunk away and screamed, closing his eyes.

Wallis grabbed the bloody scalpel from the countertop and buried it deep in Blassingame's sternum.

Blassingame lurched forward, clutching at Wallis's gown and spraying blood in a stream as he fell face-first on the floor.

Wallis caught his own reflection in the mirror and smashed it with his fist. He turned his attention to me, breathing heavily. Pus, blood, and clear fluids oozed from his face.

"I had to do it," Wallis said. "Look what he did to me!"

I made a sympathetic noise and shook at my bonds.

"I don't know you." Wallis undid the strap on my right wrist. "And you can't know me. You can undo the rest yourself."

Wallis turned away from me. "I'm glad I got to you in time," he said, and fled the room.

I untied the gag and unbuckled the rest of the straps.

I heard Wallis out in the lobby of the clinic, cursing and screaming and smashing the mirrors. The glass tinkled to the floor. Then, no sound at all. I hoped Hugo was gone. I couldn't know for sure.

I stepped off the table and into a pool of warm blood.

Thirty

I went over to the sink and washed my foot and scrubbed away the blood drips and smears on my head and neck. I stepped carefully around Blassingame's body and all the blood and left the room.

Under ordinary circumstances, I would have phoned the police and remained on the scene to render an accounting. They would be here soon enough, whether I called or not. Hugo Wallis wasn't going to get very far on the outside looking the way he did. If he knew what was good for him, he would head straight to the emergency department at Mt. Sinai up the block. He was bound to tell them who had done his face, and where.

I didn't have much time.

He might have tripped a security alarm. I found the control box behind the receptionist's desk, but I saw that no one had turned it on. The receptionist's computer was asleep beneath a frosty plastic dustcover. I made a check of each room at the clinic but found no one else around.

The large operating room across the hall was dripping with blood. Blassingame's footprints marked paths around the head of the operating table where Wallis had lain. Floating in a bucket of ice water was a whole-head mask of flesh that had been Hugo Wallis's famous face.

I went into Blassingame's private office and turned on the lights. A red plastic garbage bag sat in the middle of his desk. White lettering all over the bag said: HAZARDOUS MATERIALS – MEDICAL WASTE – TO BE DESTROYED. I went to an empty examination room and found a pair of latex gloves. I put them on, went back to the bag, and opened it up, steeling myself for more gore.

Instead, it was my clothing, wallet, boots, shoulder holster, and pistol—everything Todd Curwen had relieved me of except the keys to the 'Cuda. Curwen must have expected Blassingame to dispose of my effects along with my person.

I removed the latex gloves and put on my clothes. I checked my Glock to confirm I still had a round in the cylinder and took out the clip to make sure it was still full. I replaced the Glock in my shoulder holster and put on my jacket.

Blassingame's office contained several filing cabinets, all locked. I wanted a peek at his files. I put the latex gloves back on to avoid leaving fingerprints. I checked the top drawer of Blassingame's desk but found no keys. I went back to the examination room and stooped over his body, carefully avoiding the blood. I lifted up his smock, reached into his pockets, and found a key ring with keys of all sizes, jangling.

I went back and hastily tried the smaller keys until I found one that opened the filing cabinets. Blassingame kept his files well organized, in alphabetical order by the patient's name. I pulled all the files I wanted a look at: BLASSINGAME, CALLIE, CURWEN, TODD, DOWNEY, MADELEINE, GILBERT, JIMMY, GILBERT, JULIANNA, GILBERT, MARCIA, RESTON, NATALIE, and WALLIS, HUGO.

Some of them took up several file folders. I had no time to sift through them page by page. All I could do was thumb.

I started with BLASSINGAME, CALLIE, which was second only to Jimmy Gilbert's in bulk. I fanned the pages and found evidence of operation after operation, almost all of them involving her face. Included in the file were photos not only of her progress but also of the procedures themselves, in all their gory detail. The first procedure had been performed twenty-five years ago, when she was Callie Hewitt, employed as Blassingame's nurse. She underwent ten more operations over the next twenty years. Then, five years ago, she had her riding accident, necessitating twelve surgeries over the next twelve months merely to restore her to some semblance of a normal face. After that, Blassingame had performed an additional ten operations—two a year—in an attempt to restore her beauty. No wonder she had become addicted to painkillers. I got the impression she was happiest at the beginning, when she was Callie Hewitt, R.N.

CURWEN, TODD had undergone a handful of minor procedures, including a slight facelift, a chin implant, a nose job, some liposuction around his waist and hips, and collagen injections to smooth out chicken scratches at his eyes. Nothing in his file might have explained why he expected Troy Blassingame to do any dirty work for him, such as kill me.

It took only a moment to review DOWNEY, MADELEINE. She had been given a slimmer nose, and her ears had been fixed so they didn't stick out so much. Both procedures predated her success as a model. Without the operations, she would never have made the cover of *Vogue* or landed any lucrative cosmetics contracts. For that matter, she never would have married Jimmy Gilbert.

Jimmy Gilbert's history of plastic surgery was now in my hands: GILBERT, JIMMY. It took up several folders; all I could do was glance at a document here, a document there. Jimmy had allowed himself to be a human guinea pig on whom Blassingame could experiment with new techniques and procedures. I found evidence of several major facial reconstructions. Jimmy's nose had been reshaped at least eight times. He had chin, jaw, and cheekbone implants installed—and removed. He had the crease above his eyelids smoothed out to look more Asian—then had the crease restored. He had his earlobes removed and later changed his mind and had them reconstructed. Most recently, before production of his "more macho" music video, Jimmy received saline pectoral implants to give the appearance of a muscular chest. He underwent liposuction on several occasions, which I failed to understand, since he always appeared scrawny as a scarecrow.

I could spend hours with Gilbert's file alone, but I didn't have the time. I glanced at the simpler procedures that he had undergone as a teenager. I was curious to know what his first operation was, so I turned to the back of the first folder.

It took place twenty-five years ago. Jimmy was ten years old at the time. It didn't strike me as plastic surgery at all. Blassingame's handwriting revealed that Jimmy's testicles had become twisted up within his scrotum; surgery was necessary to go in and untangle the cords. As with all his files, Blassingame included before and after Polaroids, but there were no shots of the procedure in progress. There were simply two photos, before and after, nearly identical, showing Jimmy's immature genitalia. Blassingame's work had been neat, with no visible scars—I supposed the incision had been made just beneath the scrotum. I wasn't sure why Marcia Gilbert had taken her son to a plastic surgeon for this operation, except perhaps she thought Jimmy would wind up with a more pleasing cosmetic result.

The file for GILBERT, JULIANNA was far less extensive than her brother's. Julianna had had cheekbone implants, two nose jobs, and a series of collagen injections in her lips. She had stopped going to Blassingame two years ago. It was possible she was now seeing a different plastic surgeon.

GILBERT, MARCIA had an extensive history of liposuction and facelifts going back twenty-five years. She shied away from facial implants, nose work, and other more obvious modifications. Hers was a simple story of nip, tuck, and suck. I wasn't sure what the point of it all was, considering the condition she was in when I met her. Perhaps she was due for more work.

I had only one reason for checking out RESTON, NATALIE. I hoped to find the secret of Facegate. The official story was that she had raided a public fund earmarked for White House renovations and had promptly paid it all back. The investigative reporters had never been able to rake enough muck to keep it alive as a political scandal, and it had eventually disappeared. Paging through Natalie Reston's file, I found the smoking gun those reporters would have killed for. It was a photocopy of a check bearing the First Lady's signature. The amount matched the total due for two facelift procedures in the early years of the Reston presidency. The check was not drawn on the personal account of the Restons, nor was it drawn on the account of the White House restoration fund. It was from the Just Don't Do Drugs Foundation, Natalie Reston, National Chair. The check was countersigned by the foundation's treasurer, Callie Blassingame.

The last file was WALLIS, HUGO. On opening the folder, I came face-to-face with another check. This one was not a photocopy. It was a real check, unendorsed, made out to Blassingame Cosmetic Surgery Associates, in the amount of eight hundred thousand dollars, drawn on the account of Curgil Productions, Inc. It bore only one signature—Todd Curwen's. The memo line had the notation *For Services Rendered.*

The police would need some of these files as evidence in Callie Blassingame's murder. I put them back where I'd found them—all except Natalie Reston's, which I tucked inside my jacket. I turned out the lights on my way out.

I opened the door to the alley and was relieved to find that the 'Cuda was still parked out back. There was no sign of Curwen or Angel. They must have left in a cab. I checked to make sure no one else was around to witness me leaving the scene.

Curwen had left the keys in the 'Cuda's ignition.

I was amazed at my good fortune.

That didn't last long. When I got behind the wheel of the 'Cuda, the dome light came on. I set Natalie Reston's file on the passenger seat next to me and noticed that the door to the glove compartment was hanging open. I rifled the contents but knew immediately that my copy of David Loeb's blue file was long gone.

Thirty-One

I started up the 'Cuda and got the hell out of there. I circled the block and came back around in front of Blassingame Cosmetic Surgery Associates. An N.Y.P.D. marked squad had just pulled up in front with its lights on, and two burly cops were getting out. They hitched up their utility belts and headed toward the entrance. I drove on by and saw in my rearview that another squad was joining them. I hoped Mt. Sinai was taking good care of Hugo Wallis.

I stopped on Lexington Avenue, grabbed a pay phone, and called Loeb. I got his voice mail: Alex Clements had left for the evening. I didn't leave a message. Instead, I called Loeb's home number. His answering machine came on. I decided to leave a message on the chance he might be screening.

"David, it's Greg. It's urgent that we talk. Please call me back." I left my beeper number and hung up.

From the moment Loeb failed to pick up, I felt a stronger sense of urgency than I conveyed in my message. If anything happened to him because of the blue file, I would be responsible.

David Loeb lived at the Carnegie Hall Tower, a credit-card-thin skyscraper of recent vintage on West 57th Street right next to the old music hall. Living there was one way of knowing you'd never be late for a concert. I didn't think I'd be able to park on West 57th, so I found a spot on West 56th in the middle of the block, in front of a solitary old five-story brownstone dwarfed by dullish office buildings ten times its size. I locked up the 'Cuda and took a shortcut through the block-long lobby of the Hotel Parker Meridien. Uniformed doormen at either entrance were kind enough to hold the doors open for me. The one who let me out onto West 57th was a gorgeous North African guy of about twenty with teeth as white as a parsnip and smooth skin the color of extra virgin olives. Not that I had time to notice.

It looked like a police convention in front of the Carnegie Hall Tower. Parked out front in a chaotic tableau were two marked N.Y.P.D. squads, two plain Caprices, a plain Crown Vic with New Jersey plates, and an ambulance. The vehicles had their roof lights swirling, casting red, white, and blue flashes all around, to the astonishment of jaw-dropping tourists queuing up in front of Planet Hollywood.

I pushed my way through a small crowd of the curious and entered the tower. The doorman stopped me. This guy wasn't extra virgin—he was about sixty-five, with black olives for eyes and crusty, pitted skin like dried pizza dough.

"Eh, don't tell me," the doorman said. "More backup."

"I'm a private detective." I showed him my license. "I'm working with the police on this case. It's unit forty-one-oh-one, isn't it? David Loeb's apartment?"

"Yeah, yeah, okay, go ahead." He handed me back my license and gave me a nod of approval. I got the impression he'd already had to let through a number of official personnel and was getting tired of it. I glanced at his tiny TV and saw that he had a Yankees game going. He was already turning back to it.

I went over to the elevators. "Forty-first floor?"

He turned back to stare at me. "You some kind of super genius or something?"

The ambulance crew was waiting with their stretcher outside the open door of Loeb's apartment. I took it they weren't needed just yet. Inside the apartment, camera flashes were going off. I got as far as the doorway before I was stopped by a patrolman.

"Hey, where do you think you're going?"

"In there." I was about to dig out my license.

A woman's voice came from inside, sounding a little raspy. "Go on, let him in. I know the guy."

I stepped into the apartment and saw that my savior was Det. Paula Ozwick of the Somerset County Sheriff's Department. She stood back from the crime scene along with a couple of New York City plainclothes detectives. Specialists from the Crime Scene Unit were taking photographs and stooping over a body that lay face-up in the middle of the living room carpet.

"You're looking even worse for wear than before," Ozwick said. "How'd you get those bruises on your face?"

"Never mind. Long story."

"You know this guy?"

"I sure do." I was staring down at the last face I'd seen before the postal bag was shut and locked over my head, the face that had left me strapped down on the operating table of a deranged plastic surgeon. The only thing different was the tasteful small-caliber bullet hole in the center of his forehead. "That's Todd Curwen. He's Jimmy Gilbert's manager." ·

"I've heard the name," Ozwick said. "He was on my list. Strange, though. I came up here to see David Loeb."

"Where is Loeb?" I asked, craning my neck.

"The doorman saw him leaving here about twenty minutes ago in the company of a woman."

"His wife?"

"No. According to the doorman, Mrs. Loeb has been on vacation in Switzerland for the past two weeks and isn't due back until next Thursday."

"Did the doorman get a good look at the woman?"

"Unfortunately, no. He saw her from the back, and all he can say is that she had a scarf on her head and was wearing a big fur coat."

"Hot weather for a fur coat," I said.

"People who wear fur coats don't give a damn if it's too hot or not," Ozwick pointed out.

"How'd you get into Loeb's apartment?"

"The door was wide open when I got up here."

"That's unusual."

"Not when a noisy murder's just been committed. Looks like Loeb and his lady friend picked up and got the hell out of here."

"Did the doorman notice her legs?"

"I didn't ask." Ozwick regarded me quizzically.

"Not that I'm into women's legs," I said. "I was just wondering whether they were skinny, fat, or just right."

"I told you, I didn't ask."

"They were probably too fat or too skinny. No straight guy's likely to miss them if they're just right."

"Maybe he's one of us."

"Or the Yankees made a run the same time Loeb and his friend were leaving."

"Sure, Quaintance. Maybe they timed their exit to coincide with a triple play."

"Haven't been any triple plays," piped up an N.Y.P.D. detective who had a discreet black earphone wired to his radio.

"What's the score?" Ozwick asked over her shoulder. She cocked her ear and held up a finger to beg my patience.

"Five to four, Orioles, bottom of the seventh."

"Thanks," she said with a disheartened sigh.

"There isn't another body around here, is there?" I asked.

"You mean in this apartment? Why, you expecting one?"

"I wasn't expecting any. But with Curwen lying here, I was wondering what happened to this guy he was with. Good-looking young Puerto Rican guy. Angel. Curwen's houseboy."

"There's no second body here. Though they do have a related homicide elsewhere in the city. Would you care to take a guess?"

"I have no idea," I lied.

"Troy Blassingame. Can you believe that? I've been trying all day to see him. He's one of my top suspects."

"I thought you'd arrested Jimmy Gilbert."

"No, no." Ozwick's face crinkled up like she was in pain. "We're only holding him for questioning. Not that we can do any questioning without Mr. Loeb present. We haven't charged Gilbert with anything yet. After our initial questioning, *I* didn't think we needed to hold him. My captain second-guessed me and sent us back out to retrieve him. He considers Gilbert a flight risk, if you can believe that. All we did was inflict more embarrassment on the poor guy. Loeb was livid, I can tell you. He threatened to sue me for all I was worth. I told him he was welcome to my debts if he wanted them."

"What happened to Blassingame?" I asked, wanting to know what Ozwick knew.

"Well, it's strange," she said. "Since early this morning, I've been calling and trying to arrange an interview with Callie's husband, and each time I was put off by this smarmy receptionist. Said he was tied up in surgery. She could never put me through to him, even though his damn wife had been murdered. When I came up here to see Loeb, I found this and called it in. When the New York dicks arrived, they told me what their buddies had just discovered up on the East Side."

"How was Blassingame killed?" I asked.

"Scalpel driven straight into his heart." Ozwick mimicked the action, bringing her right arm down against my chest.

"Any idea who did it?"

"They already have a solid suspect. Efficient, huh?"

"Anyone we know?"

"Would you believe Hugo Wallis?"

"Get out of here," I said. "What's his connection?"

"Haven't the faintest," Ozwick said. "Wallis ran into the emergency room at Mt. Sinai, screaming and blabbering. Now, you'd think just about everybody on the planet could recognize Hugo Wallis after all that trial coverage, but guess what? His face was gone. All the skin and hair around his head, in fact."

"Jesus." I didn't have to try hard to produce a shudder.

"He *told* them who he was. He said Troy Blassingame had promised to give him a new face."

"A new face?"

"That's what he told the nurses. He went on blabbering about how he'd killed Blassingame. The nurses evaluated his injuries and hustled him into an operating room. Right now he's under anesthesia, getting some skin grafts. We won't be able to get any more out of him for a day, at least. I don't suppose he's going to look very pretty when they're done with him."

"I don't see how this rules out Troy Blassingame as a suspect in Callie's murder, though," I said.

"I didn't say I've ruled him out. But after this—"

The ambulance guys were in the apartment now, zipping Todd Curwen into a black vinyl body bag. All that plastic surgery and liposuction didn't do him much good in the end.

"Blassingame could've hired Wallis to kill Callie," I said.

"Anything's possible," Ozwick said.

"Maybe he was paying Wallis back by giving him a new face. Wallis can't stand being recognized now that everyone in the world believes he murdered his own wife."

"Why hire Wallis and not some professional?"

"Wallis is from the same social circle as the Blassingames," I suggested. "If Blassingame wanted to hire someone to kill his wife, why not someone he can trust? More important, someone who's done it before? Someone with experience?"

"A proven record," Ozwick said.

"You got it."

"You'd have me convinced if we didn't have all this."

All this was now a sizable bloodstain on the carpet. Curwen was heading down the elevator on a stretcher and getting a speedy delivery to the city morgue.

"Chances are," Ozwick went on, "David Loeb or his lady friend shot Curwen. Meanwhile, Blassingame's dead, and Wallis is out of commission. The only motivation I can think of for what Blassingame did to Wallis is plain old-fashioned revenge."

"Out of love for Callie?" I said. "Blassingame must have snapped a little."

"That is a distinct possibility, Greg. It's been all over the press that Wallis had no money left. Someone else may have hired Blassingame to fix up Wallis, only Blassingame didn't keep his part of the bargain. What he did to Wallis was bound to be discovered. I'll say he snapped."

"What were you coming up to see Loeb about?" I asked. "Any developments in the case? Besides the obvious—"

"No, just routine questions," Ozwick said. "What were you coming up here for, Greg? If I may ask—"

"To warn Loeb about Curwen."

"Explain."

"Curwen came into possession of some private documents of Loeb's. I had a run-in with Curwen earlier today that gave me an indication he could be violent."

"The bruises on your face?"

"That's right," I said. "Once Curwen got these documents, I had reason to be concerned about Loeb's welfare."

"Maybe you should have been concerned about Curwen's. Did you have a look at these documents?"

"I sure did."

"Where are they now?"

"I don't know," I said. "I'd imagine Curwen brought them up here with him. You didn't see anything lying around?"

"No."

"Then Loeb must have taken them. They're copies of an original file Loeb keeps at his office. In a blue file folder, to be exact, in the top drawer of his desk. Just in case you want to ask some judge for a search warrant."

Ozwick raised an eyebrow. "Would you mind telling me what's in these documents?"

"All I can say is, it had to do with Callie. It's not any kind of smoking gun. It won't tell you who wanted her dead. If you don't obtain Loeb's original file, I'll be able to tell you all about it—but later, not now. I don't have the time."

"Where are you off to?"

"Back to Jersey."

As I tried leaving the apartment, yet another plainclothes detective entered, blocking my exit. He was a tall man with a bald pate, a bushy black mustache, and a four-gallon beer belly.

"Can you tell me who's in charge here?" he asked me.

"Who are you?" I asked.

He pulled out his badge and identification and said, "Detective Don McGarrity, Atlantic City Homicide. I was coming up here to have a few words with Mr. Loeb."

"David Loeb's not here," Ozwick said, coming over to join us. "Detective Paula Ozwick, Somerset County Sheriff's Department. I came up here to have some words with David Loeb about a homicide of my own. Right now Loeb's a suspect in a fresh homicide that just took place here in his apartment."

"Did you say *Loeb* is a suspect?" McGarrity asked.

"He's at least a party to the crime, yes," Ozwick said. "What were you seeing him about?"

"Well." McGarrity cleared his throat. "Our homicide took place at the Trump Castle, late Thursday or early Friday. The victim, Angelo Ferrante, used to do detective work for Loeb. I spoke with Loeb earlier this morning, but I didn't know enough to ask him all the right questions. Now we've got a solid suspect who also happens to be one of Loeb's most famous clients—"

"Hugo Wallis?" I said.

Ozwick stared at me.

"I saw his picture in one of the newspapers," I said. "He was at a roulette table, must have been Thursday or Friday."

"Who is this guy?" McGarrity asked Ozwick.

"Greg Quaintance, private investigator," I said, and showed him my identification. I didn't say that I was Ferrante's replacement. I wasn't even sure if I was really working for Loeb anymore, and I didn't have time to get bogged down answering a slew of McGarrity's questions. I had my own work to do.

"Detective McGarrity," Ozwick said, "if you're looking for Hugo Wallis, you'll find him at Mt. Sinai Medical Center. He's in surgery right now and won't be much use to you for a day or two. The N.Y.P.D. has first dibs on him. I want a crack at him after that. Then you can have your turn."

"You think he'll talk?" McGarrity asked.

"They said he was singing like a jaybird until the anesthesiologist got to him," Ozwick said.

The N.Y.P.D. detectives joined our circle, and they all started comparing notes. I took this opportunity to sneak out.

* * *

On my way out the Carnegie Hall Tower, I stopped and asked the doorman if he'd noticed the legs on the woman in the fur coat.

"Nope." His eyes were glued to the Yankees-Orioles game. "Sorry, pal, can't help you. You have a good night, now."

Thirty-Two

Juan opened the door with the chain on. The only light came from the flickering emissions of the TV set within.

"Sorry, Gregory," Juan said, sounding groggy. "Hallway's too dark—I couldn't make you out through the peephole."

The door slammed shut, and I heard the chain being undone. When the door came open again, Juan was standing there rubbing his eyes and yawning. I stepped in.

"Hey, Gregory," he said, kissing my face.

Juan locked the door behind me and threw the chain back on.

"Are you the only one here?" I asked, scanning the room.

"Of course I am. What, you think I'm having a party?" Juan was dressed only in a clinging pair of black boxer briefs. I was used to seeing Juan's well-developed pecs outlined by his skin-tight shirts, but here they were naked before me.

"Are you okay?"

"A little tired is all. I guess I fell asleep."

Juan's futon couch was folded out before the TV set and showed the indentation his body had just been making. It was a warm night in the city, and he'd been napping without covers, with the windows open. A muggy breeze blew in.

"The tapes are that boring?"

"I'll say," he said. "See for yourself."

Juan's TV screen showed a steady black-and-white image taken by a security camera with a wide-angle lens from high up in the corner of a bedroom. The light in the room came from a dim table lamp at the far side of the bed. On top of the covers lay two people sleeping, wearing identical pajama bottoms and no tops. Though they took up a small portion of the screen, their faces were identifiable to me. The longer figure, the man, was Jimmy Gilbert. His arm was draped around the shorter, a blond boy—Jason Blassingame. Neither figure moved. They looked asleep.

"That's it?"

"Yeah, that's it."

"They ever do anything?"

"What do you want them to do? They move around, they change positions, they snuggle up, they split apart, they lie still for a while. Just like regular folks."

"Do you recognize either one of them?"

"Sure, that's Jimmy Gilbert. I don't know the kid."

"They never have sex?"

"No, they don't. Are they supposed to?"

"I don't know. How many tapes have you watched?"

"This is the last one, but I didn't exactly watch them all. It must be thirty hours of stuff. It's pretty boring, and nothing much happens. I fast-forwarded a lot."

"You watched it while you were fast-forwarding, though."

"Sure, and if I saw anything going on, I'd play it out at normal speed. It would only be Jimmy Gilbert or the kid rolling over or kicking his legs like during a nightmare or whatever."

"Do they ever get naked, play games, anything?"

"No. Each tape starts when they go to bed, and they're always wearing their little matching pajama bottoms. A couple of the tapes, they lie there and talk for a while before going to sleep. They hug a little, and Jimmy likes to give the kid a kiss before they go to bed. Just a peck, you know. They usually snuggle for a while, then they fall asleep."

"And they always keep that light on?"

"Yeah, always. Maybe the kid's afraid of the dark."

"Maybe Jimmy is," I said. "There's no sound?"

"No, nothing. I tried turning it all the way up, but no. You can never hear what they say to each other or anything."

"Do they ever get under the covers?"

"Sometimes."

"You're sure they're never having sex under the covers?"

"Positive. You'd see the thrusting or whatever, and there's nothing like that going on. Jimmy acts real protective."

"How do you mean, protective?"

"You know, he's usually got his arm around the kid. Sometimes, when the kid's asleep and Jimmy's awake, Jimmy props himself up on a pillow and just watches the kid sleep."

"How much more on this last tape?"

"I don't know. Like I said, I fell asleep. Are you disappointed, Gregory? You trying to catch Jimmy Gilbert having sex with this boy?"

"Not necessarily," I said. "I'm certainly not disappointed. It doesn't prove Jimmy never had sex with the kid, but still, there's something in this. I'm not sure what."

"You want me to watch the last tape again from the beginning to make sure I didn't miss something?"

"You don't have to watch it again if you don't want. I can look at it myself later, if you like."

"No, I'll do it. I'll make some coffee." Juan padded into the kitchen, scratching at his lower back. "You want some?"

"If you make it fast," I said. "I have to get back out to Jersey. If you see anything abnormal on the tape, call my beeper right away, okay?"

"Abnormal?" Juan said. "You mean like if they start humping?"

"Sure, anything like that."

"If they haven't by now, they're not going to."

"You're probably right." I stared at the TV screen. Jimmy Gilbert shifted back toward his side of the bed and let his arm fall off Jason. "That's just one more thing bugging me."

"What is?"

"Juan, you've had a good enough look at the kid," I said. "Don't you think he's kind of cute?"

"Yeah, he's kind of cute."

"Tell me honestly, now. If you were snuggling up all night with this kid, wouldn't it make you just a little horny?"

"I'm not into little boys, Gregory."

"Neither am I, but Jimmy Gilbert is supposed to be obsessed with this boy. Put yourself in his shoes. He's thirty-five, and he's inviting this fourteen-year-old boy into his bed. If these tapes were taken on different nights, we can assume they've slept together on at least five occasions, probably more. Jimmy acts affectionate and protective. Aside from hugs and a peck on the cheek, he doesn't force himself. Yet Jimmy's an adult— he must have a libido. Assuming he loves the boy, don't you think it's requiring a lot of self-control for him to keep his hands off?"

"I've always thought of Jimmy Gilbert as being asexual," Juan said, setting the coffee to brew. "Never thought of him as having a sex drive. Maybe he just likes to cuddle, Gregory."

"And there's no law against that."

Thirty-Three

The 'Cuda was happy to be going over the General Pułaski Skyway again after all that city driving. It hummed along as if I'd just given it a tune up. I promised it that once the case was over, I'd give it at least an oil change and maybe a body waxing.

Ennis was working the guardhouse at Somerset Hills. He was ready to let me roll on through without asking any questions, but I wanted to stop and ask him some. I parked the 'Cuda at the side of the road and went over to his window. He offered me a cup of coffee, and I took it. I also lit up a cigarette.

"How's the investigation going?" Ennis asked.

"We're getting there. I don't want to jinx myself."

"Of course not."

"You've been here all day without a break, right?"

"That's right."

"You haven't seen Jason Blassingame today, coming or going?"

"No, I sure haven't."

"You know his car?"

"Black Eagle Talon, isn't it?" Ennis said. "Jason brought it out and showed it off to me once. His dad doesn't let him drive it outside the grounds. I haven't seen it today, though."

"That's what I thought," I said. "You aren't aware of Jason's whereabouts at all, are you?"

"Nope. That dyke detective asked me the same thing."

"Detective Ozwick happens to be a friend of mine."

"Why didn't you say so? I don't mean nothing by it."

"Yeah, sure." I downed the last of the coffee. It wasn't as good as Juan's. "You took Bert's shift here last Saturday night so he could go up to Gilbert's for that party. Do you remember who else you logged in that night who went up there?"

"Without the log book, I wouldn't know," Ennis said.

"You'd remember David Loeb, wouldn't you?"

"Sure, he went up there."

"And you'd remember Hugo Wallis, certainly."

"Him too."

"You knew who he was without asking, right?"

"Everybody knows what he looks like. The next time I saw Bert, he couldn't stop talking about Hugo Wallis."

"How so?"

"Bert said he had a good time at the party, except he felt agitated the whole time because Wallis was there. He felt constantly like he ought to go over and arrest him for something. Bert couldn't stand being there, trying to have a good time in the presence of a man who'd killed his wife in cold blood."

"Did Wallis know how Bert felt?"

"I wouldn't know."

"They didn't have words or anything?"

"Bert didn't say nothing about it. Just that it made him uncomfortable. He said it kind of spoiled the party for him."

"He didn't tell you what went on at the party, did he?"

Ennis shrugged. "Who knows?"

"You saw the people who came through here. Weren't there a lot of teenage boys?"

"Yeah, Yuri Zetlin brought some kids in his van. So?"

"What do you think they were up to?"

"Hey, I don't care. What do people do at parties? Drink, do drugs, and screw. They didn't have any women up there, so I guess they weren't screwing."

"How would Bert have felt about smoking dope with teenage boys? Or encouraging minors to drink?"

"Hey, I get high myself—off duty, of course. Bert was off duty, too, and I always say whatever a guy does in his private life is his business."

"So basically, Bert had a good time, except Wallis rubbed him the wrong way. You have no idea if the feeling was mutual?"

"How would I know?" Ennis said.

I thanked him for his time and asked him to let me through.

I drove to the end of the road, to the Secret Service checkpoint. Two Secret Servicemen got out of the booth and flanked the 'Cuda.

"What's your business?" asked the one on my side. The other one got busy inspecting my Michelin radials.

"I have to speak with Natalie Reston. It's urgent."

"I'm afraid that's impossible," the first agent said. The other one scowled at my passenger door.

"Let me be perfectly straight with you, mister—" I said.

"Agent Michaels."

"My name's Greg Quaintance. I'm a private investigator. Here's my license, issued by the State of New York. See that? Here's my photo D.L. You can run it if you want. My driving record is clean."

Agent Michaels handed me back my IDs. "That won't be necessary, Mr. Quaintance. You're not going in."

"I think you'll have no choice but to let me in," I said.

"Is that so? Did you hear that, Stevens? This guy's not going to give us a choice."

Agent Stevens, who was now at the 'Cuda's tailpipe writing down my license plate number, let out a curt chuckle.

"You wouldn't want to tell me whether or not President and Mrs. Reston have got a fourteen-year-old boy in there by the name of Jason Blassingame, would you?"

Agent Michaels was momentarily mum. He was about to try bluffing, but he'd already screwed it up. "Sir, I have no idea what you're talking about. Please step out of the vehicle."

"All right." I did as instructed.

"Place your hands on the hood of the car and spread your legs, please."

Agent Michaels proceeded to pat me down from my feet up.

"I've got a gun in my shoulder holster," I informed him when he was up to my crotch. "And a license for it in my wallet."

"That's very good," he said, plucking out my gun. "We'll just check on that."

"You didn't answer my question about Jason Blassingame."

"There is no such person on this estate, to my knowledge."

"Ah, plausible deniability," I said. "Can I take my hands away from the car now?"

"Go ahead."

I turned around to face them. Both agents stood close to me, making sure that if I tried to run, I wouldn't get far.

"Maybe you guys should phone up to the house and ask the boys up there. Because I'm telling you, if this kid is being kept on the Reston estate, it constitutes kidnapping."

"Kidnapping?" Agent Michaels turned to Agent Stevens and laughed. Stevens didn't find it funny. "The Secret Service is not in the business of kidnapping. Neither is President Reston."

"Like I said, maybe you should phone up to the house and find out.

Jason Blassingame is a minor, and he is in the sole custody of his father, Troy Blassingame. Jason is not old enough to go anywhere without his father's full knowledge and explicit permission. I happened to be with his father last night when we discovered Jason missing. Troy asked me then to find his son and bring him back home safely. If I found Jason, I would have full legal authority to take him and bring him back to his father."

Agents Michaels and Stevens pondered this.

I hoped Troy's death was not yet public knowledge; it would only complicate my line of reasoning, which was credible so far.

"Did Troy Blassingame give you any written authority?" Agent Michaels asked. Stevens was glowering deeper by the minute.

"No, but I swear to you as a legally commissioned agent of the State of New York that Troy gave me full verbal authority. What's more to the point, the Restons *have* no such authority. If they are harboring Jason, if they refuse to let me see him, and if they refuse to let him leave, they could be charged with kidnapping. Any Secret Service agents with knowledge of Jason's presence in the house or grounds can be charged as accessories."

Agent Stevens nodded at Agent Michaels.

"Maybe neither of you have any knowledge of it," I allowed. "Like I said, maybe you should phone up to the house and check. All I want is to see Jason Blassingame, make sure he's safe, and make sure he's not being held against his will. Tell them that."

"Wait here." Agent Michaels trudged back over to the security booth and got on the phone.

Agent Stevens stayed with me, but he made sullen company.

"Cigarette?" I offered smilingly.

Stevens eyed me suspiciously and pulled out his own pack.

"I suppose they train you never to take cigarettes from strange men," I said.

Agent Stevens didn't laugh.

"Nice lapel pin," I said.

That also failed to start a conversation.

We smoked together in silence until Agent Michaels returned.

"The old witch says to send him on up," Michaels said.

Thirty-Four

Agent Michaels said he would nurse my Glock for me at the front gate. No guns could be allowed to enter the grounds. That was fine by me. I never felt safer in my life.

Agent Stevens accompanied me in the passenger seat of the 'Cuda up to the front entrance of the Reston house. It was an odd modern house, with a number of nonsensical gables, sharply angular roofs, and that weird tower I'd seen before that looked like it ought to have a clock or a bell or a beacon.

When I got out of the 'Cuda, I grabbed my canvas book bag.

Agent Stevens took it out of my hands. "What's this?"

"Nothing nefarious," I said. "See for yourself."

He unclasped the bag carefully and pulled the contents out into the dim illumination from the 'Cuda's dome light.

"What are you doing with Mrs. Reston's medical records?"

"It's only the records of her plastic surgeries."

"I'll ask you again," Agent Stevens said coldly. "What are you doing with them?"

"Her plastic surgeon is the boy's father," I said. "I've been instructed to trade this file for the boy—though I wouldn't call it ransom."

"*Ransom?*" Stevens was angered by my insinuations.

"But I do find it curious that Mrs. Reston would persist in holding onto the child until she could get her hands on this. Let's just consider that Dr. Blassingame is turning this over to Mrs. Reston as a favor to an old friend."

Agent Stevens whispered the word I was sure was anathema in the Reston household: "Facegate." He shut the file fast, replaced it in my book bag, and handed it all back over to me.

"The truth's in there," I said.

"Don't tell me anything more, okay? I don't want to know. I'm just here for my pension."

I told him that was fair enough.

Agent Stevens escorted me through the house, most of which was done in staid modern decor reminiscent of Jacqueline Kennedy's Camelot. Maybe Natalie Reston had gotten away with nabbing an item or two from White House storage. We passed other Secret Service agents on the way, looking like well-dressed servants with nothing better to do than make shifty eye movements. They passed the time by playing walkie-talkie. I felt like asking one of them to make himself useful by fetching me a drink.

Natalie Reston's private office broke with the rest of the house. It was all Louis Quatorze, with enough gold leaf tapped into the trim, moldings, and furnishings to blind the sun god. Mirrors had been placed on every wall. The crystal chandelier was massive enough to feel at home at Versailles. Then again, Natalie Reston would have felt home at Versailles.

She sat behind a hefty, bowlegged writing desk of highly polished dark wood. From my vantage point, it looked more like a piano. Its legs and body were encrusted with gilded vines, like kudzu that had crept up and been touched by King Midas.

"I want Jason Blassingame," I said.

"You and who else," she said, mildly amused. Her faux platinum hair was stacked and curled and sprayed firmly into place. She wore a pearl choker and a double-breasted ivory jacket with Joan Crawford shoulder pads and gold buttons. She didn't seem to realize that the slim look she'd asked Blassingame to sculpt for her made her look like a grave-robbing ghoul.

"Has anyone else been here asking for him?"

"No. Relax, have a seat." She motioned toward a stiff antique chair before her desk with the practiced hand movement of a trade show model. I recalled vaguely that she had been a Miss America sometime in the late forties and had been in old live TV commercials, opening refrigerators like Betty Furness.

"I'd rather stand," I said.

"You're that man from earlier today," she said perceptively. The way she said *man* was dated and somehow disparaging—the way I'd sound if I were to call her a broad. "Greg Quaintance, the detective. The one we caught speaking to Ralph at the fence."

"Hardly a crime, ma'am."

"No, but you disturbed him." She swiveled in her desk chair from one side to the other, chastising me with her eyes.

"The old Tiger already looks pretty disturbed."

"He has senile dementia," she said. "Not as trendy as Alzheimer's—but bad enough, believe me. He spends more time talking with his imaginary friends than he does with me."

"He didn't seem very happy with how he's being treated."

"Ralph is entitled to his feelings." Natalie Reston was impressively cold. "But I wouldn't put much stock in what he says. He's got the best of care here."

"Like a private sanatorium," I said. "A place to himself where he can't give out state secrets. Or other secrets."

I took the file folder from out of my book bag.

"What's that?" Natalie Reston's eyes went as wide as her surgically stretched epidermis would allow.

"Troy Blassingame took meticulous records of all your operations. And all monetary transactions related thereto."

"He didn't," she said, as if it were in very bad taste.

"I'm afraid he did."

"Let me see that!"

I laid it out on her desk but didn't let her have it. I leafed through it and turned to the relevant page, the copy of his bill and her check from the Just Don't Do Drugs Foundation.

"That idiot!" she said, grinding her dentition.

I closed it up and put it safely back under my arm.

"I was surprised to see that Callie was your treasurer."

"Why should that surprise you?"

"Her drug problem was well known."

"Not then, it wasn't." Natalie Reston leaned back in her chair, looking flushed. Reflections of her hairdo stretched off into the distance behind her. "Don't start thinking Callie was some kind of hypocrite, Mr. Quaintance. She volunteered her time for my foundation. She thought getting involved would help get her over her addictions. But she needed more help than that."

"If it makes you feel any better," I said, "I was kind of relieved to see that check."

"Why is that?" She pressed her fingers to her temples. She was fast growing weary of me.

"At least you didn't spend my hard-earned tax dollars."

"Spoken like a true blue-collar man, a working stiff," she said contemptuously. "I bet your father's an autoworker or some such thing, the kind of person who always voted in lockstep with the unions against Ralph and me."

"Actually, ma'am, my father was an Army man who died in Vietnam before he ever laid eyes on me." I couldn't hold myself back. "I must have had a death wish, because I followed in his footsteps. I fought in the Gulf

War and put my life on the line for Exxon and Texaco. Only I got kicked out afterward without so much as a thank you, because I happen to be homosexual."

"I stand corrected." She looked shocked and embarrassed.

"Your husband was very aggressive in kicking gays out of the military, and his successor followed his lead. If it weren't for them, I wouldn't be here with you now. I'd be a sergeant or better by now, and my mother would have been proud of me."

"Sounds like you have a lot of resentment," she said. "Is that why you're trying to persecute me and Ralph?"

"I don't give a damn about you or your husband. I'm here to pick up Jason Blassingame. His father wanted me to find him and bring him home. He's been here in this house without Troy's consent. As I told the Secret Service agents, if it goes on any longer, it might be regarded as kidnapping."

"Kidnapping! How dare you come in here and make threats!"

"I'm not making threats," I said. "It's really very simple. You give me Jason, and I'll give you the file. That's the deal."

The former First Lady sat there and stewed, swiveling back and forth in her chair and clacking her wedding ring on the desk.

She stood up. Her desk chair went rolling back against the wall. She reached out her clawlike hand. "Give it to me."

I held it back from her like candy from a grabbing child.

"You can have that little faggot," she said. "I don't care what you do with him. I was just doing it as a favor to Jimmy."

"That's right," I said. "Jimmy Gilbert believed in you. He probably did more than anyone else to raise money for your foundation. You couldn't have stolen the money for your face without him. And Jason Blassingame was one of your poster boys, in those public service spots directed by Yuri Zetlin. You're the one who introduced him to Zetlin, isn't that right?"

"As a matter of fact, I was. Not that I grasp your point."

"I'll spare you the details of what you set in motion," I said. "Just let me get a few things straight. Jimmy asked you to look after Jason for a couple of days until he was ready to leave on his tour. He was going to take Jason with him."

"That's correct. And you're right, I owe Jimmy a lot. He's a good friend, and he's been very kind to Ralph since he became ill. I did it as a favor. It certainly was *not* kidnapping."

"I'm curious, did you have a look at Jason's things when he arrived? Did he have a bottle of Ritalin with him?"

She stared bug-eyed at me. "How did you know that?"

"Callie found it missing from her apartment last night, after Troy came and picked Jason up."

"Yes, I saw it, and I confiscated it. I know how kids abuse it. I won't tolerate drugs in this household. Jason acted very sorry. I've been using the incident as a way of shaming him into helping out a little around here."

"Once a mom, always a mom," I said.

"I had to keep him occupied," she said. "He knows about what happened to his mother."

"Where is Jason now?"

"Upstairs, in the observation tower. Ralph likes it up there, and Jason's been sitting and reading to him. I didn't let Ralph finish listening to the audiobook of *Jane Eyre*. It was having too destructive an influence on him."

"Delusions of being locked in the tower," I put in.

"Anyhow, a live voice is better. It keeps Jason busy, and it's a way of keeping Ralph company so he doesn't have to dream up imaginary companions."

"You ever do much of this sort of thing yourself for Ralph?"

"I'm afraid I don't have the energy. Now, if you'll leave that file with me, I'll be more than happy to take you up there."

I hesitated for a moment.

"Come, Mr. Quaintance, you can trust me. I won't bite."

I handed it over. Her hands snatched it from my grasp. She took it to her writing desk and locked it inside with a gold skeleton key. She slipped the key into her jacket pocket and smiled up at me with a rictus grin.

We rode the elevator up to the top of the tower. Natalie Reston kept smiling like she couldn't get her face to relax. It was the sort of automatic smile she used to use on the campaign trail. I think it was designed to ward off further conversation.

The elevator doors opened onto a single large room, square in shape, with windows on all sides. Against the black void of the outside, the windows acted like the mirrors in Natalie's office. But the furnishings here were stark: two single beds with rumpled sheets, a widescreen TV with stereo speakers, a VCR, a table, some chairs, and scuffed linoleum. Sitting on the table were a pair of binoculars and a pair of night vision goggles like I'd used on many occasions on night patrol in Saudi.

Jason Blassingame was sitting cross-legged on the bed, reading a book to Ralph Reston, who was next to the bed in his wheelchair and listening intently to Jason's words like he'd never heard this story before. Maybe he hadn't:

"When breakfast was ready, we lolled on the grass and eat it smoking hot. Jim laid it in with all his might, for he was most about starved. Then when we had got pretty well stuffed, we laid off and lazied. By-and-by Jim says: 'But looky here, Huck, who wuz it dat 'uz killed in dat shanty, ef it warn't you?'"

"Jason?" Natalie Reston said. "Do you know this man?"

Jason turned to look at me, and he smiled. "Sure I do. Hi, Greg. How's it going?"

I nodded at him, feeling tongue-tied once more. He already knew about Callie, but it was going to be up to me to tell him Troy was dead. Not exactly his father—at least I wouldn't have to explain that to him.

"It's that Martian nurse," Ralph Reston said, looking confused. "Is it that time again already, Mommy?"

"No, dear," Natalie said.

"Go on, Huck, keep reading," Ralph said.

I was worrying whether I was doing the right thing, removing Jason from what seemed the safest of environments. It came down to the fact that I never felt I could trust anyone else to do a job that had to be done. Jason was my responsibility, and I couldn't trust him to a senile old man, a greedy old lady, or Secret Service agents who were just in it for their pensions.

"Come on, Jason," I said. "I'm taking you out of here."

"Jimmy sent you, didn't he?" Jason asked, beaming.

"Yeah. I'm taking you to him. Come on, hurry up."

Jason handed the book to Ralph, leaped off the bed, and started packing his things into a black DKNY Athletic duffel bag.

Thirty-Five

I carried Jason's duffel out to the 'Cuda and tossed it onto the back seat, where it landed with a solid *thunk* on the stitched vinyl. I held the passenger door open and felt compelled to place my hand on top of Jason's hair and say "Watch your head" as he got in, as if he were a handcuffed prisoner being helped out by kindly Mr. Policeman.

I got in and made sure Jason put his seatbelt on and locked his door. He was in a white T-shirt, jeans shorts, and sandals.

"What about my car?" Jason said. "It's in their garage."

"The Eagle Talon? You're too young to be driving it. We'll get it back safe and sound. I'll take care of it myself if I have to, but later. You and I have got stuff to sort out first."

I put the car in gear and drove down to the Restons' gate. It remained closed while Agent Michaels came out of his booth to meet me. He handed my Glock back over to me.

"Nice weapon, by the way," he said.

"You didn't try it out, did you?" I said, checking the chamber and removing the clip so I could count the rounds.

"No, of course not."

"You never know." I slammed the clip back home and put the gun back in my shoulder holster.

Agent Michaels peeked across at Jason and smiled. "Hi, kid. How'd you enjoy your stay with us?"

"It sucked," Jason said. "Who wants to babysit a stupid old man who believes in Martians and has to wear diapers?"

"Now you know how I feel," Agent Michaels said dryly. He went back to his booth, opened the gate, and waved us on through.

When I hit the Somerset Hills Road and upshifted into third gear, my knuckles brushed accidentally against Jason's bare knee.

"I hate people who call me *kid*," Jason said.

Jason grew anxious as we passed by the turnoff to the Gilbert estate. "You're not taking me to Jimmy's?"

"Nope."

"I thought he sent you."

"Not really."

"He told me he wouldn't tell anyone where I was!"

"He didn't. I figured it out myself." I realized I was scaring him now. I tried to calm him down. "Look, Jason, you're safe with me, okay? Nobody's going to hurt you. Trust me."

Jason eyed me warily—still too young and innocent to wonder why he should take my word for it. At least he didn't try to open the car door while we sped past the turnoff to his house.

"Where are you taking me?"

"To see Jimmy. He's being held at the Somerset County Jail. They were thinking of charging him with your mother's murder, but they're beginning to realize they were mistaken. I wanted you to be there when they let him go. Jimmy's your godfather, and he may be the only one left to take care of you."

"What do you mean?"

"I'll explain in a minute."

We were pulling up to the guardhouse. The gate remained closed. Ennis came out, looked in through my window, and smiled.

"Well, it sure is good to see you, Master Jason," he said. "I was very sorry to hear about your mother. And your father. You have my condolences. If there's anything I can do—"

"My father?" Jason's eyes grew watery. He mumbled, "Thanks, Mr. Ennis."

Yeah, thanks a lot, I thought.

"Ennis," I said as he was leaving my window.

He came back. "Yes?"

"Is that standard operating procedure, seeing who's in the vehicles before you let them out the gate?"

"Yes, why?"

"Just thinking about Bert."

"I don't get you."

"Bert was found on the other side of the gate. That's the side you'd get out on if you were letting someone in, not out."

"That's right," Ennis said. "So?"

"Nothing," I said.

Scratching his head, Ennis went back into his booth and opened the gate.

We drove on through and headed for the highway.

"My father's dead?" Jason said, staring at the dashboard.

"Yes, Jason."

"Which one?" It sounded as if he were talking to himself.

"Troy," I said. "Not your biological father. David Loeb was alive and well—the last time I saw him, anyway."

"David told you he was my real father?"

"No," I said. "Maria Arcos told me. Your mother told her. She told her a lot of things. Maria gave me your suitcase, the one Callie took from your bedroom. I'm keeping it safe for you."

"You saw what's inside?" Jason turned away from me.

"Yes," I said. "Nothing to be ashamed of. I started a similar collection when I was sixteen. What I'm worried about is what's missing. Some Polaroids of you taken in Jimmy's bedroom."

"They're missing?"

"Who took those photos?" I asked. "Was it Jimmy?"

"No, no. Jimmy would never! Yuri Zetlin took those!"

"Some day when Jimmy wasn't around?"

"Yes," Jason said. "He . . . we . . . wouldn't have done anything if Jimmy was there."

"Who let Yuri in when Jimmy was away? Madeleine Downey?"

"Yes, it was Maddy. They go way back. He made her career."

"Why couldn't you meet Yuri at his place in the city?"

"Dad—Troy—wouldn't let me go into the city by myself."

"So whenever Yuri wanted to see you, he'd arrange it with Madeleine, and you'd tell Troy you were going over to see Jimmy."

"Something like that," Jason mumbled.

"Those magazines in your suitcase. They came from Yuri?"

"Yes."

"But not the videotapes."

"You watched my tapes?"

"Not myself. I hired a disinterested friend to watch them."

"Those tapes are personal!" Jason snapped. "Private!"

"What are you worried about?" I said. "Nothing happens. You and Jimmy never do anything."

"Those are my tapes!" he shouted. "You had no right!"

"Calm down," I said. "I was just doing my job."

Jason sat on his side of the front seat and sulked.

I understood why he was so angry. He saw the stuff between him and Yuri as just sex, a game. With Jimmy it was different—romance, intimacy, a bond, a kinship—maybe love. Jimmy and Jason existed in a world unto themselves, and nobody else was privileged to sneak a peek inside. I'd felt that way about my own first love, and I'd set myself up for a big letdown. I wished Jason could retain his illusions.

"Jason, I know this is a difficult time for you, but I'm trying my best to sort out what's been going on. You know your mother was killed last night. Your father—Troy, I mean—was killed this evening. I have a strong feeling that one person was behind it all. I have an idea who, but I don't know why."

"I can't help you," Jason said.

I had to pass every car in my lane. Nobody seemed to want to drive fast anymore, even though the speed limit had been raised again. I was trying to get to the jail as fast as I could. The sooner Jason could see that Jimmy was alive and well, the better off he would be. Jimmy was the only thing left in Jason's world that hadn't completely fallen apart.

"You may know more than you think you do," I said. "If you can tolerate me prying into your personal life a little more—"

"Ask me whatever you want. I can take it if you can."

"And you'll tell me the truth?" I looked over at him.

"Yes, Greg." He sighed and rolled his eyes. "I promise."

"Good boy," I said. "I mean, good man. Good, period."

Jason laughed lightly. "Do I make you uncomfortable?"

"However you make me feel is totally irrelevant," I said, wanting to put it to rest. "I'm the one asking the questions."

"Before you start, will you tell me if you believe in Jimmy? I mean, you believe he didn't kill my mother or anything?"

"He didn't do it," I said. "I'm sure of it."

"Then I trust you, and I believe in you." Jason leaned across the seat and gave me a chaste kiss on my unshaven cheek.

"Jason," I said warningly.

"Go ahead, ask away. I'll tell you whatever you want."

"You mind if I have a smoke?"

"No." Jason opened up my ashtray and depressed the cigarette lighter for me.

I tapped out a Lucky Strike and did not offer him one. He didn't seem to want it, anyway. When the lighter sprang out, Jason beat me to it and pressed it up against my cigarette.

"Thanks," I said. "I could have done it myself."

"I like doing things for people," Jason said. "I didn't used to know that. Jimmy pointed it out. Jimmy says I don't know how to say no to people. He thinks I won't reject somebody even if I ought to know better. He says some people are just out to use me and I have to learn how to turn them down. But I can't help it. I like to make people happy. That's me, I guess."

"You should listen to Jimmy." The smoke felt good going down my gullet. It calmed my keyed-up nerves, focused my brain.

"I always listen to him. He says I don't always hear."

"Jimmy sounds wise."

"Oh, he is. If only you could know him the way I do."

"Jason, we're beating around the bush. I have to ask you my questions before we get to the jail."

"I'm ready," he said.

"First, I need to know about late last night, or early this morning. Were you up in the Restons' tower?"

"Yes, I was. That's where I stayed most of the time."

"Did Ralph Reston let you use his night vision goggles?"

"Yeah, they're pretty cool. But I know what you're getting at. You want to know if I saw what happened at Jimmy's pool."

"Did you?"

Jimmy nodded, looking down at the floorboards. "I didn't know it was my mom. I couldn't see their faces."

"They?"

"There were two of them at the pool. It was a long ways away, and all I could see were these green shapes. Old Ralph thought they were his Martians."

"Yeah, I know. What were they doing?"

"One of them was dragging this body—my mom's body—across the yard, and then he dumped her in the pool. The other shape came out waving its arms, and they got into an argument."

"Can you describe the shapes? Tall, short, fat, thin?"

"Sure, the one who dumped mom in the pool was kind of tall, regular build, I guess. Looked like a man. The one who came running out was a lot fatter."

"Man or woman?"

"Couldn't tell."

"How fat?"

"Hard to say," Jason said. "It was just this green blob, you know? It could have been someone wearing a big coat, I guess. I don't know who it was."

"What happened after the argument?"

"They split up. The tall one went running off around the side of the house. The big blob went back inside."

"And they left your mom in the pool?"

"Yes. I didn't know it was her. I told Ralph what I'd seen, but he was no use. The Secret Service guys wouldn't allow me to wake up Natalie. I told them what I saw, and they said they'd look into it."

"Did you see anything else?"

"I went back and watched. Someone came back—I think it was the same tall guy—and tried to fish Mom out of the pool. Then the blob came back out and hit him on the head, knocked him in the pool. The blob went running off, and the tall guy got out of the pool. Then someone else came out of the house and gave the tall guy mouth-to-mouth. That's when the police got there."

"I see. You don't think either of the first two shapes could have been Jimmy Gilbert, do you?"

"No, I'd know Jimmy even through those goggles," Jason said. "He's too skinny, and I don't think he'd be strong enough to handle a body like that."

"Okay," I said. "You've been acquainted with the Restons all your life, haven't you? Because of Troy?"

"Yeah, he even brought me to the White House, but I was too young to remember that."

"Natalie Reston picked you to star in those public service announcements Zetlin directed. You never met him before that?"

"No, never before that."

"When was that?"

"Two years ago. I was twelve."

"Twelve," I said. "And you developed a friendship of sorts with Zetlin? How soon did that start?"

"Right away," Jason said. "He liked me from the start."

"When did you and he first have sex?"

"Depends on what you mean by sex."

"I don't want you to go into any details, Jason. Just tell me when Zetlin started wanting more from you than friendship."

"It took about six months for it to get to that point."

"You were still twelve?"

"Maybe thirteen by then, I don't know."

"That's about when he started putting you in the ads for those jeans?"

"Yeah."

"You and other boys and girls about your age."

"Yeah."

"Was that about the same time Jimmy learned what Zetlin was doing to you?"

"Yuri wasn't doing anything to me," Jason said. "I wanted to. He wasn't the first guy I messed around with."

"Maybe you messed around with other guys your age, but I bet Zetlin was your first adult."

"Yeah, so?"

"And that's what Jimmy means when he says that other people try to use you, isn't it? He's talking about Zetlin and others like him. Zetlin's not even sexy. You feel sorry for him?"

"Yeah, I guess so."

"So when did Jimmy learn what was going on?"

"When we were doing those photo shoots. I let something slip when I was talking with Jimmy. He got real mad about it."

"This was last year, when you were thirteen? The same time Jimmy started spending so much time with you, right?"

"Uh-huh," Jason agreed.

"And then he took you away with him on his Asian tour?"

"Yeah, that was just after he found out."

"Yuri Zetlin wasn't part of this tour, was he?"

"No."

"Neither was David Loeb."

"No, none of those people ever go with Jimmy on his tours. Not Yuri, not David, not Todd. Just his mother, Marcia."

"When you came back from Asia, you started back at your private school right away?"

"Actually I was a couple days late for the start of school."

"Where do you go to school?"

"New Hampshire."

"They don't ever let you out, say, on the weekends?"

"No."

"So you never went down to New York to see Zetlin while you were in school, and he never came up to New Hampshire?"

"I didn't see him while I was in school, no."

"And during Christmas break, Jimmy took you skiing in the Swiss Alps, right?"

"Jesus, Greg," Jason said. "You know everything."

"Not really," I said. "So it's only since school was let out for summer that you started seeing Zetlin again."

"I can do what I want. People say I'm mature for my age."

"Never mind that," I said. "You don't think of it as going behind

Jimmy's back?"

"No, why should I? It's not like Jimmy and I have sex."

"You don't?" I said. "Everyone seems to think you do."

"I hope they do. I don't care what anyone thinks."

"Do you want to have sex with Jimmy?"

"Yeah, I do. I think he does, too, but he says I'm too young and he doesn't want to take advantage of me."

"Good for him," I said. "You mean to tell me Jimmy's never even tried anything?"

"Jimmy says what he and I have is a romantic friendship. We cuddle, we hug, we kiss. Jimmy likes to kiss. But it doesn't get erotic."

"It doesn't? You're sure?"

"Not for him, it doesn't. Maybe that's why I love him."

"Because he respects you."

"Yeah, I guess so. Jimmy's special. I've never known anyone as nice as him."

"You've known some pretty bad people," I observed.

"Maybe," Jason said. "I don't know. Jimmy tells me Yuri's bad, but Yuri's never hurt me. He never forced me into anything. I still like him."

"Wait a few years, and you won't like him very much. Jason, I've got to ask you this, and not because I'm being judgmental or anything—"

"Ask me what?"

"I can't believe I'm going to ask a fourteen-year-old this," I said, almost to myself. "Did you always know you were gay?"

"Yeah, of course, didn't you?"

"Yes—but I was never molested as a child. I got to learn about myself on my own. Yuri Zetlin molested you. Whatever you and he did together—even if it was only taking pornographic photos, he molested you, okay? Do you understand that? I guess I just want to know whether you think he corrupted you, made you gay or anything like that."

"Corrupted me? No." Jason laughed. "I told you I messed around with other guys before I met him. I already knew all about gay sex."

"All about it," I repeated. "You're sure about that?"

"Sure, I'm sure."

I found myself pulling up into the parking lot of the Somerset County Jail before I even knew what I was doing. I felt as if I'd been driving on autopilot. I shut off the engine.

"Thanks for talking to me, Jason," I said, squeezing his hand. "I know now why Jimmy's worked so hard to try to protect you. You *are* still a kid, whether you like it or not—a kid who's going to need a lot of protecting."

Jason looked at me soberly without saying a word.

"Come on, let's go in," I said.

"This is all my fault, isn't it?" he blurted out. "Mom's dead, and now Troy's dead, and it's all my fault!"

"No, it isn't." I lightly touched his nape. "It's not your fault at all. I don't think it has anything to do with you."

Thirty-Six

I kept my arm around Jason until we reached the counter. After I let go, he remained close to me like a loyal dog. The bell on the counter said RING FOR SERVICE, so I did; it sang out through the bureau, mingling with the chirps of phones. Deskbound deputies were jawing on their phones and drinking coffee out of styrofoam cups. A pair of younger deputies were unhandcuffing an arrested person and placing him in a holding cell.

A uniformed deputy hefted his utility belt and stepped up to the counter. Thick chestnut hair formed a horseshoe-shaped ring around his pink scalp, which bore only a sparse, wispy growth of translucent filaments shining like a halo.

"Hey," he said, silencing the bell with the first and second fingers of his right hand—the only fingers he had left on that hand. Some kind of accident must have taken him off the streets and landed him here to oversee arrests, take citizen complaints, and process paperwork, night after night. He carried a .38 on his right; some catch-22 of departmental regulations was making him wear a gun that he would never be allowed to use. "Enough with the bell, pal. I got a headache, all right? Geez Louise."

"I want Detective Ozwick."

"That's the first time I ever heard a man say that!" He looked over his shoulder to soak up the chortles of his deskbound buddies. Their bellies jiggled when they giggled like bowls full of Jell-O. I let it go. The deputy was only trying to lighten up their lives a bit, and he wasn't going to repent even if I started preaching.

"Good one, Carter!" someone shouted.

"Is she in?" I said.

"And who are you?" Deputy Carter was tidying some papers into neat little stacks and not looking at me. He was chewing a piece of gum that smelled cloyingly of artificial grape.

I told him who I was and showed him my license.

"Private eye, huh? What's your business here?"

"I've been working with Detective Ozwick on a case."

"She's not in the station," he said, looking at his watch. "But she's due back any minute. Had to go into the city. What case are you working with her on?"

"The one she's working on right now." I didn't want to say *Blassingame* and *murders* in front of Jason. I thought I'd better let Deputy Carter in on who was standing next to me before he opened his mouth again. I put my hand on Jason's shoulder and said, "Deputy, this is Jason Blassingame."

Deputy Carter's jaw fell open, and one of his deskbound buddies stood up to look. "Jason Blassingame?" Carter said. "We've been looking all over for that kid. He's next of kin!"

"You're a master of tact, Deputy," I said through gritted teeth. I wanted to punch him in the nose. I held Jason closer to me, and he seemed to welcome the touch. The kid was beat.

"Carter," came a sharp voice. It was the tall plainclothes deputy who had stood up at mention of Jason. He had short-cropped black hair and a lopsided mustache, and half the tail of his shirt was untucked. "I'll handle this from here."

"Yes, sir," Carter said, going back to his desk with his tail between his legs. He glanced back up at us while he munched on an oversized, saltless pretzel.

"Vincent Pagliani, captain of detectives." He shook Jason's hand and smiled a friendly, professional smile. He shook mine and sized me up. "Why don't both of youse come with me, huh?"

Pagliani turned Jason over to the staff psychologist for some counseling. I asked Jason if he was going to be okay, and he said he would be. I made Pagliani promise that they would look after Jason while we were in the station. He told me Jason wouldn't be going anywhere at all until they could find the nearest blood relative who could take legal custody.

Once we were in the privacy of Pagliani's glass-enclosed office, I said, "You know you're holding the wrong guy. Jimmy Gilbert didn't kill Callie Blassingame or anyone else."

"Ozwick said something to that effect over the horn with me, but this case is too delicate for us to discuss it on the open air, so I axed her to come in. Meanwhile, I got Gilbert's hotshot lawyer in here breathing down my neck. I was watching this jerk on *Dateline* a couple days ago, and now he's in here pushing his way around."

"David Loeb is here?"

"Yeah, he's speaking to Gilbert now."

"I don't think that's such a good idea."

"I'm with you. I never think it's a good idea to let them speak with their lawyers, but what can you do?" Pagliani threw up his hands. "It's his friggin' Constitutional right."

"No, you don't understand. David Loeb is in this up to his eyeballs— aside from being Jimmy's lawyer. The N.Y.P.D. wants him, at least for questioning, if not more. He was seen earlier tonight leaving the scene of Todd Curwen's murder."

"Who's Todd Curwen?" He crinkled up his face like he didn't like the sound of the name. He had good instincts, this cop.

"Check your wires—there's probably a warrant out for Loeb's arrest by now. You shouldn't be letting him anywhere near Jimmy Gilbert. Look, I'm doing you a favor by tipping you off to this. Can you do me one?"

"What?" Pagliani's tone said he was making me no promises.

"Let me have five minutes alone with Loeb."

"Youse ain't going to bust his face or nothing—not that I wouldn't like to see it. The last thing I need is a complaint of police brutality from some friggin' entertainment lawyer."

"No, no rough stuff," I said. "There's just some things I have to straighten out. You have to let me ask him some questions. Just five minutes alone, then you can slap the cuffs on him and hold him till the N.Y.P.D. can come and get him."

"Why should I do that?"

"Call Paula Ozwick. She trusts me."

"Trust ain't the issue here. If Loeb's wanted, I shouldn't be wasting no time."

"You can raise Ozwick, can't you?"

"Sure, she's got a cel phone. I'll ax for her learned opinion on youse. Hold on." Pagliani picked up his phone and punched some numbers. "Ozwick? Pagliani here. Youse heard of a Greg Quaintance? Yeah, that's right, private dick. I got him right here. Says he needs five minutes alone with David Loeb. Excuse me? Loeb? Yeah, we got him. He's in here talking with Gilbert. Yeah, this Quaintance told me. How's I to know? It's his client, for Chrissakes. A live one, huh? Possibly dangerous? Yeah, I gotcha. What? The dick says he just wants to talk with him, ax him a few questions before we read him his Miranders. That square with youse, Ozwick? Okay, right. Gotcha. Don't worry, we'll hold him for youse." He hung up.

"Well?"

"Youse got your wish. I'll have the jail deputies retrieve Loeb and bring him on down. We'll lock youse guys in a room and post a guard outside. We won't be watching or listening, 'cause it might violate his friggin' rights and blow the friggin' case. What goes on between the two of youse stays between the two of youse. New York'll have their own crack at him, I guess."

Pagliani slammed his fist into his other palm with a *smack*.

I thanked him. He said it was his pleasure.

I was waiting in the interview room when they brought Loeb in. He was shouting, "Hey, what the hell is this?" as they slammed the steel door on us. The window had wire mesh through which could be seen the back of a young deputy's cute buzzcut.

"Put your briefcase down and have a seat, David," I said.

Loeb set his case down atop the table and sat in the chair opposite me. His hair was out of place. Gravity was pulling at the bags under his eyes, and the corners of his mouth weren't faring much better. His tie was askew.

"You look like shit," I said.

"I could say the same for you, what with the stitches and the bruises. What's going on, Greg? Why are you here?"

"It's unraveling, David."

"What is?" Loeb stared at me, breathing rapidly.

"Todd Curwen is dead."

"Todd?" He was playing dumb.

"In your apartment."

"In . . . my apartment?"

"You know it, David. You were there. Witnesses saw you leaving the scene with a woman. This is going to hold up in court. You won't be able to say you were chipping golf balls—"

"I didn't kill Todd." He shook his head from side to side and began repeating himself. "I did *not* kill Todd."

"Curwen was shot point-blank with a small-caliber weapon—

probably a twenty-two—right on your living room carpet."

"I told you, I didn't do it."

"Somebody pulled the trigger, David. Who was it?"

"It was her."

"Her who?" I asked.

Loeb just sat there shaking his head. He was beginning to realize that his whole world was caving in on him.

"Never mind," I said. "You won't tell me. Let me take a guess. Marcia Gilbert."

"Yes," he whispered, not looking at me.

"Marcia Gilbert fired the round that killed Todd Curwen?"

"Yes, yes."

"You had nothing to do with it?"

"No, Greg, I tried to stop her. It was so rash!"

"Why didn't you stay and report it? Why did you run?"

"I—I don't know—she made me go with her."

"What, she held a gun to your head and made you go with her? There are witnesses, David. Nobody saw you leaving with a gun to your head. What made you go with her?"

"She was going to use the pictures, Greg," he said. "The ones you copied illegally from my office."

He was trying to turn the conversation around to his advantage, but I refused to be intimidated.

"I have no regrets about copying your blue file folder, David. Otherwise, I would never have known how you were using me. Tell me how Marcia was going to use the pictures."

"Any way she could. If she couldn't get them printed somewhere, she would have sold them to an investigative reporter or sent them to the bar association—or who knows what! My career would have been ruined."

"Wake up, David. It's ruined already. Did you think you were going to get away with it?"

"Get away with what?"

"With leaving the scene of Curwen's murder. At the very least, you'll be charged as an accessory."

"What else could I do?" Loeb grabbed a lock of his hair in his fist and looked about ready to tear it out. "It's not just what I was doing in those photos. It's who I was with."

"Who do you mean?" I said with a turn of the screw. I wanted him to spell it all out for me in plain English.

"With Jason! My own son! Not that I knew that then. You read Callie's letter. You know all about it. I did *not* know that Jason was my son, Greg. Not when those photos were taken."

"Oh, and that makes it okay?"

Loeb didn't answer that.

"You never even suspected?" I said. "Don't tell me you forgot ever sleeping with Callie? Nine months later, *presto!*"

"Callie never told me. I thought it was Troy's, honest."

"David, you're a big-time lawyer with a reputation. You really cleaned up with Hugo Wallis. Everybody wants you. You mean to tell me that all Marcia had to do was wave this over you, and you'd do what she says?"

"It's more complicated than that."

"I'm sure it is. There's not only what you did to Jason. There's what you did to Callie."

"I did not murder Callie, Greg. You should know that."

"I'm not saying you killed her. I'm saying you set her up."

"That's ludicrous," Loeb said. "I had nothing to do with it. Nobody ever told me they were going to take care of Callie."

"Look, David, they're not giving me much time with you—"

"And you're about to waste the rest of it," he said. "You can't pin Callie's murder on me."

"Shut up," I said. "You're a master lawyer, David. You know how to work all the angles. That's why people hand over their family jewels to you. Callie wrote that letter after she saw you at Yuri Zetlin's pool party, and you found yourself backed into a corner. You didn't want to give in to her demands. You couldn't resist playing out all possible scenarios in your head and finding a way to come out of it unscathed."

Loeb's jaw was set, and he was gnawing on his lower lip. He looked like he wanted to spring across the table and throttle me.

"Am I being too cynical?" I said. "I don't think so. I think I'm close to the truth. You have no comment?"

Loeb gave me a stony stare. He was livid, but powerless.

"You didn't want to give Callie any money, and you didn't want to represent her. You presented her with this scheme in which she would threaten Jimmy with criminal prosecution for child molestation. *You're* the one who put that idea in her head. You wouldn't handle her case, but you'd obtain representation for her and give her any other help she needed from you. You were ready to work against Jimmy—your own client."

"You can't prove any of this."

"That's not my job," I said. "That's irrelevant to me. You and I both know what's true. You kept up your role as Jimmy's lawyer, and you sent Angelo Ferrante to help you negotiate the settlement. You were only trying to distance yourself from the main action. You never counted on Ferrante's going to the *Enquirer*. That's where you lost control of the situation. A lawyer like you doesn't like losing control. You're supposed to have a case all scripted out beforehand, down to the letter. You didn't anticipate Ferrante's move. Apparently, he had money troubles and didn't feel he could turn to you or anybody else."

"What, you going to testify at my trial, Greg?" Loeb said. "Huh? Where's your evidence?"

"Just bear with me."

"Bear with you? *Fuck* you, Greg."

"I have to know the truth, David. Not for my sake, but for Jason's. He told me he thinks this is all his fault. Enough people have lied to him. Someone has to be able to tell him the truth. He's going to be living with this the rest of his life."

"Yeah? So will I."

"I need to know the rest, David. Ferrante wasn't supposed to sell the story. It wasn't supposed to go public. Callie's threats were only supposed to remain threats, right? It had to be a legitimate threat for it to work, because it was Jimmy's money, not yours. Jimmy had to be convinced of the need to pay Callie off, even if he hadn't committed any crime."

"Don't make me laugh!" Loeb said. "Jimmy's been fucking Jason for the last year, at least!"

"How can you be so sure of that?"

"It's pretty obvious."

"Where's your evidence?" I said. "How do you know?"

"Jimmy's as guilty of fucking Jason as I am, and I don't need to see any photos of them to prove it."

"You can go on believing that if it makes you feel any better, but I happen to know otherwise. Jason told me so himself, and he hasn't been shy about telling me who he *has* had sex with. If he'd done it with Jimmy—his idol—he would have been bragging about it. Jimmy hasn't been fucking Jason. He's been trying to protect him from men like you and Zetlin."

"That's a load of bull, Greg. You've been duped."

"The only person who duped me is you. You sent me to finish what Ferrante started, but things were already spinning out of control. The people around Jimmy were pretty alarmed by the turn of events. Here Jimmy was about to be accused publicly of child molestation, and there was no stopping Callie."

Loeb swallowed hard. His forehead was beaded with sweat.

"That's the crux of it, isn't it?" I asked. "Callie was determined to see that Jason would have a future. I'm sure she firmly believed what you told her, that Jimmy had been molesting Jason. She would not have rested until she got satisfaction. She needed two things: money and Jason."

"She never could have had Jason," Loeb said, as if anything he said now could change what had happened. "She was unfit."

"Maybe you're right, maybe not. But you knew the kind of people who live off of Jimmy Gilbert. He's a one-man industry. He made part of your fortune, and without him, Madeleine Downey and Todd Curwen would have been hurting, but all of you would have surived just fine. As far as I can figure, Jimmy is Marcia Gilbert's only source of income. Jimmy was her livelihood. She'd already burned her bridges with Julianna. She had nothing to fall back on. If Jimmy was ruined, Marcia would be ruined. Callie was going to do it. She had to be stopped."

"You'll have to discuss this with Marcia," Loeb said. "I know nothing about her role in any of this."

"Sure you don't. That's how you set it up. Maybe you learned the practice from Ralph Reston: plausible deniability. Ralph Reston could deny all he wanted that he knew anything about Facegate, because it was true. He didn't want to pay for Natalie's facelift, and he didn't want to know where she came up with the money. He was safe. He insulated himself. You were doing the same thing. You created a situation that was untenable, considering the players involved. Like I said, you set Callie up. You can deny all you want that this was ever your intention. Maybe it wasn't. But I think you could see it coming, and there wasn't a thing you would have done to stop it."

"You can't pin this on me," Loeb said confidently. "Not you, not the police. What Marcia did is her responsibility. She's going to have to take the fall."

"That's between you and her, I guess."

My chair scraped the linoleum as I stood. My time was up.

Loeb stayed seated.

I rapped on the door and said, "Deputy, let me out."

"Tell Jason I'm sorry," Loeb said.

"Tell him yourself," I said.

I watched my back as the steel door was unlocked and opened. Loeb continued to sit there, staring at the empty space I'd left behind. Once I was out, the young deputy slammed the door shut.

"You got what you wanted?" Pagliani asked, coming over.

"Yeah," I said. "He's all yours."

"I've been talking with the New York dicks. They're real interested in this low-life." Pagliani thumbed in the direction of the interview room.

It was then that we heard the gunshot.

Pagliani and I both looked through the mesh window, but neither of us rushed to get the door open. It wouldn't have been any use. Loeb's briefcase lay open on the table. His chair was toppled over. He lay on the floor, a nine-millimeter semi-automatic pistol still gripped in his fingers. Blood and brain matter had erupted randomly all over the back wall and were dripping down in rivulets like a work of art in progress.

Thirty-Seven

I was still in the station when Detective Ozwick arrived. After Pagliani let her have a look at Loeb, the three of us met for a little confab in Pagliani's office. Ozwick was not happy about Loeb, and she berated me for not knowing that he had a gun in his briefcase. Pagliani was more understanding; if he'd known, he would never have let Loeb into the jail to visit Jimmy Gilbert or any other prisoner. After a cup of black coffee, Ozwick managed to calm down enough to forgive us our trespasses.

I recounted to the two of them the parts of my conversation with Loeb that they needed to hear. I left out some of the more complicated details. They were going to need time to sift through the layers of this case themselves, and they would probably do a better job of it than I had so far.

"I don't understand what Loeb was doing here in the first place," she said, swirling the silt at the bottom of her cup. She tossed it into the back of her throat like a shot and winced.

"Maybe we'll find out when we talk to Jimmy," I said. "But I don't think Loeb was all there anymore. He'd worked with Todd Curwen a long time, and seeing him shot right in front of his eyes must have been a shock. It impaired his judgment."

"N.Y.P.D. is looking for Marcia Gilbert," Ozwick said. "The doorman didn't see her face, but someone on the street gave good-enough descriptors on her. Loeb claimed she was the shooter?"

"Why should we believe him?" Pagliani said.

"Different gun," I said. "Loeb fired a high-velocity nine-millimeter slug into his mouth. You saw the damage it caused. Curwen's wound was small, with minimal damage. I believe Marcia shot Curwen, and with her own gun, probably a twenty-two. Loeb described it as a rash act. He didn't see it coming."

"What did you say to him in there?" Ozwick asked.

"I didn't give him the idea to kill himself, if that's what you mean. I was only trying to make him appreciate the reality of his situation. As soon as I was finished, you guys were going to arrest him."

"It probably helped us more than it hurt us," Pagliani said. "He would have been a tough bird to nail in court."

"It wasn't my fault," I persisted.

"At least you found the kid," Ozwick said. "I was worried we might never find him, or that he might be dead somewhere."

"Not dead," I said, "but he'll have some permanent scars. How's it going trying to locate a relative?"

"He has none," Pagliani said. "Zippo. Troy had two older brothers, but they're both dead. Callie was an only child. Jason's grandparents are all dead, too. We'll have to place him with Social Services until we can find a better situation."

"You are releasing Jimmy Gilbert, aren't you?"

"Yes," Ozwick said, offering Pagliani a glare. "Like we should have done before. That was going to be the first thing I was going to discuss with my honorable captain when I got in. We can't charge him with the Callie Blassingame murder, Vince."

"Then who do we charge?" Pagliani said. "Loeb?"

"Marcia Gilbert," I said. "And Hugo Wallis."

"If you can believe that," Ozwick said.

"You're yanking my chain," Pagliani said. "Hugo Wallis? He just got off one murder. Why would he go and do another?"

"Marcia hired him," I said. "He wanted a new face."

"It's a long story, Vince," Ozwick said. "We'll be learning a lot more once Wallis wakes up. I think he's going to sing."

"Wakes up?" Pagliani said.

"He's in surgery. I'll tell you all about it later."

"I got all night. I'm not going anywhere."

"You guys need somewhere to place Jason, place him with Jimmy," I said. "He's the kid's godfather. Official."

"We'll have Social Services look into that. They won't be doing anything about it tonight, I can tell youse that much."

"Jason won't be wanting for money," I said, stroking my chin like an archfiend. "Maybe I ought to adopt him myself."

Ozwick and Pagliani both looked at me with a start.

"Guys," I said. "I'm kidding."

I stuck around until they processed Jimmy Gilbert out of jail. I waited by the elevator for him to appear. The doors opened, revealing him and a chubby jail deputy. Jimmy was wearing a loose white cotton shirt, black leather pants, black belt with silverwork and turquoise stones, and black snakeskin boots. He was bedraggled and worn and looked older somehow, even though his face was still baby smooth—no hint of five o'clock shadow.

As he came out, I stepped up and shook his hand.

"You," he said in his usual quiet voice.

"Quaintance," I said. "Greg Quaintance. I haven't thanked you yet for saving my life."

"Don't mention it," he said with true modesty. "They told me what happened to David."

"What was he doing here?" I asked.

"He had the gall to tell me to hang in there and 'stay the course.' He said this would probably go to trial, but he would get me acquitted like he did Wallis. I couldn't believe what he was telling me. You're not still working for him, are you?"

"I don't work for dead men," I said. "Anyway, he hired me to help you, and I've been doing that."

"You helped me get out of here?" he said breathily.

"I can't take all the credit."

"No press," Jimmy said, looking around. "Thank God. They're such wolves. Is that story still going to appear in next week's *Enquirer*?"

"I can't stop it."

"What are you doing here? Did you come with David?"

"No. I thought you might need a ride."

"I guess I do."

"I also brought Jason. They were looking for him."

"Jason's here?" His eyes lit up like crystals in the sun.

"He's got no blood kin left, and they're trying to figure out where to place him. I suggested they give him over to you."

"You did?"

"It's going to be up to the family court, but I suppose you could enter a bid or whatever it is you do."

"That won't be necessary. They'll give him to me anyway."

"How can you be so sure?"

"That's what Troy and Callie wanted," he said matter-of-factly. "They put it in their will. If both of them predecease Jason, I get legal guardianship."

"Oh?" Maybe I shouldn't have been surprised by this, but I was. "How do you know this?"

"They discussed it with me a few years ago. They were worried what would happen to Jason if both of them went. Troy's two brothers died of heart attacks, and they weren't that old. And Callie had her . . . incidents."

"Attempted suicides?"

"Yes. She wasn't healthy, anyway. Poor thing."

"How do you know they didn't change their will?"

"You think they did?" Jimmy looked aghast, like the thought had never occurred to him.

"I wouldn't know. I'm just saying keep your fingers crossed until the will is opened."

Chances were, the will still read the way Jimmy expected. If Jason had no relatives left, it wasn't going to be contested.

"I want to see Jason," Jimmy said.

"I was hoping you would."

Pagliani was resistant at first, but I explained that it would do a lot to boost Jason's spirits, and he relented. He took us down the hall to the departmental psychologist's office and knocked on the door. A thin blond woman wearing glasses and no makeup let us in. She seemed annoyed by the interruption.

"Jimmy!" Jason stood up and hugged Jimmy tightly. He came up to just under Jimmy's chin. Tears started dripping from his eyes. "They're letting you go?"

"Yes, Jason." Jimmy stroked Jason's hair.

"Jimmy, I was so worried about you!"

"I thought about you all the time. Are you all right?"

Jason nodded rapidly, convincingly. He sniffled a little.

"Everything's going to be okay," Jimmy said. "Trust me."

I felt embarrassed to be watching—like a voyeur—so I looked over at the psychologist and smiled. She looked at me with wide eyes and pursed lips, like a startled owl.

"Are you taking me with you tomorrow?" Jason said.

Jimmy glanced over at me. "I think I'm going to have to postpone my tour for a while. The deputies are going to take care of you tonight, but we'll be seeing each other soon."

"You promise?" Jason looked up at him.

Jimmy wiped Jason's tears away with his thumb. "I promise."

The psychologist cleared her throat rudely, and Pagliani made a production out of pointing at his watch dial.

Jimmy got the hint. "I have to go now, Jason. But I'll check in tomorrow and see what they plan on doing with you."

"When are they reading the will?" Jason asked.

"Shh," Jimmy said. "I don't know anything about that. Now you stay here, and the deputies will take care of you, okay?"

"Okay."

"Be strong."

"I will."

Jason broke his hug with Jimmy and threw his arms around me.

"Thanks, Greg," he said, nestling his head against my chest.

"For what?" I was startled by Jason's display of affection.

"For talking to me, and . . . well, for everything!"

Standing as I was under the gaze of all those witnesses, my whole bald head must have turned a bright shade of ultramaroon.

"Whatever I did to deserve this," I said, "you're welcome."

Jimmy took me up on the offer of the ride and asked me to drive him back to his estate in Somerset Hills. I was glad to oblige.

"I love your car," Jimmy said, stroking the 'Cuda's dash. "It's so retro-seventies. Brings back a lot of memories."

"I guess the seventies were a big decade for you," I said. "'Come Play With Me' was what, nineteen seventy-two?"

"No, nineteen seventy. My first hit single."

"You were what, seven years old?"

"Eight," he said. "I was eight. How do you know that song? It must have been before your time."

"Well, I must have been two when it came out, but it's gotten a lot of airplay over the years. I've heard it plenty."

"It's still one of my favorites," Jimmy admitted. "Every song I write, I hope I'll be able to catch some of that quality that's in 'Come Play With Me.'"

"Your voice still has that same quality."

"Yeah," he said, sounding sad. "Amazing, isn't it?"

"Your face has changed so much over the years, but your voice has stayed the same," I remarked.

"Not really. I've improved my technique. My singing is much more mature. My vocal cords are much better developed."

"I'm talking about the tonal quality."

"That's an illusion. I always sing in a falsetto."

"That's not what I think. I know what falsetto sounds like. The Bee Gees sang falsetto. Andy Gibb sang falsetto. You have a high-pitched voice, Jimmy. There's no way around it. It's almost like a girl's voice, but it's not. Something about it still tells you it's a man. You're like a countertenor, only—"

"Yes, that's right." Jimmy cut me off. It was something to grasp on to. "I am a countertenor. Do you listen to opera?"

"Yes, I do," I said. "I'm a gay man and I listen to opera—no big surprise. I've seen a few operas with roles for countertenors. Juilliard did one a few months ago by Monteverdi. Only I think in his day they weren't countertenors but castrati."

Jimmy didn't pursue the subject of opera any further.

"Too bad we don't have any castrati today," I went on. "I'd love to hear one."

"That's a selfish idea," Jimmy said. "Selfish."

"What's selfish about it? Castrati were supposed to be divine. Their singing is lost to us. I wish I could hear it."

"At what cost?" Jimmy's emotions were getting worked up.

"I'd pay anything," I said, pretending to misunderstand him.

"I mean to the child!" Jimmy's voice rose to the strongest level I'd ever heard it in person, and still it dripped from his throat like the finest honey. "I've read about the castrati— deprived of their manhood before they ever got a chance to know what it was! They didn't have any choice! They were nothing more than slaves to other people's pleasure!"

"The best of them made great fortunes," I pointed out.

"They made even bigger fortunes for the theater managers and the composers! It was a good thing when castrati fell out of fashion. What was done to those poor boys was barbaric!"

"Of course you're right. I wasn't thinking of that."

"I know how you've been trying to protect Jason," I said. "You want to tell me why you were hiding him out at the Reston's?"

"It's complicated," Jimmy said, thinking that would end it.

"You wanted him on the tour, I know," I said. "Only this time, Troy wasn't going to allow it, was he?"

"No. He refused, and I couldn't do anything to change his mind. I even gave him those two Arabian mares. I almost had him, but then Callie started throwing a fit last week."

"Did Jason tell you why?"

"Yes," Jimmy said. "Did he tell you?"

"He didn't have to. I learned about Zetlin's pool party on my own. You were in the city and knew nothing about it."

"I would never have let it take place. Yuri's a predator. I've told him to stay away from Jason, but he won't listen."

"Haven't you also told Jason to stay away from Zetlin?"

"Yes," Jimmy said, "but Jason's a boy who can't say no."

"When did you first learn Zetlin was seeing Jason?"

"The moment I heard about the commercial Yuri was directing for Natalie. Jason was at just the right age for Yuri."

"How do you know that?"

"I was about the same age when Yuri started on me. It's not something I really want to talk about."

"I'm sorry. Can we keep talking about Jason, though?"

"Sure. I didn't want Yuri doing to Jason what he did to me. I didn't realize it was already too late. I took Jason away from him and started spending all my time with him. But I never victimized him. I couldn't hurt Jason for the world."

"You took him on your Asian tour to get him away from Zetlin?"

"Yes."

"And then Jason went back to school. You took him skiing over Christmas break, also to keep him away from Zetlin."

"Yes."

"Now it's summer again, and Yuri's back to his old tricks. You wanted to give Jason sanctuary with you to South America."

"Yes, but Troy forbade it. I pretended to give in, but secretly I planned to take Jason with me. Our plans almost got screwed up when Callie took Jason into the city with her. Troy finally went over and picked him up and brought him back to New Jersey. I didn't want to take any more chances, and I saw this as our last window of opportunity. I called Natalie Reston and arranged everything. She was going to look after Jason just until I was ready to leave for Buenos Aires. Then I called Jason and told him to get himself over there. You know the rest."

"And you've never had sex with Jason?"

"No, of course not."

"Everybody in your entourage seems to think so," I said. "Next week, the whole world's going to think so."

"I know," he said with a heavy sigh. "But I'll survive. And Jason will be safe. With me."

Ennis was still at the guardhouse. He took a look inside and practically ignored me. "Oh, good to see you again, Jimmy!"

"I've only been gone since this afternoon," Jimmy said. "Would you mind letting us in? And no visitors, Ennis. Anyone wants to see me—anyone at all, I don't care who they are—you buzz me first and check with me, you got it?"

"Yes, Jimmy, I got it."

"That includes my mother."

"Your mother?" Ennis's face fell. "I'm sorry, Jimmy. She's up at the house already. I let her through an hour ago."

"You let her in?" I said. "Ennis, don't you have a police scanner or anything? Marcia Gilbert's wanted by the N.Y.P.D."

"Sorry," Ennis said. "I must not have been paying attention. I was watching the Yankees game."

"Let us in," I said. "And call the sheriff's department. Tell Detectives Ozwick and Pagliani that Marcia is up at the Gilbert estate. If Marcia tries to come down here and get out, don't let her. Don't leave your booth. She's considered armed and dangerous."

"Marcia Gilbert? Armed and dangerous?" Ennis was baffled.

"And when the detectives get here, let them in!"

Ennis went back inside the booth and let us on through. The 'Cuda's radials squealed a little when I let out the clutch.

"Your mother had Callie Blassingame killed," I said as I upshifted. We were doing seventy miles an hour in a few seconds.

"She did?"

"How much do you know about it?"

"Nothing, honest," Jimmy said. "I was asleep."

"You were asleep when?"

"When whatever happened happened. When Callie was drowned or whatever. I heard something going on outside and woke up, but that was you struggling in the pool."

"Me and who else? You saw her running away from me."

"I saw someone," he said.

"Come on, Jimmy, cooperate with me!" I took my hand off the gearshift knob and grabbed the collar of Jimmy's shirt. "If you try to protect her, they'll charge you as an accessory to murder! That could mean a good decade or more in prison!"

"I can't, I can't!" His voice rose with emotion, still rapturous and pristine.

"If you don't care about your career, think about Jason! He needs you, Jimmy. Don't throw it all away."

"I can't."

"Yes, you can. Tell me who it was who tried to kill me at the swimming pool. I know who it was. I want you to tell me."

"How can I tell the police what she did?" he said, his face wet with tears. "How can I, after all she's done for me?"

"After all she's done for you? Are you kidding me? Jimmy, I know about the operation."

"What operation?" he mumbled.

"The operation Troy Blassingame performed on you when you were ten years old. The one your mother paid him a fortune for. His nurse at the time was named Callie Hewitt. She married him shortly afterward. I think she blackmailed Troy into marrying her because of what he did to you. She could have anything she wanted as Troy's wife, so she grabbed her chance. She held it over him all these years. But she wasn't the only one who knew. Marcia was the one who asked Troy to do it. She's the one who paid him for it. All three of them were safe because any one of them could have let out the secret at any time."

"I don't know what you're talking about."

"They castrated you, didn't they?"

"What?" Jimmy laughed, but it didn't convince me. "Oh, that is funny! You can't believe that my voice is simply the result of God-given talent, can you? You have to believe that they cut off my balls! See for yourself and tell me it's true!"

Jimmy unbuckled his belt, unzipped his leather pants, and pulled them and his underwear down around his knees. I kept looking between him and the road, even though I knew what I was going to see. Jimmy had a normal-looking uncircumcised adult penis and a normal-looking scrotum with average-sized testicles. There was no pubic hair, however.

"See?" Jimmy said, turning toward me. "I'm not a freak! I've got balls just like you! My voice is a gift from God that I nurtured with proper training from the—"

"You have no pubic hair," I said.

"Maybe I shave it. A lot of guys do that. Bodybuilders—"

"They're fake." I reached over and grabbed Jimmy's scrotum. I rolled his balls around and around in my fingers as if they were dice, over and over each other. It caused him no pain at all. "Your testicles are fake. Troy Blassingame constructed them for you. He gave you a smaller pair when you were a child and a larger one when you grew older, so no one would ever know. What are they, Jimmy, silicone? Don't tell me you didn't know."

"Of course I knew," Jimmy said. He pulled his pants back up. "But only after they did it. I didn't have a choice. I was ten years old. They told me I had testicular cancer."

"They lied to you."

"Yes, I've known that for a few years now. *She* lied to me."

"Then why would you want to protect her?"

"I don't know. She's my mother."

"That's what makes it so horrible," I said. It was going to be painful, but I had to get through to him. "She's been living off you all these years like a parasite. What was it you said about the castrati? They were deprived of their manhood? Slaves to other people's pleasure? You made a fortune for your mother because she made sure you'd stay a male soprano the rest of your life. What kind of a mother is that?"

"Greg, help me," Jimmy said. "What am I going to do?"

We were approaching the house. It was dark. A metallic gold Rolls-Royce convertible was parked in the circular drive.

"That's her Rolls," Jimmy said.

"She could have parked it in the garage, couldn't she?"

"Yeah, sure. She usually does."

"Don't do anything to get her excited, Jimmy," I said. "All we want is to get her safely into custody. Nobody wants to hurt her. You should leave it to me."

"No, I want to see her. I want to tell her."

"Tell her what?"

"You know what I mean, Greg," Jimmy growled. "I want to *tell* her. I'm just not sure how. You've got to help me."

"Okay, Jimmy," I said, "but first you've got to calm down and tell me what you want."

Thirty-Eight

Basically, Jimmy wanted the chance to tell his mother off. All the anger he'd pent over thirty-five years was getting ready to explode like Krakatoa. I didn't want to be the cause of another family tragedy. I told Jimmy he should wait at least until she was safely in police custody, perhaps until she was confined in jail, before he made any attempt to confront her. She was bound to be emotional right now as well as armed, and she could direct her anger at anybody. I didn't want Jimmy getting hurt.

I didn't want to get hurt myself. I considered waiting to go in until Detective Ozwick and her back-up could arrive, but the thought of David Loeb offing himself kept nagging at me. I didn't want another suicide on my hands, and there was no telling what Marcia Gilbert was doing in there. I had to go in.

"Here." Jimmy plunged his electronic key card into its slot. The little green LED came on, and the latch made a noise.

The sound made me wince. I wanted to go in quietly. I drew my Glock from its holster and held it up toward the overhanging eaves. I turned the knob slowly and stepped in.

"Stay behind me," I said in a stage whisper. I lowered my Glock now and held it straight out in front of me. I didn't need Jimmy crossing in front of my line of fire from here on out. I didn't want him along at all, but I needed him to shut off the security alarm and to lead me around the long, winding corridors. There hadn't been time for Jimmy to draw me a map; the place must have had about a million square feet, give or take.

We stepped into the darkened foyer, and I did the best I could to clear it. Jimmy closed the front doors quietly. I covered him while he disarmed the alarm.

"Got it," Jimmy said.

"Okay," I said. "Where to first?"

"When she's here, she spends most of her time in her room."

"Her room, then. Take me there."

"First go straight down this hall," Jimmy said.

Blue moonlight filtered in through the small horizontal windows just below the eaves. My boots made a clopping noise on the tiles that echoed off the walls; Jimmy's shoes had a squeak. I removed my boots and socks and made Jimmy do the same.

As we passed open rooms, I stepped in with my gun extended, checking the main points for Marcia. There was no sign of her.

"Turn right," Jimmy said. "Watch your step."

I turned with my gun ahead of me and cleared the main points. We went down a half flight of stairs and met another hall, this one carpeted. I was still glad to be in bare feet. This part of the house seemed more insulated from the rest, and less moonlight made its way in. The rooms we passed were pitch black, but I didn't bother to clear them. We merely rushed past.

"Down again, and turn left," Jimmy said. "Be careful."

It was another half flight, then a jot to the left. We were in near-total darkness, and I could hardly see a thing. I kept to the center of the hall, not wanting to brush up against an object and send it crashing to the floor.

Jimmy tapped me on the shoulder and leaned into my ear to whisper, "The door at the end of this hall."

"Her room?"

"Yes."

"Okay," I said. "Stay back, will you?"

I stepped carefully toward the door ahead, which I could barely make out as a darker object against a lighter wall. It appeared to be closed, though I couldn't be sure. No light came from the crack at the base of the door. I was aware of a slight creaking noise my feet made as they fell on the plush carpet, but I doubted whether anyone behind the door could hear it.

I placed my left hand carefully on the cold doorknob and turned it slowly, standing to one side of the jamb. Before the latch could click, I eased the door open a few inches. Jimmy was right behind me, standing back and away from the door.

I felt for the light switch and fumbled for a moment. I was expecting a flip switch, but it was a dimmer. I slapped it hard and kicked the door open, putting my gun arm and half my body into the doorway and yelling, "Freeze!"

A gun went off, and a bullet went whizzing past my ear. Marcia Gilbert was kneeling on her bed in a black nightgown, shielding her eyes from the glare of the lights, holding out a revolver with a wisp of smoke at its tip. I caught that brief glimpse of her before I tucked myself back behind the wall.

"Stay away from me!" Marcia said from her sanctum. Her speech was slurred enough to convince me she'd been drinking.

"It's Greg Quaintance, Marcia," I said. "Put the gun down!"

"Not on your life!"

"I don't want to hurt you. I just want to talk to you."

"Ha!" she said. "My mother told me never to trust men!"

Jimmy made a movement behind me, but I held him back and gave him a glare. I wanted him to keep his place. I didn't want Marcia to know he was with me. The outcome was bound to be better if I handled this myself.

"I'm coming in, Marcia," I said. "And I want to see you put that gun down. You don't want to hurt anybody."

"Shows how much *you* know," she said.

"I'm coming around the corner, all right? I don't want to hurt you. I only want to talk."

"I'm not making any promises," she said.

I took that as a first step. I stuck my gun hand in first, counting on the assumption that Marcia was a lousy shot. Most people were lousy shots unless they practiced all the time at a firing range. Marcia didn't strike me as the type. Anyway, she had put the gun an inch away from Curwen's forehead instead of shooting him from across the room. And it was only a small .22.

"Don't shoot me now," I said.

"Don't come any closer," she said.

I poked my head around and saw her pointing her gun in my general direction, but her grip was shaky. The tip of her gun was veering off in all directions. She couldn't control it. All she could see were my gun arm and my head—two small targets. If I went in any farther, she'd have my entire body to aim at; she might not kill me, but if she hit me I'd be in big trouble.

"It's over, Marcia," I said. "The police know you killed Todd Curwen. They're on their way over here now to arrest you. I thought if I came first, I could spare you their indignities."

"How did you get in here?" she said, screwing up her face like she was trying to take aim. "I didn't hear you come in."

"Put the gun down, Marcia."

"I don't want to."

"You don't want to hurt me. You've hurt enough people already. Now calm down—"

"I am quite calm, thank you very much."

"And throw your gun on the floor, right there at the base of your bed. Go on, Marcia, throw it down there on the floor."

"I can't," she said.

"Marcia, I'm counting on you to do the right thing."

"You didn't tell me how you got in here." She cocked the hammer on her revolver.

I nudged the trigger on my Glock to within a hair of firing.

"Mother, don't shoot!" Jimmy yelled.

I was too focused on Marcia to stop him. He came rushing into the room and stood between me and her, blocking our lines of fire. I relaxed my finger; he had come this close to stepping directly into my bullet. He held his hands up and away from him to show her that he was unarmed.

"Get out of here, Jimmy!" I said, stepping fully into the doorway. If he moved out of the way, I was ready to shoot her.

"Jimmy, I'm warning you," his mother said. "Don't come any closer. Don't let them trick you into helping them, honey. The only person a boy can ever trust is his Mama. You know that."

"I'm not afraid of you, Mother." Jimmy took a step forward. "Not anymore."

Marcia's gun arm shook more than before. I hadn't heard her uncock her gun. It could go off from the motion alone.

"Jimmy, don't!" I said.

"Go ahead, kill me," Jimmy said, moving slowly toward her. "Put me out of my misery. You took something away from me that no one can ever give back."

"I don't know what you mean, darling! You know I love you!"

"You don't love me. You love the money you make off me. You're like a vampire keeping me just enough alive so you can suck my blood every now and then. Whenever you get hungry."

"Jimmy, stop it! You're scaring Mama, honey! Stop scaring Mama! I'm warning you!"

"Give me the gun, Mother," Jimmy said.

"No! No! Stay away from me, God help me!"

Jimmy was within a few feet of her gun—close enough that she couldn't miss. Her wobbly aim was directed at his heart.

"I despise you," Jimmy said. "You make me sick."

"Don't talk that way to your Mama!" Marcia was crying now —out of horror, out of fear. She was backed into a corner. "You can't talk to your Mama that way! I won't tolerate it!"

Jimmy reached out and knocked the gun from her hand. It fired, harmlessly, into the vanity mirror above Marcia's dresser. It made a clean bullethole in the glass. The mirror cracked.

Marcia screamed, took in a deep breath, and screamed again. Her world was being taken away from her. No more holidays in Rio, no more nights in Bangkok.

I came into the room and covered her with my gun.

Jimmy reached back and slapped Marcia hard across the cheek.

"You cunt!" he screamed. "You goddamned, fucking *cunt!*"

"Jimmy, don't," I said. "Stand back, let me cuff her."

But he wouldn't leave her alone. She was sitting there helpless like a beached whale, blubbering. Jimmy didn't hit her anymore, but he kept abusing her with his words.

"You bitch!" he said. "All my life, I've hated you!"

"I'm sorry," Marcia mumbled.

"It's too late for sorry, mother! You *castrated* me! I was just a boy! You never let me be a man!"

"I'm sorry, honey," Marcia said feebly. "It was for your own good. You had cancer, and we—"

"Don't give me that! That's a lie! I never had cancer!"

"I did it for your career, darling," she said, shaking her head from side to side as if she couldn't figure out why all this was happening to her. "I clothed you, I raised you. I made you everything you are today. If we hadn't cut out that cancer, you would have been a nobody, *washed up* at age *ten*. A *nobody.*"

"You cut off my balls and then threw me to the wolves!"

"What wolves?" she said in a voice almost as young and pure as Jimmy's own. "I don't remember any wolves."

Jimmy grabbed her by the shoulders and shook her.

"Jimmy," I said. "Cut it out. You'll have plenty of time to talk to her later."

"David Loeb!" he said. "Yuri Zetlin! *Those* wolves! Now do you remember? You knew what they wanted me for!"

"I . . . I don't know . . . I don't know what you mean."

"Everything you did was for my career," he said. "As if that makes it all okay! You paid Troy to cut off my balls, and then you had Troy in your pocket! The best plastic surgeon! Then you gave me to David, because you wanted the best lawyer! And to Yuri, the best fashion photographer! All for my career!"

"That's right, Jimmy, I did it all for you, everything!"

"Mother, how could you? I was only a boy. Do you have any idea what those men did to me? Huh? Do you? *Do you?*"

"Stop it!" Marcia threw her hands up over her ears. "Lies! Lies! I've never heard so much filth out of your mouth, boy!"

"I'm not a boy anymore, Mother! I'm as much of a man as I'm ever going to be. But I won't let you run my life anymore!"

"What are you saying?"

"You're fired!"

"What?"

"You heard me, you cunt! You're no longer my mother!"

With that, Jimmy pushed Marcia against the bed, and she started wailing again. She grabbed her magenta hair in tufts and started pulling at it as if in mourning. Jimmy went and stood against the vanity, like he wanted to get far away from her.

I holstered my Glock and got onto the bed.

"On your stomach, Marcia," I said "I have to cuff you."

She didn't pay any attention to me. She was lost.

"Come on, Jimmy, help me," I said.

Reluctantly, he helped me roll Marcia over. I grabbed my handcuffs out of my jacket and slapped them over her wrists.

"The police will be here any minute, Marcia," I said. "But I need to ask you a few questions. You hear me?"

"Yes," she said, beginning to calm down. "Yes, I hear you."

"Let's sit her up," I said to Jimmy, "get her comfortable."

We helped Marcia sit up on the bed with her legs dangling over the side, her arms still cuffed behind her.

"Do you need to blow your nose?"

Marcia nodded. I grabbed a tissue from her vanity and held it for her while she blew. I had to do it a few more times.

"Hugo Wallis is in surgery right now in Manhattan," I said. "He's going to wake up tomorrow and tell us everything."

"Why should he do that?" she said, sniffling.

"Because of what Troy did to him. I bet you don't know, do you? You thought Troy was going to help you out, didn't you? He was going to give Hugo Wallis what he wanted, a new face."

Marcia looked at me with alarm. She hadn't realized that I knew so much already.

"Wallis may have liked fame, but he doesn't like infamy. He's tired of being recognized everywhere he goes. Callie was threatening Jimmy, and you wanted her dead. You probably didn't think you were up to it, so you hired Wallis to do it. Wallis agreed as long as you'd buy him a new face. You also had him kill Angelo Ferrante, to shut him up for good."

"Hugo told you this?" she said.

"He may as well have," I said. "You paid Troy to perform the operation. You directed Todd Curwen to write out the check on the account of the film production company the two of you share. That's the only place where you had that kind of money readily available, isn't it? And a big expense like that is a drop in the bucket for a production company. No one would question it."

"There's no way you could know any of this!"

"Curwen wrote the check without even asking why, I bet."

"Todd was a lapdog," she said with contempt. "Always wanting to get in on everything. I should have kept him out."

"Out of Callie's murder? You sure should have."

"He didn't know about it. He began to suspect, and he thought he could use it to buy out my half of our production company. When he found that file in your car, he brought it straight to me. What a fool he was to trust me!"

"You were a fool to trust Troy," I said. "Maybe he would do your bidding under most circumstances. But you were asking him to give a new face to the man who'd murdered his wife. I believe Troy really loved Callie, right up to the end."

"The end?"

"Troy had a little fun with Wallis. Instead of giving him a new face, he ripped off the old one. Skinned him alive, under anesthesia. When Wallis came out of it, he didn't like what he saw. He found Troy and killed him with a scalpel."

Marcia clutched at her throat.

"Wallis went looking for a hospital and started spilling the beans when he got there. The nurses sedated him, though. He'll finish his story tomorrow, and you'll be nailed to the wall."

"That rat!" she said. "He deserved what Troy did to him. After the way he double-crossed me!"

"What was the double-cross?" I asked.

Marcia sighed. Jimmy came around to stand in front of her, but she wouldn't look at him. He held something in his hands.

"Mother, what are these?" Jimmy asked. He showed her a stack of square, white-bordered photographs all tied together with a rubber band. "They were sitting on your vanity."

"Oh, those pictures of your little nastyboy!" Marcia laughed bitterly. "That's how I lured Callie out here. I called and said that I'd give her the

Polaroids if she was willing to strike a deal and keep it out of the courts. I told her to go out to the Duke Island lot, park her car there, and wait for me to show up. I would have liked to see the look on Callie's face when she saw Hugo and his gun! He was a little late, of course. Callie was out there a couple hours, I guess. Hugo got the photos from Ferrante, of course. Nice camera work, by the way, Jimmy! Such beautiful flesh tones!"

"I didn't take these!" Jimmy said. "I would never—"

"Zetlin took them, Marcia," I said. "Jason told me so himself. Tell me about Wallis's double-cross."

"Hugo wasn't supposed to bring Callie here," she said, turning closer to me. The smell of alcohol was strong on her breath. "He was supposed to kill her at the park and dump her in the Raritan River. Instead, he brought her back here!"

"And killed Bert Ferrigno on his way in," I said. "Bert would never have let him in, would he? Wallis had to kill him."

"I had nothing to do with that!" Marcia said. "You can't pin that on me. That was pure Hugo. Hugo all the way."

"Why did you come back to the house yourself?" I asked. "The last I saw you, you'd left for the city with Todd Curwen."

"I threw a fit in his car and made Todd bring me back. I was supposed to be there to take Hugo's call after he'd finished the job. I couldn't have let Jimmy answer. I told Todd I wanted to pack my things for Argentina. I said I'd ride back with Jimmy." "You heard Wallis dumping Callie in the pool," I said. "You ran outside and started arguing with him. We have a witness."

"He was ruining everything!" Marcia said. "He was connecting us to it directly!"

"You were hoping attention would be directed elsewhere, like Troy Blassingame."

"They always go after the husband." Marcia was confident.

"But Hugo put her in your pool and wanted what?"

"I told him to take her out. He said not unless I paid him another half a million dollars on top of the operation. I told him I didn't have that much on hand. He said take it or leave it. I didn't budge. He went back to his car and drove it over to Blassingame's, like we'd planned. I went over to the toolshed to find something I could use to fish Callie out."

"That's when I came along," I said. "I reached out for Callie, and you leaped on top of me and tried to kill me."

"Nothing personal," she said.

"You didn't have your gun. What did you hit me with?"

"A monkey wrench."

"But you didn't have time to finish me off. Jimmy heard the noises and came out to see what was going on. You fled."

"I couldn't let him see his mama doing something like that!"

"So Jimmy never knew anything about your plans."

"Of course not," she said, giving Jimmy a smile. "If he'd known, he would have never let me go through with it. He's a good boy, but weak. He doesn't realize that you have to be ruthless to survive. Without Jimmy's father around, I've had to be strong for him all these years. Without me, he'd be nothing."

Jimmy looked down at her with revulsion.

"You killed Callie because she knew," I said. "She was Troy's nurse during that first operation on Jimmy."

"She was trying to break away from us," Marcia said. "She couldn't be trusted. Things were happening too fast. She told too much to Angelo Ferrante, and he was going to sell it off in bits and pieces to the press. They were going to know everything! Jimmy would have been ruined! She had to go."

"And so did Ferrante," I said. "You sent Hugo Wallis down to Atlantic City to do the job on him."

"Hugo didn't mind doing it. Ferrante could have sold dirty secrets about him, too. But Hugo was seen at the Castle! His picture was taken there! That's why he wanted a new face."

"What really worried you was the idea of Jimmy being tried in court for statutory rape," I said. "The truth was bound to come out. It would be Jimmy's best defense, the fact that he'd been castrated as a boy. Everyone in the world would know the secret that you, Troy, and Callie were keeping all these years. That's the real reason you wanted Callie killed, isn't it?"

"I did it all for Jimmy." Marcia threw him a loving glance.

"Come on, get up," I said. "We have to go. You have something we could put over you?"

"My robe," she said, looking down at her pale shoulders.

Jimmy found her robe on the door to her private bathroom. He helped me get Marcia to her feet and threw the robe over her.

Marcia smiled her thanks up at him.

Jimmy looked away. He looked disgusted with himself as well, for the things he'd said to her. She was still his mother.

We took Marcia through the halls, turning on lights as we went so she wouldn't stumble. We brought her out the front door and into the clear, still night.

The red lights and sirens were coming fast up the drive.

"So many stars!" Marcia said, breathing in the fresh air. "I love nights in the country, don't you?"

Thirty-Nine

I was at the Somerset County Sheriff's Department for several more hours, explaining to Ozwick and Pagliani everything they didn't already know. By the time I was finished, I was looking forward to crossing the General Pułaski Skyway one last time and getting back to the coziness of Chelsea.

I drove the 'Cuda into the entrance of Ahmed Kotby's garage at 3:30 in the morning. I got out and stretched.

Alejandro came out of the office, grinning wildly and pointing at his head. He had shaved it bald. It looked great.

"Alejandro!" I said. "You didn't!"

"Hey, I did," he said. "What you think, man?"

"Very sexy."

"You think so?" He rubbed his hand across the top, still shocked that he had actually gone through with it.

"Trust me, everyone's going to go crazy for you."

"Everyone?" Alejandro smiled. "How about you, eh? Does it make you go crazy for me?"

"Naturally."

"What you going to do about it?"

"Nothing," I said. He was probably kidding with me. "Right now I have to get some sleep. I left the keys in the ignition. Take good care of my 'Cuda for me, Alejandro."

"I will, Greg. Hey, when you going to use your car again?"

"Not for a long time, I hope," I said, and walked away.

It was a quarter of four when I buzzed Juan's apartment on West Fifteenth Street. I was surprised he even answered.

"Who is it?" came his sleepy voice.

"Greg," I said, almost expecting him to say *who?*

The door buzzer sounded, and I entered the building. I went up the stairs slowly to his third-floor walk-up and rapped lightly on his door.

Juan opened it in his black boxer briefs.

"Gregory," he said, yawning. "What time is it?"

"Almost four. Can I come in?"

"Yeah, sure."

Juan let me in and closed the door. Only the dim bulb over the sink was on. Some light filtered in from the streetlights.

"Oh," he said, slowly waking. "I checked the rest of that tape. Nothing on it."

"Nothing?" I took off my jacket and shoulder holster.

"I mean, there's no sex. Same old stuff as on the other tapes. All they do is lie there sleeping."

"You're sure that's all?"

"It was kind of sweet." Juan draped his arms around me and gave me a kiss on the lips. "Are you through with your case?"

"I am."

"Good," he said. "Take off your clothes and get into bed."

"I will."

I gave him a kiss back.

Juan helped me off with my clothes. My muscles ached, and my eyelids felt heavy.

We fell together in a heap on top of his futon and started sorting ourselves out into some kind of position. I began to grow exceedingly comfortable. I closed my eyes and relaxed.

"I'm glad you're okay, Gregory," Juan said, nestling into the crook of my arm with his head on my chest and his arm draped around me. "Gregory? Hey, Gregory, don't fall asleep on me!"

He shook me slightly, but it was too late.

THE END

GREG QUAINTANCE RETURNS IN
THE FALL OF LUCIFER

§   §   §

ABOUT THE AUTHOR

John Peyton Cooke was born in Amarillo, Texas, in 1967, and grew up in Laramie, Wyoming. His other novels include STINK LAKE, OUT FOR BLOOD, TORSOS, THE CHIMNEY SWEEPER, HAVEN, and THE FALL OF LUCIFER. His short fiction has been published in several magazines and anthologies, including *Christopher Street, The Magazine of Fantasy & Science Fiction,* DARK LOVE, and *Best American Mystery Stories 2003*, and are collected in AFTER YOU'VE GONE AND OTHER OUTRÉ TALES. John currently lives in London with his husband.